Also by Jhumpa Lahiri

The Namesake

Interpreter of Maladies

Unaccustomed Earth

Unaccustomed Earth

Jhumpa Lahiri

Alfred A. Knopf New York • Toronto 2008

This Is a Borzoi Book Published by Alfred A. Knopf and
Alfred A. Knopf Canada

Copyright © 2008 by Jhumpa Lahiri

www.aaknopf.com

www.randomhouse.ca

"Hell–Heaven," "Nobody's Business," "Once in a Lifetime,"
and "Year's End" originally appeared in The New Yorker.

Knopf, Borzoi Books, and the colophon are registered trademarks of
Random House, Inc. Knopf Canada and colophon are trademarks.

Library of Congress Cataloging-in-Publication Data
Lahiri, Jhumpa.
Unaccustomed earth : stories / by Jhumpa Lahiri.—1st ed.
p.   cm.
ISBN 978-0-307-26573-9
1. Bengali Americans—Fiction. 2. Bengali (South Asian
people)—United States—Fiction. I. Title.
PS3562.A316U53 2008
813'.54—dc22   2007017612

Library and Archives Canada Cataloguing in Publication
Lahiri, Jhumpa
Unaccustomed earth / Jhumpa Lahiri.
ISBN 978-0-676-97934-3
I. Title.
PS3562.A316U54 2008   813'.54   C2007-905080-8

Manufactured in the United States of America
Published April 4, 2008
Reprinted Eight Times
Tenth Printing, August 2008

With thanks to the National Endowment for the Arts,
and special thanks to Robin Desser.

For Octavio, for Noor

Human nature will not flourish, any more than a
potato, if it be planted and replanted, for too long
a series of generations, in the same worn-out soil.
My children have had other birthplaces, and, so far
as their fortunes may be within my control, shall
strike their roots into unaccustomed earth.

—NATHANIEL HAWTHORNE,
"The Custom-House"

CONTENTS

PART ONE

Unaccustomed Earth

After her mother's death, Ruma's father retired from the pharmaceutical company where he had worked for many decades and began traveling in Europe, a continent he'd never seen. In the past year he had visited France, Holland, and most recently Italy. They were package tours, traveling in the company of strangers, riding by bus through the countryside, each meal and museum and hotel prearranged. He was gone for two, three, sometimes four weeks at a time. When he was away Ruma did not hear from him. Each time, she kept the printout of his flight information behind a magnet on the door of the refrigerator, and on the days he was scheduled to fly she watched the news, to make sure there hadn't been a plane crash anywhere in the world.

Occasionally a postcard would arrive in Seattle, where Ruma and Adam and their son Akash lived. The postcards showed the facades of churches, stone fountains, crowded piazzas, terra-cotta rooftops mellowed by late afternoon sun. Nearly fifteen years had passed since Ruma's only European adventure, a month-long EuroRail holiday she'd taken with two girlfriends after college, with money saved up from her salary as a paralegal. She'd slept in shabby pensions, practicing a frugality that was foreign to her at this stage of her life, buying nothing but variations of the same postcards her father sent now. Her father wrote succinct, impersonal accounts of the things he had seen and done: "Yesterday the Uffizi Gallery. Today a walk to the other side of the Arno. A trip to Siena scheduled tomorrow." Occasionally there was a sentence about the weather. But there was never a sense of her father's presence in those places. Ruma was reminded of the telegrams her parents used to send to their relatives long ago, after visiting Calcutta and safely arriving back in Pennsylvania.

The postcards were the first pieces of mail Ruma had received from her father. In her thirty-eight years he'd never had any reason to write to her. It was a one-sided correspondence; his trips were brief enough so that there was no time for Ruma to write back, and besides, he was not in a position to receive mail on his end. Her father's penmanship was small, precise, slightly feminine; her mother's had been a jumble of capital and lowercase, as though she'd learned to make only one version of each letter. The cards were addressed to Ruma; her father never included Adam's name, or mentioned Akash. It was only in his closing that he acknowledged any personal connection between them. "Be happy, love Baba," he signed them, as if the attainment of happiness were as simple as that.

In August her father would be going away again, to Prague. But first he was coming to spend a week with Ruma and see the house she and Adam had bought on the Eastside of Seattle. They'd moved from Brooklyn in the spring, for Adam's job. It was her father who suggested the visit, calling Ruma as she was making dinner in her new kitchen, surprising her. After her mother's death it was Ruma who assumed the duty of speaking to her father every evening, asking how his day had gone. The calls were less frequent now, normally once a week on Sunday afternoons. "You're always welcome here, Baba," she'd told her father on the phone. "You know you don't have to ask."

Her mother would not have asked. "We're coming to see you in July," she would have informed Ruma, the plane tickets already in hand. There had been a time in her life when such presumptuousness would have angered Ruma. She missed it now.

Adam would be away that week, on another business trip. He worked for a hedge fund and since the move had yet to spend two consecutive weeks at home. Tagging along with him wasn't an option. He never went anywhere interesting—usually towns in the Northwest or Canada where there was nothing special for her and Akash to do. In a few months, Adam assured her, the trips would diminish. He hated stranding Ruma with Akash so often, he said, especially now that she was pregnant again. He encouraged her to hire a babysitter, even a live-in if that would be helpful. But Ruma knew no one in Seattle, and the prospect of finding someone to care for her child in a strange place seemed more daunting than looking after him on her own. It was just a matter of getting through the summer— in September, Akash would start at a preschool. Besides, Ruma wasn't working and couldn't justify paying for something she now had the freedom to do.

In New York, after Akash was born, she'd negotiated a part-time schedule at her law firm, spending Thursdays and Fridays at home in Park Slope, and this had seemed like the perfect balance. The firm had been tolerant at first, but it had not been so easy, dealing with her mother's death just as an important case was about to go to trial. She had died on the operating table, of heart failure; anesthesia for routine gallstone surgery had triggered anaphylactic shock.

After the two weeks Ruma received for bereavement, she couldn't face going back. Overseeing her clients' futures, preparing their wills and refinancing their mortgages, felt ridiculous to her, and all she wanted was to stay home with Akash, not just Thursdays and Fridays but every day. And then, miraculously, Adam's new job came through, with a salary generous enough for her to give notice. It was the house that was her work now: leafing through the piles of catalogues that came in the mail, marking them with Post-its, ordering sheets covered with dragons for Akash's room.

"Perfect," Adam said, when Ruma told him about her father's visit. "He'll be able to help you out while I'm gone." But Ruma disagreed. It was her mother who would have been the helpful one, taking over the kitchen, singing songs to Akash and teaching him Bengali nursery rhymes, throwing loads of laundry into the machine. Ruma had never spent a week alone with her father. When her parents visited her in Brooklyn, after Akash was born, her father claimed an armchair in the living room, quietly combing through the *Times,* occasionally tucking a finger under the baby's chin but behaving as if he were waiting for the time to pass.

Her father lived alone now, made his own meals. She could not picture his surroundings when they spoke on the phone. He'd moved into a one-bedroom condominium in a part of Pennsylvania Ruma did not know well. He had pared down his possessions and sold the house where Ruma and her younger brother Romi had spent their childhood, informing them only after he and the buyer went into contract. It hadn't made a difference to Romi, who'd been living in New Zealand for the past two years, working on the crew of a German documentary filmmaker. Ruma knew that the house, with the rooms her mother had decorated and the bed in which she liked to sit up doing crossword puzzles and the stove on which she'd cooked, was too big for her father now. Still, the news had been shocking, wiping out her mother's presence just as the surgeon had.

She knew her father did not need taking care of, and yet this very fact caused her to feel guilty; in India, there would have been no question of his not moving in with her. Her father had never mentioned the possibility, and after her mother's death it hadn't been feasible; their old apartment was too small. But in Seattle there were rooms to spare, rooms that stood empty and without purpose.

Ruma feared that her father would become a responsibility, an added demand, continuously present in a way she was no longer used to. It would mean an end to the family she'd created on her own: herself and Adam and Akash, and the second child that would come in January, conceived just before the move. She couldn't imagine tending to her father as her mother had, serving the meals her mother used to prepare. Still, not offering him a place in her home made her feel worse. It was a dilemma Adam didn't understand. Whenever she brought up the issue, he pointed out the obvious, that she already had a small child to care for, another on the way. He reminded her that her father was in good health for his age, content where he was. But he didn't object to the idea of her father living with them. His willingness was meant kindly, generously, an example of why she loved Adam, and yet it worried her. Did it not make a difference to him? She knew he was trying to help, but at the same time she sensed that his patience was wearing thin. By allowing her to leave her job, splurging on a beautiful house, agreeing to having a second baby, Adam was doing everything in his power to make Ruma happy. But nothing was making her happy; recently, in the course of conversation, he'd pointed that out, too.

How freeing it was, these days, to travel alone, with only a single suitcase to check. He had never visited the Pacific Northwest, never appreciated the staggering breadth of his adopted land. He had flown across America only once before, the time his wife booked tickets to Calcutta on Royal Thai Airlines, via Los Angeles, rather than traveling east as they normally did. That journey was endless, four seats, he still remembered, among the smokers at the very back of the plane. None of them had the energy to visit any sights in Bangkok during their lay-over, sleeping instead in the hotel provided by the airline. His wife, who had been most excited to see the Floating Market, slept even through dinner, for he remembered a meal in the hotel with only Romi and Ruma, in a solarium overlooking a garden, tasting the spiciest food he'd ever had in his life as mosquitoes swarmed angrily behind his children's faces. No matter how they went, those trips to India were always epic, and he still recalled the anxiety they provoked in him, having to pack so much luggage and getting it all to the airport, keeping documents in order and ferrying his family safely so many thousands of miles. But his wife had lived for these journeys, and until both his parents died, a part of him lived for them, too. And so they'd gone in spite of the expense, in spite of the sadness and shame he felt each time he returned to Calcutta, in spite of the fact that the older his children grew, the less they wanted to go.

He stared out the window at a shelf of clouds that was like miles and miles of densely packed snow one could walk across. The sight filled him with peace; this was his life now, the ability to do as he pleased, the responsibility of his family absent just as all else was absent from the unmolested vision of the clouds. Those returns to India had been a fact of life for him, and for all their Indian friends in America. Mrs. Bagchi was an exception. She had married a boy she'd loved since girlhood, but after two years of marriage he was killed in a scooter accident. At twenty-six she moved to America, knowing that otherwise her parents would try to marry her off again. She lived on Long Island, an anomaly, an Indian woman alone. She had completed her doctorate in statistics and taught since the seventies at Stony Brook University, and in over thirty years she had gone back to Calcutta only to attend her parents' funerals. Meenakshi was her name, and though he used it now when he addressed her, in his thoughts he continued to think of her as Mrs. Bagchi.

Being the only two Bengalis in the tour group, naturally they'd struck up a conversation. They started eating together, sitting next to one another on the bus. Because of their common appearance and language, people mistook them for husband and wife. Initially there was nothing romantic; neither of them had been interested in anything like that. He enjoyed Mrs. Bagchi's company, knowing that at the end of a few weeks she would board a separate plane and disappear. But after Italy he'd begun thinking of her, looking forward to receiving her e-mails, checking his computer five or six times a day. He searched MapQuest for the town she lived in to see how long it would take him to drive to her home, though they had agreed, for the time being, to see each other only when they were abroad. Part of the route was familiar to him, the same path that he and his wife used to take to visit Ruma in Brooklyn.

He would soon see Mrs. Bagchi again, in Prague; this time, they'd agreed, they would share a room, and they were thinking, in the winter, of taking a cruise in the Gulf of Mexico. She was adamant about not marrying, about never sharing her home with another man, conditions which made the prospect of her companionship all the more appealing. He closed his eyes and thought of her face, which was still full, though he guessed she was probably almost sixty, only five or six years younger than his wife. She wore Western clothing, cardigans and black pull-on slacks and styled her thick dark hair in a bun. It was her voice that appealed to him most, well modulated, her words always measured, as if there were only a limited supply of things she was willing to say on any given day. Perhaps, because she expected so little, he was generous with her, attentive in a way he'd never been in his marriage. How shy he'd felt, asking

Mrs. Bagchi for the first time in Amsterdam, after they had a tour of the Anne Frank House, to pose for a photograph in front of a canal.

Ruma had offered to drive to the airport and greet her father, but he insisted on renting a car and following directions off the Internet. When she heard the sound of tires on the gravel drive, she started picking up the toys that were scattered across the living-room floor, putting away the plastic animals and closing the books that Akash insisted on leaving open to his favorite pages. "Turn off the television, Peanut," she called out to him now. "Don't sit so close to the screen. Come, Dadu's here."

Akash was lying motionless on the floor, on his stomach, his chin cupped in his hands. He was a perfect synthesis of Ruma and Adam, his curly hair they'd never cut and his skin a warm gold, the faint hair on his legs gold as well, reminding her of a little lion. Even his face, with its slanted, narrow green eyes, had a faintly leonine aspect. He was only three, but sometimes she already felt the resistance, the profound barrier she assumed would set in with adolescence. After the move he'd grown difficult. It was a combination, she knew, of the new surroundings, and her lack of energy, and Adam being away so much. There were times Akash would throw himself without warning on the ground, the body she'd nurtured inside of her utterly alien, hostile. Either that or he was clingy, demanding that she hold him while she was trying to make a meal.

Though she'd mentioned nothing about the baby, she was convinced that he'd figured it out already, that already he felt replaced. She'd changed, too—she was less patient, quicker to say no instead of reasoning with him. She hadn't been prepared for how much work it was, how isolating it could be. There were mornings she wished she could simply get dressed and walk out the door, like Adam. She didn't understand how her

mother had done it. Growing up, her mother's example—
moving to a foreign place for the sake of marriage, caring exclusively for children and a household—had served as a warning, a
path to avoid. Yet this was Ruma's life now.

She walked across the living room, turned off the television.
"Answer me when I talk to you, Akash. Get up, let's go."

The sight of her father's rental car, a compact maroon sedan,
upset her, freshly confirming the fact that she lived on a separate coast thousands of miles from where she grew up, a place
where her parents knew no one, where neither of her parents,
until today, had set foot. The connections her family had formed
to America, her parents' circle of Bengali friends in Pennsylvania
and New Jersey, her father's company, the schools Ruma and
Romi had gone through, did not exist here. It was seven
months since she'd last seen her father. In the process of selling
and packing up their old apartment, moving and settling into
the new house, and her father's various trips, over half a year
had gone by.

Akash got up and trailed behind her, and together they
watched as her father opened the trunk of the car, lifting out a
small black suitcase with wheels. He was wearing a baseball cap
that said POMPEII, brown cotton pants and a sky-blue polo
shirt, and a pair of white leather sneakers. She was struck by the
degree to which her father resembled an American in his old
age. With his gray hair and fair skin he could have been practically from anywhere. It was her mother who would have stuck
out in this wet Northern landscape, in her brightly colored
saris, her dime-sized maroon bindi, her jewels.

He began to pull the suitcase along the driveway, but
because of the inconvenience of the gravel under the wheels, he
picked it up by the handle and walked across the grass up to the
house. She saw that it was a slight struggle for him, and she
wished Adam were there to help.

"Akash, is that you?" her father called out in mock bewilderment, in English. "So big you have become." By now Akash had forgotten the little Bengali Ruma had taught him when he was little. After he started speaking in full sentences English had taken over, and she lacked the discipline to stick to Bengali. Besides, it was one thing to coo at him in Bengali, to point to this or that and tell him the corresponding words. But it was another to be authoritative; Bengali had never been a language in which she felt like an adult. Her own Bengali was slipping from her. Her mother had been strict, so much so that Ruma had never spoken to her in English. But her father didn't mind. On the rare occasions Ruma used Bengali anymore, when an aunt or uncle called from Calcutta to wish her a Happy Bijoya or Akash a Happy Birthday, she tripped over words, mangled tenses. And yet it was the language she had spoken exclusively in the first years of her life.

"How old now? Three? Or is it three hundred?" her father asked.

Akash did not respond, behaving as if her father did not exist. "Mommy, I'm thirsty," he said.

"In a minute, Akash."

Her father seemed the same to her. For a man of seventy, the skin of his hands and face was firm and clear. He had not lost weight and the hair on his head was plentiful, more so, she feared, than her own after Akash's birth, when it had fallen out in clumps on her pillow each night, the crushed strands the first thing she noticed every morning. Her doctor assured her it would grow back, but her bathtub was still filled with shampoos that promised to stimulate scalp growth, plump the shafts. Her father looked well rested, another quality Ruma did not possess these days. She'd taken to applying concealer below her eyes, even when she had no plans to leave the house. In addition she'd been putting on weight. With Akash she'd lost weight in her first trimester, but this time, at just twelve weeks, she was already ten pounds heavier. She decided that it must have been the food she found herself always finishing off of Akash's plate and the fact that now she had to drive everywhere instead of walk. She'd already ordered pants and skirts with elastic waistbands from catalogues, and there was a solidity to her face that upset her each time she looked in the mirror.

"Akash, please say hello to Dadu," she said, giving him a gentle push behind the shoulder. She kissed her father on the cheek. "How long did it take you to get here? Was there traffic?"

"Not so much. Your home is twenty-two miles from the airport." Her father always made it his business to know the distances he traveled, large and small. Even before MapQuest existed, he knew the exact distance from their house to his office, and to the supermarket where her parents shopped for food, and to the homes of their friends.

"Gasoline is expensive here," he added. He said this matter-of-factly, but still she felt the prick of his criticism as she had all her life, feeling at fault that gas cost more in Seattle than in Pennsylvania.

"It's a long flight. You must be tired."

"I am only tired at bedtime. Come here," her father said to Akash. He set down the suitcase, bent over slightly, and put out his arms.

But Akash pressed his head into Ruma's legs, refusing to budge.

They came inside, her father leaning over to untie the laces of his sneakers, lifting one foot at a time, wobbling slightly.

"Baba, come into the living room, you'll be more comfortable doing that sitting down on the sofa," Ruma said. But he continued removing his sneakers, setting them in the foyer next to the mail table before straightening and acknowledging his surroundings.

"Why does Dadu take his shoes off?" Akash asked Ruma.

"He's more comfortable that way."

"I want shoes off, too." Akash stomped his sandals on the floor.

It was one of the many habits of her upbringing which she'd shed in her adult life, without knowing when or why. She ignored Akash's request and showed her father the house, the rooms that were larger and more gracious than the ones that had sheltered her when she was a child. Akash trailed behind them, darting off on his own now and then. The house had been built in 1959, designed and originally owned by an architect, and Ruma and Adam were filling it slowly with furniture from that period: simple expensive sofas covered with muted shades of wool, long, low bookcases on outwardly turned feet. Lake Washington was a few blocks down a sloping street. There was a large window in the living room framing the water, and beyond the dining room was a screened-in porch with an even more spectacular view: the Seattle skyline to the left, and, straight ahead, the Olympic Mountains, whose snowy peaks seemed hewn from the same billowing white of the clouds drifting above them. Ruma and Adam hadn't planned on living in a suburb, but after five years in an apartment that faced the backs of other buildings, a home so close to a lake, from which they could sit and watch the sun set, was impossible to resist.

She pointed out one of the two bridges that spanned the lake, explaining that they floated on pontoons at their centers because the water was too deep. Her father looked out the window but said nothing. Her mother would have been more forthcoming, remarking on the view, wondering whether ivory curtains would have been better than green. It appeared, as her father walked from one end of the living room to another, that he was inwardly measuring its dimensions. She remembered him doing this when he helped her to move in the past, into dorm rooms and her first apartments after college. She imagined him on his tours, in public squares, walking from one end to another, pacing up and down a nave, counting the number of steps one had to ascend in order to enter a library or a museum.

She took him downstairs, where she had prepared the guest room. The space was divided into two sections by an accordion door. On one side was the bed and a bureau, and on the other, a desk and sofa, bookcase and coffee table. She opened the door to the bathroom and pointed to the wicker basket where he was to put his laundry. "You can close this off if you like," she said, pulling at the accordion door to demonstrate.

"It's not needed," her father said.

"All the way, Mommy," Akash said, tugging at the handle, causing the folded cream-colored panel to sway back and forth. "Close it all the way."

"No, Akash."

"This is my room when I get bigger," Akash announced.

"That little TV in the corner works, but it's not hooked up to cable," Ruma told her father. "Nine is the PBS station,"she added, knowing those were the programs he was fond of.

"Hey, don't walk on my bed with your shoes on," her father said suddenly to Akash, who had gotten onto the bed and was walking with large, deliberate steps around the bedcover. "Peanut, get off the bed."

For a moment Akash continued exactly as he was doing, ignoring them. Then he stopped, looking suspiciously at his grandfather. "Why?"

Before Ruma could explain, her father said, "Because I will have nightmares."

Akash dropped his head. Quickly, to Ruma's surprise, he slithered onto the floor, briefly crawling as if he were a baby again.

They went back upstairs, to the kitchen. It was the room Ruma was most proud of, with its soapstone counters and cherry cupboards. Showing it off to her father, she felt self-conscious of her successful life with Adam, and at the same time she felt a quiet slap of rejection, gathering, from his continued silence, that none of it impressed him.

"Adam planted all this?" her father asked, taking in the garden that was visible through the kitchen window, mentioning Adam for the first time.

"No. It was all here."

"Your delphiniums need watering."

"Which are they?" she asked, embarrassed that she did not know the names of the plants in her own backyard.

He pointed. "The tall purple ones."

It occurred to her that her father missed gardening. For as long as she could remember it had been his passion, working outdoors in the summers as soon as he came home from the office, staying out until it grew dark, subjecting himself to bug bites and rashes. It was something he'd done alone; neither Romi nor Ruma had ever been interested in helping, and their father never offered to include them. Her mother would complain, having to keep dinner waiting until nine at night. "Go ahead and eat," Ruma would say, but her mother, trained all her life to serve her husband first, would never consider such a thing. In addition to tomatoes and eggplant and zucchini, her father had grown expert over the years at cultivating the things her mother liked to cook with—bitter melon and chili peppers and delicate strains of spinach. Oblivious to her mother's needs in other ways, he had toiled in unfriendly soil, coaxing such things from the ground.

He glanced at the gleaming six-burner stove with its thick red knobs and then, without asking, began to open one of the cupboards.

"What are you looking for?"

"Do you have a kettle?"

She opened the pantry. "I'll make tea, Baba."

"Let me water your delphiniums. They won't survive another day." He took the kettle from her hands and filled it at the sink. Then he carried it, slowly and carefully, through the kitchen door outside, taking oddly small steps, and for the first time since his arrival she saw that in spite of his clear eyes and skin, her father had become an old man. She stood by the window and watched her father water the flowers, his head bent, his eyebrows raised. She listened to the sound of the water hitting the earth in a forceful, steady stream. It was a sound that vaguely embarrassed her, as if he were urinating in her presence. Even after the sound stopped, her father stood there for a moment, tipping the spout and pouring out the final drops that the kettle contained. Akash had followed her father outside, and now he stood a few feet away, looking up at his grandfather with curiosity.

Akash had no memory of her mother. She had died when he was two, and now, when she pointed her mother out in a photograph, Akash would always say, "she died," as if it were something extraordinary and impressive her mother had done. He would know nothing of the weeks her mother had come to stay with Ruma after his birth, holding him in the mornings in her kaftan as Ruma slept off her postpartum fatigue. Her mother had refused to put him into the bassinet, always cradling him, for hours at a time, in her arms. The new baby would know nothing of her mother at all, apart from the sweaters she had knit for Akash, which he'd already outgrown and which the new baby would eventually wear. There was a half-knit cardigan patterned with white stars still on its needles, one of the few items of her mother's Ruma had kept. Of the two hundred and eighteen saris, she kept only three, placing them in a quilted zippered bag at the back of her closet, telling her mother's friends to divide up the rest. And she had remembered the many times her mother had predicted this very moment, lamenting the fact that her daughter preferred pants and skirts to the clothing she wore, that there would be no one to whom to pass on her things.

. . .

He went downstairs to unpack, arranging his two pairs of pants in one of the drawers of the bureau, hanging his four checkered summer shirts on hangers in the closet, putting on a pair of flip-flops for indoors. He shut his empty suitcase and put it in the closet as well and placed his kit bag in the bathroom, at the side of the sink. The accommodations would have pleased his wife; it had always upset her, the fact that Ruma and Adam used to live in an apartment, with no separate room for them to sleep in when they stayed. He looked out at the yard. There were houses on either side, but the back felt secluded. One could not see the water or the mountains from here, only the ground, thick with the evergreen trees he'd seen on the sides of the highway, that were everywhere in Seattle.

Upstairs, Ruma was serving tea on the porch. She had brought everything out on a tray: a pot of Darjeeling, the strainer, milk and sugar, and a plate of Nice biscuits. He associated the biscuits deeply with his wife—the visible crystals of sugar, the faint coconut taste—their kitchen cupboard always contained a box of them. Never had he managed to dip one into a cup of tea without having it dissolve, leaving a lump of beige mush in the bottom of his cup.

He sat down and distributed gifts. For Akash there was a small wooden plane with red propellers and a marionette of Pinocchio. The boy began playing with his toys immediately, tangling up Pinocchio's strings and demanding that Ruma fix them. There was a handpainted cruet that had the word "olio" on its side for Ruma, and a marbled box for Adam, the sort of thing one might use for storing paper clips. Mrs. Bagchi had chosen everything, spending nearly an hour in a toyshop, though she had no grandchildren. He had mentioned nothing to Ruma or Romi about Mrs. Bagchi, planned to say nothing.

He saw no point in upsetting them, especially Ruma now that she was expecting again. He wondered if this was how his children had felt in the past, covertly conducting relationships back when it was something he and his wife had forbidden, something that would have devastated them.

It was Ruma and his wife who were supposed to have gone on the first of his trips to Europe. In the year before she died, his wife had begun to remark that although she had flown over Europe dozens of times in the process of traveling from Pennsylvania to Calcutta, she had never once seen the canals of Venice or the Eiffel Tower or the windmills and tulips of Holland. He had found his wife's interest surprising; throughout most of their marriage it had been an unquestioned fact that visiting family in Calcutta was the only thing worth boarding a plane for. "They show so many nice places on the Travel Channel," she would remark sometimes in the evenings. "We can afford it now, you have vacation days that are wasting away." But back then he had had no interest in taking such a trip; he was impervious to his wife's sudden wanderlust, and besides, in all their years, they had never taken a vacation together, alone.

Ruma had organized as a sixty-fourth birthday present a package tour to Paris for her mother and herself. She scheduled it during the summer, a time Adam could take Akash to her in-laws' place on Martha's Vineyard. Ruma put down a deposit at the travel agency and sent her mother tapes to learn conversational French and a guidebook filled with colorful pictures. For a while he would come home from work and hear his wife up in her sewing room, listening to the tapes on a Walkman, counting in French, reciting the days of the week. The gallstone surgery was scheduled accordingly, the doctor saying that six weeks would be more than enough time for her to recover before traveling. Ruma took the day off from work and came down with Akash for the procedure, insisting on being there even though he'd said there was no need. He remembered how irritated he'd felt in the waiting room over how long it was taking, that feeling vivid in a way the surgeon's news still was not. That information, and the chronology of events that followed, remained hazy to him: listening to the surgeon say his wife was dead, that she had reacted adversely to the Rocuronium used to relax her muscles for the procedure, he and Ruma taking turns with Akash as they went in to see the body. It was the same hospital where Ruma had been a candy striper, where he had once rushed to the emergency room after Romi broke his arm on a soccer field. A few weeks after the funeral one of his colleagues at work suggested that he take a vacation, and it was then that he'd remembered the trip Ruma and his wife had planned. He'd asked Ruma if she still intended to go, and when she said no, he asked if it would be all right for him to reserve the tour in his own name.

"Did you like Italy?" Ruma asked him now. She sat with the Pinocchio on her lap, clumsily untwisting the strings. He wanted to tell her that she was going about it wrong, there was a knot in the center that needed to be undone first. Instead, he replied to her questions, saying that he had liked Italy very much, commenting on the pleasant climate, the many piazzas, and the fact that the people, unlike most Americans, were slim. He held up his index finger, waving it back and forth. "And everyone still smokes. I was nearly tempted to have a cigarette myself," he said. He had smoked when she was little, a habit he'd acquired in India but abandoned in his forties. He remembered Ruma, never Romi or his wife, pestering him about quitting, hiding his packs of Winstons, or removing the cigarettes when he wasn't aware of it and replacing them with balled-up tissue paper. There was the time she'd cried all night, convinced, after her teacher at school had talked about the dangers of smoking, that he would die within a handful of years.

He had done nothing, back then, to comfort her; he'd maintained his addiction in spite of his daughter's fear. He'd been attached to a small brass ashtray in the house, shaped like a nagrai slipper with a curling, pointed toe. After he quit he threw out all the other ashtrays in the house, but Ruma, to his puzzlement, appropriated his favorite, rinsing it out and keeping it among her toys. He recalled that she and her friends would pretend it was the glass slipper in Cinderella, trying to get it to fit over the unyielding plastic feet of her various dolls.

"Did you?" she asked him now.

"What?"

"Have a cigarette in Italy."

"Oh no. I am too old for such things," he said, his eyes drifting over to the lake.

"What did you eat there?" she asked.

He remembered one of the first meals the group had had, lunch at a restaurant close to the Medici Palace. He'd been shocked by the amount of food, the numerous courses. The marinated vegetables were enough for him, but then the waiters brought out plates of ravioli, followed by roasted meat. That afternoon a number of people in the group, including him, went back to the hotel to recover, forgoing the rest of the sightseeing. The next day their guide told them that the restaurant lunches were optional, as long as everyone met back at the next designated place and time. And so he and Mrs. Bagchi began to wander off together, picking up something small, commenting with amazement that there had once been a time when they, too, were capable of eating elaborate lunches, as was the custom in India.

"I tried one or two pasta dishes," he said, sipping his tea. "But mainly I ate pizza."

"You spent three weeks in Italy and all you ate was pizza?"

"It was quite tasty pizza."

She shook her head. "But the food there is so amazing."

"I have videos," he said, changing the subject. "I can show them later if you like."

They ate dinner early, Ruma saying her father must be hungry from the journey and her father admitting that he was eager to turn in, that it was after all three hours later on the East Coast. She'd spent the past two days cooking, the items accumulating one by one on the shelves of the refrigerator, and the labor had left her exhausted. When she cooked Indian food for Adam she could afford to be lazy. She could do away with making dal or served salad instead of a chorchori. "Is that all?" her mother sometimes exclaimed in disbelief on the phone, asking Ruma what she was making for dinner, and it was in such moments that Ruma recognized how different her experience of being a wife was. Her mother had never cut corners; even in Pennsylvania she had run her household as if to satisfy a mother-in-law's fastidious eye. Though her mother had been an excellent cook, her father never praised her for it. It was only when they went to the homes of others, and he would complain about the food on the way home, that it became clear how much he appreciated his wife's talent. Ruma's cooking didn't come close, the vegetables sliced too thickly, the rice overdone, but as her father worked his way through the things she'd made, he repeatedly told her how delicious it was.

She ate with her fingers, as her father did, for the first time in months, for the first time in this new house in Seattle. Akash sat between them in his booster seat, wanting to eat with his fingers, too, but this was something Ruma had not taught him to do. They did not talk about her mother, or about Romi, the brother with whom she had always felt so little in common, in spite of their absurdly matching names. They did not discuss her pregnancy, how she was feeling compared to last time, as she and her mother surely would have. They did not talk very much at all, her father never one to be conversant during meals. His reticence was one of the things her mother would complain about, one of the ways Ruma had tried to fill in for her father.

"It is still so light outside," he said eventually, though he had not lifted his eyes from his plate since he'd started eating, had seemed, as he so often did to Ruma, oblivious to his surroundings.

"The sun doesn't set until after nine in the summer," she said. "Sorry the begunis broke apart," she added. "I didn't let the oil get hot enough."

"It doesn't matter. Try it," he told Akash, who for the past four months refused to eat anything other than macaroni and cheese for dinner. To Ruma he added, pointing to Akash's plate, "Why do you buy those things? They are filled with chemicals." When Akash was younger she had followed her mother's advice to get him used to the taste of Indian food and made the effort to poach chicken and vegetables with cinnamon and cardamom and clove. Now he ate from boxes.

"I hate that food," Akash retorted, frowning at her father's plate.

"Akash, don't talk that way." In spite of her efforts he was turning into the sort of American child she was always careful not to be, the sort that horrified and intimidated her mother: imperious, afraid of eating things. When he was younger, he'd eaten whatever her mother made for him. "You used to eat Dida's cooking," she said. "She used to make all these things."

"I don't remember Dida," Akash said. He shook his head from side to side, as if denying the very fact that she was ever alive. "I don't remember it. She died."

She was reading stories to Akash before his bedtime when her father knocked softly on the door, handing her the receiver of the cordless phone. He was holding up his right hand awkwardly in front of his chest, and she saw that it was soapy from dishwater. "Adam is on the phone."

"Baba, I would have done those. Go to sleep."

"It is only a few things." Her father had always done the dishes after the family had eaten; he claimed that standing upright for fifteen minutes after a meal helped him to digest. Unlike Ruma, unlike her mother, unlike anyone Ruma had ever known, her father never ran the water while he soaped everything. He waited until the plates and pans were ready to be rinsed, and until then it was only the quiet, persistent sound of the sponge that could be heard.

She took the phone. "Rum," she heard Adam say. That was what he'd begun to call her, soon after they met. The first time he wrote her a letter, he'd misspelled her name, beginning, "Dear Room—"

She pictured him collapsed on the bed in a hotel room in Calgary, where he'd gone this time, his shoes off, his tie loosened, ankles crossed. At thirty-nine he was still boyishly handsome, with the generous, curling brown-blond hair that Akash had inherited, a whittled marathoner's body, cheekbones she secretly coveted. Were it not for the powerful depth of his voice and the glasses he wore these days for distance he could still pass for one of the easy-going, athletic boys she went to college with.

"My dad's here."

"We spoke."

"What did he say?"

"The usual questions: 'How are you? How are your parents?' " It was true; this was all her father ever had to say to Adam.

"Have you eaten?"

There was a pause before he replied. She realized he must have been watching something on the television as they were speaking. "I'm about to head off to dinner with a client. How's Akash?"

"Right here." She put the receiver to his ear. "Say hi to Daddy."

"Hi," Akash said, without enthusiasm. Then silence. She could hear Adam saying, "What's going on, buddy? Having fun with Dadu?" But Akash refused to engage any further, staring at the page of his book, and eventually she put the phone back to her own ear.

"He's tired," she said. "He's about to fall asleep."

"I wish I could fall asleep," Adam said. "I'm wiped."

She knew he'd been traveling since early morning, that he'd been working all day, would have to work through his dinner. And yet she felt no sympathy. "I can't imagine my father living here," she said.

"Then don't ask him to."

"I think the visit is his way of suggesting it."

"Then ask."

"And if he says yes?"

"Then he moves in with us."

"Should I ask?"

She heard Adam breathing patiently through his nose. "We've been over this a million times, Rum. It's your call. He's your dad."

She turned a page of Akash's book, saying nothing.

"I need to get going," Adam said. "I miss you guys."

"We miss you, too," she said.

She hung up the phone, putting it beside the framed photograph on the bedside table, of Ruma and Adam on their wedding day, slicing into the tiered white cake. She could not explain what had happened to her marriage after her mother's death. For the first time since they'd met, at a dinner party in Boston when she was a law student and he was getting his MBA, she felt a wall between them, simply because he had not experienced what she had, because both his parents were still living in the house in Lincoln, Massachusetts, where Adam had been raised. It was wrong of her, she knew, and yet an awareness had set in, that she and Adam were separate people leading separate lives. Though his absences contributed to her isolation, sometimes it was worse, not better, when Adam was home. Even with Akash to care for, part of her was beginning to prefer the solitude, without Adam hovering around, full of concern about her state of mind, her mood.

Ten years ago her mother had done everything in her power to talk Ruma out of marrying Adam, saying that he would divorce her, that in the end he would want an American girl. Neither of these things had happened, but she sometimes thought back to that time, remembering how bold she'd had to be in order to withstand her mother's outrage, and her father's refusal to express even that, which had felt more cruel. "You are ashamed of yourself, of being Indian, that is the bottom line," her mother had told Ruma again and again. She knew what a shock it was; she had kept her other involvements with American men a secret from her parents until the day she announced that she was engaged. Over the years her mother not only retracted her objections but vehemently denied them; she grew to love Adam as a son, a replacement for Romi, who had crushed them by moving abroad and maintaining only distant ties. Her mother would chat with Adam on the phone, even when Ruma was not at home, e-mailing him from time to time, carrying on a game of Scrabble with him over the Internet. When her parents visited, her mother would always bring a picnic cooler filled with homemade mishti, elaborate, syrupy, cream-filled concoctions which Ruma had never learned to make, and Adam loved.

It was after she'd had a child that Ruma's relationship with her mother became harmonious; being a grandmother transformed her mother, bringing a happiness and an energy Ruma had never witnessed. For the first time in her life Ruma felt forgiven for the many expectations she'd violated or shirked over the years. She came to look forward to their nightly conversations, reporting the events of her day, describing what new things Akash had learned to do. Her mother had even begun to exercise, getting up at five in the morning, wearing an old Colgate sweatshirt of Ruma's. She wanted to live to see her grandchildren married, she'd said. There were times Ruma felt closer to her mother in death than she had in life, an intimacy born simply of thinking of her so often, of missing her. But she knew that this was an illusion, a mirage, and that the distance between them was now infinite, unyielding.

After finishing with the dishes he dried them and then scrubbed and dried the inside of the sink, removing the food particles from the drainer. He put the leftovers away in the refrigerator, tied up the trash bag and put it into the large barrel he'd noticed in the driveway, made sure the doors were locked. He sat for a while at the kitchen table, fiddling with a saucepan whose handle he'd noticed while washing it—was wobbly. He searched in the drawers for a screwdriver and, not finding one, accomplished the task with the tip of a steak knife. When he was finished he poked his head into Akash's room and found both the boy and Ruma asleep. For several minutes he stood in the doorway. Something about his daughter's appearance had changed; she now resembled his wife so strongly that he could not bear to look at her directly. That first glimpse of her earlier, standing on the lawn with Akash, had nearly taken his breath away. Her face was older now, as his wife's had been, and the hair was beginning to turn gray at her temples in the same way, twisted with an elastic band into a loose knot. And the features, haunting now that his wife was gone—the identical shape and shade of the eyes, the dimple on the left side when they smiled.

In spite of his jet lag he had trouble falling asleep, was distracted by the sound of a motorboat cutting now and then across the lake. He sat up in bed flipping absently through an issue of *U.S. News & World Report*, which he'd taken from the seat pocket on the plane, and then opened a guidebook to Seattle that had been placed on the bedside table, he guessed, for his benefit. He glanced at the photographs, of the new library and coffee shops and whole salmon displayed on beds of ice. He read about the average yearly rainfall, and the fact that it seldom snowed. Studying a map, he was surprised by how far he was from the Pacific Ocean, not realizing until now that mountains stood in the way. Though he had traveled such a distance, his surroundings did not feel foreign to him as they had when he went to Europe. There he was reminded of his early days in America, understanding only a word or two of what people said, handling different coins. Here, as on a summer night in Pennsylvania, moths fluttered against the window screen, and sometimes an insect would bang against it, startling him with its force.

From his position in bed he took in the spacious, sparsely furnished room. When he was Ruma's age, he had lived with his wife and children in a small apartment in Garden City, New Jersey. They'd converted a walk-in closet into a nursery when Romi and then Ruma were born. He had worried for his family's safety in that apartment complex, the surveillance cameras in the lobby making him nervous rather than putting him at ease, but at the time, still working on his PhD in biochemistry, it was the best he could afford. He remembered his wife making meals on the electric stove in the tiny kitchen, the rooms smelling afterward of whatever she'd prepared. They lived on the fourteenth floor and she would dry her saris one by one over the narrow balcony railing. The bedroom in which Romi and Ruma had both been conceived was dreary, morning light never penetrating, and yet he considered it, still, the most sacred of spaces. He recalled his children running through the rooms, the pitch of their young voices. It was a part of their lives only he and his wife carried with them. His children would only remember the large house he'd bought in the suburbs with willow trees in the backyard, with rooms for each of them and a basement filled with their toys. And compared to where Ruma now lived even that house was nothing, a flimsy structure that he always feared could burn down from the flame of a match.

Now that he was on his own, acquaintances sometimes asked if he planned to move in with Ruma. Even Mrs. Bagchi mentioned the idea. But he pointed out that Ruma hadn't been raised with that sense of duty. She led her own life, had made her own decisions, married an American boy. He didn't expect her to take him in, and really, he couldn't blame her. For what had he done, when his own father was dying, when his mother was left behind? By then Ruma and Romi were teenagers. There was no question of his moving the family back to India, and also no question of his eighty-year-old widowed mother moving to Pennsylvania. He had let his siblings look after her until she, too, eventually died.

Were he to have gone first, his wife would not have thought twice about moving in with Ruma. His wife had not been built to live on her own, just as morning glories were not intended to grow in the shade. She was the opposite of Mrs. Bagchi that way. The isolation of living in an American suburb, something about which his wife complained and about which he felt responsible, had been more solitude than she could bear. But he enjoyed solitude, as Mrs. Bagchi did. Now that he had retired he spent his days volunteering for the Democratic Party in Pennsylvania, work he could do from his computer at home,

and this, in addition to his trips, was enough to keep him occupied. It was a relief not to have to maintain the old house, to
mow and rake the lawn, to replace the storm windows with
screens in summer, only to have to reverse the process a few
months later. It was a relief, too, to be living in another part of
the state, close enough so things were still familiar, but far
enough to feel different. In the old house he was still stuck in
his former life, attending by himself the parties he and his wife
had gone to, getting phone calls in the evenings from concerned friends who routinely dropped off pots of chicken curry
or, assuming he was lonely, visited without warning on Sunday
afternoons.

He was suddenly tired, his vision blurring and the words in
the guidebook lifting off the page. Beside the small pile of
books there was a telephone. He set down the book, lifted the
receiver, checked for a dial tone, and set it down again. Before
coming to Seattle he had given Mrs. Bagchi his daughter's
phone number in an e-mail, but it was understood that she was
not to call. She had loved her husband of two years more than
he had loved his wife of nearly forty, of this he was certain. In
her wallet she still carried a picture of him, a clean-shaven boy
in his twenties, the hair parted far to one side. He didn't mind.
In a way he preferred knowing that her heart still belonged to
another man. It was not passion that was driving him, at seventy, to be involved, however discreetly, however occasionally,
with another woman. Instead it was the consequence of being
married all those years, the habit of companionship.

Without his wife, the thought of his own death preyed on
him, knowing that it might strike him just as suddenly. He'd
never experienced death up close; when his parents and relatives had died he was always continents away, never witnessing
the ugly violence of it. Then again, he had not even been present, technically, when his wife passed away. He had been reading a magazine, sipping a cup of tea from the hospital cafeteria.

But that was not what caused him to feel guilty. It was the fact that they'd all been so full of assumptions: the assumption that the procedure would go smoothly, the assumption that she would spend one night in the hospital and then return home, the assumption that friends would be coming to the house two weeks later for dinner, that she would visit France a few weeks after that. The assumption that his wife's surgery was to be a minor trial in her life and not the end of it. He remembered Ruma sobbing in his arms as if she were suddenly very young again and had fallen off a bicycle or been stung by a bee. As in those other instances he had been strong for her, not shedding a tear.

Sometime in the middle of the night she'd woken up in Akash's bed and stumbled into her own. Normally Akash came into her bed at dawn, falling asleep beside her for another few hours before waking her up and wanting cereal. She didn't mind Akash coming into her bed, especially when Adam was out of town. But this morning the bed was empty. She no longer felt sick in the mornings. Instead, her first thought was of food; she wanted a burrito, or one of the egg and cheese sandwiches from the bagel shop near their old apartment in Park Slope, a reminder that all through the night, as she slept, her body had been hard at work. In the kitchen she saw that the dinner dishes, washed and dried, were at one side of the countertop. In the drainer was a clean bowl, spoon, juice glass, and mug. Beside the stove, on a saucer, was a drying tea bag, reserved for a second use. She heard Akash's voice coming from somewhere outside, but couldn't see him through the window. She went onto the porch, where the sound of his voice was more distinct. "But I didn't see a turtle," she heard him say, and she gathered that he and her father had taken a walk down to the lake.

She took her prenatal vitamin, put on water for tea. She was making toast when her father and Akash came in through the kitchen door.

"We went to the lake and Dadu put me into a movie," Akash said excitedly, pointing to the video camera strung around her father's neck.

"You're wet," she observed, noticing that the straps of his sandals and the front of his shorts were darkened by water. She turned to her father. "What happened?"

"Nothing, nothing. We thought we saw a turtle, and Akash wanted to touch it," he said to Ruma. "He is asking for cereal."

"Come on, first you need to change," she said to Akash. When she returned she saw that her father had opened up the cupboard. "Is this the one he takes?" he asked, holding up a box of Cheerios.

She nodded. "When did you wake up, Baba?"

"Oh, I was up before five. I sat on the porch and had my breakfast, and then Akash joined me and we went outside."

"I can take over," she said, watching her father pour milk into the cereal bowl.

"I don't mind. Have your food."

She opened the fridge for butter and jam, prepared her tea. When she was finished, her father took the kettle, put the dried-out tea bag into the same cup that was in the dish drainer, and added the remaining hot water.

"Dadu, outside?" Akash said, tugging on her father's pants.

"Soon, Babu. Let me finish."

As she ate her breakfast she mentioned the places they could see during the course of his visit—before his arrival she had looked up hours of admission, ticket prices, and in her mind she'd already conceived of an itinerary, something to keep them occupied each day. She hadn't had the time or energy to explore much of downtown Seattle, and thought the week with her father would provide the opportunity. "There's the Space Needle of course," she began. "And Pike Place Market. There's an aquarium along the waterfront I've been meaning to take Akash to. They have ferry rides across Puget Sound that are supposed to be nice. We could go to Victoria for the day. And then there's the Boeing factory, if you're interested. They give tours."

"Yes," her father said. He looked tired to her, his eyes small behind his glasses. "To be honest," he said, "I wouldn't mind a rest from all that."

She was confused; she had assumed her father would want to see Seattle with his video camera, just as he was interested in seeing so many other places in the world these days. "Well, otherwise, there's not much else to do here."

"I don't need to be entertained."

"That's not what I meant. Whatever you'd like, Baba." Her confusion was followed by worry. She wondered if there was something he wasn't telling her. She wondered how it was in the condominium, whether there were too many stairs to climb, if he had any neighbors who knew or cared about him. She remembered a statistic she'd heard, about long-term spouses typically dying within two years of one another, the surviving spouse dying essentially of a broken heart. But Ruma knew that her parents had never loved each other in that way.

"Are you all right?"

He looked up at her; he'd been leaning close to Akash, making faces to distract him as he finished the cereal. "What do you mean?"

"I mean, are you feeling all right?"

"I am feeling fine. I was just hoping for a vacation from my vacations," he said. "The tours are work, in their own way."

She nodded. "I understand." She did understand, for deep down she knew that there was nothing wrong with her father. Though it upset her to admit it, if anything, he seemed happier now; her mother's death had lightened him, the opposite of what it had done to her.

He took a worn white handkerchief from his pocket, wiped remnants of milk and cereal off Akash's face. The gesture reminded her of being small, and the little ways her father had come to her rescue, pulling out a handkerchief if she'd spilt food on her clothes, or needed to blow her nose, or had scraped her knee. "Let a few days go by. Maybe then we can take a boat ride."

After breakfast Akash had his weekly swimming lesson. She expected her father to stay at home, but he said he wanted to go, bringing his video camera along. He offered to drive them to the pool in the rental car, but because the car seat was in the SUV, Ruma drove. She had learned to drive in high school, but then for years she had lived in cities and not owned a car, so that until now it was an activity she associated only with visiting her parents: taking the car to drop off videos, or going with her mother to the mall. It was something she had to get used to in Seattle—having to fill the car with gas, making sure there was air in the tires. Though she was growing familiar with the roads, with the exits and the mountains and the quality of the light, she felt no connection to any of it, or to anyone. She had exchanged only pleasantries with her neighbors—a retired husband and wife on one side, two gay professors at the University of Washington on the other. There were some women she would talk to as she sat watching Akash in the swimming pool, but at the end of each class they never suggested getting together. It felt unnatural to have to reach out to strangers at this point in her life.

She was used to the friends she'd left behind in Brooklyn, women she met in prenatal yoga and through a mommy group she'd joined after Akash was born, who had known the every-day details of her life. They'd kept her company when she went into labor, handed down the clothes and blankets their children had outgrown. Those friends had been a five- or ten-minute walk from her apartment, some of them in the building itself, and back when she worked part time they could meet her at a moment's notice, pushing their strollers through Prospect Park. They had gotten to know Ruma's mother when she came to visit on weekends, and some of them had driven down to Pennsylvania for the funeral. At first, after the move, these friends sent Ruma e-mails, or called from their cell phones as they sat in the playground without her. But given the time change and the children always at their sides, it was impossible to carry on a meaningful conversation. For all the time she'd spent with these women the roots did not go deep, and these days, after reading their e-mails, Ruma was seldom inspired to write back.

The car was silent apart from the sound the tires made on the road, and the slicing sound of cars passing in the opposite direction. Akash was playing with one of his toy trains, running its wheels along the surface of the door and the back of Ruma's seat. She was aware of her father quietly monitoring her driving, glancing now and then at the speedometer, looking along with her when she was about to switch lanes. She pointed out the grocery store where she now shopped, the direction of Mount Rainier, not visible today.

"There's the exit Adam takes to go to work," she said.

"How far it is?"

When she was younger she would have corrected him; "How far is it?" she would immediately have said, irritated, as if his error were a reflection of her own shortcomings. "I don't know. I think it takes him about forty minutes each way."

"That's a lot of driving. Why didn't you choose a house closer by?"

"We don't mind. And we fell in love with the house." She wondered whether her father would consider this last remark frivolous.

"And you? Have you found work in this new place?"

"Part-time litigation work is hard to find," she said. "Pre-school is only until noon, and Adam and I don't want Akash in a daycare."

"In order to practice here you will have to take another bar exam?" her father asked.

"No. There's reciprocity with New York."

"Then why not look for a new job?"

"I'm not ready yet, Baba." She had not bothered to contact any firms in Seattle, not called up the trusts and estates attorney one of the partners at her old firm had given her the name of, suggesting maybe Ruma could write briefs on a case-by-case basis. She realized she'd never explicitly told her father that she intended, for the next few years, to be at home. "We're still getting settled."

"That I understand. I am only asking if you have a time frame in mind."

"Maybe when the new baby starts kindergarten."

"But that is over five years from now. Now is the time for you to be working, building your career."

"I am working, Baba. Soon I'll be taking care of two children, just like Ma did."

"Will this make you happy?"

She didn't answer him. Her mother would have understood her decision, would have been supportive and proud. Ruma had worked fifty-hour weeks for years, had earned six figures while Romi was still living hand to mouth. She'd always felt unfairly cast, by both her parents, into roles that weren't accurate: as her father's oldest son, her mother's secondary spouse.

"They won't be young forever, Ruma," her father continued. "Then what will you do?"

"Then I'll go back."

"You'll be over forty. It may not be so simple."

She kept her eyes on the road, pushing a button that turned

on the radio, filling the car with the determined drone of a reporter's voice. She had never been able to confront her father freely, the way she used to fight with her mother. Somehow, she feared that any difference of opinion would chip away at the already frail bond that existed between them. She knew that she had disappointed him, getting rejected by all the Ivy Leagues she'd applied to. In spite of Romi's itinerant, uncertain life, she knew her father respected him more for having graduated from Princeton and getting a Fulbright to go abroad. Ruma could count the arguments she'd had with her father on one hand. In high school, after she'd gotten her license, he'd refused to insure her on the family car so that she could drive it on her own. In college, when it was time to declare her major, he'd tried to convince her to choose biology instead of history. He had balked at the cost of law school, but when she'd gotten into Northeastern he had paid for it all the same. And he had argued, when she and Adam were planning their wedding, that an outdoor ceremony was unwise, recommending an institutional banquet hall instead of the bluff on Martha's Vineyard she and Adam desired as a location. As it turned out the weather was perfect, the sun beating brilliantly on the ocean as they exchanged their vows. And yet, even to this day, Ruma suffered from nightmares of the white tent and folding chairs and hundreds of guests soaked by rain.

She pulled into the parking lot where the swimming pool was. Inside the building, she told her father to wait on the benches where they could watch the class through a window, while she went into the locker room to change Akash into his bathing suit. When she joined her father he was busy with his camera, putting in a new tape and adjusting the settings. "There's Akash," she said, pointing to where he sat, wrapped in a towel, waiting for the class to begin. She had thought Akash was too young to go into the pool without her, that they would have to take the earlier class, in which parents went into the water as well. But there were no spots in that class, and from the very beginning Akash had separated from her willingly, leaping into the arms of the instructor, an auburn-haired teenage girl.

For the next thirty minutes her father taped Akash continuously: having the flotation device strapped on his back, jumping into the pool, blowing bubbles and practicing kicks. Her father stood up from the bench where Ruma sat, the lens of the video camera nearly touching the window. He had not paid this sort of attention when Ruma and Romi were growing up. Back then it was their mother who sat watching their swimming lessons, who held her breath, terrified, as they climbed the ladder and waved at her, then plunged off the high diving board. Her father had not taught Romi to throw a baseball, and he had not taken them to learn to skate on the pond, a short walk through the woods behind their neighborhood, that froze every winter.

In the car on the way home, her father brought up the topic of her career again. "Work is important, Ruma. Not only for financial stability. For mental stability. All my life, since I was sixteen, I have been working."

"You're retired."

"But I cannot stay unoccupied. That is why I am traveling so much. It is an extravagance, but I don't need all the money I've saved up.

"Self-reliance is important, Ruma," he continued. "Life is full of surprises. Today, you can depend on Adam, on Adam's job. Tomorrow, who knows."

For a split second she took her eyes off the road, turning to him. "What are you suggesting? What are you saying?"

"Nothing. Only, perhaps, that it makes me nervous that you are not employed. It is not for my sake, you understand. My concern is for you. I have more than enough money to last until I am dead."

"Who else is dead?" Akash called out from the backseat.

"No one. We are only talking silly things. Oh dear, what a nice train you have, has it left the station?" her father inquired, turning back to Akash.

That night after dinner he showed his videos. First, to Akash's delight, they watched the footage of the swimming class, and then he showed videos of Europe: frescoes in churches, pigeons flying, the backs of people's heads. Most of the images were captured through the window of the tour bus, as a guide explained things about the monuments they were passing. He had always been careful to keep Mrs. Bagchi out of the frame, but as he watched the video enlarged on his daughter's television, he realized there were traces throughout—there was Mrs. Bagchi's arm resting on the open window of the bus, there was her blue leather handbag on a bench.

"That's Luigi," he said, as the camera focused briefly on their Italian guide.

"Who goes on these tours with you?" Ruma asked.

"They are mostly people like me, retired or otherwise idle," he said. "A lot of Japanese. It is a different group in each country."

"Have you made any friends?"

"We are all friendly with one another."

"How many of you are there?"

"Perhaps eighteen or twenty."

"And are you stuck with them all day, or do you have time on your own?"

"An hour here and there."

"Who's that?" she asked suddenly.

He stared, horrified, at the television screen, where for a few seconds Mrs. Bagchi choppily appeared, sitting at a small table at a café, stirring sugar with a tiny spoon into a tiny cup. And then he remembered offering to let Mr. Yamata, one of his

Japanese companions, look through the lens. Without his realizing, Mr. Yamata must have pressed the record button. Mrs. Bagchi vanished, did not appear again. He was grateful the room was dark, that his daughter could not see his face. "Who do you mean?"

"She's gone now. A woman who looked Indian."

It was an opportunity to tell Ruma. It was more difficult than he'd thought, being in his daughter's home, being around her all day. He felt pathetic deceiving her. But what would he say? That he had made a new friend? A girlfriend? The word was unknown to him, impossible to express; he had never had a girlfriend in his life. It would have been easier telling Romi. He would have absorbed the information casually, might even have found it a relief. Ruma was different. All his life he'd felt condemned by her, on his wife's behalf. She and Ruma were allies. And he had endured his daughter's resentment, never telling Ruma his side of things, never saying that his wife had been overly demanding, unwilling to appreciate the life he'd worked hard to provide.

Like his wife, Ruma was now alone in this new place, overwhelmed, without friends, caring for a young child, all of it reminding him, too much, of the early years of his marriage, the years for which his wife had never forgiven him. He had always assumed Ruma's life would be different. She'd worked for as long as he could remember. Even in high school, in spite of his and his wife's protests, she'd insisted, in the summers, on working as a busgirl at a local restaurant, the sort of work their relatives in India would have found disgraceful for a girl of her class and education. But his daughter was no longer his responsibility. Finally, he had reached that age.

"That is one thing I have observed on my travels," he said as Siena's sloping pink piazza flashed across the screen, Mrs. Bagchi concealed somewhere in the throng. "Indians are everywhere these days."

. . .

Akash woke her the following morning, running into her room
and tugging her arm. "Dadu went away."

"What are you talking about?"

"He's not here."

She got up. It was quarter to eight. "He's probably gone for
a walk, Akash." But when she looked out the window, she saw
that the rental car wasn't in the driveway.

"Is he coming back?"

"Hold on, Akash, let me think." Her heart was pounding
and she felt as she would sometimes on a playground, unable,
for a few seconds, to spot Akash. In the kitchen she saw that her
father had not had his breakfast; there was no bowl and spoon
in the dish drainer, no dried-out tea bag on a plate beside the
stove. She wondered if he'd been feeling ill, if he'd driven off in
search of a pharmacy for aspirin or Alka-Seltzer. It would be
like him, to do that and not wake her up. Once he'd had root
canal surgery without telling anyone, coming home in the
evening with his mouth swollen and full of gauze. Then she
wondered if he'd discovered the boats moored to the dock they
shared at the edge of the lake and taken one onto the water.
There was no way to reach him; her father did not carry a cell
phone. As for calling the police, she didn't know the number of
the rental car's license plate. She picked up the phone anyway,
deciding to call Adam, to ask him what to do. But just then she
heard the sound of gravel crackling under tires.

"Where on earth did you go?" she demanded. There was
nothing to indicate that her father was in any type of distress;
he was carrying a flat box tied with string that looked like it had
come from a bakery.

"I remembered, yesterday on the way to swimming, passing
by a nursery. I thought I would drive by and see their hours."

"But we've already decided on a nursery school for Akash."

"Not a school. A place that sells plants. You get a fair amount of sun in the back, and the soil looks rich," he said, looking out the window. "A rainy climate is good for the garden. I can plant a few shrubs, some ground covering if you like."

"Oh," she said.

"It is just six miles from your home. Next to it is a place that sells pastries. Here," he said, opening the box and showing it to Akash. "Which would you like?"

"You don't have to work on our garden, Baba. You said you wanted to rest."

"It is relaxing for me."

Flowers in the backyard had not occurred to her until now. And yet his offer appealed to her. She felt flattered by his interest in the place in which she lived, by his desire to make it more beautiful.

"You could have let me know you were going out," Ruma said.

"I did," he replied. "I left a note on the bureau downstairs, saying I was going for a drive."

She turned to Akash, who had pulled apart a croissant and scattered flakes of dough across the front of his pajamas. She was about to blame him for being hasty in his search of her father's room. But of course Akash was too small to see the top of the bureau, too young to read a note.

When the nursery opened her father went out again, taking Akash with him this time, transferring the car seat into the sedan. As they drove off, she realized that this was the first time she was leaving Akash exclusively in her father's care. It was odd being alone in the house, and she worried that perhaps Akash would suddenly demand her presence. She used to feel that way in his infancy, when he would nurse every two hours, when being without him, even briefly, felt abnormal. An hour later her father and Akash returned, with bags of topsoil, flats full of flowers, a shovel, a rake, and a hose. Her father asked if he could borrow some old clothes of Adam's, and Ruma gave him a pair of khakis and a torn oxford shirt, things Adam had set aside to give to the Salvation Army, and lent him a pair of Adam's running shoes. The clothes were large on her father, the shoulders of the shirt drooping, the cuffs of the pants rolled up. For the rest of the day, with Akash playing at his side in a growing mountain of soil, her father pushed the shovel into the ground, hacking away at grass with a soft, forceful sound, wearing his baseball cap to protect his head from the sun. He worked steadily, pausing briefly at midday to eat a peanut butter and jelly sandwich along with Akash, coming in at dusk only because he said the mosquitoes were out.

The next morning her father drove back to the nursery to get more things: a bale of peat moss, bags of mulch and composted manure. This time, in addition to the gardening supplies, he brought back an inflatable kiddie pool, in the form of a crocodile spouting water from its head, which he set up in the yard and filled with the hose. Akash spent all day outdoors, splashing in the pool and squirting water into the garden, or searching for the worms her father dug up. Again her father worked almost continuously until dusk. With Akash outside all day, Ruma had time to do a few things around the house, small and large things she'd been putting off. She paid the bills that were due at the month's end, filed away piles of the paperwork her life with Adam generated, and then began to sort through Akash's clothing, weeding drawers of what he'd outgrown, bringing up larger things from plastic tubs stored in the basement. Depending on whether she had a boy or a girl, she'd have to save the smaller clothes or give them away. It would be another four weeks until the amnio, allowing them to learn the sex. She wasn't showing significantly, had yet to feel any kicks.

But unlike the last time she didn't doubt the presence of life inside her.

She dug out her maternity wear, the large-paneled pants and tunics that she would soon require. After sorting through the clothing, she turned to the unfinished bookcase in Akash's room, which she'd been meaning to paint ever since she bought it, over ten years ago in Boston, to hold her law books. She removed all the toys and books and began to put them in the corner. She would ask her father to help her carry it outside, so that she could paint in the yard. At one point Akash came into the room, surprising her. He was barefoot, his golden legs covered with dirt. She wondered if he would be upset with her for touching his things, but he regarded the pile as if it were perfectly normal and then began picking items out of it.

"What are you up to?" she asked him.

"Growing things."

"Oh? What are you planting?"

"All this stuff," he said, his arms full, walking out of the room. She followed him outside, where she saw that her father had created a small plot for Akash, hardly larger than a spread-open newspaper, with shallow holes dug out at intervals. She watched as Akash buried things into the soil, crouching over the ground just as her father was. Into the soil went a pink rubber ball, a few pieces of Lego stuck together, a wooden block etched with a star.

"Not too deep," her father said. "Not more than a finger. Can you touch it still?"

Akash nodded. He picked up a miniature plastic dinosaur, forcing it into the ground.

"What color is it?" her father asked.

"Red."

"And in Bengali?"

"*Lal.*"

"Good."

"And *neel!*" Akash cried out, pointing to the sky.

While her father was in the shower, she made tea. It was a ritual she liked, a formal recognition of the day turning into evening in spite of the sun not setting. When she was on her own, these hours passed arbitrarily. She was grateful for the opportunity to sit on the porch with her father, with the teapot and the bowl of salted cashews and the plate of Nice biscuits, looking at the lake and listening to the vast breeze work its way through the treetops, a grander version of the way Akash used to sigh when he was a baby, full of contentment, in the depths of sleep. The leaves flickered as if with internal light, shivering though the air was not cold. Akash was asleep, exhausted from playing outdoors all day, and the house was filled with silence.

"If I lived here I would sleep out here in the summers," her father said presently. "I would put out a cot."

"You can, you know."

"What?"

"Sleep out here. We have an air mattress."

"I am only talking. I am comfortable where I am.

"But," he continued, "if I could, I would build a porch like this for myself."

"Why don't you?"

"The condo would not allow it. It would have been nice in the old house."

When her father mentioned their old house, tears sprang to her eyes. In a way it was helpful to be in a place her mother had never seen. It was one of the last conversations she had had with her mother, telling her about Adam's new job, which back then was only a remote possibility, as they rode together to the hospital. "Don't go," her mother had said from the front seat.

"It's too far away. I'll never see you again." Six hours after saying this, her mother was dead. Ruma suddenly wanted to ask her father, as she'd wanted to ask so many times, if he missed her mother, if he'd ever wept for her death. But she'd never asked, and he'd never admitted whether he'd felt or done those things.

"If you were to have built one, where would you have put it?"

He considered. "Off the dining room, I suppose. That side of the house was coolest."

She tried to think of her parents' house transformed this way. She imagined a wall in the dining room broken down, imagined speaking to her mother on the telephone, her mother complaining as the workmen hammered and drilled. Then she saw her parents sitting in the shade, in wicker chairs, having tea as she and her father were now. For when she pictured that house in her mind, her mother was always alive in it, impossible not to see. With the birth of Akash, in his sudden, perfect presence, Ruma had felt awe for the first time in her life. He still had the power to stagger her at times—simply the fact that he was breathing, that all his organs were in their proper places, that blood flowed quietly and effectively through his small, sturdy limbs. He was her flesh and blood, her mother had told her in the hospital the day Akash was born. Only the words her mother used were more literal, enriching the tired phrase with meaning: "He is made from your meat and bone." It had caused Ruma to acknowledge the supernatural in everyday life. But death, too, had the power to awe, she knew this now—that a human being could be alive for years and years, thinking and breathing and eating, full of a million worries and feelings and thoughts, taking up space in the world, and then, in an instant, become absent, invisible.

"I'm sorry we haven't seen your new apartment," she said to

her father. "Adam doesn't have any vacation for a while. But we'll come after the baby's born."

"There is nothing to see there. Just a TV and a sofa and my things. There is no space for all of you to stay. Not like here."

"I'd like to see it anyway," she said. "We can stay in a hotel."

"There is no need, Ruma. No need to travel all that way, just to see an apartment," her father said. "You are a mother now," he added. "No need to drag your children."

"But that's what you and Ma did, taking us to India all those times."

"We had no alternative. Our parents weren't willing to travel. But I will come here again to see you," he said, looking approvingly into the distance and taking a sip of his tea. "I like this place."

"My dad's planting flowers in the backyard," she told Adam that night on the phone.

"Does he plan to be around to take care of them?"

His flippancy irritated her, and she felt defensive on her father's behalf. "I don't know."

"It's Thursday, Ruma. How long are you going to torture yourself?"

She didn't feel tortured any longer. She had planned to tell Adam this, but now she changed her mind. Instead she said, "I want to wait a few more days. Make sure everyone gets along."

"For God's sake, Ruma," Adam said. "He's your father. You've known him all your life."

And yet, until now, she had not known certain things about him. She had not known how self-sufficient he could be, how helpful, to the point where she had not had to wash a dish since he'd arrived. At dinner he was flexible, appreciating the grilled fish and chicken breasts she began preparing after the Indian food ran out, making do with a can of soup for lunch. But it was Akash who brought out a side of her father that surprised Ruma most. In the evenings her father stood beside her in the bathroom as she gave Akash his bath, scrubbing the caked-on dirt from his elbows and knees. He helped put on his pajamas, brush his teeth, and comb back his soft damp hair. When Akash had fallen asleep one afternoon on the living-room carpet, her father made sure to put a pillow under his head, drape a cotton blanket over his body. By now Akash insisted on being read to at night by her father, sleeping downstairs in her father's bed.

The first night Akash slept with her father she went downstairs to make sure he'd fallen asleep. She saw a sliver of light under her father's door and heard the sound of his voice, reading *Green Eggs and Ham*. She imagined them both under the covers, their heads reclining against the pillows, the book between them, Akash turning the pages as her father read. It was obvious that her father did not know the book by heart, as she did, that he was encountering it for the first time in his life. He read awkwardly, pausing between the sentences, his voice oddly animated as it was not in ordinary speech. Still, his effort touched her, and as she stood by the door she realized that for the first time in his life her father had fallen in love. She was about to knock and tell her father that it was past Akash's bedtime, that he should turn out the light. But she stopped herself, returning upstairs, briefly envious of her own son.

The garden was coming along nicely. It was a futile exercise, he knew. He could not picture his daughter or his son-in-law caring for it properly, noticing what needed to be done. In weeks, he guessed, it would be overgrown with weeds, the leaves chewed up by slugs. Then again, perhaps they would hire someone to do the job. He would have preferred to put in vegetables, but they required more work than flowers. It was a modest planting, some slow-growing myrtle and phlox under the trees, two azalea bushes, a row of hostas, a clematis to climb one of the posts of the porch, and in honor of his wife, a small hydrangea. In a plot behind the kitchen, unable to resist, he also put in a few tomatoes, along with some marigolds and impatiens; there was just time for a small harvest to come in by the fall. He spaced out the delphiniums, tied them to stalks, stuck some gladiola bulbs into the ground. He missed working outside, the solid feeling of dirt under his knees, getting into his nails, the smell of it lingering on his skin even after he'd scrubbed himself in the shower. It was the one thing he missed about the old house, and when he thought about his garden was when he missed his wife most keenly. She had taken that from him. For years, after the children had grown, it had just been the two of them, but she managed to use up all the vegetables, putting them into dishes he did not know how to prepare himself. In addition, when she was alive, they regularly entertained, their guests marveling that the potatoes were from their own backyard, taking away bagfuls at the evening's end.

He looked over at Akash's little plot, the dirt carefully mounded up around his toys, pens and pencils stuck into the ground. Pennies were there, too, all the spare ones he'd had in his pocket.

"When will the plants come out?" Akash called out from the swimming pool, where he stood crouching over a little sailboat.

"Soon."

"Tomorrow?"

"Not so soon. These things take time, Akash. Do you remember what I taught you this morning?"

And Akash recited his numbers in Bengali from one to ten.

In bed that night, after Akash had fallen asleep beside him, he wrote Mrs. Bagchi a postcard. It was safer, he decided, than

sending an e-mail from Ruma's computer, a mode of communication he could not bring himself fully to trust. He had
bought the card off a rack at the hardware store where he had
bought Akash's swimming pool. The picture was a view of fer-
ries on Elliott Bay, a sight he had not seen. In Europe he was
always careful to buy postcards only of places he'd been to, feeling dishonest otherwise. But here he had no choice. He composed the letter in Bengali, an alphabet Ruma would not be
able to decipher. "I am planting Ruma a garden," he began.
"Akash has grown and is learning to swim. The weather is
pleasant, no rain here in summer. I am looking forward to
Prague," he ended. He did not sign his name. He looked
through his wallet, where on a folded slip of paper he had written down Mrs. Bagchi's mailing address. He carried only a few
addresses with him: his son and his daughter and now Mrs.
Bagchi, all written on slips of paper that lived behind his driver's license and Social Security card. He filled out the address
in English, and finally, at the top, her name.

He wondered where the nearest post office was. Would
Ruma find it odd if he were to ask her for a stamp? He could
take it back with him to Pennsylvania and mail it from there,
but that seemed silly. He decided he could tell Ruma that he
needed to mail a bill. There was a public mailbox two miles
down the road; at some point before leaving he could drop it
there. He didn't know where to put the postcard now. It was
not an easy room to hide things in: the surfaces were clear, the
corners visible, the closet bare apart from his few shirts. At
some point in the day Ruma came downstairs—he never could
tell when—in order to make his bed and check the hamper for
laundry and wipe away the water that he splattered, in the
course of brushing his teeth and shaving, at the sides of the
sink. He considered putting the postcard in the pocket of his
suitcase, but was too tired to get out of bed. Instead, he tucked
it between the pages of the Seattle guidebook on the side table,

and then, as an extra precaution, put the book into the table drawer.

He turned to face his sleeping grandson, the long lashes and rounded cheeks reminding him of his own children when they were young. He was suddenly conscious that he would probably not live to see Akash into adulthood, that he would never see his grandson's middle age, his old age, this simple fact of life saddening him. He imagined the boy years from now, occupying this very room, shutting the door as Ruma and Romi had. It was inevitable. And yet he knew that he, too, had turned his back on his parents, by settling in America. In the name of ambition and accomplishment, none of which mattered anymore, he had forsaken them. He kissed Akash lightly on the side of his head, smoothing the curling golden hair with his hand, then switched off the lamp, filling the room with darkness.

Saturday morning, the day before her father was scheduled to leave, the garden was finished. After breakfast, he showed Ruma what he'd done. The shrubs were still small, with mulch around their bases and enough space to distinguish one from the next, but he said they'd grow taller and closer together, showing her with his hand the height she could anticipate by next summer. He told her how often to water, and for how long, to wait until the sun had gone down. He showed her the bottle of fertilizer he'd bought, and told her when to add it to the watering. Patiently she listened as Akash dashed in and out of his pool, but she absorbed little of what her father said.

"Watch out for these beetles," he said, plucking an insect off a leaf and flicking it away. "The hydrangea won't bloom much this year. The flowers will be pink or blue depending on the acidity of your soil. You'll have to prune it back, eventually."

She nodded.

"They were always your mother's favorite," her father added. "In this country, that is."

Ruma looked at the plant, at the dark green leaves with serrated edges. She had not known.

"Make sure to keep the tomatoes off the ground." He leaned over, readjusting one of the plants. "This stake should be enough to support them, or you could use a little string. Don't let them dry out. If the sun is strong check them twice a day. If frost comes before they've ripened, pick them and wrap them up in newspaper. And cut down the delphinium stalks in the fall."

"Maybe you could do that," she suggested.

He stood up awkwardly, a hand gripping the front of his thigh. He took off his baseball cap and wiped his forehead with his arm. "I have a trip scheduled. I've already bought the ticket."

"I mean after you get back, Baba."

Her father had been looking down at his dirt-rimmed fingernails, but now he raised his face and looked around him, at the garden and at the trees.

"It is a good place, Ruma. But this is your home, not mine."

She had expected resistance, so she kept talking. "You can have the whole downstairs. You can still go on your trips whenever you like. We won't stand in your way. What do you say, Akash," she called out. "Should Dadu live with us in here? Would you like that?"

Akash began jumping up and down in the pool, squirting water from a plastic dolphin, nodding his head.

"I know it would be a big move," Ruma continued. "But it would be good for you. For all of us." By now she was crying. Her father did not step toward her to comfort her. He was silent, waiting for the moment to pass.

"I don't want to be a burden," he said after a while.

"You wouldn't. You'd be a help. You don't have to make up your mind now. Just promise you'll think about it."

He lifted his head and looked at her, a brief sad look that seemed finally to take her in, and nodded.

"Would you like to do anything special on your last day here?" she asked. "We could drive into Seattle for lunch."

He seemed to brighten at the suggestion. "How about the boat ride? Is that still possible?"

She went inside, telling him she was going to get Akash ready and look up the schedule. He was suddenly desperate to leave, the remaining twenty-four hours feeling unbearable. He reminded himself that tomorrow he would be on a plane, heading back to Pennsylvania. And that two weeks after that he would be going to Prague with Mrs. Bagchi, sleeping next to her at night. He knew that it was not for his sake that his daughter was asking him to live here. It was for hers. She needed him, as he'd never felt she'd needed him before, apart from the obvious things he provided her in the course of his life. And because of this the offer upset him more. A part of him, the part of him that would never cease to be a father, felt obligated to accept. But it was not what he wanted. Being here for a week, however pleasant, had only confirmed the fact. He did not want to be part of another family, part of the mess, the feuds, the demands, the energy of it. He did not want to live in the margins of his daughter's life, in the shadow of her marriage. He didn't want to live again in an enormous house that would only fill up with things over the years, as the children grew, all the things he'd recently gotten rid of, all the books and papers and clothes and objects one felt compelled to possess, to save. Life grew and grew until a certain point. The point he had reached now.

The only temptation was the boy, but he knew that the boy would forget him. It was Ruma to whom he would give a new reminder that now that his wife was gone, even though he was still alive, there was no longer anyone to care for her. When he saw Ruma now, chasing Akash, picking up after him, wiping his urine from the floor, responsible for his every need, he realized how much younger his wife had been when she'd done all that, practically a girl. By the time his wife was Ruma's age, their children were already approaching adolescence. The more the children grew, the less they had seemed to resemble either parent—they spoke differently, dressed differently, seemed foreign in every way, from the texture of their hair to the shapes of their feet and hands. Oddly, it was his grandson, who was only half-Bengali to begin with, who did not even have a Bengali surname, with whom he felt a direct biological connection, a sense of himself reconstituted in another.

He remembered his children coming home from college, impatient with him and his wife, enamored of their newfound independence, always wanting to leave. It had tormented his wife and, though he never admitted it, had pained him as well. He couldn't help thinking, on those occasions, how young they'd once been, how helpless in his nervous arms, needing him for their very survival, knowing no one else. He and his wife were their whole world. But eventually that need dissipated, dwindled to something amorphous, tenuous, something that threatened at times to snap. That loss was in store for Ruma, too; her children would become strangers, avoiding her. And because she was his child he wanted to protect her from that, as he had tried throughout his life to protect her from so many things. He wanted to shield her from the deterioration that inevitably took place in the course of a marriage, and from the conclusion he sometimes feared was true: that the entire enterprise of having a family, of putting children on this earth, as gratifying as it sometimes felt, was flawed from the start. But these were an old man's speculations, an old man who was him self now behaving like a child.

Her father left early the next morning, while Akash was still asleep. Again she'd offered to go to the airport, but this time he was even more adamant, telling her he didn't want to upset Akash's schedule. They were all tired from their day in Seattle. After the ferry ride they'd gone up the Space Needle and then had dinner in Pike Place Market before driving home. Joining her father in the kitchen, she saw that he'd already finished his cereal, the bowl and spoon in the drainer. The tea bag normally saved for a second cup later in the day had been tossed out.

"You've got everything?" she asked, seeing his suitcase by the door. He'd come bearing gifts but had bought nothing to take back with him. Everything he'd purchased in the past week, all the things from the nursery and the hardware store, the coiled-up hose and tools and bags of leftover topsoil now neatly arranged under the porch, had been for her.

"Call when you get home," she said, something her mother would say to her children when they parted. She asked for his flight information, writing it on the bottom of the same sheet of paper that was on the refrigerator door with Adam's itinerary.

"Adam will be here tonight?"

She nodded.

"Good. Things will return to normal then."

She wanted to tell him how normal it had felt, to have her father there. But she couldn't bring herself to say the words. Her father glanced at his watch, then poured a bit of his tea into his saucer in order to cool it more quickly. He raised the saucer to his lips, sipping from the rim.

"It has been a marvelous week, Ruma. I have enjoyed each day."

"Me too."

"These days with Akash have been the greatest gift," he added, his voice softening. "If you like, I can come for a while after you have the baby. I won't be as useful as your mother would have been."

"That's not true."

"But please understand, I prefer to stay on my own. I am too old now to make such a shift."

His gentle words fell on her thickly, too quickly. She understood that he had not had to think it over, that he had never intended to stay.

"Make time to look into law firms here," he continued. "Don't let all that hard work go to waste."

He stood up, and before she could stop him, rinsed out his cup and saucer and put those into the drainer as well. It was time to go.

"Let me go downstairs and give Akash a kiss," he said. He turned to leave the room, then stopped. "Do you have a spare stamp? I need to put a bill into the mail."

"In the drawer of the little table in the hall," she said. "There's a roll there."

She heard the drawer opening, then closing, then the sound of his flip-flops hitting the stairs. When he returned, he went to the entryway to put on his shoes, tied his laces, fit the flip-flops into the front pocket of his suitcase. He kissed Ruma on the cheek. "Take care of yourself. Let me know how the garden comes along." He glanced at her stomach and added, "I am waiting for the good news." He turned and walked outside to his car, putting the suitcase into the trunk. She stood watching as he turned on the engine and backed out, wondering when she would see him again. At the mailbox he paused, and for a moment she thought he was about to open the window and put his bill inside. But he only waved through the closed window, leaning toward her, looking lost, and a few seconds later he was gone.

"Where's Dadu?" Akash asked as she was finishing her tea.

"He went home today."

"Why?"

"Because that's where he lives."

"Why?" In her son's small face she saw the disappointment she also felt.

"Daddy's coming back tonight," she said, trying to change the subject. "Should we make a cake?"

Akash went to the kitchen door and tried the knob, looking through the glass at the yard. "I want Dadu."

She opened the door for him and followed him out, both of them padding barefoot, Ruma treading gingerly, Akash not fearful of stones or twigs. It was chillier than she expected, still too early for the warmth of the day to have gathered. She considered going back in for sweaters. "Sweetpea? You cold?" she asked, folding her arms across her chest, but Akash did not reply. He picked up the empty watering can her father had left underneath the porch and pretended to water things in his little plot. She looked at the items poking out of the ground: pens and pencils, a straw, a Popsicle stick. There were papers, too: old envelopes from junk mail, the cards that fell out of magazines, seeking subscribers, folded up like little tents on the soil. Her eye fell to another piece of paper, stiffer than the rest. She bent down to look at it, recognizing her father's handwriting. She assumed it was a postcard her father had sent to her, one Akash had removed from the front of the refrigerator door, or the basket on the hall table. But this postcard bore no postmark, had not been sent. It was composed in Bengali and addressed in English to someone on Long Island. A Mrs. Meenakshi Bagchi.

She picked it up. "Akash, what's this?"

He reached out, attempting to snatch it back from her. "It's mine."

"What is it?" she asked, more harshly this time.

"It's for my garden."

"Did Dadu give this to you?"

He shook his head angrily, and then he started to cry.

She stared at the card and instantly she knew, just as she'd known from the expression on the surgeon's face what had happened to her mother on the operating table. The woman in the video, the reason for her father's trips, the reason for his good spirits, the reason he did not want to live in Seattle. The reason he'd wanted a stamp that morning. Here, in a handful of sentences she could not even read, was the explanation, the evidence that it was not just with Akash that her father had fallen in love.

He was in a bookshop in the airport, buying a newspaper to read at the gate, when he saw, propped by the register on a metal stand, a copy of the same guidebook to Seattle that had been at his bedside in Ruma's house. He'd searched everywhere for the book, overturning all the sheets, nearly waking up Akash in the process. He opened drawers he'd never used, peering on the shelf of the closet, wedging his hand as far as it would go under all sides of the mattress, cursing himself for not making the time to mail the card earlier. At last he spotted the book on the floor beneath the bed, on the side where Akash slept. He searched frantically through each page, shaking the book by its spine, but the postcard was missing. For an instant he'd been tempted to wake the boy, to ask if he'd seen it, put it somewhere. He looked in the bathroom, in the laundry hamper, in the tub where just that morning he'd bathed. Finally, unable to justify his search any longer, knowing that he would miss his plane, he left, the unused stamp from Ruma still floating in his shirt pocket, its value more than a postcard needed, a weightless thing that filled him with dread.

She took Akash inside, wiped his tears and held him, and then, when he was calm, prepared his breakfast. She said yes when he asked if he could watch television, setting him with his cereal bowl behind the coffee table, and returned to the kitchen to look at the postcard again. Her first impulse was to shred it, but she stopped herself, staring at the Bengali letters her mother had once tried and failed to teach Ruma when she was a girl. They were sentences her mother would have absorbed in an instant, sentences that proved, with more force than the funeral, more force than all the days since then, that her mother no longer existed. Where had her mother gone, when life persisted, when Ruma still needed her to explain so many things?

She walked back outside, across the grass and looked at the hydrangea her father had planted, that was to bloom pink or blue depending on the soil. It did not prove to Ruma that her father had loved her mother, or even that he missed her. And yet he had put it there, honored her before turning to another woman. Ruma smoothed out the postcard in her hand, scraping away, with her fingernail, the dirt that obscured a bit of the Zip code. She turned the postcard around and looked at the front, at the generic view her father had chosen to commemorate his visit. Then she went back into the house, to the table in the hall. From the drawer she took out the roll of stamps and affixed one to the card, for the mailman, later in the day, to take away.

Hell–Heaven

Pranab Chakraborty wasn't technically my father's younger brother. He was a fellow Bengali from Calcutta who had washed up on the barren shores of my parents' social life in the early seventies, when they lived in a rented apartment in Central Square and could number their acquaintances on one hand. But I had no real uncles in America, and so I was taught to call him Pranab Kaku. Accordingly, he called my father Shyamal Da, always addressing him in the polite form, and he called my mother Boudi, which is how Bengalis are supposed to address an older brother's wife, instead of using her first name, Aparna. After Pranab Kaku was befriended by my parents, he confessed that on the day we met him he had followed my mother and me for the better part of an afternoon around the streets of Cambridge, where she and I tended to roam after I got out of school. He had trailed behind us along Massachusetts Avenue and in and out of the Harvard Coop, where my mother liked to look at discounted housewares. He wandered with us into Harvard Yard, where my mother often sat on the grass on pleasant days and watched the stream of students and professors filing busily along the paths, until, finally, as we were climbing the steps to Widener Library so that I could use the bathroom, he tapped my mother on the shoulder and inquired, in English, if she might be a Bengali. The answer to his question was clear, given that my mother was wearing the red and white bangles unique to Bengali married women, and a common Tangail sari, and had a thick stem of vermilion powder in the center parting of her hair, and the full round face and large dark eyes that are so typical of Bengali women. He noticed the two or three safety pins she wore fastened to the thin gold bangles that were behind the red and white ones, which she would use to replace a missing hook on a blouse or to draw a string through a petti-coat at a moment's notice, a practice he associated strictly with his mother and sisters and aunts in Calcutta. Moreover, Pranab Kaku had overheard my mother speaking to me in Ben-gali, telling me that I couldn't buy an issue of *Archie* at the Coop. But back then, he also confessed, he was so new to America that he took nothing for granted and doubted even the obvious.

My parents and I had lived in Central Square for three years prior to that day; before that, we lived in Berlin, where I was born and where my father had finished his training in microbi-ology before accepting a position as a researcher at Mass General, and before Berlin my mother and father had lived in India, where they were strangers to each other, and where their mar-riage had been arranged. Central Square is the first place I can recall living, and in my memories of our apartment, in a dark brown shingled house on Ashburton Place, Pranab Kaku is always there. According to the story he liked to recall often, my mother invited him to accompany us back to our apartment that very afternoon and prepared tea for the two of them; then, after learning that he had not had a proper Bengali meal in more than three months, she served him the leftover curried mackerel and rice that we had eaten for dinner the night before. He remained into the evening for a second dinner after my father got home, and after that he showed up for dinner almost every night, occupying the fourth chair at our square Formica kitchen table and becoming a part of our family in practice as well as in name.

He was from a wealthy family in Calcutta and had never had to do so much as pour himself a glass of water before moving to America, to study engineering at MIT. Life as a graduate student in Boston was a cruel shock, and in his first month he lost nearly twenty pounds. He had arrived in January, in the middle of a snowstorm, and at the end of a week he had packed his bags and gone to Logan, prepared to abandon the opportunity he'd worked toward all his life, only to change his mind at the last minute. He was living on Trowbridge Street in the home of a divorced woman with two young children who were always screaming and crying. He rented a room in the attic and was permitted to use the kitchen only at specified times of the day and instructed always to wipe down the stove with Windex and a sponge. My parents agreed that it was a terrible situation, and if they'd had a bedroom to spare they would have offered it to him. Instead, they welcomed him to our meals and opened up our apartment to him at any time, and soon it was there he went between classes and on his days off, always leaving behind some vestige of himself: a nearly finished pack of cigarettes, a newspaper, a piece of mail he had not bothered to open, a sweater he had taken off and forgotten in the course of his stay.

I remember vividly the sound of his exuberant laughter and the sight of his lanky body slouched or sprawled on the dull, mismatched furniture that had come with our apartment. He had a striking face, with a high forehead and a thick mustache, and overgrown, untamed hair that my mother said made him look like the American hippies who were everywhere in those days. His long legs jiggled rapidly up and down wherever he sat, and his elegant hands trembled when he held a cigarette between his fingers, tapping the ashes into a teacup that my mother began to set aside for this exclusive purpose. Though he was a scientist by training, there was nothing rigid or predictable or orderly about him. He always seemed to be starving, walking through the door and announcing that he hadn't had lunch, and then he would eat ravenously, reaching behind my mother to steal cutlets as she was frying them, before she had a chance to set them properly on a plate with red onion salad. In private, my parents remarked that he was a brilliant student, a star at Jadavpur who had come to MIT with an impressive assistantship, but Pranab Kaku was cavalier about his classes, skipping them with frequency. "These Americans are learning equations I knew at Usha's age," he would complain. He was stunned that my second-grade teacher didn't assign any homework and that at the age of seven I hadn't yet been taught square roots or the concept of pi.

He appeared without warning, never phoning beforehand but simply knocking on the door the way people did in Calcutta and calling out "Boudi!" as he waited for my mother to let him in. Before we met him, I would return from school and find my mother with her purse in her lap and her trench coat on, desperate to escape the apartment where she had spent the day alone. But now I would find her in the kitchen, rolling out dough for luchis, which she normally made only on Sundays for my father and me, or putting up new curtains she'd bought at Woolworth's. I did not know, back then, that Pranab Kaku's visits were what my mother looked forward to all day, that she changed into a new sari and combed her hair in anticipation of his arrival, and that she planned, days in advance, the snacks she would serve him with such nonchalance. That she lived for the moment she heard him call out "Boudi!" from the porch and that she was in a foul humor on the days he didn't materialize.

It must have pleased her that I looked forward to his visits as well. He showed me card tricks and an optical illusion in which he appeared to be severing his own thumb with enormous struggle and strength and taught me to memorize multiplication tables well before I had to learn them in school. His hobby was photography. He owned an expensive camera that required thought before you pressed the shutter, and I quickly became his favorite subject, round-faced, missing teeth, my thick bangs in need of a trim. They are still the pictures of myself I like best, for they convey that confidence of youth I no longer possess, especially in front of a camera. I remember having to run back and forth in Harvard Yard as he stood with the camera, trying to capture me in motion, or posing on the steps of university buildings and on the street and against the trunks of trees. There is only one photograph in which my mother appears; she is holding me as I sit straddling her lap, her head tilted toward me, her hands pressed to my ears as if to prevent me from hearing something. In that picture, Pranab Kaku's shadow, his two arms raised at angles to hold the camera to his face, hovers in the corner of the frame, his darkened, featureless shape superimposed on one side of my mother's body. It was always the three of us. I was always there when he visited. It would have been inappropriate for my mother to receive him in the apartment alone; this was something that went without saying.

They had in common all the things she and my father did not: a love of music, film, leftist politics, poetry. They were from the same neighborhood in North Calcutta, their family homes within walking distance, the facades familiar to them once the exact locations were described. They knew the same shops, the same bus and tram routes, the same holes-in-the-wall for the best jelabis and moghlai parathas. My father, on the other hand, came from a suburb twenty miles outside Calcutta, an area that my mother considered the wilderness, and even in her bleakest hours of homesickness she was grateful that my father had at least spared her a life in the stern house of her in-laws, where she would have had to keep her head covered with the end of her sari at all times and use an outhouse that was nothing but a raised platform with a hole, and where, in the rooms, there was not a single painting hanging on the walls. Within a few weeks, Pranab Kaku had brought his reel-to-reel over to our apartment, and he played for my mother medley after medley of songs from the Hindi films of their youth. They were cheerful songs of courtship, which transformed the quiet life in our apartment and transported my mother back to the world she'd left behind in order to marry my father. She and Pranab Kaku would try to recall which scene in which movie the songs were from, who the actors were and what they were wearing. My mother would describe Raj Kapoor and Nargis singing under umbrellas in the rain, or Dev Anand strumming a guitar on the beach in Goa. She and Pranab Kaku would argue passionately about these matters, raising their voices in playful combat, confronting each other in a way she and my father never did.

Because he played the part of a younger brother, she felt free to call him Pranab, whereas she never called my father by his first name. My father was thirty-seven then, nine years older than my mother. Pranab Kaku was twenty-five. My father was a lover of silence and solitude. He had married my mother to placate his parents; they were willing to accept his desertion as long as he had a wife. He was wedded to his work, his research, and he existed in a shell that neither my mother nor I could penetrate. Conversation was a chore for him; it required an effort he preferred to expend at the lab. He disliked excess in anything, voiced no cravings or needs apart from the frugal elements of his daily routine: cereal and tea in the mornings, a cup of tea after he got home, and two different vegetable dishes every night with dinner. He did not eat with the reckless appetite of Pranab Kaku. My father had a survivor's mentality. From time to time, he liked to remark, in mixed company and often with no relevant provocation, that starving Russians under Stalin had resorted to eating the glue off the back of their wallpaper. One might think that he would have felt slightly jealous, or at the very least suspicious, about the regularity of Pranab Kaku's visits and the effect they had on my mother's behavior and mood. But my guess is that my father was grateful to Pranab Kaku for the companionship he provided, freed from the sense of responsibility he must have felt for forcing her to leave India, and relieved, perhaps, to see her happy for a change.

In the summer, Pranab Kaku bought a navy-blue Volkswagen Beetle and began to take my mother and me for drives through Boston and Cambridge, and soon outside the city, flying down the highway. He would take us to India Tea and Spices in Watertown, and one time he drove us all the way to New Hampshire to look at the mountains. As the weather grew hotter, we started going, once or twice a week, to Walden Pond. My mother always prepared a picnic of hard-boiled eggs and cucumber sandwiches and talked fondly about the winter picnics of her youth, grand expeditions with fifty of her relatives, all taking the train into the West Bengal countryside. Pranab Kaku listened to these stories with interest, absorbing the vanishing details of her past. He did not turn a deaf ear to her nostalgia, like my father, or listen uncomprehending, like me. At Walden Pond, Pranab Kaku would coax my mother through the woods, and lead her down the steep slope to the water's edge. She would unpack the picnic things and sit and watch us as we swam. His chest was matted with thick dark hair, all the way to his waist. He was an odd sight, with his pole-thin legs and a small, flaccid belly, like an otherwise svelte woman who has had a baby and not bothered to tone her abdomen. "You're making me fat, Boudi," he would complain after gorging himself on my mother's cooking. He swam noisily, clumsily, his head always above the water; he didn't know how to blow bubbles or hold his breath, as I had learned in swimming class. Wherever we went, any stranger would have naturally assumed that Pranab Kaku was my father, that my mother was his wife.

It is clear to me now that my mother was in love with him. He wooed her as no other man had, with the innocent affection of a brother-in-law. In my mind, he was just a family member, a cross between an uncle and a much older brother, for in certain respects my parents sheltered and cared for him in much the same way they cared for me. He was respectful of my father, always seeking his advice about making a life in the West, about setting up a bank account and getting a job, and deferring to his opinions about Kissinger and Watergate. Occasionally, my mother would tease him about women, asking about female Indian students at MIT or showing him pictures of her younger cousins in India. "What do you think of her?" she would ask. "Isn't she pretty?" She knew that she could never have Pranab Kaku for herself, and I suppose it was her attempt to keep him in the family. But, most important, in the beginning he was totally dependent on her, needing her for those months in a way my father never did in the whole history of their marriage. He brought to my mother the first and, I suspect, the only pure happiness she ever felt. I don't think even my birth made her as happy. I was evidence of her marriage to my father, an assumed consequence of the life she had been raised to lead. But Pranab Kaku was different. He was the one totally unanticipated pleasure in her life.

In the fall of 1974, Pranab Kaku met a student at Radcliffe named Deborah, an American, and she began to accompany him to our house. I called Deborah by her first name, as my parents did, but Pranab Kaku taught her to call my father Shyamal Da and my mother Boudi, something with which Deborah gladly complied. Before they came to dinner for the first time, I asked my mother, as she was straightening up the living room, if I ought to address her as Deborah Kakima, turning her into an aunt as I had turned Pranab into an uncle. "What's the point?" my mother said, looking back at me sharply. "In a few weeks, the fun will be over and she'll leave him." And yet Deborah remained by his side, attending the weekend parties that Pranab Kaku and my parents were becoming more involved with, gatherings that were exclusively Bengali with the exception of her. Deborah was very tall, taller than both my parents and nearly as tall as Pranab Kaku. She wore her long brass-colored hair center-parted, as my mother did, but it was gathered into a low ponytail instead of a braid, or it spilled messily over her shoulders and down her back in a way that my mother considered indecent. She wore small silver spectacles and not a trace of makeup, and she studied philosophy. I found her utterly beautiful, but according to my mother she had spots on her face, and her hips were too small.

For a while, Pranab Kaku still showed up once a week for dinner on his own, mostly asking my mother what she thought of Deborah. He sought her approval, telling her that Deborah was the daughter of professors at Boston College, that her father published poetry, and that both her parents had PhDs. When he wasn't around, my mother complained about Deborah's visits, about having to make the food less spicy, even though Deborah said she liked spicy food, and feeling embarrassed to put a fried fish head in the dal. Pranab Kaku taught Deborah to say *khub bhalo* and *aacha* and to pick up certain foods with her fingers instead of with a fork. Sometimes they ended up feeding each other, allowing their fingers to linger in each other's mouth, causing my parents to look down at their plates and wait for the moment to pass. At larger gatherings, they kissed and held hands in front of everyone, and when they were out of earshot my mother would talk to the other Bengali women. "He used to be so different. I don't understand how a person can change so suddenly. It's just hell–heaven, the difference," she would say, always using the English words for her self-concocted, backward metaphor.

The more my mother began to resent Deborah's visits, the more I began to anticipate them. I fell in love with Deborah, the way young girls often fall in love with women who are not their mothers. I loved her serene gray eyes, the ponchos and denim wrap skirts and sandals she wore, her straight hair that she let me manipulate into all sorts of silly styles. I longed for her casual appearance; my mother insisted whenever there was a gathering that I wear one of my ankle-length, faintly Victorian dresses, which she referred to as maxis, and have party hair, which meant taking a strand from either side of my head and joining them with a barrette at the back. At parties, Deborah would, eventually, politely slip away, much to the relief of the Bengali women with whom she was expected to carry on a conversation, and she would play with me. I was older than all my parents' friends' children, but with Deborah I had a companion. She knew all about the books I read, about Pippi Longstocking and Anne of Green Gables. She gave me the sorts of gifts my parents had neither the money nor the inspiration to buy: a large book of Grimm's *Fairy Tales* with watercolor illustrations on thick, silken pages, wooden puppets with hair fashioned from yarn. She told me about her family, three older sisters and two brothers, the youngest of whom was closer to my age than to hers. Once, after visiting her parents, she brought back three Nancy Drews, her name written in a girlish hand at the top of the first page, and an old toy she'd had, a small paper theater set with interchangeable backdrops, the exterior of a castle and a ballroom and an open field. Deborah and I spoke freely in English, a language in which, by that age, I expressed myself more easily than Bengali, which I was required to speak at home. Sometimes she asked me how to say this or that in Bengali; once, she asked me what *asobbho* meant. I hesitated, then told her it was what my mother called me if I had done something extremely naughty, and Deborah's face clouded. I felt protective of her, aware that she was unwanted, that she was resented, aware of the nasty things people said.

Outings in the Volkswagen now involved the four of us, Deborah in the front, her hand over Pranab Kaku's while it rested on the gearshift, my mother and I in the back. Soon, my mother began coming up with reasons to excuse herself, headaches and incipient colds, and so I became part of a new triangle. To my surprise, my mother allowed me to go with them, to the Museum of Fine Arts and the Public Garden and the Aquarium. She was waiting for the affair to end, for Deborah to break Pranab Kaku's heart and for him to return to us, scarred and penitent. I saw no sign of their relationship foundering. Their open affection for each other, their easily expressed happiness, was a new and romantic thing to me. Having me in the backseat allowed Pranab Kaku and Deborah to practice for the future, to try on the idea of a family of their own. Countless photographs were taken of me and Deborah, of me sitting on Deborah's lap, holding her hand, kissing her on the cheek. We exchanged what I believed were secret smiles, and in those moments I felt that she understood me better than anyone else in the world. Anyone would have said that Deborah would make an excellent mother one day. But my mother refused to acknowledge such a thing. I did not know at the time that my mother allowed me to go off with Pranab Kaku and Deborah because she was pregnant for the fifth time since my birth and was so sick and exhausted and fearful of losing another baby that she slept most of the day. After ten weeks, she miscarried once again and was advised by her doctor to stop trying.

By summer, there was a diamond on Deborah's left hand, something my mother had never been given. Because his own family lived so far away, Pranab Kaku came to the house alone one day, to ask for my parents' blessing before giving her the ring. He showed us the box, opening it and taking out the diamond nestled inside. "I want to see how it looks on someone," he said, urging my mother to try it on, but she refused. I was the one who stuck out my hand, feeling the weight of the ring suspended at the base of my finger. Then he asked for a second thing: he wanted my parents to write to his parents, saying that they had met Deborah and that they thought highly of her. He was nervous, naturally, about telling his family that he intended to marry an American girl. He had told his parents all about us, and at one point my parents had received a letter from them, expressing appreciation for taking such good care of their son and for giving him a proper home in America. "It needn't be long," Pranab Kaku said. "Just a few lines. They'll accept it more easily if it comes from you." My father thought neither ill nor well of Deborah, never commenting or criticizing as my mother did, but he assured Pranab Kaku that a letter of endorsement would be on its way to Calcutta by the end of the week. My mother nodded her assent, but the following day I saw the teacup Pranab Kaku had used all this time as an ashtray in the kitchen garbage can, in pieces, and three Band-Aids taped to my mother's hand.

Pranab Kaku's parents were horrified by the thought of their only son marrying an American woman, and a few weeks later our telephone rang in the middle of the night: it was Mr. Chakraborty telling my father that they could not possibly bless such a marriage, that it was out of the question, that if Pranab Kaku dared to marry Deborah he would no longer acknowledge him as a son. Then his wife got on the phone, asking to speak to my mother and attacked her as if they were intimate, blaming my mother for allowing the affair to develop. She said that they had already chosen a wife for him in Calcutta, that he'd left for America with the understanding that he'd go back after he had finished his studies and marry this girl. They had bought the neighboring flat in their building for Pranab and his betrothed, and it was sitting empty, waiting for his return. "We thought we could trust you, and yet you have betrayed us so deeply," his mother said, taking out her anger on a stranger in a way she could not with her son. "Is this what happens to people in America?" For Pranab Kaku's sake, my mother defended the engagement, telling his mother that Deborah was a polite girl from a decent family. Pranab Kaku's parents pleaded with mine to talk him out of it, but my father refused, deciding that it was not their place to get embroiled. "We are not his parents," he told my mother. "We can tell him they don't approve but nothing more." And so my parents told Pranab Kaku nothing about how his parents had berated them and blamed them, and threatened to disown Pranab Kaku, only that they had refused to give him their blessing. In the face of this refusal, Pranab Kaku shrugged. "I don't care. Not everyone can be as open-minded as you," he told my parents. "Your blessing is blessing enough."

After the engagement, Pranab Kaku and Deborah began drifting out of our lives. They moved in together, to an apartment in Boston, in the South End, a part of the city my parents considered unsafe. We moved as well, to a house in Natick. Though my parents had bought the house, they occupied it as if they were still tenants, touching up scuff marks with leftover paint and reluctant to put holes in the walls, and every afternoon when the sun shone through the living-room window my mother closed the blinds so that our new furniture would not fade. A few weeks before the wedding, my parents invited Pranab Kaku to the house alone, and my mother prepared a special meal to mark the end of his bachelorhood. It would be the only Bengali aspect of the wedding; the rest of it would be strictly American, with a cake and a minister and Deborah in a long white dress and veil. There is a photograph of the dinner, taken by my father, the only picture, to my knowledge, in which my mother and Pranab Kaku appear together. The picture is slightly blurry; I remember Pranab Kaku explaining to my father how to work the camera, and so he is captured looking up from the kitchen table and the elaborate array of food my mother had prepared in his honor, his mouth open, his long arm outstretched and his finger pointing, instructing my father how to read the light meter or some such thing. My mother stands beside him, one hand placed on top of his head in a gesture of blessing, the first and last time she was to touch him in her life. "She will leave him," my mother told her friends afterward. "He is throwing his life away."

The wedding was at a church in Ipswich, with a reception at a country club. It was going to be a small ceremony, which my parents took to mean one or two hundred people as opposed to three or four hundred. My mother was shocked that fewer than thirty people had been invited, and she was more perplexed than honored that, of all the Bengalis Pranab Kaku knew by then, we were the only ones on the list. At the wedding we sat, like the other guests, first on the hard wooden pews of the church and then at a long table that had been set up for lunch. Though we were the closest thing Pranab Kaku had to a family that day, we were not included in the group photographs that were taken on the grounds of the country club, with Deborah's parents and grandparents and her many siblings, and neither my mother nor my father got up to make a toast. My mother did not appreciate the fact that Deborah had made sure that my parents, who did not eat beef, were given fish instead of filet mignon like everyone else. She kept speaking in Bengali, complaining about the formality of the proceedings, and the fact that Pranab Kaku, wearing a tuxedo, barely said a word to us because he was too busy leaning over the shoulders of his new American in-laws as he circled the table. As usual, my father said nothing in response to my mother's commentary, quietly and methodically working though his meal, his fork and knife occasionally squeaking against the surface of the china, because he was accustomed to eating with his hands. He cleared his plate and then my mother's, for she had pronounced the food inedible, and then he announced that he had overeaten and had a stomachache. The only time my mother forced a smile was when Deborah appeared behind her chair, kissing her on the cheek and asking if we were enjoying ourselves.

When the dancing started, my parents remained at the table, drinking tea, and after two or three songs they decided that it was time for us to go home, my mother shooting me looks to that effect across the room, where I was dancing in a circle with Pranab Kaku and Deborah and the other children at the wedding. I wanted to stay, and when, reluctantly, I walked over to where my parents sat, Deborah followed me. "Boudi, let Usha stay. She's having such a good time," she said to my mother. "Lots of people will be heading back your way, someone can drop her off in a little while." But my mother said no, I had had plenty of fun already and forced me to put on my coat over my long puff-sleeved dress. As we drove home from the wedding I told my mother, for the first but not the last time in my life, that I hated her.

The following year, we received a birth announcement from the Chakrabortys, a picture of twin girls, which my mother did not paste into an album or display on the refrigerator door. The girls were named Srabani and Sabitri but were called Bonny and Sara. Apart from a thank-you card for our wedding gift, it was their only communication; we were not invited to the new house in Marblehead, bought after Pranab Kaku got a high-paying job at Stone & Webster. For a while, my parents and their friends continued to invite the Chakrabortys to gatherings, but because they never came, or left after staying only an hour, the invitations stopped. Their absences were attributed, by my parents and their circle, to Deborah, and it was universally agreed that she had stripped Pranab Kaku not only of his origins but of his independence. She was the enemy, he was her prey, and their example was invoked as a warning, and as vindication, that mixed marriages were a doomed enterprise. Occasionally, they surprised everyone, appearing at a pujo for a few hours with their two identical little girls who barely looked Bengali and spoke only English and were being raised so differently from me and most of the other children. They were not taken to Calcutta every summer, they did not have parents who were clinging to another way of life and exhorting their children to do the same. Because of Deborah, they were exempt from all that, and for this reason I envied them. "Usha, look at you, all grown up and so pretty," Deborah would say whenever she saw me, rekindling, if only for a minute, our bond of years before. She had cut off her beautiful long hair by then, and had a bob. "I bet you'll be old enough to babysit soon," she would say. "I'll call you—the girls would love that." But she never did.

I began to grow out of my girlhood, entering middle school and developing crushes on the American boys in my class. The crushes amounted to nothing; in spite of Deborah's compliments, I was always overlooked at that age. But my mother must have picked up on something, for she forbade me to attend the dances that were held the last Friday of every month in the school cafeteria, and it was an unspoken law that I was not allowed to date. "Don't think you'll get away with marrying an American, the way Pranab Kaku did," she would say from time to time. I was thirteen, the thought of marriage irrelevant to my life. Still, her words upset me, and I felt her grip on me tighten. She would fly into a rage when I told her I wanted to start wearing a bra, or if I wanted to go to Harvard Square with a friend. In the middle of our arguments, she often conjured Deborah as her antithesis, the sort of woman she refused to be. "If she were your mother, she would let you do whatever you wanted, because she wouldn't care. Is that what you want, Usha, a mother who doesn't care?" When I began menstruating, the summer before I started ninth grade, my mother gave me a speech, telling me that I was to let no boy touch me, and then she asked if I knew how a woman became pregnant. I told her what I had been taught in science, about the sperm fertilizing the egg, and then she asked if I knew how, exactly, that happened. I saw the terror in her eyes and so, though I knew that aspect of procreation as well, I lied, and told her it hadn't been explained to us.

I began keeping other secrets from her, evading her with the aid of my friends. I told her I was sleeping over at a friend's when really I went to parties, drinking beer and allowing boys to kiss me and fondle my breasts and press their erections against my hip as we lay groping on a sofa or the backseat of a car. I began to pity my mother; the older I got, the more I saw what a desolate life she led. She had never worked, and during the day she watched soap operas to pass the time. Her only job, every day, was to clean and cook for my father and me. We rarely went to restaurants, my father always pointing out, even in cheap ones, how expensive they were compared with eating at home. When my mother complained to him about how much she hated life in the suburbs and how lonely she felt, he said nothing to placate her. "If you are so unhappy, go back to Calcutta," he would offer, making it clear that their separation would not affect him one way or the other. I began to take my cues from my father in dealing with her, isolating her doubly. When she screamed at me for talking too long on the telephone, or for staying too long in my room, I learned to scream back, telling her that she was pathetic, that she knew nothing

about me, and it was clear to us both that I had stopped needing her, definitively and abruptly, just as Pranab Kaku had.

Then, the year before I went off to college, my parents and
I were invited to the Chakrabortys' home for Thanksgiving.
We were not the only guests from my parents' old Cambridge
crowd; it turned out that Pranab Kaku and Deborah wanted
to have a sort of reunion of all the people they had been
friendly with back then. Normally, my parents did not celebrate
Thanksgiving; the ritual of a large sit-down dinner and the
foods that one was supposed to eat was lost on them. They
treated it as if it were Memorial Day or Veterans Day—just
another holiday in the American year. But we drove out to
Marblehead, to an impressive stone-faced house with a semicir-
cular gravel driveway clogged with cars. The house was a short
walk from the ocean; on our way, we had driven by the harbor
overlooking the cold, glittering Atlantic, and when we stepped
out of the car we were greeted by the sound of gulls and waves.
Most of the living-room furniture had been moved to the basement and extra tables joined to the main one to form a giant U.
They were covered with tablecloths, set with white plates and
silverware, and had centerpieces of gourds. I was struck by the
toys and dolls that were everywhere, dogs that shed long yellow hairs on everything, all the photographs of Bonny and Sara
and Deborah decorating the walls, still more plastering the
refrigerator door. Food was being prepared when we arrived,
something my mother always frowned upon, the kitchen a
chaos of people and smells and enormous dirtied bowls.

Deborah's family, whom we remembered dimly from the
wedding, was there, her parents and her brothers and sisters
and their husbands and wives and boyfriends and babies. Her
sisters were in their thirties, but, like Deborah, they could have
been mistaken for college students, wearing jeans and clogs and
fisherman sweaters, and her brother Matty, with whom I had

danced in a circle at the wedding, was now a freshman at Amherst, with wide-set green eyes and wispy brown hair and a complexion that reddened easily. As soon as I saw Deborah's siblings, joking with one another as they chopped and stirred things in the kitchen, I was furious with my mother for making a scene before we left the house and forcing me to wear a shalwar kameez. I knew they assumed, from my clothing, that I had more in common with the other Bengalis than with them. But Deborah insisted on including me, setting me to work peeling apples with Matty, and out of my parents' sight I was given beer to drink. When the meal was ready, we were told where to sit, in an alternating boy-girl formation that made the Bengalis uncomfortable. Bottles of wine were lined up on the table. Two turkeys were brought out, one stuffed with sausage and one without. My mouth watered at the food, but I knew that afterward, on our way home, my mother would complain that it was all tasteless and bland. "Impossible," my mother said, shaking her hand over the top of her glass when someone tried to pour her a little wine.

Deborah's father, Gene, got up to say grace, and asked everyone at the table to join hands. He bowed his head and closed his eyes. "Dear Lord, we thank you today for the food we are about to receive," he began. My parents were seated next to each other, and I was stunned to see that they complied, that my father's brown fingers lightly clasped my mother's pale ones. I noticed Matty seated on the other side of the room and saw him glancing at me as his father spoke. After the chorus of Amens, Gene raised his glass and said, "Forgive me, but I never thought I'd have the opportunity to say this: Here's to Thanksgiving with the Indians." Only a few people laughed at the joke.

Then Pranab Kaku stood up and thanked everyone for coming. He was relaxed from alcohol, his once wiry body beginning to thicken. He started to talk sentimentally about his early days in Cambridge, and then suddenly he recounted the story of meeting me and my mother for the first time, telling the guests about how he had followed us that afternoon. The people who did not know us laughed, amused by the description of the encounter, and by Pranab Kaku's desperation. He walked around the room to where my mother was sitting and draped a lanky arm around her shoulder, forcing her, for a brief moment, to stand up. "This woman," he declared, pulling her close to his side, "this woman hosted my first real Thanksgiving in America. It might have been an afternoon in May, but that first meal at Boudi's table was Thanksgiving to me. If it weren't for that meal, I would have gone back to Calcutta." My mother looked away, embarrassed. She was thirty-eight, already going gray, and she looked closer to my father's age than to Pranab Kaku's; regardless of his waistline, he retained his handsome, carefree looks. Pranab Kaku went back to his place at the head of the table, next to Deborah, and concluded, "And if that had been the case I'd have never met you, my darling," and he kissed her on the mouth in front of everyone, to much applause, as if it were their wedding day all over again.

After the turkey, smaller forks were distributed and orders were taken for three different kinds of pie, written on small pads by Deborah's sisters, as if they were waitresses. After dessert, the dogs needed to go out, and Pranab Kaku volunteered to take them. "How about a walk on the beach?" he suggested, and Deborah's side of the family agreed that that was an excellent idea. None of the Bengalis wanted to go, preferring to sit with their tea and cluster together, at last, at one end of the room, speaking freely after the forced chitchat with the Americans during the meal. Matty came over and sat in the chair beside me that was now empty, encouraging me to join the walk. When I hesitated, pointing to my inappropriate clothes and shoes but also aware of my mother's silent fury at the sight of us together, he said, "I'm sure Deb can lend you something." So I went upstairs, where Deborah gave me a pair of her jeans and a thick sweater and some sneakers, so that I looked like her and her sisters.

She sat on the edge of her bed, watching me change, as if we were girlfriends, and she asked if I had a boyfriend. When I told her no, she said, "Matty thinks you're cute."

"He told you?"

"No, but I can tell."

As I walked back downstairs, emboldened by this information, in the jeans I'd had to roll up and in which I felt finally like myself, I noticed my mother lift her eyes from her teacup and stare at me, but she said nothing, and off I went, with Pranab Kaku and his dogs and his in-laws, along a road and then down some steep wooden steps to the water. Deborah and one of her sisters stayed behind, to begin the cleanup and see to the needs of those who remained. Initially, we all walked together, in a single row across the sand, but then I noticed Matty hanging back, and so the two of us trailed behind, the distance between us and the others increasing. We began flirting, talking of things I no longer remember, and eventually we wandered into a rocky inlet and Matty fished a joint out of his pocket. We turned our backs to the wind and smoked it, our cold fingers touching in the process, our lips pressed to the same damp section of the rolling paper. At first I didn't feel any effect, but then, listening to him talk about the band he was in, I was aware that his voice sounded miles away, and that I had the urge to laugh, even though what he was saying was not terribly funny. It felt as if we were apart from the group for hours, but when we wandered back to the sand we could still see them, walking out onto a promontory to watch the sun set.

It was dark by the time we all headed back to the house, and I dreaded seeing my parents while I was still high. But when we got there Deborah told me that my parents, feeling tired, had left, agreeing to let someone drive me home later. A fire had

been lit and I was told to relax and have more pie as the leftovers were put away and the living room slowly put back in
order. Of course, it was Matty who drove me home, and sitting
in my parents' driveway I kissed him, at once thrilled and terrified that my mother might walk onto the lawn in her nightgown and discover us. I gave Matty my phone number, and for
a few weeks I thought of him constantly, and hoped foolishly
that he would call.

In the end, my mother was right, and fourteen years after that
Thanksgiving, after twenty-three years of marriage, Pranab
Kaku and Deborah got divorced. It was he who had strayed,
falling in love with a married Bengali woman, destroying two
families in the process. The other woman was someone my
parents knew, though not very well. Deborah was in her forties
by then, Bonny and Sara away at college. In her shock and
grief, it was my mother whom Deborah turned to, calling and
weeping into the phone. Somehow, through all the years, she
had continued to regard us as quasi in-laws, sending flowers
when my grandparents died and giving me a compact edition
of the O.E.D. as a college-graduation present. "You knew him
so well. How could he do something like this?" Deborah asked
my mother. And then, "Did you know anything about it?" My
mother answered truthfully that she did not. Their hearts had
been broken by the same man, only my mother's had long ago
mended, and in an odd way, as my parents approached their old
age, she and my father had grown fond of each other, out of
habit if nothing else. I believe my absence from the house, once
I left for college, had something to do with this, because over
the years, when I visited, I noticed a warmth between my parents that had not been there before, a quiet teasing, a solidarity,
a concern when one of them fell ill. My mother and I had also
made peace; she had accepted the fact that I was not only her

daughter but a child of America as well. Slowly, she accepted that I dated one American man, and then another, and then yet another, that I slept with them, and even that I lived with one though we were not married. She welcomed my boyfriends into our home and when things didn't work out she told me I would find someone better. After years of being idle, she decided, when she turned fifty, to get a degree in library science at a nearby university.

On the phone, Deborah admitted something that surprised my mother: that all these years she had felt hopelessly shut out of a part of Pranab Kaku's life. "I was so horribly jealous of you back then, for knowing him, understanding him in a way I never could. He turned his back on his family, on all of you, really, but I still felt threatened. I could never get over that." She told my mother that she had tried, for years, to get Pranab Kaku to reconcile with his parents, and that she had also encouraged him to maintain ties with other Bengalis, but he had resisted. It had been Deborah's idea to invite us to their Thanksgiving; ironically, the other woman had been there, too. "I hope you don't blame me for taking him away from your lives, Boudi. I always worried that you did."

My mother assured Deborah that she blamed her for nothing. She confessed nothing to Deborah about her own jealousy of decades before, only that she was sorry for what had happened, that it was a sad and terrible thing for their family. She did not tell Deborah that a few weeks after Pranab Kaku's wedding, while I was at a Girl Scout meeting and my father was at work, she had gone through the house, gathering up all the safety pins that lurked in drawers and tins, and adding them to the few fastened to her bracelets. When she'd found enough, she pinned them to her sari one by one, attaching the front piece to the layer of material underneath, so that no one would be able to pull the garment off her body. Then she took a can of lighter fluid and a box of kitchen matches and stepped outside, into our chilly backyard, which was full of leaves needing to be raked. Over her sari she was wearing a knee-length lilac trench coat, and to any neighbor she must have looked as though she'd simply stepped out for some fresh air. She opened up the coat and removed the tip from the can of lighter fluid and doused herself, then buttoned and belted the coat. She walked over to the garbage barrel behind our house and disposed of the fluid, then returned to the middle of the yard with the box of matches in her coat pocket. For nearly an hour she stood there, looking at our house, trying to work up the courage to strike a match. It was not I who saved her, or my father, but our next-door neighbor, Mrs. Holcomb, with whom my mother had never been particularly friendly. She came out to rake the leaves in her yard, calling out to my mother and remarking how beautiful the sunset was. "I see you've been admiring it for a while now," she said. My mother agreed, and then she went back into the house. By the time my father and I came home in the early evening, she was in the kitchen boiling rice for our dinner, as if it were any other day.

My mother told Deborah none of this. It was to me that she confessed, after my own heart was broken by a man I'd hoped to marry.

A Choice of Accommodations

From the outside the hotel looked promising, like an old ski lodge in the mountains: chocolate brown siding, a steeply pitched roof, red trim around the windows. But as soon as they entered the lobby of the Chadwick Inn, Amit was disappointed: the place was without character, renovated in pastel colors, squiggly gray lines a part of the wallpaper's design, as if someone had repeatedly been testing the ink in a pen and ultimately had nothing to say. By the front desk a revolving brass rack was filled with tourist brochures about the Berkshires, and Megan grabbed a handful as Amit checked in. Now the brochures were scattered across one of the two double beds in their room. Megan unfolded the cover of a brochure to reveal a map. "Where are we, exactly?" she asked, her finger trailing too far to the north.

"Here," Amit said, pointing to the town. "There's the lake, see? The one that sort of looks like a rabbit."

"I don't see it," Megan said.

"Right here." Amit took Megan's finger and drew it firmly to the spot.

"I mean, I don't get how the lake's supposed to look like a rabbit."

It had been a long drive from New York and Amit was in the mood for a drink. But there was no minibar, and no room service. The two double beds were covered in flowery maroon quilts, and across from them, a wide dresser held a television set at its center. A small paper pyramid sat on a square table between the beds, listing the local cable channels. The only pleasant feature in the room was a cathedral ceiling with exposed beams. In spite of this the room was dark; even with the curtains to the balcony drawn apart, all the lights needed to be turned on.

They were here for Pam Borden's wedding, which was to take place that evening at Langford Academy, a boarding school where Pam's father was headmaster, and from where Amit had graduated eighteen years ago. There had been an option to sleep, for twenty dollars a person, at one of the Langford dorms, empty now because it was August. But Amit had decided to splurge on the Chadwick Inn, which was slightly removed from campus, and offered a pool, a tennis court, a restaurant with two stars, and access to the shaded lake in which he'd been taught, as a teenager, to kayak and canoe. Talking it over with Megan, they'd agreed to drop off the girls at her parents' place on Long Island and book a room for both Saturday and Sunday, making a short vacation out of Pam's wedding, just the two of them.

Amit unlocked the sliding glass door and stepped out onto the balcony, a strip of cement containing two plastic chairs. The Northeast was in the middle of a heat wave and even up in the mountains it was sultry, but the purity of the air, with its sharp scent of pine, felt restorative. He was unsettled by how quiet it was. No little girls' voices calling out to one another, no reprimands or endearments coming from Megan. The car ride had been the same, Megan asleep, the backseat empty even though he kept looking in the rearview mirror, expecting to see his daughters' faces as they dozed or quarreled or chewed on bagels. He sat down now in one of the chairs, which was not very comfortable. He felt cheated. "I can't believe they charge two hundred and fifty dollars a night for this," he said.

"It's crazy," Megan said, joining him. "But I guess they can get away with it, given that we're in the middle of nowhere."

It was true, they were in the middle of nowhere, though he did not feel the same way. He'd known, without having to review a map, which roads to take after exiting the highway, remembered which direction the town was in. But he had never been to this hotel. His parents had not stayed here for parents' weekends; when Amit was at Langford they had lived in India, in New Delhi. They hadn't made it to his graduation, either. They'd been planning to, but Amit's father, an ophthalmologist at one of Delhi's best hospitals, was requested to perform cataract surgery on a member of Parliament, and so Bengali acquaintances of his parents' from Worcester attended in their stead. After graduating, Amit had not kept in touch with his Langford friends. He had no nostalgia for the school, and when letters came seeking alumni contributions or inviting him to the succession of reunions, he threw them out without opening them. Apart from his loose connection with Pam, and a sweatshirt he still owned with the school's wrinkled name across the chest, there was nothing to remind him of those years of his life. He couldn't imagine sending his daughters to Langford—couldn't imagine letting go of them as his parents had let go of him.

He looked out at the hotel grounds. A pine tree growing directly in front of their balcony obstructed most of the immediate view. The pool was small and uninviting, surrounded by a chain-link fence, with no one swimming or sunbathing on its periphery. To the right were the tennis courts, concealed by more pine trees, but he could hear the soft *thwack* of a ball flying back and forth, a sound that made him tired.

"It's a shame about this tree," he said.

"If only it were a few feet that way," Megan agreed.

"Maybe we should ask for another room. It wouldn't be the first time."

Amit and Megan had a tradition, in their relationship, of switching hotel rooms. On the first trip they'd taken together after they met, to Puerto Rico, they'd gotten a room on the ground floor, and there was a dead lizard in the bathroom. Megan complained and they were switched to a deluxe suite overlooking the mesmerizing blue-green ocean and the contrasting blue of the sky. For the entirety of their stay they kept the curtains open to that view, making love sideways on the bed as they faced it, waking to it in the mornings, the effect being as if the whole room, and the bed, and they themselves, were somehow afloat on the sea. A similar thing had happened in Venice, where they'd gone to celebrate their first anniversary— after one night facing a stone wall, they moved to a room by a canal, where a small barge docked each morning selling fruits and vegetables. In this case, Amit reflected, they were already on the desirable side of the hotel—the rooms at the front would overlook the parking lot.

"It's not worth it, for just two nights," Megan said. She leaned slightly forward in her chair and peered over the railing of the balcony, craning her neck. "Is the wedding here at the hotel?"

"I told you, it's at Langford."

"Well, another couple is about to get married in that gazebo. I see bridesmaids."

Amit looked on the other side of the pine tree and saw people filing out along a flagstone path that led from the terrace of the hotel restaurant. A photographer leaned over a tripod, surrounded by bags of equipment, and in front of him, a group of young women posed in matching lavender dresses.

"Pam's wedding will be different," he said.

"What do you mean?"

"She won't have bridesmaids."

"How do you know?"

"She's not the type."

"You never know," Megan said. "A lot of women do things that are out of character on their wedding day. Even women like Pam."

Her slight derision washed over him, not penetrating. He knew Megan had been surprised that he'd accepted the invitation to Pam's wedding, given that he and Pam rarely saw each other. And though Megan hadn't protested, he understood that on some level he had dragged her here, to an unfamiliar place full of unfamiliar people, to a piece of his past that had nothing to do with the life he and Megan shared. He knew that though Megan refused to admit it, she was insecure about Pam, defensive the one or two times they'd met, as if Amit and Pam had once been lovers. When Amit and Megan had first met they'd traded their histories, divulging the succession of romantic interests that led them to each other, but he'd never mentioned Pam in that context. He had loved her, it was true, but because she'd never been his girlfriend there had been nothing to explain.He slouched in his chair, resting his neck on the hard plastic edge and shut his eyes. "I could use a drink."

They stepped back into the air-conditioned room and he opened the suitcase they were sharing for the weekend. He pulled out the thick envelope containing the invitation, directions, a small map of Langford's campus with the ceremony and reception locations marked with a highlighter. He sat on the bed, leaning against a pile of extremely soft pillows, sinking down. Then he looked at the digital clock that was beside the paper pyramid on the bedside table. "The wedding starts in an hour. We should get pillows like this at home."

"Then we'd better get ready." Megan regarded him with a look of professional concern, as if he were a patient on her rounds. "What's wrong?"

"Nothing. I was just hoping we'd have some time before-hand, to go for a walk or swim in the lake. I was thinking about a swim all the way up here. I didn't think the traffic would be so bad."

"We'll swim tomorrow," she said. "We have a whole weekend."

He nodded. "Right." He stood up and went into the bath-room, to shave and to shower. These everyday rituals felt like a chore. He was uninspired to put on his suit and socialize with ghosts from his adolescence. He undressed, then stood in front of the mirror spreading shaving cream on his face. Since Monika's birth three years ago, this was their first trip without either of the girls. They were overdue for a vacation. Normally, every summer, they rented a cabin for two weeks in the Adiron-dacks. But Megan was in the last year of her residency at Mount Sinai, and her schedule did not allow it. She'd just finished a rotation in the cardiac intensive-care unit, working thirty-six-hour shifts, returning to the apartment at dawn, falling asleep just as Amit and the girls were beginning their day. Amit, who worked as the managing editor for a medical journal, had a more flexible schedule. Summer was a slow time at the journal, and since June he'd been overseeing the girls' breakfasts and baths, scheduling playdates, dropping Maya off at a day camp in the mornings and picking her up again. Reducing their nanny's hours for the summer months was one of the ways he and Megan had decided to cut back on expenses; the down payment on their new apartment, two stories of a brownstone on West Seventy-fifth Street, had depleted their savings.

He sensed Megan's relief at not having Maya and Monika around, at being free. Amit wanted to share that relief, that sense of escape he'd been looking forward to all summer, after the invitation to Pam's wedding had come and they'd made their plan. But now that they were alone he was nagged by the thought of Monika's runny nose, and wondered if his mother-in-law would remember that strawberries gave Maya a rash. He was tempted to ask Megan, but he stopped himself, knowing that she would accuse him of not trusting his in-laws. As a parent she was less fussy, less cautious than he was. On her days off she indulged them, baking with them in the kitchen, not minding if they skipped dinner because they were too full of cookies and cake. He knew that it was partly out of guilt that she tended to be lenient, but it was also her nature. She had not been horrified, as he had, when Maya found a wad of flattened chewing gum at the playing ground and put it into her mouth, or when Monika wandered off during a picnic they were having in Central Park and began playing, with her tiny fingers, with dog shit. Megan laughed at such moments, wiping off their hands and faces, convinced that her children could survive anything. She spent her days with people who were fighting for their lives, and could not be shaken by a scraped elbow or a hundred-degree fever.

It was Amit, who had studied enough about the body to know its inherent fragility, who had dissected enough cadavers to know what a horizontal chest incision would reveal, who was plagued by his daughters' vulnerability, both to illness and to accidents of all kinds. He was still haunted by an incident in the cafeteria of the Museum of Natural History, when Monika, a year old, had nearly choked on a piece of dried apricot. A woman at a neighboring table who happened to be a nurse had leapt up at the sound of Monika's coughing and efficiently swept her finger through the girl's mouth; in spite of two years of medical school, Amit lacked the simple instinct, the confidence, to do such a thing. He had been unable to look at either of his daughters for the rest of the day, to enjoy their time at the museum. He kept picturing the apricot piece lodged in Monika's windpipe, and how it might have silenced her forever. When he read articles in the newspaper about taxis suddenly swerving onto sidewalks and killing half a dozen pedestrians, it was always himself he pictured, holding Monika and Maya by the hand. Or he imagined a wave at Jones Beach, where he had been taking them once a week during the summer, dragging one of them down, or a pile of sand suffocating them as he was flipping, a few feet away, through a magazine. In each of these scenarios, he saw himself surviving, the girls perishing under his supervision. Megan would blame him, naturally, and then she would divorce him, and all of it, his life with her and the girls, would end. A brief glance in the wrong direction, he knew, could toss his existence over a cliff.

He lay down his razor and turned on the shower to warm up the room. He heard a knock, and then Megan opened the door.

"I can't go to the wedding," she said, shaking her head. She said this definitively, the way she told the girls that they weren't allowed to watch another program on television, or spend another five minutes in the tub.

"What are you talking about?"

"Look," she said, pointing to the skirt she'd put on. Above it she wore only her bra, flesh-colored and dingy at the straps. The skirt reached her ankles, and it was made of a diaphanous, smoky gray material, layered over a silk panel of a slightly darker shade. She held up a section, and his eyes went immediately to a spot in the fabric. At first he thought it was a stain, but then he realized it was a burn that had created a small empty patch, charred around the edges. Beneath it, the silk lining looked unsightly, like the bright flesh exposed when a scab is forcibly lifted away.

"It looks awful," she said. "There's no way to hide it."

"Did you pack a spare outfit?"

She shook her head, looking at him with annoyance. "Did you?"

Amit wiped his hands on a towel and sat on the lid of the toilet seat. Running his hands between the two layers of fabric, he felt the gauzy material brushing his palm, the silk at the back of his fingers. In medical school he'd considered being a surgeon, learning to piece together the most minuscule tissues of the body. But he'd never made it to any rotations, had only learned from textbooks and labs. As far as he could see there was no hope for repairing the skirt. It was so simple, so sheer, that the missing patch, through which the pad of one of his fingers was now visible, had ruined it.

"I can't believe I didn't notice when I was packing," Megan said. "It must have happened the last time I wore it. Sparks from a cigarette or something."

He knew it wasn't her fault, and yet he couldn't stop himself from blaming her a little, for not paying closer attention. And he couldn't help but wonder if it was an unconscious move on her part, to avoid Pam's wedding, to sabotage things. It occurred to him that with the excuse of Megan's skirt they might blow off the wedding altogether and spend the night in the hotel, watching movies in bed. Their absence would go unnoticed in such a big crowd, their place settings ignored as the waiters circled the tables. Had the Chadwick Inn been nicer he might have been tempted.

"Is there a store nearby?" Megan asked. "Somewhere I could dash out and buy something else while you get ready?"

"There used to be a mall, but it was about an hour's drive from here. I don't remember any clothing stores in town. Not nice ones."

She turned the skirt to one side, so that the burn was no longer visible from the front. Then she stood beside him in front of the mirror over the sink, their bare arms touching. Normally Megan did not wear makeup, but for the occasion she had painted her mouth with a reddish lipstick. He found it distracting, preferred the intelligent, old-fashioned beauty of her face. It was the face of someone he could imagine living in a previous era, a simpler time, in an America that was oblivious to India altogether. Her dark brown hair was wound up as always, pulled away without fuss from her face and her long pale neck. She wore glasses, frameless oval lenses that seemed necessary to protect her sensitive gaze. They were the same height, five foot nine, tall for a woman but short for a man, and she was five years older, forty-two. And yet of the two of them it was Amit who already looked, at first glance, middle-aged, for by the age of twenty-one his hair had turned completely gray. It was here, at Langford, that it had begun, when he was in the sixth form. At first it was just a few strands, well concealed in his black hair. But by the time he was a junior at Columbia it was the black hairs he could count on one hand. He'd read it was possible, after a traumatic experience, for a person's hair to turn gray in youth. But there had been no sudden death he could point to, no accident. No profound life change, apart from his parents sending him to Langford.

"I suppose if you stood right next to me all night, no one would notice," Megan said, pressing up against him. He felt the warmth of her arms and a twitch of desire, too mired by exhaustion to act upon.

"Do you really think you can survive a whole evening without leaving my side?" he asked her.

"I can if you can." There was a note of challenge in her voice, and Amit smiled, amused by the idea, motivated to go to the wedding now that he would have a specific task to perform. At the same time he thought that in the early days of their love this would not have been an issue, their bodies continuously touching through the course of an evening, something that would have been taken for granted.

"It's a deal," he said.

They looked at their reflections in the mirror, she in her torn skirt and dingy bra, he naked, his penis flaccid, his face covered with bright white shaving cream. Megan shook her head. "What a vision we'll be."

.   .   .

He'd assumed they'd walk to the school—it was just across the road, a few minutes over a sloping field. But Megan was wearing heels and didn't want to get them muddy, so they got into the car. The seats were still full of evidence of their daughters— abandoned books, tiny dolls, the plastic horses Maya had begun collecting. Only the car seats were gone, transferred into his in-laws' car for the weekend. He thought of the girls now at their grandparents', playing in the treehouse his father-in-law had built for their occasional visits, his mother-in-law providing slices of pound cake and juice boxes for a tea party. His daughters looked nothing like him, nothing like his family, and in spite of the distance Amit felt from his parents, this fact bothered him, that his mother and father had passed down nothing, physically, to his children. Both Maya and Monika had inherited Megan's coloring, without a trace of Amit's deeply tan skin and black eyes, so that apart from their vaguely Indian names they appeared fully American. "Are they yours?" people sometimes asked when he was alone with them, in stores, or at the playground in the park.

After just two minutes they pulled off the road and turned up the wide tree-lined drive that led to the gates of the school. The leaves were glossy and abundant, but his memories were of the blazing branches of autumn and the purplish light of the mountains, the shadows that spread in their curves and dips, and the snow that covered the tops of the gates in winter. The school itself was more or less as he remembered it, embarrassingly large and well maintained, pieces of rounded abstract sculpture here and there on the grass.

"This place is nicer than where I went to college," Megan said as they walked across the campus, taking in the pristine buildings, the sculptures.

"It's a bit over the top," he said. When they'd first met

Megan had been impressed by his prep school education, but at the same time she'd teased him about it. She was not bitter toward the privileged, but she was sometimes judgmental; were he not Indian, Megan would have probably avoided someone like him. She was the youngest of five children, her father a policeman, her mother a kindergarten teacher. She'd gotten a job after graduating from high school, in a photocopy store during the days and as a telemarketer in the evenings, not beginning college until she was twenty, going part time because she'd had to continue working. In that sense, she worked harder than anyone he'd ever known, including his own father and his parents' uniformly successful crowd of Bengali friends. Megan's ordinary background had displeased his parents, as had the fact that she was five years older than he was. Her stark prettiness, her refusal to wear contact lenses, her height, had not charmed them. The fact that she was a doctor did not make up for it. If anything, it made their disappointment in Amit worse.

He noticed new wings tacked onto some of the buildings, modern elements of steel and glass alongside the brick and white cupolas. His parents had plucked him out of public school in Winchester, Massachusetts, where he'd been raised, and sent him here, for they'd decided when Amit was in the ninth grade to move back to India. He still remembered the night his parents told him their plans. They were sitting in a seafood restaurant on the Cape, in Cotuit, overlooking the water, the table heaped with the bright red claws and shells from which his father had effortlessly extracted the meat for all of them. His father began by saying he was growing restless on the faculty of Harvard Medical School, that there was a hospital in Delhi where he believed he was needed. Amit had been stunned by his parents' decision—his parents, unlike most other Bengalis in Massachusetts, had always been dismissive, even critical, of India, never homesick or sentimental. His mother had short hair and wore trousers, putting on saris only for special occasions. His father kept a liquor cabinet and liked a gin and tonic before his meals. They both came from wealthy families, had both summered in hill stations and attended boarding schools in India themselves. The relative affluence of America never impressed them; in many ways they had lived more privileged lives in India, but they left the country and had not looked back.

At the restaurant his father pulled out the admissions packet for Langford, showing photographs of the campus, smiling students gathered around classroom tables, teachers standing in front of blackboards, caught midsentence by the camera's lens. Academically it was far superior to the school he'd been attending, his father told him, mentioning the percentage of Langford graduates who went on to Ivy League colleges. Amit realized, as his father spoke, that the position in Delhi had been accepted, their house in Winchester already put up for sale. There was no question of his going to school in Delhi; it wasn't worth the trouble to adjust to education in a different country, his father said, given that eventually Amit would be attending an American college.

From Langford, during Christmas and after each academic year came to an end, Amit went to Delhi to be with his parents, staying in their flat full of servants in Chittaranjan Park, in a barren room set aside for his stays. He never enjoyed his visits to Delhi, his broken Bengali of no use in that city. It made him miss Calcutta, where all his relatives lived, where he was used to going. His parents had moved to Delhi the year of Indira Gandhi's assassination, and the riots that subsequently raged there, the curfews and the constant vigilance with which his parents had to live, meant that Amit remained cooped up inside, without friends, without anything to do. In that sense it was a relief to him to return to this peaceful town. Four years later his parents were back in America, moving to Houston. In Delhi his father had perfected a laser technique to correct astigmatism that earned him invitations to work and teach in hospitals all over the world. After five years in Houston they'd moved yet again, to Lausanne, Switzerland. They lived in Saudi Arabia now.

At Langford, Amit was the only Indian student, and people always assumed that he'd been born and raised in that country and not in Massachusetts. They complimented him on his accent, always telling him how good his English was. He'd arrived when he was fifteen, for sophomore year, which at Langford was called the fourth form, and by that time friendships and alliances among the boys of his class were already in place. At his high school in Winchester he'd been a star student, but suddenly he'd had to work doggedly to maintain his grades. He had to wear a jacket every morning to his classes and call his teachers "masters" and attend chapel on Sundays. Quickly he learned that his parents' wealth was laughable compared to the majority of Langford boys. There was no escape at the end of the day, and though he admitted it to no one, especially not his parents when they called from Delhi every weekend, he was crippled with homesickness, missing his parents to the point where tears often filled his eyes, in those first months, without warning. He sought traces of his parents' faces and voices among the people who surrounded and cared for him, but there was absolutely nothing, no one, at Langford to remind him of them. After that first semester he had slipped as best as he could into this world, swimming competitively, calling boys by their last names, always wearing khakis because jeans were not allowed. He learned to live without his mother and father, as everyone else did, shedding his daily dependence on them even though he was still a boy, and even to enjoy it. Still, he refused to forgive them.

Every Thanksgiving, he and the other students who had nowhere to go were taken in by Pam's family—boys who were from Santiago and Tehran and other troubled parts of the world, or were the sons of diplomats and journalists who moved around even more frequently than Amit's parents. They would eat in the Bordens' house, located at one end of the campus, with Pam and her three brothers, all of whom went to different boarding schools but always came home for the holidays. For Amit it was the highlight of each year. He and all the other boys were in love with Pam, who was the only girl in her family, the only girl on campus, the only girl, it had felt back then, in the world. They would pray to be seated close to her at the table, and for weeks afterward they would talk about her, imagining her life at Northfield Mount Hermon, imagining what her breasts looked like, or the feel of her light brown poker-straight hair, wondering what it was like in the morning, messily trailing over her back. They wondered about the room upstairs, where Pam slept when she came home. They noticed if she ate white meat or dark, and they noticed the year she did not eat any turkey at all.

She seemed fully aware of their admiration, flattered but off-limits. She was that rare, unsettling thing, a teenage girl already conscious of her power over men while at the same time uninterested in them. She was comfortable with the opposite sex in a way most girls were not, perhaps because she'd grown up in a house full of boys. The Bordens were forthright people, all of them, even the children, trained to act as friendly hosts for the students who washed up at their holiday table. Pam would talk to Amit and the others, asking each of them about their courses as if she were her mother's age and not a girl of fifteen. And then they would disappear from her consciousness until the following year. After the meal, Headmaster Borden would take them out onto the lawn for a game of touch football with Pam's brothers. Or they stayed inside, where Mrs. Borden, who taught French at the school, would conduct complicated word games or charades.

In his final year at Langford Amit was admitted to Columbia University. No one else from his class was going there, but then one day Headmaster Borden told Amit that Pam had decided on Columbia, too. "Keep an eye on her for me," the headmaster said, but it was Pam who'd called first in that same ambassadorial way her parents had, even though New York City, and the world of college, was as foreign to her as it was to him. Suddenly, because she had decided so, they were friends. They would go to dinner twice a week after the religion class they took together, either to Café Pertutti, treating themselves to creamy plates of pasta, or to La Rosita for caffè con leche and rice and beans. After that they would study in the same small room in Butler Library, sitting across from each other on armchairs, reading Milton and Marx. Odd things made him love her. The fact that she never put her books into a backpack or a bag, hugging them instead against her chest. That she always appeared somehow underdressed, still wearing a fringed suede jacket at a time of year when everyone else was bundled in wool and down. That the last two letters in her name were the first two in his, a silly thing he never mentioned to her but caused him to believe that they were bound together.

He'd wondered at first if it was romantic but quickly realized that she was involved in affairs, that he was just a friend. She was used to being surrounded by men who, like her brothers, were protective of her, loyal to her, who paid court without seducing her. And she had appointed Amit to play that role while they were in college. She would ask him to investigate boys she was curious about, learning about their reputations, their history, before deciding whether to pursue them. In exchange she would give him advice on how to approach other girls, how most effectively to flirt with them. It was Pam who had coached Amit through his first college relationship, with

Ellen Craddock, going out of her way and befriending Ellen just for the sake of being able to throw her and Amit together on College Walk.

Only once had Amit worked up the nerve to make a pass at Pam, in their sophomore year, kissing her after getting drunk at a party and putting his hand on her breast, on top of a dark green turtleneck sweater she was wearing. She had kissed him back, allowed him to touch her, but then she'd drawn away, as if she'd known all along that one day this would happen. "Now we know what that feels like," she told him, and he knew then that it was impossible, that she did not like him in that way. She had indulged him, just as her family had indulged him once a year in their home, offering a small piece of herself and then shutting the door.

Although Pam still lived in New York, selling foreign rights at a literary agency, these days they saw each other, at best, once or twice a year, usually by accident, on a subway or a street corner or a crowded exhibit at the Metropolitan. But he was permanently on her mailing list, and therefore he received cards at Christmas, and even on his birthday—she was the type to remember that sort of thing. When she learned that Amit and Megan had gotten married, she sent them candlesticks from Tiffany's. And when the girls were born, expensive gifts arrived, European dresses and cashmere blankets for their strollers. There had been no phone call from her to tell him she was getting married, only the invitation. And after all these years, Amit felt both quietly elated and solicitous, as contact from Pam and the Bordens had always made him feel, causing him to set aside whatever it was that he was doing and pay them his full attention.

Guests were gathered under a beautiful tree where a bar had been set up, offering cocktails before the ceremony. On the

lawn were rows of white folding chairs, overlooking the decep-
tively gentle milky-blue mountains. Over them, the sun was
just beginning to set. It was here, at this precise spot, that he'd
graduated. He'd looked different that day, leaner in frame, his
hair still predominantly black. It was Pam, in college, who'd
forbidden him to color it, telling him it was distinguished, that
women would be drawn to it. He hadn't believed her but she
was right; every woman he'd ever been involved with had confessed, at one point or another, that they found his gray hair
sexy.

"Other side," Megan said as they approached the crowd. He
moved over to her left and matched his stride to hers. Side by
side they took their place in the line for drinks. There was the
usual array of bottles, and two punch bowls full of lemonade.
"Spiked or unspiked?" the bartender asked. They got two
glasses of the spiked and approached the lawn, sipping their
sweet, potent drinks. He looked around at the faces, at men
carrying toddlers on their shoulders, mothers shushing babies
in their carriers, nannies chasing after older children. The nannies seemed young, high school students, he guessed, hired for
the occasion. The fathers were pointing to the trees, to the
clouds that spread and shifted over the valley. He recognized
no one and missed his daughters.

"Lots of kids here," Megan said.

"The girls would have enjoyed this."

"But then we wouldn't be able to enjoy ourselves. Cheers."

"Cheers." Because they were standing side by side they
raised their glasses into the air in front of them, without looking at each other.

It felt strange to be drinking at the school. He remembered
the covert parties, the bottles that would be smuggled into the
dorms and consumed Friday and Saturday nights, always fearful of the proctor's rounds.

"I feel old," he said to Megan. He saw a face that was familiar, smiling at him, walking over. The stylish tortoiseshell glasses were new, but he remembered the friendly blue eyes, the wavy brown hair, the cleft in the chin. They had shared a number of classes, been lab partners, he suddenly remembered, in chemistry. His father and Pam's father had grown up together; he had always referred to the headmaster as "Uncle Borden." He remembered the last name, Schultz, but not the first.

"Sarkar," Schultz said. "Amit Sarkar, right?"

Amit extended a hand, Schultz's first name coming to him just then. "Great to see you. This is my wife, Megan. Megan, this is Tim."

The smile disappeared from Schultz's face. "It's Ted."

"Ted, of course, Ted. I'm so sorry. Ted, meet my wife, Megan." He felt like an idiot, as mortified by his error as he would have been in his first term at Langford, when he worked so hard to please. He berated himself for using a name at all, for not letting it emerge naturally in the course of conversation. "I'm sorry," he said again as Ted and Megan shook hands. "It's been a long day. A long drive."

"Don't worry about it," Ted said, in a way that only made Amit feel worse. "Your parents still in India?"

"They came back. And then they left again."

"Where are you living these days?"

It turned out that Ted lived in Manhattan, too. He was divorced and working at a law firm.

"Do you guys know this guy Pam's marrying? The one she's finally going to settle for instead of one of us?"

"I've never met Ryan," Amit said, wondering what Megan would make of Ted's comment.

"All I know is he writes for television," Ted said. "One of those law shows that makes my job look glamorous. That's why they're moving to L.A. Apparently one of the actors for the show is supposed to be here."

They looked around for someone who might be a celebrity. It was an attractive crowd, many of the women in black cocktail dresses. Amit remembered Megan's skirt and took a step toward her, putting his arm around her waist.

"How did you two meet?" Ted asked.

"Med school," Megan said.

"Oh. Dr. Sarkar, I'm impressed."

"Just her," Amit said. "She stuck it out. I didn't."

A string quartet began to play and people drifted toward their seats. Amit and Megan chose chairs at the back, Megan complaining that her heels were sinking into the grass. They put their empty glasses under their seats. Everyone turned around as the man Pam was about to marry walked between the chairs and took his place at the center where a clergyman was standing. Ryan looked well into his forties, tall, tanned, with a salt and pepper beard, his handsome features lined. And then Pam appeared, coming down the aisle with her father, then her mother and her brothers behind. Mrs. Borden was unchanged, her cropped sandy hair styled in the same practical way, her figure still trim. She turned her head to smile reassuringly at the guests on either side of her. All their lives the Bordens had presided over similarly large gatherings, weekly assemblies and homecoming games and graduations, and in a way this was no different. The only person he didn't recognize was a girl of about twelve or so, with a long, pretty face and a somber expression, carrying a bouquet of flowers. He guessed it was one of Pam's nieces or younger cousins. Pam wore a sleeveless dress with a train, made of crumpled ivory material. The effect was not so much a dress as a long bedsheet that she had wrapped around herself, a careless yet perfect vision. She carried yellow freesias casually in one hand, smiling and waving to people with the other. To this day she was the most beautiful woman he had ever known.

The couple stood with their backs to the guests, facing the

minister and the mountains and the setting sun. It was a brief, simple ceremony, without bridesmaids or a best man, as Amit had predicted. Someone got up and read a poem he could not hear because there was no microphone. Still, visually, it was spectacular, the sky deepening into a combination of dark peach and plum over the mountains, the lush grounds of the school unpopulated save for the spot where the wedding was taking place. He watched strands of Pam's hair, loosened by the wind that had settled over them, causing women to put shawls around their shoulders, that cold mountain air that always replaced the day's heat. She was thirty-seven now, his age, but from the back she looked like a girl of nineteen. And yet she was marrying late, so much later than he had.

As he witnessed the ceremony he felt grateful for the faint connection he and Pam had maintained, enough for him to be sitting there, watching her marry, witnessing the very beginning of that phase of her existence. Amit anticipated only a continuation of the things he knew: Megan, his job, life in New York, the girls. The most profound thing, having Maya and Monika, had already happened; nothing would be more life-altering than that. He wanted to change none of it, and yet a part of him sometimes longed to return to the beginning of his relationship with Megan, if only for the pleasure of anticipating and experiencing those things again.

There was a round of applause as Pam and Ryan kissed, their eyes open from the excitement, and then the music started up and the wedding party receded down the grassy aisle. Amit rose, this time positioning himself on Megan's left without having to be told, and together they took their places behind the others in the receiving line. Pam tossed back her head and laughed at things people said, leaning over to kiss them or put a hand comfortingly to their upper arms. "Where are your beautiful little girls?" she cried out as soon as she saw Amit, extending her neck so that he could kiss her on one cheek, then the other. Her skin was the same, disconcertingly soft, but now that he faced her he saw Mrs. Borden's crow's-feet forming around her eyes.

"We left them with Megan's parents. It's our weekend of reckless freedom."

"I want to stay up until five in the morning," Megan announced cheerfully. "I want to celebrate all night and watch the sun rise from our balcony."

Amit glanced at Megan, puzzled that she'd never mentioned this to him. He had assumed her main objective for the weekend was to sleep undisturbed. "You do?"

Megan didn't answer him. Instead she said to Pam, "You look lovely. It's such a pretty dress." She said this genuinely, not intimidated by Pam as she'd been in the past. Amit wondered if it was because Pam was married now, belonging to another man and therefore not even a little bit to Amit.

They shook hands with Ryan. "Pam's told me so much about you," Ryan said to Amit.

"Congratulations," Amit replied. "All the best."

"We'll see if I can make a California girl out of her."

"Ryan's kids are running around here, somewhere," Pam said. "That was Claire, carrying the flowers." She corrected herself, kissing Ryan on the cheek. "Sorry, sweetie. Our kids." She caught Amit's eye, as if to say, Can you believe I'm a stepmother? So this was a second marriage for Ryan, another woman's children involved. The long-faced girl in the wedding procession was now Pam's stepdaughter. It was not what Amit would have predicted for Pam, such complications, Pam who could have had any man.

"I was really hoping to see your girls," Pam said. "Do you have a picture?"

Megan looked in her bag, but she was carrying a small beaded evening purse and had left her wallet in the hotel room.

"I've got some," Amit said. He flipped to two pictures, each taken when Maya and Monika were newborns, their eyes beady, their mouths drawn to fine points. "They look nothing like that now."

"You'll have to bring them to L.A. You'll all have to come and stay with us at Ryan's beach house." She laughed. "I mean, our beach house."

"We'd love that," Megan said. But Amit knew it would never happen, that this was the end of the road, that there would never be a reason for him to step into Pam's world again.

"There's a brunch tomorrow, on campus," Pam said. "We'll see you there?" She said it in her old way, looking at Amit as if there were something of extreme urgency she needed to discuss with him—notes for an exam they were about to take together, or an analysis of his latest college infatuation.

"Of course," he told her.

"It's great of you to come, Amit. It's so good to see you," Pam said. For a moment he felt a flicker of their old bond, their odd friendship. He had always been devoted to her, more so, she'd once admitted, than even her brothers, and he felt that she was acknowledging that again, now, in her glance.

"We wouldn't have missed it," he said.

The line pushed them along, into the crowd of the party. Megan said she needed to use the restroom. "Do you know where one is?"

He looked around. Across the lawn where people stood eating hors d'oeuvres was the admissions building, a massive Victorian mansion with wraparound porches. The double doors at the back were open, and waiters dashed in and out with their trays. He remembered going there with his parents, being interviewed by an unpleasant man named Mr. Plotkin. Mr. Plotkin had asked Amit why he wanted to attend Langford, and because his parents were sitting outside the room, Amit had replied, truthfully, that his parents were moving to India and didn't want him to go to school there. "I'm afraid that reply isn't the mark of a Langford boy, Mr. Sarkar," Mr. Plotkin told him across the desk where Amit's report cards and recommendations lay. And then he folded his hands together and waited until Amit had provided a more adequate reply.

"There's probably bathrooms in there," he said now to Megan. He walked with her, still positioned faithfully at her left, toward the building, but inside they discovered a long line for the ladies' room.

"What should we do?" Megan whispered.

"Well, I can't wait in that line with you. It's all women. I'm sure no one will notice the skirt."

"You think?" She fiddled with her purse, adjusting her wrist so that the purse rested over the burnt material. Over the skirt she was wearing a white buttoned shirt, open to reveal part of a pink camisole below. Her neck was bare. She never wore the jewels his mother had given her eventually, that were too ornate for her taste.

"You look great," he said. He meant it, but he hadn't told her yet. "I'll get us more drinks and meet you back here. Another lemonade?"

"Okay."

He left her there, still fiddling with the purse. It took him longer than he expected to get the drinks. The line at the bar contained a few of his old teachers, most of them in advanced middle age, a few looking on the brink of retirement. There was Mrs. Randall, his physics teacher, to whom he waved, and Mr. Plotkin, whose eyes he avoided. Then he saw Mr. Nagle, one of his English teachers, who'd also been the adviser for the school newspaper, *The Langford Legend,* that Amit wrote for and eventually edited. Mr. Nagle had been one of the youngest members of the faculty, just out of college when Amit was a student, and he still looked refreshingly young, his dark hair and drooping mustache reminding Amit of a shorter, thinner version of Ringo Starr. Mr. Nagle was originally from

Winchester, a graduate of the high school there, and Amit always felt a connection with him because of that.

"Let me guess. You're writing for *The New York Times*," Mr. Nagle said.

"Actually, I work for a medical journal."

"Is that right? I didn't think you were interested in the sciences."

He hadn't been. He'd wanted to be a journalist, it was true. He had loved working on the eight-page weekly paper, loved going with Mr. Nagle and the rest of the editorial staff to the offices of the local town paper once a week to do the layout. He remembered sitting in the library, thinking up story ideas, interviewing members of the faculty, and the famous people who sometimes came to Langford to speak at assemblies. Taking an active, reporter's interest in the life of the school had helped him to endure the fact that he hated it there. But he knew that journalism wasn't an option as a career, that his parents would never indulge such thinking. It was the one battle he hadn't had the courage to fight—his parents' expectation that he go to medical school, their assumption that he become a doctor like his father.

He'd had the aptitude for science and so he'd gone ahead with it, majoring in biology at Columbia and then starting medical school there. He lasted two years, mainly because he met Megan and fell in love with her. But the more he got to know her, the clearer it became that he lacked her dedication, her drive. One night in the middle of studying for a pharmacy exam, he'd gone out for a cup of coffee. He walked a few blocks to stretch his legs, and then a few more. He kept walking down Broadway, one hundred blocks from his dorm in Washington Heights to Lincoln Center, and then continuing all the way to Chinatown where, at daybreak, feeling close to delirious, he finally stopped. Fish and vegetables were being unloaded from trucks, life creeping back onto the streets. He entered a bakery, had hot tea and coconut bread, watched a group of Chinese women sitting at a round table at the back, sorting through a mountain of spinach. He took the train back uptown, slept through his exam. He began to cut one class, then another. A week went by, and in spite of his total passivity, he felt that he was accomplishing the greatest feat of his life. He dropped out, not telling his parents until the semester ended. He'd expected Megan to break up with him, but she'd respected his decision and remained. On a lark, after dropping out of med school, he applied to the journalism school at Columbia but was not accepted. Megan urged him to write anyway, to work freelance and put together some clips. But the job at the medical journal was easier, more predictable work. It demanded less of him, and Amit could no longer imagine doing anything else.

"I had you pegged as a newspaperman," Mr. Nagle said. "We won that wonderful award the year you graduated. Never managed to win it again. They still have the plaque up in the library."

A third person joined them, a man who was introduced to Amit as the newly appointed director of alumni affairs. He took an immediate interest in Amit, asking whether he planned to attend the next reunion, talking about plans for Langford's new gymnasium.

"Excuse me," Amit said when there was a pause in the conversation, "I need to find my wife." He realized that in the course of talking to Mr. Nagle he'd finished his drink and now had only the one for Megan. So he stood in the line again and got another spiked lemonade. He began to weave among the guests, going into the admissions building, looking for her. But she wasn't there, and he realized she'd probably gone out to look for him. It was getting dark, and the only lit-up area was the tent where they would all sit to dine. When he found Megan she was talking to Ted Schultz, her left hand still placed strategically over her skirt. The sight of Ted made Amit feel foolish all over again, for calling him by the wrong name.

"I got you this," Amit said, handing Megan the lemonade.

"Oh." She looked at the drink, shaking her head. There was a glass of champagne in her other hand. "I got this off a tray."

"I was just telling Megan about what it was like here when we were students," Ted said. "Before these ugly new buildings went up. Where did you live?"

"Ingalls my first year. And then Harkness." He felt unsure about the names, as if they, too, might be incorrect.

"Guess what," Megan said. "Our cell phone doesn't work up here. I tried to call the girls but there's no service."

"I'm sure there's a pay phone somewhere," Amit said. "I'll call them before their bedtime." He was tired of standing, longed for the opportunity to sit down and fill his stomach with something solid. A few elderly people were already under the tent, along with some mothers nursing their babies, and he wondered if it would be improper of him to take his seat as well. He waited for a gap in Ted and Megan's conversation, to suggest going to their table, but then he felt a tap on the back and turned to see Pam's parents. He proceeded to catch up with them, congratulating them, pulling out his wallet again and showing the pictures of the girls. "They look just like their mother," Mrs. Borden said in her usual forthright way.

When he turned back to Megan he saw that her champagne glass was empty. She had moved closer to Ted, and her hand was playing with her diamond earring, a habit of hers when she was nervous. Could it be that Megan was flirting with Ted? Instead of being jealous Amit felt oddly liberated, relieved of his responsibility to Megan, to show her a good time. His head was pounding. He needed a glass of water, needed to dilute the alcohol that had rushed too quickly into his brain. The evening had barely begun but it was as if he'd been drinking for hours. Then he saw that the hand by Megan's ear was the one that had been formerly concealing her skirt. Now that she'd had a few drinks herself she no longer cared, and Amit realized he was free of his duty to stand by her side.

At dinner they were seated at a table with three other couples. Two of them were friends of Ryan's from California, and after introductions were made they talked among themselves. The women were in their fifties, both dressed in silk jackets and with heavy pieces of silver jewelry, and Amit suspected they had something to do with television. The men were dark-haired and voluble and seemed to be very old friends. The other couple was engaged to be married. The woman, Felicia, was a friend of Pam's, and her fiancé's name was Jared. Jared was an architect, with very fair wispy hair, who seemed to be faintly smiling at everyone and everything, until Amit realized it was the set expression of his face, his thin mouth permanently pulled back at the corners. Jared's current commission was a new wing in a hospital, and he and Megan immediately fell into conversation, Megan telling him all the things that needed to be improved, in her opinion, when it came to the design of hospitals.

As their wine and water glasses were filled and a salmon terrine was served, Felicia talked to Amit about her and Jared's wedding plans. She was a petite woman, her girlish figure encased in a high-necked beige sleeveless dress. Her features, though pleasant, seemed too small for her face, as if yet to fill it up properly, the distance between the bottom of her nose and her top lip distracting. She spoke in a tired way, each word weighted down. They were in the process of deciding on a venue, Felicia said, and weren't sure of the number of guests.

"This wedding is huge," she remarked. "How many people, would you guess?"

He looked around at the tables, counted eight bodies at

each. "Around two hundred, I think." He drained his water glass and looked over at Megan, her animated face without a trace of discomfort.

"Where was your wedding?" Felicia asked.

"We eloped eight years ago. City Hall." It had seemed like the right thing to do at the time—instead of asking his parents to fly in from Lausanne, and Megan's parents to go to the expense, and figuring out how to make everybody happy. He was twenty-nine, Megan thirty-four. It had been exhilarating— the joy of getting married combined with the fact that it would all be in secret, without planning, without involvement from anyone else. His parents had not even met her. He was aware of what an insult it was to them. For all their liberal Western ways he knew they wanted him to marry a Bengali girl, raised and educated as he had been.

"Do you regret it at all?" Felicia asked.

"I think our daughters do." For they were at the age now when they expected tales of a wedding cake, pictures of their mother in a white gown.

Felicia asked how old the girls were, and again, clumsily, he pulled out the photos in his wallet. "Megan has better ones. More recent, I mean. But they're at the hotel."

"Did you have to try for a while?"

He thought it a bold question, coming from a stranger. But he was honest with her, his thoughts still loose from the spiked lemonade. "Would you believe, with Maya it happened the first time," he said. He remembered how proud he'd felt, how powerful. The first time in his life he'd had sex without contraception a life had begun.

"Will you go for a third?"

"It's hard to imagine." He thought back to when his daughters were infants, when swings and play-saucers crowded the rooms and the sticky tray of the high chair had to be scrubbed in the shower at the end of each night. His girls had already turned mysterious, both out of diapers, withdrawing to their room to read or play games, talking in secret languages, bursting into peals of laughter at the table for no apparent reason. He'd been more eager than Megan to start a family. It was exotic, the world of parenting, fulfilling him in a way his job did not. It was Amit who'd pushed for a second. Megan was content with one, telling him she'd paid the price for being from a large family. But Amit hadn't wanted Maya to be an only child, to lead the lonely existence he remembered. Megan had given in, gotten pregnant again even though she was almost forty, but since Monika's birth she'd worn an IUD.

A spoon clinked on a glass and they all turned their attention to the front of the tent, to the first round of toasts. They listened to friends of Pam's from prep school and then from college, a few of whom he vaguely remembered drinking with at the Marlin. They were followed by members of both families, and coworkers of Pam's and Ryan's. Amit was distracted by a pale gray spider that crawled up the side of the tablecloth and then into the space between the cuff of Jared's shirt and jacket. He was tempted to say something, but Jared hadn't noticed; instead he sat there, the same faint smile still fixed on his face, no doubt anticipating the day people would stand up and offer toasts at his own wedding.

The entrée was served, plates of prime rib with asparagus and potatoes.

"How was it, going from one child to two?" Felicia inquired, picking up the conversation where they'd left it. "A friend of mine told me that one plus one equals three. Is it true?" She sliced into her prime rib, causing blood from the meat to seep into the potatoes.

He considered for a moment. "Actually, it was after the second that our marriage sort of"—he paused, searching for the right word—"disappeared." He realized it was a funny word to use, but something had been lost, something had fallen through their fingers, and that was the only way he could put it.

"What do you mean?" Felicia asked. She set down her fork and squinted at him with her small eyes, her voice suddenly cold.

He looked over at Megan, full of the radiance that had graced her this evening, still talking to Jared. In the hotel they had vowed not to leave each other's side, but she was miles away from him. He felt the same resentment that often seized him after he cleaned up the kitchen and bathed Maya and Monika and put them to bed, and then watched television alone, knowing that he had seen his children through another day, that again Megan had not been a part of it. She lived in the apartment, she slept in his bed, her heart belonged to no one but him and the girls, and yet there were times Amit felt as alone as he had first been at Langford. And there were times he hated Megan, simply for this. Had he been sober he would have repressed the thought, reminding himself that it was for his sake, and the girls, that she worked so hard. He would have reminded himself that in a year or so their lives would change, that Megan hoped to find a job in a private practice, so they would once again be able to go on family vacations and throw dinner parties for their friends. But tonight nothing censored his peevishness; he embraced it, felt justified by his very ability to acknowledge what was true.

"It disappeared," he repeated, with more force this time. "I guess it does for everyone, sooner or later."

But Felicia's face had hardened. "What an awful thing to say," she said, not hiding her disgust. "At a wedding, of all places."

And yet he felt justified. Wasn't it since Monika's birth that so much of his and Megan's energy was devoted not to doing things together but devising ways so that each could have some time alone, she taking the girls so that he could go running in the park on her days off, or vice versa, so that she could browse in a bookstore or get her nails done? And wasn't it terrible, how much he looked forward to those moments, so much so that sometimes even a ride by himself on the subway was the best part of the day? Wasn't it terrible that after all the work one put into finding a person to spend one's life with, after making a family with that person, even in spite of missing that person, as Amit missed Megan night after night, that solitude was what one relished most, the only thing that, even in fleeting, diminished doses, kept one sane?

He considered explaining this to Felicia, but he saw that she no longer wanted to talk to him. She'd been hanging on his every word but now she turned her attention to one of the women in silver jewelry. He looked at his watch and saw that it was almost eight thirty. The girls would be in their nightgowns, reading stories before bedtime. He had not finished his meal, had eaten very little of it in fact, but the plate was cleared away and strawberry shortcake was in its place. He looked up and saw that most of the tables were empty. Dancing had begun, couples clinging to each other under a neighboring tent, surrounded by the mountains, the black night. The band was playing a Gershwin song. Jared led Felicia away, and though Amit knew he would never have to see her again, he was relieved to see her go, taking away the depressing evidence of their conversation. Jared was bending down to hear something Felicia was whispering and Amit wondered if she was relaying what he'd said to her. How inappropriate, they would think, to talk that way to a person who was engaged. And they would promise each other not to let that happen in their own marriage, that even after twelve children they would never feel that way.

He saw Ted drifting over, asking Megan if it was all right to sit in the empty chair beside her. "That was quite a meal. I didn't eat half as well at my own wedding," he said.

"I should call the girls," Megan said. "We promised them we would."

"I'll go," Amit offered. "You stay, Meg. Enjoy yourself."

"I won't run off with her," Ted said, winking. "I promise."

"Are you sure you're okay?" Megan asked Amit. From the way she was looking at him he saw, without his having to say anything, that she knew he'd had too much to drink, that she had still paid attention to him while speaking to other men all evening.

"I'm fine. I'll go find a pay phone and then I'll be right back. A walk will do me good."

"But then we dance the night away and watch the sun rise, okay?" She smiled at him, and he felt her love for him suddenly—that unshakable belief in him and in their marriage that she never questioned, never denigrated, as he had tonight.

"Okay." He walked over to where she was sitting, bent down and kissed her on the cheek, then went up to the admissions building where the bathrooms were. Two large rooms had been opened up for the children to play in. Some were running around, some crying, others sprawled fast asleep on the leather club chairs and sofas. He wandered around, looking for a pay phone. There were only the kind limited to the campus exchange, or private ones, sitting on desks. He saw them through the glass doors of offices. But when he tried the knobs they were all locked.

He walked outside, to see if maybe there was a phone there. He found nothing. And yet he had to call the girls, wanted to hear their voices, this was the sole thought in his mind. He began to cut across the field in the dark, in the direction of the hotel, forgetting that the car was parked at the school. Instead he stumbled across the field, silent except for the faint sound of the music carried across the air, and the sound of his own breathing. He stopped and looked up at the sky and the stars, the constellations that were so piercing outside the city. He thought of Megan, thought maybe he should go back and tell her he was going to the hotel. But he continued walking, unable to see his feet as they marched across the ground.

There were no lights apart from the stars and he was unsure which direction the hotel was in. And then again he stopped, to listen to the serenade of the frogs that lived around the lake, like the repeated, random plucking of a bowed instrument in an orchestra, endlessly tuning itself before a performance. It was a sound he had forgotten, one that had haunted him and kept him awake his first nights in a Langford dormitory, at the end of another August when he was fifteen years old. All the incoming students heard it as they slept in their new rooms, in their strange beds, missing their parents, their homes; they were told at their first assembly that the frogs were calling for their mates, defending their territory by the water's edge before burying themselves under mud for the winter. The deafening thrum spoke to Amit tonight as it had then, of everything in the world that teemed beyond his vision, that was beyond his grasp.

He saw the hotel. It had taken no time at all; Megan wouldn't even notice he'd been gone. He went into the room and sat on the bed that was empty, as opposed to the one used for their discarded clothes and luggage, and picked up the telephone. He looked around the room, and what he had earlier found disappointing he now found comforting. He dialed his in-laws' area code. But he could not remember the rest of the number.

He sat there for a long time, the phone in his lap, trying to remember the digits. But he did not know them by memory, it was Megan who always called. He studied the paper pyramid from all sides, as if that might hold the answer. But no, those were television channels. He would have to go back to the wedding, ask Megan, and then come back again to the hotel. That was what he would do. He stood up, walking across the room to the door. Then he remembered that he could call directory assistance. He returned to the phone and was about to press the buttons. But his head throbbed and things began to spin, the paper pyramid on the bedside table no longer where it had been a second ago, and the need to be horizontal overwhelmed him, pulling him back to the pillows on the bed.

He woke up dressed in his suit, polished black shoes on his feet. The light was on in the dark room, the curtain to the balcony drawn. He first thought that it was still nighttime and that he had to get back to the wedding. But then he looked at the digital clock on the bedside table and saw that it was eleven in the morning.

"Megan?" he called out. He could barely form the word. His voice was ragged, and he realized that for a long time in his sleep he'd been craving a glass of water. He sat up a little and became aware of an excruciating band of pressure around his head. Looking at the neighboring bed he saw that it had not been slept in, that the open suitcase and clothes had not been moved aside.

He sat up fully and then stood. "Megan?" he called out again. He took off his jacket, went to the bathroom, drank water from the basin. He couldn't bear to turn the light on. The night began to come back to him in pieces. He remembered sitting on the toilet seat, just minutes ago, it seemed, inspecting Megan's skirt. Then he remembered watching Pam Borden getting married and waiting in a long line for a drink, and a conversation at dinner with a woman who was engaged. He remembered leaving Megan at the table with another man. Suddenly he jerked on the light and saw that her glasses were not by the basin where she normally left them during the night, that she had not come back to the hotel.

He returned to the bed in which he'd slept, searching for some sign of her on the other side of it. But the cover had not been turned back; there were only the creases indicating where he'd lain. Again he crossed the room. He yanked open the closet, which contained just a few empty hangers on the rod. He decided to go to the front desk and ask if she'd returned. He felt chilly and put on his jacket again. Then he saw that the door to the balcony was partly open.

She was sitting in a chair, in jeans and a fleece pullover she'd wisely packed, thinking it might be cold in the mountains. The diamond studs he'd given her after Maya's birth sparkled in her ears. She was sipping coffee from a paper cup and was staring at the pine tree that blocked the view.

"Well, I made it to watch the sun rise, like I said I would," she said. "Only the sunrise wasn't visible today." He looked at the sky. It was full of daylight but uniformly gray. The air was cool and rain seemed imminent.

He eyed the empty chair next to Megan, knowing he wasn't welcome. She had not turned around to face him, had not looked up, and he stood partly behind her, shivering, his arms crossed in front of him. "When did you get back?" he asked her.

"Oh, it must have been around three. That was when the party finally broke up. My feet are killing me. I haven't danced like that in years."

Her words made him think that perhaps his memories had been part of a terrible dream. "Did we dance last night at the wedding?"

"It was only for about an hour that I was out of my mind with worry. We looked for you everywhere. I asked strange men to check underneath bathroom stalls. I even considered calling the police. But then something told me you'd ended up back here, and when I called the hotel that's exactly what they told me." She said all of this calmly, as if addressing the tree in front of her, and yet he felt her fury in each word.

"I couldn't find a pay phone," he said.

She turned to him then, jerking the chair around while still sitting in it, her eyes wet with tears. "Neither could I. But I asked Pam's father and he opened up one of the offices."

Amit looked down at his feet, at his muddied wing tips. "I left the car up there. Did you drive it back?"

"How could I, when the keys were in your pocket?"

"How did you get here, then?" He felt as if he might be sick, remembering Ted, thinking of him accompanying her to the hotel in the middle of the night.

"Oh, that nice couple at our table gave me a ride. Jared and Felicia."

He knew that she'd been virtuous, that she was telling him the truth. At the same time, feeling sick again, he wondered if Felicia had told Megan what he'd said. "How are the girls?"

"They're fine, they're having a blast. I told my parents we'll be there by afternoon."

"But we're staying here until tomorrow. That was the plan."

"It's a bit silly, don't you think, given the weather? The concierge said it's only supposed to get worse."

Ten years ago it wouldn't have mattered. They would have laughed at the rain, gone for a walk anyway, then holed up in the room and made love.

"I'm sorry, Meg. The drinks went straight to my head. I don't even remember having that many. I didn't mean to abandon you."

She didn't acknowledge his apology. Instead she said, "I've had breakfast. I can go get the car before the rain starts, while you pack up. The hotel restaurant's not bad. You should probably eat something. I'm tired, and I want you to be able to drive back."

"You're always tired," he wanted to tell her. "The only time you haven't been tired in years was last night." But he knew that he was in no position to accuse her.

"Well?" she said.

"There's a brunch," he remembered, and suddenly he felt hopeful, that there was still a bit of the wedding left, that he could make an appearance, make up for what he'd missed. "I can eat there. I'd like to go and say good-bye to Pam and Ryan," he said. "Let's go over together. Please."

She opened her mouth to say something, then stopped. His head was pounding and his voice was cracking, and from the sad look in her eyes he knew that he looked pathetic, that it was out of pity that she refused to raise her voice, to berate him. Eventually she said, "If that's what you want."

"You'll go with me?"

"I've spent enough time at this wedding by myself."

She sat on the balcony reading the local paper while he changed out of his suit and into his ordinary clothes. Then he packed up their things, throwing all the tourist brochures into the garbage. They walked across the road and across the field to Langford. They were halfway there when the rain started. It was an undramatic drizzle, filling the air with the faintest sound, but by the time they reached the edge of campus their hair was damp, their feet drenched and cold. At one point they paused to take in a view of the lake. In spite of the rain, a man swam in the dark gray water, quite far out.

They went past the small cemetery on the grounds of the school, along a path that led them to a sign taped to a stake that said BRUNCH, with an arrow. They headed in that direction, keeping their eye out for another sign. The tents under which people had dined and danced were still up, empty now, the tables folded and stacked in piles. The chairs on which they'd sat to watch the ceremony were still arranged more messily, on the lawn. There was a truck parked in front of the alumni building, where two maintenance men in overalls were clearing up.

"Is the brunch in here?" Amit asked.

"Don't know anything about a brunch," one of them said.

They walked in the direction of the chapel and the observatory. They passed the parking lot, where a few cars stood, including their own. They reached the front gates of the school, then turned back again.

"I don't see any other signs," Megan said. "Did she say which building?"

Amit shook his head, and they continued on. United in their quest, he wondered if her rage was dissipating. And yet they did not walk side by side; she was ahead of him, leading the way even though she did not know it. When doors were open they entered, wandering down musty carpeted hallways, into naked stairwells, past empty classrooms with clean blackboards and the round wooden tables at which Langford students always sat. In less than a month students would return to those tables. He was free of the school, it no longer touched his life in any way. But instead of feeling grateful, he wanted to relive those confused days, that life of discovery, to be bound to those round tables and lectures and exams. There were things he had always meant to understand better: Russian history, the succession of Roman emperors, Greek philosophy. He wanted to read what he was told each evening, to do as he was told. There were the great writers he had never read, would never read. His daughters would begin that journey soon enough, the world opening up for them in its awesome entirety. But there was no time now, not even to look at the whole paper on Sundays.

In the music complex, they found a room with an assortment of couches and practice stands. There was a baby grand piano in the corner, and in front of it, two trash bins filled with coffee cups and crushed boxes from a bakery. A long folding table held a coffee percolator, a stack of unused cups.

"We found it," Amit said, feeling triumphant. And then, just as instantly, he felt thwarted. He saw an open box on the table containing a few eclairs. The sight made his stomach churn up in hunger, and he picked one up, consumed it without pause.

"Looks like we missed brunch," Megan said. After a while she added, "You have chocolate icing around your mouth."

Lacking a napkin or the wipes he always had with him when he was with the girls, he drew the back of his hand across his lips. The bells of the chapel chimed as if for the two of them alone. He thought of Pam and Ryan on their way to the airport, to their honeymoon in Scotland. He thought of the other guests heading back, pleasantly hungover, and the Bordens relaxing at home, commenting on the evening, saluting themselves on a job well done.

They headed toward the parking lot to get the car. The rain was heavy now, the sound of it percussive against the leaves of the trees. Had the wedding been today instead of yesterday, Amit thought to himself, everything would have been different; they would have gathered in the chapel, everyone would have remarked what a shame it was. The rain came down harder and they both began picking up their pace, half-jogging side by side, Megan keeping a hand pressed over her head. They approached Standish Hall, the dorm in which they could have stayed. The front door was open, held by a large rock.

"Let's wait this out for a few minutes," Amit said, panting for breath. "I need to use the bathroom."

In the entryway, on a bulletin board, was a list of room assignments for the wedding guests. He left Megan standing there, reading the names on the list, while he went to the bathroom. All along the hallway the doors were open, beds stripped, sheets folded up on top of them. In the bathroom, the shower stalls, separated by slabs of gray marble, still had beads of water on them from the morning's use. When he returned, Megan was no longer in the entryway. He began walking down the remaining length of the hall and found her in one of the rooms, perched on the edge of a desk. She was looking at a xeroxed sheet of paper that someone had stepped on, leaving the dusty imprint of a shoe's sole. "The brunch ended at eleven," she said.

The arrangement of the room was familiar to him but things had been redone since his time here. There was a new fire alarm, blond wood furniture. The mattress looked firmer, without the black-and-white ticking he remembered. There was a tan carpet covering the floor. The shade half-pulled on the window was fresh, with a ring attached to the string. The effect was more sanitized, less charming, a lot like the inside of the Chadwick Inn. He opened the closet, barely deep enough for a hanger.

"You know, we should have just stayed here," Megan said. "We would have saved two hundred dollars, and I wouldn't have spent half the night worried you'd vanished into thin air."

He closed the closet, then shut the door to the room. There was no way to lock it from the inside. "My fault for trying to have a romantic getaway."

"But this is so much more romantic." She spoke objectively, but he also detected a note of regret. When he turned to her she was preoccupied, slightly frowning. She had removed her glasses, raised her fleece pullover, and was wiping the delicate lenses on the T-shirt underneath. Her pulled-back hair was slick against her head, her cheeks flushed from running. She held out the glasses in front of her face, inspecting them before putting them back on. "Was it in a room like this that you had sex for the first time?"

It was something, after all these years, that she didn't know about him. In spite of her anger his past still preyed on her, if only because she hadn't been a part of it. "I didn't have sex at Langford. Anyway, it was a boys' school back then."

"I refuse to believe there weren't ways to sneak girls in."

"There were, but I never did. I've told you a million times I was miserable here."

"What about Pam?" Megan asked, folding her arms across her chest, glancing over at the bed. "Did you ever have sex with her?"

"No."

She took a step toward him, looking at the shirt that clung coldly to his body, then directly into his eyes. "What, then? Something passed between you two, it's obvious."

"It was nothing, Meg. We were friends and for a while I had a crush on her. But nothing happened. Is that so terrible?"

The information fell between them, valuable for the years he'd kept it from her, negligible now that he'd told. Through the window he saw the workmen in the rain, folding up the chairs and stacking them onto a cart. He went to the window and pulled down the shade completely, darkening the room. Then he turned back to Megan, close to her now. He kneeled on the floor and put his arms around her legs, pressing his face against her jeans. She did not walk away as he feared, did not detangle herself from his awkward embrace. Then he felt her hand on top of his head, her long fingers grazing the gray hairs of his skull, and instantly, powerfully, he felt an erection. He began to kiss her legs, grasping at her belt loops and pulling her down so that she was kneeling on the carpet, too. He put a hand up against the thick inseam of her jeans, knowing exactly what it was like to touch her there, the combination of skin and bone and hair. He looked at her and he saw that although her face was turned away, she had relaxed her body, adjusting herself to accommodate his hand.

"We can't do this here," she whispered, and yet she was tipping back her head, allowing him to push up her fleece pullover.

"Why not?" He was kissing her neck now, and then her mouth, strong, open-mouthed kisses that she was returning. He took her hand and placed it under his belt.

She looked at him then, with slight tenderness, and shook her head. "It's a dorm room, Amit. Kids live here."

But he continued, guiding her hand to his belt buckle while forcing off her clothes, the fleece, the soft T-shirt below that. Her hair came undone. He pulled down her jeans, revealing thighs that were chilled and reddened, as if from a sunburn. They took off their shoes and socks, a mess of wet grass clippings falling onto the carpet, then positioned themselves on the mattress. He couldn't remember the last time they'd done this outside their apartment, outside their bedroom, where they were always nervous that the girls would walk in. They were nervous now, but they were excited, too, knowing they could get caught. He entered her and felt her hands on his back, warming him, her ankles around the backs of his legs, and the shock of her tongue in his ear. She offered to turn over, knowing this was the quickest way. But he wanted to face her. He placed his hands on her hips, over the stretch marks that were like inlaid streaks of mother-of-pearl that would never fade, whose brilliance spoke only for the body's decay. He put his mouth to one of her breasts, flattened and drained after nursing two children, tasting the film of perspiration that had gathered. Her breathing became audible and then she cried out, loudly enough for anyone in the neighboring rooms to know what was taking place. But no one discovered them, no workmen came to clean up, no guest from the wedding strayed in, no little girls intruded giggling into the room. He came inside her and sat up, knowing they could not linger. He was looking at the clothes they needed to put on again. Megan's eyes were on his face, an arm stretched in front of her and a hand pressed to his chest, as if to prevent him, now that they were finished, from collapsing on top of her again. But he hoped that he was forgiven, and for a few moments they remained together on the narrow bed in the little room, his heart beating rapidly, vigorously, plainly striking the skin of her palm.

Only Goodness

It was Sudha who'd introduced Rahul to alcohol, one weekend he came to visit her at Penn—to his first drink from a keg and then, the next morning in the dining hall, his first cup of coffee. He'd pronounced both beverages revolting, preferring Schnapps to the beer and emptying a dozen packets of sugar in his coffee cup. That had been his junior year of high school. When she was home the following summer he asked her to buy him some six-packs, planning to have a party one weekend when their parents were going to be in Connecticut overnight. He'd shot up to six feet, braces off his teeth, whiskers sprouting around his mouth, dark pimples occasionally studding his cheekbones, her little brother in name only. She went to a local liquor store, helping Rahul divvy up the cans between his room and hers so that their parents wouldn't discover them.

After her parents were asleep she brought some cans into Rahul's room. He snuck downstairs, bringing back a cup of ice cubes to chill down the warm Budweiser. They shared one cupful, then another, listening to the Stones and the Doors on Rahul's record player, smoking cigarettes next to the open window and exhaling through the screen. It was as if Sudha were in high school again, doing things she once hadn't had the wits or guts for. She felt a new bond with her brother, a sense, after years of regarding him as just a kid, that they were finally friends.

Sudha had waited until college to disobey her parents. Before then she had lived according to their expectations, her persona scholarly, her social life limited to other demure girls in her class, if only to ensure that one day she would be set free. Out of sight in Philadelphia she studied diligently, double-majoring in economics and math, but on weekends she learned to let loose, going to parties and allowing boys into her bed. She began drinking, something her parents did not do. They were prudish about alcohol to the point of seeming Puritanical, frowning upon the members of their Bengali circle—the men, that was to say—who liked to sip whiskey at gatherings. In her freshman year there had been nights when she got so drunk that she was sick on the streets of campus, splattering the side-walk and stumbling back to her dorm with friends. But she learned what her limits were. The idea of excess, of being out of control, did not appeal to Sudha. Competence: this was the trait that fundamentally defined her.

After Rahul graduated from high school their parents cele-brated, having in their opinion now successfully raised two chil dren in America. Rahul was going to Cornell, and Sudha was still in Philadelphia, getting a master's in international rela-tions. Their parents threw a party, inviting nearly two hundred people, and bought Rahul a car, justifying it as a necessity for his life in Ithaca. They bragged about the school, more impressed by it than they'd been with Penn. "Our job is done," her father declared at the end of the party, posing for pictures with Rahul and Sudha at either side. For years they had been compared to other Bengali children, told about gold medals brought back from science fairs, colleges that offered full schol-arships. Sometimes Sudha's father would clip newspaper articles about unusually gifted adolescents—the boy who finished a PhD at twenty, the girl who went to Stanford at twelve—and tape them to the refrigerator. When Sudha was fourteen her father had written to Harvard Medical School, requested an application, and placed it on her desk.

Sudha's example had taught her parents that there was nothing to fear about sending a child to college. Rahul took it in stride as well, not overly anxious as Sudha had been the summer before she'd gone away. He was almost indifferent to the changes ahead, his attitude reminding her that he'd always been the smarter one. Sudha had struggled to keep her place on the honor roll, to become salutatorian of her high school class. But Rahul never lifted a finger, never cracked a book unless it appealed to him, precocious enough to have skipped third grade.

At the end of the summer, Sudha went to Wayland to help him pack, but when she got there she saw that there was nothing left for her to do. He had already stuffed his bags, filled some milk crates with records, grabbed sheets and towels from the linen closet, wrapped the cord around his electric typewriter. He told her she didn't need to go all the way to Ithaca, but she insisted, riding beside him as he drove his new car, their parents following behind. The campus was on a hilltop surrounded by farms and lakes and waterfalls, nothing like Penn. She helped unload his things, carrying boxes across the quadrangle along with the other families of incoming freshmen. When it was time to say good-bye their mother wept, and Sudha cried a little, too, at the thought of abandoning her little brother, still not eighteen, in that remote, majestic place. But Rahul did not behave as if he were being either abandoned or liberated. He pocketed the money their father counted out and gave him as they parted, and he turned back toward his dormitory before Sudha and her parents had pulled away.

. . .

The next time she saw him was Christmas. At dinner he had nothing specific to say about his classes, or his professors, or the new friends he'd made. His hair had grown long enough to conceal his neck and to tuck behind his ears. He wore a checked flannel shirt, and around his wrist, a knotted woven bracelet. He did not eat the enormous amounts Sudha still did when she sat at her mother's table. He seemed bored, watching but not helping when Sudha and her mother decorated the tree with the ornaments she and Rahul had made when they were little. Sudha remembered always seeming to come down with the flu over Christmas break, collapsing once she was free of the pressure of exams, and thought that Rahul might do so, too. But later that evening, finding her upstairs where she was wrapping gifts in her room, he seemed to have perked up. "Hey. Where did you hide it?" he asked.

"Hide what?"

"Don't tell me you came home empty-handed."

"Oh," she said, realizing what he meant. "It didn't occur to me. I just thought, since you're in college—" It was true, it hadn't occurred to her this time to stick a six-pack into her bag. She preferred wine now, a glass with dinner when she went out with friends in Philadelphia, but she did not expect it when she came home to Wayland.

"I'm still not old enough to buy anything here." He glanced around the room as if it might contain what he sought, looking at her closet and her chest of drawers, at the bed that was covered with wrapping paper and a box from Filene's containing a nightgown for her mother.

"Trip to the liquor store?" he suggested, sitting on top of the bed, crushing some wrapping paper she'd unrolled. His hand sifted through the gift tags, the tape, picking up each item and then dropping it again.

"Now?" she asked.

"Do you have any other plans for the evening?"

"Well, no. But Ma and Baba are going to think it's weird if we go out all of a sudden."

He rolled his eyes. "Jesus, Didi. You're almost twenty-four. Do you really still care what they think?"

"I was about to get into my pajamas."

He picked up the scissors, his eyes focused on the slow opening and closing of the blades, as if discovering their function for the first time. "Since when did you get so boring?"

She knew he was joking, but the remark hurt her nevertheless. "Tomorrow, I promise."

He stood up, distant again as he had been at dinner, and she felt herself faltering. "I guess it's still open," she said, looking at her watch. And so she'd gone, lying to her parents that she needed to get something last minute at the mall, Rahul saying he'd drive her there.

"You're the best," Rahul told her as they headed into town. He rolled down the window on his side, filling the car with freezing air, and fished in his coat pocket for a pack of cigarettes. He pushed in the lighter on the dashboard and offered her one, but she shook her head, turning up the heat. She told him that she'd applied to go to London the following year, to do a second master's at the London School of Economics.

"You're going to London for a whole year?"

"You can visit me."

"Why do you need another master's degree?" He sounded distressed, and also disapproving. It was the sort of reaction she expected from her parents. Her parents hadn't allowed her to do a junior year abroad at Oxford, telling her then that she was too young to live in a foreign county alone. But now they were excited by the prospect of Sudha going to London, where they'd first lived after getting married and where Sudha had been born, talking about visiting and reconnecting with old friends.

She explained that LSE had one of the best programs in developmental economics, that she was thinking of doing NGO work, eventually. But Rahul didn't seem to be listening, and she was annoyed with him, with herself, really, for agreeing to go out so late at night. "You want a six-pack?" she asked when they got to the liquor store.

"I'd prefer a case."

In the past she had paid for things without a second thought, but she was aware, now, that he did not reach for his wallet.

"And a bottle of vodka, too," he added.

"Vodka?"

He drew another cigarette out of its pack. "It's a long vacation."

Their parents were in bed by the time they returned, but Sudha insisted they hide things as they had before. Thinking that their mother might have reason to enter Rahul's room for the weeks that he was home, to clean up or put away his laundry, she kept the liquor in her room, a few cans at the back of her closet, some in a gap behind a bookcase, the bottle of Smirnoff wrapped in an old pilly sweater in her chest of drawers. She told Rahul it was safer that way, and he didn't seem to care. He took a couple of cans for the night, pecking her on the cheek before he left her, not insisting when she said she was too tired to join him.

He had been born when Sudha was six, and the night her mother went into labor was the first sustained memory of her life. She remembered being at a party in the home of one of her parents' Bengali friends in Peabody, being left there overnight because her father had to take her mother straight to Boston without the suitcase Sudha had helped pack containing the toothbrush and cold cream and robe her mother would need in the hospital. Though Sudha understood that a baby was about to be born, had felt it with her hand as it sometimes threatened to pound clear through her mother's belly, she was terrified nevertheless that her mother, moaning with her forehead pressed against a wall, was dying. "Go away," she said, when Sudha tried to stroke her mother's hand, in a tone that had stung. "I don't want you to see me this way." After her parents' departure the party continued. Sudha was expected to play in the basement with the other children, among the washer and dryer, as dinner was served to adults. The host and hostess did not have children of their own. Sudha had slept on a cot in a spare room containing no permanent furniture other than an ironing board and a closet devoted to cleaning supplies. In the morning there were no Frosted Flakes for her to eat, only toast with margarine, and it was then, during that restrained and disappointing adult breakfast, that the phone rang with news of her brother's arrival.

She had been hoping for a sister but was delighted nevertheless no longer to be an only child, to have someone help fill the emptiness she felt in her parents' home. The few things they owned were always in their places, the two most current issues of *Time* in the same spot on the coffee table. Sudha preferred the homes of her American friends, crammed and piled with things, toothpaste caking their sinks, their soft beds unmade. Finally, with Rahul's arrival, there was a similar swelling and disorder: his lotions and diapers heaped on the top of the dresser, stockpots clattering with boiling bottles on the stove, an infant's strong, milky odor pervading the rooms. She remembered how excited she had been, moving her things to one side to make space in her bedroom for Rahul's bassinet, his changing table, his mobile of stuffed bumblebees. Toys and other gifts accumulated in the crib he would eventually use; her favorite was a stuffed white rabbit that played a tune if a key at its throat was turned. She had not minded when her mother came in in the middle of the night to comfort Rahul, sitting in a rocking chair, singing a song in Bengali, something about a fishbone piercing the foot of a little boy, a song that would lull Sudha back to sleep also. Birth announcements were bought at the drugstore, the card of Sudha's choosing, and she helped to put them in their envelopes, dampening stamps with her father on a wet sponge. Countless photographs were taken—Rahul sleeping in his bassinet, being bathed in a plastic tub—and she took it upon herself to arrange these in a special album, with a blue denim cover because he was a boy.

There was not the same documentation of Sudha's infancy. In London, her parents had rented two rooms in Balham from a Bengali landlord named Mr. Pal, and it was he who had taken the few baby pictures of Sudha that existed, wearing a white lace dress intended for a christening but that her mother had simply thought pretty. Mr. Pal had opened his doors to her parents when her mother was pregnant with Sudha, providing refuge from their previous landlady, an elderly British woman who did not allow children under her roof. Her parents told her that half the rentals in London in the sixties said WHITES ONLY, and the combination of being Indian and pregnant limited her parents to the point where her father considered sending her mother back to India to give birth, until they met Mr. Pal. To Sudha this story was like an episode out of a Greek myth or the Bible, rich with blessing and portent, marking her family as survivors in strange intolerant seas.

Four years later they moved to Massachusetts, her father transferring from Badger to Raytheon, transporting no evidence of their years in London, no trace apart from her mother's fondness for the McVitie's biscuits she ate every morning with tea and her lifelong belief in the quality of British brassieres, which she asked friends in the UK to mail her every so often. None of Sudha's toys had made it on the journey across the Atlantic, no baby clothing or bedding or keepsake of any kind. In grade school, when Sudha had been required to present her autobiography to the class, a project for which the other students brought in blankets and scuffed shoes and blackened spoons, she came only with an envelope containing pictures Mr. Pal had taken, boring her classmates as she stood at the front of the room.

None of this mattered after Rahul arrived. Sudha had slipped through the cracks, but she was determined that her little brother should leave his mark as a child in America. She sought out all the right toys for him, scavenging from yard sales the Fisher Price barn, Tonka trucks, the Speak and Say that made animal sounds, and other things that she'd discovered in the playrooms of her friends. She asked her parents to buy him the books she'd been read by her first teachers, *Peter Rabbit* and *Frog and Toad*. "What's the point of buying books for someone who can't read?" her parents asked, legitimately enough, and so she checked them out of her school library and read them to Rahul herself. She told her parents to set up sprinklers on the lawn for him to run through in the summer, and she convinced her father to put a swing set in the yard. She thought up elabo-rate Halloween costumes, turning him into an elephant or a refrigerator, while hers had come from boxes, a flimsy apron and a weightless mask. At times she engaged with Rahul's upbringing more than he did—it was she, too heavy by then for the seats, who would swing in the yard after school, she who spent hours building towns out of Lincoln Logs that he would destroy with a gleeful swipe of the hand.

Though she doted on him and adored him, she began to envy him in small ways. She envied him for his lean limbs while she grew slightly pudgy once her period came, and she envied him because people could call him Raoul, that he could introduce himself in crowds without questions. She envied him for his beauty; even when he was a child there was a clear sense of the handsome man he would become. His face defied the family mold. Sudha, with her father's rounded chin and her mother's low hairline, was transparently their offspring, but Rahul looked little like either of them, his genes pulled not from the surface but from some deeper, forgotten source. His complexion was darker, his skin an unmistakable brown, his pronounced features lacking the indeterminate quality she and her parents shared. He was allowed to wear shorts in summer, to play sports in school, things her mother considered inappropriate for a girl. Sudha supposed it was a combination of his being a boy and being younger, and her parents being more at ease with the way things worked in America by then. Sudha had no fondness for her younger self, no sentimental affection for the way she had looked or the things she had done. What she felt was an overwhelming sense of regret, for what exactly she did not know. She had looked, of course, perfectly ordinary, her black hair worn in pigtails or braids, grown to her waist one year and cut like Dorothy Hamill's the next. And she had done ordinary things: attended slumber parties and played clarinet in the school band and sold chocolate bars from door to door. And yet she could not forgive herself. Even as an adult, she wished only that she could go back and change things: the ungainly things she'd worn, the insecurity she'd felt, all the innocent mistakes she'd made.

Thanks to Rahul there was also someone else to witness the perplexing fact of her parents' marriage. It was neither happy nor unhappy, and the lack of emotion in either extreme was what upset Sudha most. She would have understood quarrels, she believed she would even have understood divorce. She always hoped some sign of love would manifest itself; the only things that consoled her were a few pictures taken during their London years. Her mother looked unrecognizably slim, hair styled at a salon, a woven purse shaped like a cornucopia dangling from the crook of her elbow. Even her saris were glamorous back then, tightly wrapped to show off her figure, patterned with a spidery brown batik. Her father seemed vaguely mod, wearing suits with narrow dark ties and sunglasses. Those were the days, Sudha, supposed, when immigration was still an adventure, living with paraffin heaters, seeing snow for the first time.

Wayland was the shock. Suddenly they were stuck, her parents aware that they faced a life sentence of being foreign. In London her mother had been working toward a certificate in Montessori education, but in America she did not work, did not drive. She put on twenty pounds after Rahul was born, and her father put away his mod suits and shopped at Sears. In Wayland they became passive, wary, the rituals of small-town New England more confounding than negotiating two of the world's largest cities. They relied on their children, on Sudha especially. It was she who had to explain to her father that he had to gather up the leaves in bags, not just drag them with his rake to the woods opposite the house. She, with her perfect English, who called the repair department at Lechmere to have their appliances serviced. Rahul never considered it his duty to help their parents in this way. While Sudha regarded her parents' separation from India as an ailment that ebbed and flowed like a cancer, Rahul was impermeable to that aspect of their life as well. "No one dragged them here," he would say. "Baba left India to get rich, and Ma married him because she had nothing else to do." That was Rahul, always aware of the family's weaknesses, never sparing Sudha from the things she least wanted to face.

Another semester passed before she saw him again. She was accepted at LSE, and in June she came home to Wayland for a week. During her visit, Sudha gave herself fully to her parents, watching Wimbledon with her father on television, helping her mother cook and order new blinds for the bedrooms. She was always in the house, while Rahul drifted in and out without explanation. He was waiting tables part time at a seafood restaurant out in Scituate, thirty-five miles away, sleeping most days, working dinner shifts, out with friends after that. These were no longer friends from high school, boys Sudha had known since Rahul started kindergarten. Instead, they were people he met working at the restaurant, people he never bothered to invite home.

His aloofness troubled Sudha, but her parents said nothing. He seemed always to be in a slightly bad mood and in urgent need to get somewhere—to his job, to a gym where he went to lift weights, to the video store to return one of the foreign films he would watch when everyone else was asleep. She and Rahul never argued, but there were moments, when she crossed paths with him in the hallway or asked him to pass her the remote control, when she was briefly convinced he despised her. It was nothing he said or did—even in his avoidance he was always coolly polite—but she sensed that he had revised his opinion of her, that the Rahul who had once looked up to her and confided in her was replaced by a person she could only offend. She wondered when he would approach her for another run to the liquor store, but he never mentioned it. She gathered he had his own supply, stashed away somewhere; one night, when she was up late reading a magazine, she heard the sound of the ice machine grinding in the refrigerator, cubes dropping into a glass.

She learned from her mother that his second-semester grades had been bad; the first semester the lowest was a B, but now he'd gotten mostly C's. He had dropped biology and organic chemistry and taken up film and English literature instead. "Can you talk to him?" her mother asked Sudha. "Find out what went wrong?" Sudha came to Rahul's defense, saying that it was an enormous adjustment going from high school to college, that a lot of students had a hard time. Her father did not hide his disapproval, and while he did not confront Rahul, one day he said to Sudha, "He is floundering." He did not approve of paying an astronomical tuition just so Rahul could watch French movies in a classroom. Her father had no patience for failure, for indulgences. He never let his children forget that there had been no one to help him as he helped them, so that no matter how well Sudha did, she felt that her good fortune had been handed to her, not earned. Both her parents came from humble backgrounds; both their grandmothers had given up the gold on their arms to put roofs over their families' heads and food on their plates. This mentality, as tiresome as it sometimes felt, also reassured Sudha, for it was something her parents understood and respected about each other, and she suspected it was the glue that held them together.

Late one night, she knocked on Rahul's door. He was lying in bed, listening to music on his headphones, leafing through a tattered copy of Beckett's plays. He put the book on his chest when he saw her but didn't remove the headphones. She saw a mug on the floor by the bed, filled with ice cubes and a clear liquid. He didn't offer any, was playing their old game without her.

"So, what's going on at school?" she asked.

He looked up at her. His eyes were reddish. "I'm on vacation."

"Your grades weren't good, Rahul. You need to work a little harder."

"I did work hard," he said.

"I know the first year can be tough."

"I did work hard," he repeated. "My professors hate me. Is that my fault?"

"I'm sure they don't hate you," she said. She considered

crossing the room and sitting on the edge of the bed but remained where she was.

"What the fuck do you know?" he said, giving her a start.

"Look, I'm just trying to help."

"I'm not asking you to help. You don't need to fix anything. Has it ever occurred to you that my life might be fine the way it is?"

His words silenced her, cut to the bone. She'd always had a heavy hand in his life, it was true, striving not to control it but to improve it somehow. She had always considered this her responsibility to him. She had not known how to be a sister any other way.

"You don't even live here," he continued. "You think you can stroll in and make everything perfect before you disappear to London? Is that what you want to do?"

She looked at him, and then at the mug at the side of his bed, wondering how much he'd consumed in the course of the evening, where the bottle was hidden. She thought of her parents sleeping down the hall, unaware of what he was doing, and she felt indignant on their behalf. "You're smart, Rahul. You're a lot smarter than me. I don't get it."

He leaned over and picked up the cup from the floor. He took a sip and swallowed, then slid the cup under the bed, out of sight. "You don't have to get it, Didi. You don't have to get everything all the time."

On Sudha's last night before heading back to Philadelphia he surprised them, agreeing to go out to a restaurant to celebrate her impending departure for England. Their parents were in good moods, reminiscing about London, trying to remember the order of stops on the Piccadilly Line. Rahul was jovial, too, telling Sudha about all the writers' homes and graves she should visit while she was there. He spoke with an aggressive authority, as if he'd been to Marx's tomb himself, and for the first time it occurred to Sudha that perhaps Rahul was jealous of those years she and her parents had lived in England, those years when Rahul did not exist. He ordered a Singapore Sling and nursed it slowly through the meal. He mentioned nothing about having plans later on, but before the check came he looked at his watch and leapt up from the table, saying he was late for something, and left in his own car.

Sudha went home with her parents, was up watching *Spellbound* on the VCR when the phone rang. It was Rahul calling from the local police station. He'd been pulled over on a quiet road near Mill Pond for wavering in his lane. His blood alcohol content was not extreme, but because he was under twenty-one it was enough to get him arrested. He asked Sudha to come to the station alone, to bring three hundred dollars in cash. But it was past midnight, and besides, the keys to her parents' car were in the pocket of her father's pants, in their bedroom. She woke up her father, told him to get dressed. Together they went to post bail and release Rahul from the cell. Her father drove, his face creased with sleep, seeming disoriented in the town he'd lived in for years. They stopped at an ATM and withdrew money. "You go," her father said when they reached the station. "I prefer to wait in the car." His voice faltered as he spoke, as it had the day he'd called Sudha in college, to tell her his father died. And so she spared her father that humiliation, that pain, entering a place where handcuffed criminals were brought. When she saw Rahul he was sober, the pads of his fingers blackened from ink. It was a Sunday night, the arraignment scheduled for the following day. "Will you go with me?" he asked as they walked back to the car, and he was shaken enough for her to assure him that she would.

"It's ridiculous," her mother said the next morning as Rahul slept. She blamed the police for overreacting. "It's not like he had an accident. He was only going forty miles an hour. They probably stopped him just for being Indian." Her father said nothing. He sat sipping his tea and reading the *Sunday Globe.* He'd said nothing on the way home.

"That wasn't the problem," Sudha said slowly, forcing cold butter across the surface of her toast.

"What are you saying, Sudha?" her mother asked, sounding bothered. Her father did not put down his paper, but she sensed that he had stopped reading. Sudha knew that what she was about to say was something they expected and also viscerally feared, like disobedient children who are about to be slapped. That it was up to her to deliver the blow.

"I think Rahul might have a drinking problem."

"Sudha, please," her mother said. After a pause she added, "I gather everyone at American colleges drinks." She spoke as if drinking were an undergraduate hobby, a phase one outgrew.

"Not like that."

"Didn't you drink in college?"

"Not like that," Sudha repeated. Not enough to get arrested, she was tempted to say.

"That's the problem with this country," her mother said. "Too many freedoms, too much having fun. When we were young, life wasn't always about fun."

Sudha pitied her mother, pitied her refusal to accommodate such an unpleasant and alien fact, her need to blame America and its laws instead of her son. She sensed that her father understood, but he refused to engage in the conversation, refused to confront Rahul when he eventually came downstairs, showered and penitent, promising never to do such a thing again. Her parents had always been blind to the things that plagued their children: being teased at school for the color of their skin or for the funny things their mother occasionally put into their lunch boxes, potato curry sandwiches that tinted Wonderbread green. What could there possibly be to be unhappy about? her parents would have thought. "Depression" was a foreign word to them, an American thing. In their opinion their children were immune from the hardships and injustices they had left behind in India, as if the inoculations the pediatrician had given Sudha and Rahul when they were babies guaranteed them an existence free of suffering.

She was excited to be in London, curious to know the land of her birth. Before leaving she had applied for her British passport, a document her parents had not obtained for her when she was born, and when she presented it at Heathrow the immigration officer welcomed her home. Her parents went with her and stayed ten days, settling her into her hall of residence off Tottenham Court Road. They reminded her to look right before crossing the street, bought her cardigans from Marks and Spencer's to see her through the winter. They took her to Balham on the Tube to show her the house where she'd been an infant. Together they made a trip to Sheffield, three hours away through the countryside, where their old landlord Mr. Pal now lived with his family. They did not speak of Rahul unless forced to by friends, and when they did, it was always the same unobjectionably impressive facts about him—that he was at Cornell, a sophomore now. These facts gave her parents a feeble hope: as if college, where he'd begun to fall apart, would magically put him together again.

After her parents left she grew busy with her classes, and with the new friends she made who came from all over the world, joining them to study and sightsee and visit pubs. Perhaps because it was her birthplace, she felt an instinctive connection to London, a sense of belonging though she barely knew her way around. In spite of the ocean that now separated her from her parents, she felt closer to them, but she also felt free, for the first time in her life, of her family's weight. Still, she could not drink anymore without thinking of Rahul, always conscious that the second pint she drained, satisfied at the end of a night out, would not have been enough for him. At the arraignment she'd sat next to him in the crowded courtroom, waiting for his name to be called, listening as the charges were read. She was there to stand by him, to support him, but in that place of judgment she was not on his side. His license was suspended for six months and he was ordered to attend some alcohol education classes in Ithaca. In the end her father had had to pay nearly two thousand dollars in fines and fees. The arrest was mentioned in *The Wayland Town Crier*, a paper her parents received.

In November, wandering through the National Gallery, she met a man. She had been admiring *The Arnolfini Marriage* by van Eyck, lingering in front of it after a cluster of people had passed. It was an oil painting of a couple in a bedroom holding hands, with a small dog standing at their feet. The man wore a fur-trimmed purple cape and an overly large black straw hat. The woman wore an emerald-green gown that trailed like a heavy curtain onto the floor, some of the material gathered up in her left hand. She had a white veil on her head and looked possibly pregnant, Sudha wasn't sure. There was a window behind the man, with a piece of fruit, an apricot or a tangerine, on the sill. On the wall hung a convex mirror that reflected everything in the painting.

"Come closer," the man next to Sudha said, ushering her a few steps forward so that no one could cross their line of vision. "Otherwise you can't really see." He started talking about the mirror, how it was the focal point of the painting, capturing the floor and the ceiling, the room and the world outside, and then she saw that it reflected not only the couple but also a pair of men standing in the doorway, peering into the room just as she was. "One of them is van Eyck," the man said. "That's what the inscription above the mirror says. It's Latin for *'van Eyck was here.'*" He spoke softly, as if for Sudha alone, with the singsong British cadence that was already influencing Sudha's speech. His dark hair was slightly long, and he kept raking it with his fingers away from his face. She could smell the slightly spiced soap on his skin. He wore a tweed blazer and corduroy pants, and carried a raincoat draped over one arm. He told her that the two men in the doorway of the painting were witnessing the couple's union, adding that the painting was intended to serve as a marriage certificate. "Of course, that's just one interpretation," the man said. "Some argue that it's a betrothal scene."

She studied the details he spoke of, the glow of the paint, conscious of their shared gaze. "What about the shoes? Do they mean something?" Sudha heard herself asking, pointing to a pair of abandoned wooden clogs in the foreground, and then to some red slippers by the carpet.

The man turned to Sudha then. He was older than she expected, closer to forty judging from the eyes, clear blue eyes that settled calmly upon different points of her face. His expression was serious, placidly cast, but the sides of his mouth now rose up in a smile. "I suspect it means they're standing on holy ground. Either that or she just went shopping."

She had not known that day what a famous painting it was, but the man never made her feel ignorant. They walked to other paintings, the man bending his head down toward Sudha's and talking about them, and eventually he asked if she would like to join him for tea. His name was Roger Featherstone. He had a PhD in art history, was an editor at an art magazine and had also written a book about Renaissance portraiture. He wooed Sudha consistently, romantically: flowers every time he knocked on the door, gifts of gloves and earrings and perfume. He was an only child who had grown up in English boarding schools; his father had worked overseas for Singer sewing machines and now both his parents were dead. Roger was born in India, spent the first three years of his life in

Bombay but remembered nothing. He had been married in his twenties to a girl he'd known at Cambridge; after two years she left him, renounced her possessions, and joined a Buddhist monastery in Tibet.

He took responsibility for things, booking theater tickets, making reservations at restaurants, packing picnics and dragging Sudha off to Hampstead Heath. He was the first man she'd dated who was never late, never forgot to call when he said he would, and Sudha quickly recognized in him the same strain of competence she possessed. He enjoyed food and cooking, inspired to get up early and walk to a favorite bakery for pastries, surprising Sudha, the first morning she woke up in his flat in Shepherd's Bush, with breakfast on a tray. He had lived alone for many years but quickly opened his life to her, giving her a key, lined drawers in his bureau, a glass shelf in his medicine cabinet. In his youth he had dreamed of being a painter, had enrolled at Chelsea Art School, but after a teacher told him he would not go far he never touched a canvas again. He was not bitter about this turn of events; like Sudha, he was a person who understood what his limits were. At the same time he could be exacting, writing withering reviews for his magazine, insisting on the best table at restaurants, sending back wine. Like Sudha he was moderate with alcohol, always ordering a bottle for the table but seldom consuming more than a glass or two.

As Christmas approached she told her parents she had too much work and did not come home, when in fact she and Roger went away together, to Seville and then to the Costa del Sol. When she returned from Spain there was a message at the switchboard of her dormitory from her parents, asking her to call. When she did, from one of the pay phones in the lobby of the dorm, they told her that Rahul's grades had not improved, that a letter had come from an adviser, expressing concern. He was in Wayland now for Christmas break; after one explosive fight, he'd stopped speaking to them. She was glad that Roger wasn't there to overhear the call, that he'd kissed her good-bye in the taxi and gone back to his flat. She'd painted a hazy image of her family that he absorbed as if it were an endnote in a book, something stemming from her but safely tucked out of sight. "I can't wait to meet them," he told her, words that, Sudha hoped, made his intentions clear. Beyond the basic details he did not probe. And so she did not tell Roger about Rahul's drinking, about his arrest, about the fact that she had not talked to her brother in months.

Her parents asked her to speak to Rahul, saying he'd gone out for a walk, to try in a little while. She waited a few days. She was surprised after all these months by how upset she felt. And she was upset at her parents, too, for still depending on her to help. She called from Roger's flat, putting the charges on a card while Roger was at work. Rahul had turned twenty in the first week of January, a thing she'd let pass without acknowledgment. He picked up the phone, and she wished him happy birthday now. It was noon in Massachusetts, early evening in London. The sky was dark through Roger's kitchen window; at the counter, Sudha was setting out cheese and crackers and olives for her and Roger to eat together when he got home.

"Things okay?" she asked.

"Everything's fine. Ma and Baba are getting totally hysterical over nothing." Rahul spoke as if no strain existed between them, asking her how London was.

"They said you failed two classes."

"They were lousy classes."

"Are you even going to your classes?"

"Lay off, Didi," he said, his mood turning.

"Are you?" she persisted.

There was a pause. She heard the flicking of a lighter, the first pent-up exhale of a cigarette. "I don't want to be doing this."

"What do you want to do?" she asked, not bothering to conceal her exasperation.

"I'm writing a play."

She was surprised by this information and found it promising that he was actually doing something. He had always been a good writer; once, when he was in high school, he'd written a response to one of the take-home essay questions she had on a philosophy exam at Penn, a question about Plato's *Euthyphro* that her professor had approved of with a lengthy comment.

She put an olive in her mouth, extracted the thin purple pit, and placed it on a painted dish she and Roger had bought together in Seville. "That's great, Rahul. But you have to study, too."

"I want to drop out."

"Ma and Baba aren't going to go for that. Finish college and then you can do whatever you want."

"I'm sick of wasting time. And I want my car back. I hate not driving. I feel trapped."

She controlled herself, not telling him that it was ludicrous to expect their parents to trust him on the road again. "It's just two more years of your life, Rahul. Try to stick it out. Otherwise you'll end up hating yourself."

"Jesus, you sound just like them," he said and hung up on her.

She returned to Boston in April, during the break after the Lent term, a diamond ring from Roger concealed on a chain beneath her sweater, and this made her feel dipped in a protective coating from her family. After January her parents had not bothered her again about Rahul, telling her, the one time she asked, that he'd gone back to school. She felt guilty for distancing herself but not enough to counsel her parents, not enough to speak to Rahul. She had a ten-thousand-word dissertation to write on deregulation for her degree, and she had Roger, had moved in with him by then. She was surprised to see Rahul standing at the airport with her parents. All three of them looked sad, preoccupied, her parents perking up only when they caught sight of her behind her trolley piled with bags.

"Hey," she said, walking up to him, hugging him, though initially his long arms remained at his side. "It's good to see you."

"Welcome home," he said, and when he stepped back, she saw that he was not smiling.

"Is your semester finished already?"

He shook his head, still refusing to meet her gaze, and then a small, odd-sounding laugh escaped from him. "I live here now."

She had come home to tell her family about Roger, to tell them she planned to move permanently to London and marry him, but it was Rahul they had to talk about first. During the ride home from the airport she pieced together what had happened. It was her mother who did the talking; her father drove, muttering to himself now and then about the condition of the traffic, and Rahul spent most of the time staring out the window, as if he occupied the back of a cab. Though he returned to Ithaca after Christmas break, he'd stopped going to classes, and two weeks ago, after being formally dismissed from the university, he moved back to Wayland.

From what Sudha could tell, he was living in the house as if it were simply another vacation. He stayed in his room or watched television during the day. Their parents had sold his car, and so he never went out. Previously when he'd avoided them, there was something bristling in him, something about to explode. That energy was missing now. He no longer seemed upset with them, or with the fact that he was at home. For a while her parents told their friends that he was taking a leave of absence and then that he was in the process of transferring to BU. "Rahul needs a city in order to thrive," they said; but he never applied to other schools. They told people Rahul was looking for a job, and then the lie became more elaborate, and Rahul had a job, a consulting job from home, when in fact he stayed home all day doing nothing. Their mother, who had always hoped her children would live under her roof, was now ashamed that this was the case.

Eventually he got a job managing a Laundromat in Wayland three days a week. Her parents bought a cheap used car so that Rahul could drive into town. Sudha knew that the job embarrassed her parents. They had not minded him washing dishes in the past, but now they lived in fear of the day someone they knew would see their son weighing sacks of dirty clothes on a scale. Other Bengalis gossiped about him and prayed their own children would not ruin their lives in the same way. And so he became what all parents feared, a blot, a failure, someone who was not contributing to the grand circle of accomplishments Bengali children were making across the country, as surgeons or attorneys or scientists, or writing articles for the front page of *The New York Times*.

Sudha was among those successful children now, her collection of higher degrees framed and filling up her parents' upstairs hall. She was working as a project manager for an organization in London that promoted micro loans in poor countries. And she was spoken for. In the summer, she and Roger flew to Massachusetts so that he could meet Sudha's family and ask formally for her hand. At Roger's request they stayed not in Wayland but in a hotel in Boston; by now she knew him well enough to accept that he would maintain a limited exposure to her family, just as he guarded his body, on the beach, from the rays of the sun. "Better to be up front about these things at the start," Roger had told Sudha in his kind but firm way, and she took this as another sign of his responsible nature, his vigilance toward their life together. The hotel arrangement was accepted by her parents without protest; Rahul had stripped them of their capacity to fight back. They accepted that she and Roger planned to have a registry wedding in London, that they were willing to have only a reception in Massachusetts, that Roger had been previously married, that he and Sudha had a fourteen-year gap. They approved of his academic qualifications, his ability, thanks to his wisely invested inheritance, to buy a house for himself and Sudha in Kilburn. It helped that he'd been born in India, that he was English and not American, drinking tea, not coffee, and saying "zed" not "zee," superficial things that allowed her parents to relate to him. Sudha felt that they were not so much making room for Roger in the family as allowing him to take her away. But Rahul had not loosened his grip; he asked Roger questions, combing through the current issue of Roger's art magazine that her parents had admired and set aside, doing his part to inspect his sister's future husband for flaws.

"Roger's a good guy," Rahul told her when the two of them were alone in the kitchen clearing plates. "Congratulations."

"Thanks. Thanks for being here," she said. She meant it; she'd never brought a man to the house, hadn't realized how nervous she'd be.

"Got nowhere else to go."

"So, how are things?" she asked. "It's not driving you crazy, living at home this way?"

"It's not so bad."

She was grateful that he was talking to her, afraid to pressure him. She was aware of a horrible imbalance between them. She felt accused, simply because her life wasn't broken in the same way.

"How's the Laundromat?"

He shrugged.

"Are you still writing your play?"

"It was stupid."

Not knowing what else to do she stepped forward to hug him, and it was then that she smelled the liquor, sweet, strong, unmistakable. During lunch he'd gotten up from the table once; now she realized he'd gone wherever the bottle was hidden. He was not drunk, there was nothing about his behavior to indicate that he'd had more than a single drink. But the fact that he'd consumed the alcohol in stealth, that he could not endure her family's company without it, made her realize that Rahul was not simply fond of drinking, or a social drinker, or a binge drinker, which were all the ways she'd rationalized it until now.

"You're welcome to visit us in London any time," she offered, saddened by the fact that she did not mean it.

"I don't have any money."

"I'm sure Baba would buy you a ticket."

"I don't want his money," Rahul said.

You live in his house, she wanted to point out. You eat the food Ma puts on the table. You let them put gas in your car. But she said none of this, knowing that if she did, the door he tentatively held open for her benefit would slam once more in her face.

In the months before Sudha's wedding reception, planned for the fall, Rahul began dating a woman named Elena. Elena was an aspiring actress, and she was a waitress at a diner in Waltham. He had conveyed these facts to Sudha when she came back to Wayland ten days before the reception, without Roger, who would be flying in for the party alone. "I've never felt this way before, Didi," he told her. A few days before the reception he brought Elena home. Sudha was a married woman now, but being without Roger made her anxious, that protective coating he provided suddenly thinning. Elena was thirty, eight years older than Rahul. But she could have passed for a high school student, wearing tight jeans and a tank top, her long brown hair fastened at one side with a barrette, dark liner rimming her eyes. She was quiet, speaking only when spoken to, not working to charm Sudha's parents as Roger had. She told them she'd grown up in Mattapoisett and had gone to Emerson. She did not eat the rice Sudha's mother served with lunch, saying it caused her bloating. Rahul kept his arm around her thin shoulders, kissing her dreamily in front of everyone. He spoke on Elena's behalf, saying she had once made a commercial for an allergy medicine. He kept mentioning someone named Crystal; it turned out that Crystal was Elena's daughter from a previous boyfriend.

Sudha's parents said nothing as this information was divulged. They had welcomed Elena, filled their table in her honor as they had done for Roger, making chitchat about the Big Dig and the menu for Sudha and Roger's reception. But then, as Sudha and her mother were bringing out tea and a bowl of pantuas in their syrupy bath, Rahul announced that he and Elena were engaged.

Sudha froze behind a chair, gripping the spoons she was in the process of distributing. The room seemed to tilt; she pressed down on the tablecloth as if a forceful wind were about to come and blow everything away. She looked down at the diamond on her finger, imagining the same thing on Elena's hand, wondering where in the world her brother would get the money to buy a ring. The Darjeeling brought out for special occasions grew too strong in the pot, the reddish-brown pantuas still crowded together in their serving bowl.

"That's not possible," their father said finally, breaking the silence that he had been maintaining, it seemed to Sudha, for over a year.

"What's not possible about it?" Rahul asked. He still had an arm around Elena, his index finger stroking the side of her neck.

"You are only a boy. You have no career, no goal, no path in life. You are in no position to be getting married. And this woman," their father said, registering Elena's presence only for an instant before turning away, "is practically old enough to be your mother."

They were even, equilibrium, if it could be called that, restored to the room. But Sudha knew that it was the furthest thing from equilibrium, that in fact it was war.

"You're a snob," Rahul said. "You're nothing but a pathetic old snob." There was no rage in his voice, none of the violence Sudha had expected. He stood up in a fluid motion, seeming to lift Elena to her feet as well, as if his arm were a magnet for her form, and then the two of them left the house. Sudha and her parents waited until they heard the sound of Elena's car backing out of the driveway, and then her mother began to pour the tea.

"I have been thinking," her father said, turning to Sudha, breaking the silence for the second time. "The restaurant where we will have the wedding reception. There is a bar?"

"All restaurants have bars, Baba."

"I am concerned about Rahul. He has no control when it comes to—" He paused, searching for the word he wished to use. "When it comes to that."

Sudha shut her eyes, thinking she might cry. All this time she had been waiting for her parents to acknowledge Rahul's drinking, but hearing her father say it now, after what had just happened, was too much.

"Maybe we should hold it somewhere else," her mother suggested. "Somewhere without drinks."

"It's too late for that. And it's not fair," Sudha said. Sudha and Roger expected to be able to drink at their own wedding reception, she maintained. Why should everyone be punished because of Rahul?

"Can't you ask him not to drink too much that day?" her mother asked.

"No," Sudha said, pushing back her chair and standing up. She had been fiddling all this time with her teaspoon, and she flung it now, ineffectually, on the carpeted floor of the dining room, where it fell without sound. "I can't talk to him anymore. I can't fix him. I can't keep fixing what's wrong with this family," she said, and like her brother only a little while earlier, she stormed out of the room.

During the reception Rahul made a toast. It was a tribute to Sudha and Roger, but Sudha held her breath as he spoke, wanting him only to sit down. He was without Elena. The day after walking out with her he'd returned abject, alone. Sudha wondered if Elena had broken up with him, but she didn't ask. She wondered if Rahul would not attend the reception, but he was at the restaurant an hour early, maintaining his rightful place in the family, greeting people as they arrived, showing them to the sign-in book. They were almost all friends of Sudha's parents, almost all Bengali. No one from Roger's side had come.

The toast went on, the words becoming slurred. Before the reception, her father had spoken with the bartender, paying him extra to monitor Rahul's drinks; Sudha did not have the heart to tell her father that Rahul was beyond such measures, that alcohol dwelled in his pockets where most men's wallets were, that the two glasses of champagne he'd had openly were just for show. Rahul began telling a story about Sudha's childhood, dredging up an anecdote about going on a vacation long ago in Bar Harbor, Sudha needing to use the bathroom and there not being a gas station for miles. Then their father got up, stood next to Rahul, and whispered something in his ear, motioning for him to sit down.

"Excuse me, I'm not finished." People laughed, not realizing Rahul had not meant to be funny, that it wasn't some sort of comic routine. The microphone made a screeching sound.

Their father took him by the elbow then, and Rahul flinched, giving a shove. "You—don't—touch me," Rahul hissed, the words amplified by the microphone.

One of Sudha's parents' friends got up to make another toast, but Sudha didn't hear it. She was aware of guests talking among themselves in front of their plates of pink tandoori and her brother heading toward the bar. When she got up to look for him, he was no longer there, his car missing from the parking lot. She alerted her parents, prepared herself for another call from the police. But no one was in the position to search for him in the middle of the reception, and without him there, perversely, her parents began to relax. Only Sudha couldn't relax. Roger, who had had a little too much champagne himself, told her not to worry. "He's been going through a rough time," he observed dispassionately as he led her on the dance floor. "He's young."

She stared at her husband, wanting to scream at him for believing in Rahul in a way she no longer could. She had never told Roger about the old game of hiding beer cans, a fact that now tortured her. But once again she chose not to tell Roger, fearing that he would blame her, that he would judge Rahul. It was like the painting they'd first looked at together in London, the small mirror at the back revealing more than the room at first appeared to contain. And what was the point of making Roger lean in close, to see what she was already forced to?

It turned out Rahul hadn't gone far, only back to their parents' house, where they found him, at the end of the night, in his bedroom asleep. The following morning Roger and Sudha flew off for their honeymoon. She felt neutralized in the air, sealed off in the cabin, the unnaturally strong sunlight bleaching out the events of the night before, but as soon as they touched down in St. Thomas she felt tainted all over again, hearing Rahul hissing into the microphone, insulting her father and pushing him in front of all their friends. Life went on. Sudha and Roger returned to London, settling into their new house, writing cards to thank their guests for helping to make it such a special day. But Sudha could not forgive Rahul for what had happened, those dreadful minutes he stood at the microphone the only thing she remembered when she looked at the photographs of her reception, all the posed portraits on the grass in which they were smiling, leading up to that.

And then he disappeared for good. There was no note, no explanation. He simply left one night, her parents said, and had not returned. By then his comings and goings were so erratic that their parents had not fully absorbed the fact of his absence until a few days had passed. Then they realized that his toothbrush was not in the bathroom, and that one of the big suitcases normally used for trips to India was not in the basement. He must have decided to visit a friend, her parents said, but they knew none of Rahul's new friends and were unable to make calls. They reported that the car was missing, and it was located the next day, abandoned at the bus station in Framingham. Roger, trying to be helpful, suggested they contact Elena, but they had never known Elena's last name.

After a week a letter came, with a postmark from Columbus, Ohio. It was not addressed to anyone; he had not even put their family surname on the envelope. "Don't bother looking for me here," he'd written, "I'm only spending the night. I don't want to hear from any of you. Please leave me alone." They wondered how he got to Ohio, since he had no money, wondered if he'd hitched rides. A week passed before her mother noticed that the small zippered pouches she kept hidden at the backs of her drawers, behind her jumble of British brassieres, containing all the gold jewels she'd acquired over her lifetime, all the pieces representative of her husband's success in America, much of which was intended to go to whatever woman Rahul eventually married, were missing.

He had been gone two months when Sudha discovered that she was pregnant; one night during her miserable honeymoon, her body had begun to make a life. Suddenly alongside the terrible there was now the wonderful, the good news reviving her parents. Sudha thought of Rahul often during her pregnancy, invaded by memories and dreams of their childhood, recalling the existence that had produced them both, an experience that was both within her and behind her and that Roger would never understand. In her first trimester her emotions dipped and soared without warning. On good days she believed that Rahul needed to get away in order to put his life back together. On bad days she feared that the police would call her parents saying his body had been found in a ditch. He was absent the following Christmas, which Sudha and Roger spent in Wayland, absent at the hospital in London the night she gave birth to Neel. And she got used to it, used to having a brother she never saw.

Wrapped up with Neel, her parents got used to it, too, coming to London now at every opportunity, their tiny grandson plugging up the monstrous hole Rahul left in his wake. For hours they stared into the bassinet, at the stern downy creature with Roger's pale skin and Sudha's dark hair and a destiny all his own. After a few months Sudha returned to work, first three days a week, then five, leaving the house at eight thirty and returning at six, taking Neel from the nanny and spending just two hours with him, first in the bath and then nursing him to sleep in the rocker. She felt awful, always, that it was for such a brief piece of her day that she actually cared for Neel, but she reminded herself that he was too young to resent her for it, his face lighting up at the sight of her, leaping into her arms as if she were the most wonderful being on earth.

It was then, at a time when her life was at its most demanding and also gratifying, that she returned home one cold Saturday from grocery shopping and found, on the other side of the door slot, an envelope from America addressed in Rahul's hand.

She stood in the entryway of the house, with the brown-and-gold wallpaper she and Roger kept meaning to tear down, staring at that simple but certain proof of Rahul's existence. She wondered how he'd gotten her new address, but then she remembered, when she was home for her wedding reception, writing it on a piece of paper and taping it to her parents' refrigerator. Neel napped in his stroller, not knowing the existence of his uncle, not knowing the shock that filled his mother's eyes with tears. There was a faded postmark from New York, and on the back of the envelope, a post office box somewhere upstate. Before opening the envelope she pulled out an atlas. The town was north of Ithaca. She was stunned—she had assumed he'd gone as far as possible, to Oregon or California. She never thought he'd want to return anywhere near the place where he'd so spectacularly failed. Inside was a single sheet of paper that he'd stuck into a typewriter.

Dear Didi,
I hope this is you. First, I want to say that I'm sorry. For everything. I know I screwed up, but things are better now. I have a job at a restaurant, as a line cook. I discovered that I really like cooking. Nothing fancy, but I've gotten really good at omelettes. Also, I'm writing another play. I showed it to someone I met here, a guy who's directed some things at Syracuse, and he said it still needs work but that I should stick

with it! I'm living with Elena—remember her? We got back together and I convinced her to come up here. Crystal's in fifth grade and Elena got a job doing human resources at the university. Think what you will about Elena, but she got me to start rehab. So like I said, things are better. Anyway, I'm sorry for everything and I hope you (and Roger) can forgive me for being a jerk at your wedding. I really am happy for you guys. And I'd like to come to London and see you, if that's okay. I've saved up some money and I'll have a little time off from the restaurant this summer. I'm assuming you won't mention any of this to our parents.

Rahul

She replied immediately, without rereading the letter or bothering to ask Roger if it was all right for Rahul to stay with them. She tore a sheet of paper out of the notebook they kept by the phone, for messages, and wrote:

Dear Rahul,
Yes, it's me. I've had a baby, a boy named Neel. He's ten months old, and I want you to meet him.

She stopped, then signed the letter. She had nothing more to say.

She had not seen Rahul since her wedding night, a fact that was incredible to her. "Hi, Didi," he said when she opened the door, still using the traditional term of respect their parents had taught him. She felt no awkwardness, the sight of him after over a year and a half standing under the portico of the house, completing a part of her that had been missing, like the clothes she could wear again now that the weight of her pregnancy was gone.

"Here he is," she said to Rahul, adjusting Neel in her arms. Neel stuck out a hand, his fingers gripping a digestive biscuit. He babbled softly, taking in the new person in front of him.

"That's right," Rahul said, stroking Neel's cheek with the back of his index finger. "It's your screwup uncle finally here to see you." He shook his head in disbelief, acquainting himself with the details of Neel's face, the nose and eyes and mouth and wisps of hair that Sudha felt she'd known all her life. It was Rahul who'd changed. He'd put on weight, enough so that his once refined features appeared common, his neck and waistline thick. He had acquired the stoop of an older, uncertain man. His hair was combed back from his head, receding above the temples, the sideburns long. His jeans had lost their stiffness, frayed at the hems. The pin-striped blazer looked like it had come from a thrift store and was a little short in the sleeves.

"I can't believe you were born and I didn't know it. You're absolutely perfect," he said to Neel. He looked at Sudha, then Neel, then back at Sudha. "He's got your face, totally."

"You think? I see Roger's."

Rahul shook his head. "No way, Didi. This boy is a Mukherjee through and through."

She gave him a tour of the house: the kitchen and a small toilet in the basement, the parlor above, two bedrooms and a bathroom above that, Roger's study under the eaves. In spite of all the stories the house was diminutive, and they were constantly going up and down the staircase, which these days Neel was also attempting to climb. The steps were too much for Sudha's father, who had recently developed bursitis in his knee, and when her parents last visited London they'd stayed with friends in the suburbs. But Roger had agreed to let Rahul sleep on the daybed normally covered with papers in the study.

"Feel free to take a nap," she told Rahul, but he declined, coaxing Neel into his arms and not letting go as Sudha peeled potatoes and prepared to roast a chicken. He took in the low-ceilinged space, with its black-and-white checkerboard floor, a perpetually cluttered dining table, Spode plates and copper molds hung on yellow walls. Roger had painted the walls himself, the final layer applied with a sponge. Rahul stopped in front of some shelves where the cookbooks were, along with photographs in frames. Most of the photos were of Neel: in the hours after his birth, in the arms of Sudha's parents, sitting in his stroller outside of the house. There were no pictures of Rahul. "When was this taken?" he asked.

"Which?"

"It looks like an annaprasan."

"Oh that," she said, pricking a fork into a lemon, thinking back to the day Neel was fed his first meal a few months before, her parents flying to London for the occasion. "It was just a tiny thing at home," she told him, as if that would explain away Rahul's absence. It was the maternal uncle who traditionally fed the child. In Neel's case it had been Sudha's father.

He crossed the floor to where she stood at the butcher block and removed his wallet from his back pocket. With one hand he shook it so that it displayed a school portait of a smiling young girl with freckles and two long brown ponytails. "This is Crystal," he said proudly, explaining that he arranged to be home every day when Crystal got home from school, making her a snack and then cooking her dinner before Elena returned and he went off to his shift at the restaurant. He didn't pull out a picture of Elena but Sudha remembered her clearly from that one time she'd come to lunch. Sudha didn't ask Rahul if he and Elena had gotten married, if they were going to have a child of their own. Sudha had tried to help her brother but it was Elena who had succeeded. "She's a great kid," he said, before putting away Crystal's picture. "I thought I'd get her a little tea set, you know, something really English? She'd love that."

He lifted Neel into the air, shaking him playfully, rubbing his face against Neel's belly, Neel cackling hysterically.

"Careful," Sudha warned.

Rahul obliged, stopping the game and hugging Neel tightly, then beginning to tickle him so that the cackles started up again. "Relax, Didi. I'm a parent too, now."

Sudha and Roger had white wine with dinner, but Rahul had asked only for club soda mixed with some orange juice. They ate outside, at a small table on the garden patio, overlooking the rosebushes that thrived in spite of Sudha and Roger's neglect. She had wondered about the wine, whether or not to drink it in front of Rahul. There were a few bottles of Scotch and vodka in their kitchen cabinets left over from a housewarming party she and Roger had thrown, and she stuffed them into the back of her closet and into the sweater chest at the foot of their bed, telling herself that Roger would never notice. Neel sat in Rahul's lap, eating small dollops of mashed potato from Roger's extended finger.

"First time in London, is it?" Roger asked Rahul.

"Apart from sitting in Heathrow dozens of times on the way to Calcutta," Rahul said, and Sudha was reminded of all those trips they'd taken together in childhood to see their relatives, trips that would never take place again. They had slept beside one another on the same bed, often bathed together, taken everything in with one pair of eyes.

Rahul mentioned things he wanted to see in the course of the week—the British Museum, Freud's house, the V&A—asking if it was possible to go to Stratford-upon-Avon for the day. He seemed suddenly desperate to interact with the world, after all those years of sitting up in his room. Roger told him when the museums were open, what was currently on exhibit, and it struck Sudha how little her husband and her brother were acquainted, that they remained all but strangers. "Mainly I want to spend time with Neel," Rahul said. "I can take him out to a park or a zoo, whatever."

Sudha told Rahul to enjoy himself, that Neel spent the days with a nanny, but that in the evening his nephew would be all his.

"So, when's the next one?" Rahul asked, draping Neel over his legs, jiggling them up and down.

"Next what?" Roger asked.

"The next kid."

"Have you been talking to Ma?" Sudha said, beginning to laugh before abruptly stopping herself.

"What do you want, buddy?" Rahul asked, looking down at Neel's upturned face. "A little brother like me, or a sister?"

Now that the subject of their parents had come up she decided to give Rahul their news, that their father was retiring at the end of the year and that their parents were shopping for a flat in Calcutta. "That's where they are now," she said.

"They're not in Wayland?"

"No." It was a fact that had made it easier for Sudha to honor Rahul's request and not tell her parents about his visit.

"Are they moving back for good?"

"Maybe." She told him about their father's knee trouble, that he was going to have surgery to have fluid drained. One day, she knew, it would be something more serious, and when it came, as long as Rahul stayed away, she would have to be an only child all over again.

After dinner Roger put away the leftovers while Sudha went upstairs to run Neel's bath. Rahul came with her, sitting on the toilet and blowing some bubbles he'd brought for Neel as she crouched on the floor and soaped and rinsed him. Neel was ecstatic about the bubbles, waiting wide-eyed for each to emerge from the little plastic wand, reaching out and popping them and calling out for more.

"Okay, little guy, time for bed," she said after a few minutes, lifting the rubber plug and letting the water drain out out of the claw-foot tub. She reached for Neel's towel, throwing it over her shoulder and lifting him out. She wrapped him up, scrubbing his head. "Say goodnight to Mamu," she said.

"What does he call them?" Rahul asked.

"Who?"

"Our parents."

She hesitated, though the answer was not something she had to search for. "Dadu and Dadi."

"Just like we did," he said, his voice softening. "I bet they treat you like a king," he said to Neel.

"You could say that. We still haven't unwrapped some of his Christmas presents."

"What about next Christmas? Do you guys have plans?"

"They're supposed to come to London," Sudha began, watching for a reaction. "Of course, you're welcome," she continued, knowing the idea was ludicrous. "All of you, Elena and Crystal. You guys could stay in a hotel."

She stopped then, realizing that she was holding her breath, waiting for him to walk out of her life all over again. Instead he said, "I'll think about it," leaving her even more breathless, for she realized that without a formal truce the battle had ended, that he wanted to come back.

Rahul was already awake when she came downstairs the next morning, sitting at the table with Roger, a T-shirt sticking to his thickened body, sweaty hair plastered to his face. He was wearing shorts, the hair on his dark legs curlier than she remembered. Roger was drinking his tea, showing Rahul a

Tube map, telling him which trains went where, pointing out parks in which he could run.

"Where did you go?" she asked Rahul. She prepared a pot of coffee, then warmed the milk for Neel's Weetabix, knowing he would be up soon.

"No idea," he said. "I just go for an hour. Running's my new addiction." It was the first time since he arrived that he'd alluded in any way to his drinking. "That and coffee."

When it was ready she poured him a cup, watched him add three spoons of sugar, remembered the time he'd visited her in college and she'd handed him his first beer. "What will you do today?"

Rahul shrugged. "Maybe a museum. I just want to walk around."

"Be ready in twenty minutes and I'll drop you at the tube," Roger offered.

While Sudha was at work she wondered what her brother was doing, wondered if one of the hundreds of pubs on the streets of London would tempt him. Part of her worried that something would set him off and that he would disappear again. But when she got back to the house that evening she found Rahul crawling up the staircase after Neel, pretending to be a hungry lion. That night they went out for curry and again he did not drink, covering the paper spread on the table with elaborate drawings. Again he sat with Sudha in the bathroom as she bathed Neel, and the following morning he went for his run. For the rest of the week he worked through his list of activities, always returning with a little gift for Neel. It felt strange to be at work for so much of the time that Rahul was visiting, but Sudha thought it was better, safer, that their time together was limited to mornings and evenings, times when Roger and Neel were around.

Saturday morning Rahul made omelettes, expertly chopping

mushrooms and onions the way the chefs did on television, and then at Rahul's suggestion they went to the London Zoo. Rahul had offered to take Neel himself, and though throughout the week both Sudha and Roger had taken advantage of Rahul's presence, leaving him in charge for five or ten minutes if they needed to go to the corner for eggs or bread, there was no question of that. And yet, once they were at the zoo, both Roger and Sudha felt obsolete. Rahul carried Neel on his shoulders the whole time, the stroller Sudha pushed containing nothing but her purse. Neel was equally smitten, bursting into tears when Rahul had to use the restroom. Rahul had insisted on paying for everything—buying them their tickets, their sandwiches and sodas, the ice cream for Neel, the lime-green balloon that drifted all afternoon above their heads.

"I was thinking of going to a movie later," Rahul said when they returned to the house, still carrying Neel. "But I think I'd rather stay home with this guy."

"Don't be silly," Sudha said. "You've dealt with him all day. You deserve a break."

Rahul shook his head. "I'm leaving tomorrow, and we've got a lot of catching up to do." And then he said, "You two are the ones who need a break. When was the last time you saw a movie together?"

The idea presented itself, a perfect plan that felt all wrong. She looked over at Roger, and Rahul saw her looking. "What, you guys don't trust me?"

"Of course," Roger said. He turned to Sudha. "Shall we, Su?"

She reminded herself that they had a cell phone; the movie theater was a ten-minute drive from the house. If they went to an early show, they'd be back in time for Neel's bath. "I'll call to see what's playing," she said.

. . .

"We'll be right here," Rahul promised her, looking up from the sitting room floor where he and Neel were stacking blocks, and she forced herself to believe him. They had not left him a key, there was nowhere he could go. She had left food for Neel, milk in a sippy cup, overcooked macaroni that was impossible to choke on. She had reminded Rahul to be careful with Neel on the stairs. During the movie she kept the volume of her cell phone turned on, not trusting it to vibrate in the pocket of her jeans. After the first hour she got up and called from the lobby.

"Everything okay?"

"Everything's great," Rahul told her. "He seemed hungry so I'm giving him something to eat." In the background she could hear Neel banging something, a cup or a spoon, against the tray of his high chair.

"Great. Thanks. We'll be back soon," she said.

"No need to rush," Rahul said. And so on their way back, at Roger's suggestion, they stopped at a market, for cheese and jams and a few other things they needed. They bought three nice steaks for dinner, Roger saying he would make a tart.

Rahul and Neel were not in the sitting room where she expected to find them, not playing among the toys scattered across the carpet. A children's show was on television but no one was watching it. Downstairs in the kitchen the high chair had not been wiped, and gummy bits of pasta were submerged in a puddle of water on the surface of the tray. The balloon from the zoo had been tied to the side, reaching almost to the ceiling. All the upper cupboards were open, but nothing seemed to have been removed from them. Quickly Sudha shut them, a cold sweat forming on her lips.

"They haven't left, the push chair's still here," Roger said.

As she raced up the steps she heard the sound of water splashing and chided herself for panicking. "It's okay," she called out. "He's giving Neel a bath."

She found Neel in the tub, filling his sippy cup with water

and pouring it out. He was sitting without the plastic ring they normally put him in so that he wouldn't tip over. He was trembling but otherwise happy, intent on his task, the water up to the middle of his chest, the mere sight of him sitting there, unattended, causing Sudha to emit a series of spontaneous cries and a volt of fear to seize her haunches. The water was no longer warm. One slip and he would have been facedown, his fine dark hair spread like a sunburst, the strands waving as the rest of him was still.

"Where's your uncle?" Roger demanded, even though Neel did not yet have the words to reply. He yanked Neel out of the tub, making him burst into tears.

They found Rahul in Roger's study, asleep, a glass tucked beneath the daybed. In their bedroom, the sweater chest was open, the necks of the bottles poking out, nestled in woolly arms. They went back to Roger's study and were unable to rouse Rahul, Sudha shaking his shoulder as she held Neel. Roger leaned over Rahul's duffel, stuffing it with clothes.

"What are you doing?" she asked.

"What does it look like, Sudha?"

"He'll do that when he gets up."

Roger stood up, his face not at all kind. "I'm making it easier for him. I don't want your brother to set foot in our home or come near our child ever again."

Because they could not scream at Rahul they began to scream at each other, the strange calm that had followed their discovery in the bathtub now shattered.

"You're the one who told him we trusted him," she said. "You agreed to go out."

"Don't blame this on me," Roger said. "I barely know him. Don't you dare blame a bit of this on me."

"I'm not," she said, beginning to cry. "I'm sorry. I should have told you."

"Told me what?"

She was sobbing now, too hard for any words to come out, Neel beginning to cry again in reaction. Roger went up to her, holding her by the shoulders, his arms outstretched. "Told me what?"

And somehow, in spite of how hard she was crying, she told him, about the very first time Rahul had come to visit her at Penn, and how he hadn't even liked beer, and then about all the cans they'd hidden over the years and how eventually it was no longer a game for him but a way of life, a way of life that had removed him from her family and ruined him.

Roger looked around the study with its book-lined walls, its cabinets full of files, postcards of noble portraits pinned over the desk. A disgusted look appeared on his face. And then he looked at Sudha, his disgust for her just as plain. "You lied to me. I've never lied to you, Sudha. I would never have kept something like this from you."

She nodded. She was still crying, tightly holding Neel. Roger took their son from her arms and left her there with Rahul, who was flat on his back, one leg hanging over the edge of the daybed, his slackened face to the wall.

All night she did not sleep, Roger stiff as a board on his side. They'd gone to bed hungry, the three steaks tossed into the freezer. Rahul had never woken up. She knew Roger was right, knew that if it had been his sibling she would have said and done the same. She thought of her parents, who had believed their children were destined to succeed, had fumbled when one failed. After everything Rahul had put them through they never renounced him, never banished him. They were incapable of shutting him out. But Roger was capable, and Sudha realized, as the wakeful night passed, that she was capable, too.

She drifted off around daybreak, then woke up an hour later, hearing the shower running. It ran for a long time. She became nervous and considered knocking, but then she heard the door open, and a few minutes later, footsteps padding down the stairs.

"I meant to clean up the high chair," Rahul said when she joined him in the kitchen. He was dressed in one of Roger's bathrobes, squinting, as if the subterreanean space were flooded with light. His voice was gruff, the effects of the liquor clear in the delicate yet awkward way he was moving about. He had filled the kettle with water, turned on the gas, measured coffee into the glass pot. "Sorry about that."

"I thought you were better."

He glanced at her, only for a second. He looked like an idiot to her, dull and slow.

"What the hell happened, Rahul?"

He didn't reply.

"Is it me?" she asked. For she had wondered this, during the long hours she had lain awake: wondered if seeing her had reminded him of the past, of those nights they had defied their parents together, pouring warm beer into cups of ice and forging a link all their own.

The water began to boil, the kettle emitting a thin whistle. She switched off the gas, poured the water into the coffeepot. "You have to go to the airport," she said.

"My flight isn't until evening."

"Now, Rahul. You have to get dressed and go now. You left Neel in the bathtub." Her voice quavered and at the same time it was beginning to rise, the sickening image flooding her all over again.

"I did?"

"Yes, Rahul," she said, fresh tears streaming down her face. "You passed out and you left our baby alone in a tub. You could have killed him, do you understand?"

He turned away, his back to her. He pressed his head to a cupboard, twisting it slightly to either side, swearing to himself under his breath. Then, still without facing her, he said, "But he's okay, right, Didi? I peeked into his room this morning and he was asleep in his crib just fine."

"You have to go now." Her words were coming out in almost a whisper. She was aware that she sounded like a broken record. Fury had raged through her all night; that storm cloud had unleashed its rain, and now she was simply tired.

"I've stayed away from it for months," he said. "I don't know what happened. I just had the tiniest bit—"

"Stop," she said, and he did. "I don't want to hear your explanation. Do you understand me? I don't want to hear it."

He didn't try to speak again. He went upstairs to dress and get his bag and then stood in the sitting room as she called a minicab for Heathrow. She held out fifty pounds to cover the fare and he took it from her. Then he left, going out to the street before the cab arrived. When it pulled up to the house she went to the window, held back the lace curtain, and watched him slip into the backseat. Then the cab pulled away, leaving her to stare out at the gray morning light. She wasn't aware of when she'd stopped crying. She felt wide awake suddenly. She heard Neel upstairs, stirring in his crib. In another minute he would cry out, wanting her, expecting breakfast; he was young enough so that Sudha was still only goodness to him, nothing else. She returned to the kitchen, opened a cupboard, took out a packet of Weetabix, heated milk in a pan. Something brushed against her ankles, and she saw that the balloon tied to the back of Neel's high chair was no longer suspended on its ribbon. It had sagged to the floor, a shrunken thing incapable of bursting. She clipped the ribbon with scissors and stuffed the whole thing into the garbage, surprised at how easily it fit, thinking of the husband who no longer trusted her, of the son whose cry now interrupted her, of the fledgling family that had cracked open that morning, as typical and as terrifying as any other.

Nobody's Business

Every so often a man called for Sang, wanting to marry her. Sang usually didn't know these men. Sometimes she had never even heard of them. But they'd heard that she was pretty and smart and thirty and Bengali and still single, and so these men, most of whom also happened to be Bengali, would procure her number from someone who knew someone who knew her parents, who, according to Sang, desperately wanted her to be married. According to Sang, these men always confused details when they spoke to her, saying they'd heard that she studied physics, when really it was philosophy, or that she'd graduated from Columbia, when really it was NYU, calling her Sangeeta, when really she went by Sang. They were impressed that she was getting her doctorate at Harvard, when really she'd dropped out of Harvard after a semester and was working part time at a bookstore on the square.

Sang's housemates, Paul and Heather, could always tell when it was a prospective groom on the phone. "Oh. Hi," Sang would say, sitting at the imitation-walnut kitchen table, rolling her eyes, coin-colored eyes that were sometimes green. She would slouch in her chair, looking bothered but resigned, as if a subway she were riding had halted between stations. To

Paul's mild disappointment, Sang was never rude to these men. She listened as they explained the complicated, far-fetched connection between them, connections Paul vaguely envied in spite of the fact that he shared a house with Sang, and a kitchen, and a subscription to the *Globe*. The suitors called from as far away as Los Angeles, as close by as Watertown. Once, she told Paul and Heather, she had actually agreed to meet one of these men, and he had driven her north up I-93, pointing from the highway to the corporation he worked for. Then he'd taken her to a Dunkin' Donuts, where, over crullers and coffee, he'd proposed.

Sometimes Sang would take notes during these conversations, on the message pad kept next to the phone. She'd write down the man's name, or "Carnegie Mellon," or "likes mystery novels" before her pen drifted into scribbles and stars and tick-tack-toe games. To be polite, she asked a few questions, too, about whether the man enjoyed his work as an economist, or a dentist, or a metallurgical engineer. Her excuse to these men, her rebuttal to their offers to wine and dine her, was always the same white lie: she was busy at the moment with classes, its being Harvard and all. Sometimes, if Paul happened to be sitting at the table, she would write him a note in the middle of the conversation: "He sounds like he's twelve" or "Total dweeb" or "This guy threw up once in my parents' swimming pool," waving the pad for Paul's benefit as she cradled the phone to her ear.

It was only after Sang hung up that she complained. How dare these men call? she'd say. How dare they hunt her down? It was a violation of her privacy, an insult to her adulthood. It was pathetic. If only Paul and Heather could hear them, going on about themselves. At this point, Heather would sometimes say, "God, Sang, I can't believe you're complaining. Dozens of men, successful men, possibly even handsome, want to marry you, sight unseen. And you expect us to feel sorry for you?"

Heather, a law student at Boston College, had been bitterly single for five years. She told Sang the proposals were romantic, but Sang shook her head. "It's not love." In Sang's opinion it was practically an arranged marriage. These men weren't really interested in her. They were interested in a mythical creature created by an intricate chain of gossip, a web of wishful Indian-community thinking in which she was an aging, overlooked poster child for years of bharat natyam classes, perfect SATs. Had they any idea who she actually was and how she made a living, in spite of her test scores, which was by running a cash register and arranging paperback books in pyramid configurations, they would want nothing to do with her. "And besides," she always reminded Paul and Heather, "I have a boyfriend."

"You're like Penelope," Paul ventured one evening. He had lately been rereading Lattimore's Homer, in preparation for his orals in English literature the following spring.

"Penelope?" She was standing at the microwave, heating some rice. Paul watched as she removed the plate and mixed the steaming rice with a spoonful of the dark red-hot lime pickle that lived next to his peanut butter in the door of the refrigerator.

"From the *Odyssey*?" Paul said gently, a question to match her question. He was tall without being lank, with solid fingers and calves, and fine straw-colored hair. The most noticeable aspect of his appearance was a pair of expensive designer glasses, their maroon frames perfectly round, which an attractive salesgirl in a frame shop on Beacon Street had talked him into buying. Paul had not liked the glasses, even as he was being fitted for them, and had not grown to like them since.

"Right, the *Odyssey*," Sang said, sitting down at the table. "Penelope. Only I can't knit."

"Weave," he said, correcting her. "It was a shroud Penelope kept weaving and unweaving, to ward off her suitors."

Sang lifted a forkful of the rice to her lips, blowing on it so that it would cool. "Then, who's the woman who knits?" she asked. She looked at Paul. "You would know."

Paul paused, eager to impress her, but his mind had drawn a blank. He knew it was someone in Dickens, had the paperbacks up in his room. "Be right back," he said. Then he stopped, relieved. "*A Tale of Two Cities*," he told her. "Madame Defarge."

Paul had answered the phone the first time Sang called, at nine o'clock one Saturday morning in July, in reference to the housemate ad he and Heather had placed in the *Phoenix*. The call had roused him from sleep, and he wondered, standing there, groggy in his bathrobe, what sort of name Sang was, half expecting a Japanese woman. It wasn't until she wrote out a check for her security deposit at the end of her visit that he saw that her official name was Sangeeta Biswas. This was the name he would see on her mail, on the labels of the thick, pungent *Vogue* magazines she received each month, and in the window of the electric bill she agreed to take on. Heather had been in the shower when Sang arrived and pressed the doorbell that chimed two solemn tones, so Paul greeted her alone. She had worn her long hair loose, something Paul was to learn she rarely did, and as he walked behind her he had liked the way it clung protectively to her body, over the rise of her shoulder blades. She had admired the spectacular central staircase, as most everyone did, letting her hand linger over the bannister. The staircase turned six times at right angles after every six steps and was constructed of dark gleaming wood with the lustre of cognac. It was the only thing of enduring beauty in the house, a false promise of what was above: ugly brown cabinets in the kitchen, moldy bathrooms with missing tiles, omnipresent oatmeal carpeting to protect the ears of the landlords, who lived below.

She had remarked on what a lot of space it was, pacing the landing before joining Paul in the vacant room. There was a built-in hutch in the corner, with Doric pilasters and glass-paned doors, which Sang opened and closed. Paul told her that the room had originally been the dining room, the cabinet intended to store china. There was a bathroom across the landing; Paul and Heather shared the larger one, upstairs. "I feel like I'm standing inside an empty refrigerator," she'd said, referring to the fact that the walls, once blue, had been painted over with a single coat of white; the effect, under the glare of the ceiling light, was stark and cold. She ran a hand along one wall and carefully removed a stray piece of tape. Once, there had been an arched doorway connecting the room to the kitchen, since filled in, but Sang noted that the arch was still visible, like a scar in the plaster.

While she was there, the phone rang, another person replying to the ad, but by then she had handed over her deposit. She had met Heather, and the three of them chatted in the living room with its peeling bay window and its soft filthy couch and its yellow papasan chair. They told her about their system for splitting up the chores, and about the landlords, both doctors at Brigham and Women's. They told her there was only one phone jack in the house, in the kitchen. The phone was attached to a cord so long that they could all drag it to their rooms, though at times the price to pay for dragging the cord too far was a persistent crackle.

"We thought about having another line put in, but it's pretty expensive," Heather said.

"It's not a big deal," Sang said.

And Paul, who seldom spoke on the phone to anyone, said nothing at all.

. . .

She had practically nothing to contribute to the house, no pots or appliances, nothing for the kitchen apart from an ailing hanging plant that shed yellow heart-shaped leaves. A friend helped her move in one Sunday, a male friend who was not, Paul gathered, her boyfriend (for she had mentioned one on her first visit, telling them that he was in Cairo for the summer visiting his parents, that he was Egyptian, and that he taught Middle Eastern history at Harvard). The friend's name was Charles. He wore high-top sneakers and a bright orange bowling shirt, his hair tied back in a stubby ponytail. He was telling Sang about a date he'd had the night before, as they unloaded a futon, two big battered suitcases, a series of shopping bags, and a few boxes from the back of a pickup truck. Paul had offered to help, calling out from the deck where he was trying to read the *Canterbury Tales*, but Sang said no, it was nothing. Their talk distracted him and yet he remained, watching Sang through the railing. Charles was teasingly forbidding her to buy too many things, so that moving out would be just as easy. Sang had been laughing at him, but now she stopped, her expression pensive. She looked up at the house, a balled-up comforter in her arms. "I don't know, Charles. I don't know how long I'll be here."

"He still doesn't want to live together until you're married?"

She shook her head.

"What does he say?"

"That he doesn't want to spoil things."

Charles shifted the weight of the box he was carrying. "But he acknowledges the fact that you're getting married."

She turned back to the truck. "He says things like 'When we have kids, we'll buy a big house in Lexington.' "

"You've been together three years," Charles said. "So he's a little old-fashioned. That's one of the things you like about him, right?"

. . .

The next few nights, Sang slept on the couch in the living room, her things stored temporarily in the corner, in order to paint her room. Both Paul and Heather were surprised by this; neither of them had made an effort to do much to their rooms when moving in. For the walls, she had chosen a soothing sage green; for the trim, the palest lavender, a color that the paint company called "mole." It wasn't what she imagined a mole to look like at all, she told Paul, stirring the can vigorously on the kitchen counter. "What would you have named it?" she asked him suddenly. He could think of nothing. It was only upstairs, sitting alone at his big plywood desk, piled with thick books full of tissue-thin pages, that he thought of the ice cream his mother always ordered at Newport Creamery when his family went on Sunday nights for hamburgers. His mother had died years ago, his father soon after. They'd adopted Paul late in life, when they were in their fifties, so people had often mistaken them for his grandparents. That evening in the kitchen, when Sang walked in, Paul said, "Black raspberry."

"What?"

"The paint."

She had a small, slightly worried-looking smile on her face, a smile one might give a confused child. "That's funny."

"The name?"

"No. It's just a little funny the way you picked up a conversation we had, like, six hours ago, and expected me to remember what you were talking about."

As soon as Paul opened the door of his room the next morning, he detected the fresh yet cloying smell of paint, heard the swish of the roller as it moved up and down a wall. After Heather had left the house, Sang started to play music: one Billie Holiday CD after another. They were having a spell of sticky, sweltering days, and Paul was working in the relative cool of the living room, a few paces across the landing from Sang.

"Oh, my God," she exclaimed, noticing him on her way to the bathroom. "This music must be driving you crazy." She wore cutoff jeans, a black tank top with straps like those of a brassiere. Her feet were bare, her calves and thighs flecked with paint.

He lied, telling her he often studied to music. Because he noticed it was the kitchen she went to most often, to rinse her brushes or eat some yogurt out of a big tub, the second day he moved himself there, where he made a pot of tea, and, much to her amusement, set the alarm on his wristwatch to know when to take out the leaves. In the afternoon, her sister called, from London, with a voice identical to Sang's. For a moment, Paul actually believed it was Sang herself, mysteriously calling him from her room. "Can't talk, I'm painting my room sage and mole," she reported cheerfully to her sister, and when she replaced the receiver of the dark brown phone there were a few of her mole-colored fingerprints on the surface.

He liked studying in her fleeting company. She was impressed with how far he'd got on his PhD—she told him that after she dropped out of Harvard a year ago, her mother locked herself up in her bedroom for a week and her father refused to speak to her. She'd had it with academia, hated how competitive it was, how monkish it forced one to become. That was what her boyfriend did, always blocking off chunks of his day and working at home with the phone unplugged, writing papers for the next conference. "You'll be good at it," she assured Paul. "You're devoted, I can tell." When she asked him what his exam entailed, he told her it would last three hours, that there would be three questioners, and that it would cover three centuries of English and European literature.

"And they can ask you anything?" she wanted to know.

"Within reason."

"Wow."

He didn't tell her the truth—that he'd already taken the exam the year before and failed. His committee and a handful of students were the only ones who knew, and it was to avoid them that Paul preferred to stay at home now. He had failed not because he wasn't prepared but because his mind had betrayed him that bright May morning, inexplicably cramped like a stubborn muscle that curled his foot during sleep. For five harrowing minutes, as the professors stared at him with their legal pads full of questions, as trains came and went along Commonwealth Avenue, he had not been able to reply to the first question, about comic villainy in *Richard III*. He had read the play so many times he could picture each scene, not as it might be performed on a stage but, rather, as the pale printed columns in his Pelican Shakespeare. He felt himself go crimson; it was the nightmare he had been having for months before the exam. His interrogators were patient, tried another question, which he stammered miserably through, pausing in the middle of a thought and unable to continue, until, finally, one of the professors, white hair like a snowy wreath around his otherwise naked head, put out a hand, as might a policeman stopping traffic, and said, "The candidate's simply not ready." Paul had walked home, the tie he'd bought for the occasion stuffed into his pocket, and for a week he had not left the house. When he returned to campus, he was ten pounds thinner, and the department secretary asked him if he'd fallen in love.

Sang had been living with them for a week when a suitor called. By then, the painting was finished, the dreary room transformed. She was removing masking tape from the edges of the windowpanes when Paul told her someone named Asim Bhattacharya was calling from Geneva. "Tell him I'm not in," she said, without hesitating. He wrote down the name, spelled out carefully by the caller, who had said before hanging up, "Just tell her it's Pinkoo."

More men called. One asked Paul, dejectedly, if he was Sang's boyfriend. The mere possibility, articulated by a stranger, jolted him. Such a thing had happened once before in the house, the first year Paul lived there—two housemates had fallen in love, had moved out in order to marry each other. "No," he told the caller. "I'm just her housemate." Nevertheless, for the rest of the day he felt burdened by the question, worried that he'd transgressed somehow simply by answering the phone. A few days later, he told Sang. She laughed. "He's probably horrified now, knowing that I live with a man," she said. "Next time," she advised him, "say yes."

A week afterward, the three of them were in the kitchen, Heather filling a thermos with echinacea tea because she had come down with a cold and had to spend all day in classes, Sang hunched over the newspaper and coffee. The night before, she had locked herself up in her bathroom, and now there were some reddish highlights in her hair. When the phone rang and Paul picked up, he assumed it was another suitor on the line, for, like many of Sang's suitors, the caller had a slight foreign accent, though this one was more refined than awkward. The only difference was that instead of asking for Sangeeta he asked to speak to Sang. When Paul asked who was calling, he said, in a slightly impatient way, "I am her boyfriend." The words landed in Paul's chest like the dull yet painful taps of a doctor's instrument. He saw that Sang was looking up at him expectantly, her chair already partly pushed back from the table.

"For me?"

He nodded, and Sang took the phone into her room.

"Boyfriend," Paul reported to Heather.

"What's his name?"

Paul shrugged. "Didn't say."

"Well, she must be happy as a clam," Heather remarked with some asperity, screwing the lid onto her thermos.

Paul felt sorry for Heather, with her red, chapped nose and her thick-waisted body, but more than that he felt protective of Sang. "What do you mean?" he said.

"Because her lover's back, and now she can tell all those other guys to fuck off."

The boyfriend was standing on the sidewalk with Sang, looking up at the house, as Paul returned on his bike from a day of photocopying at the library. A bottle-green BMW was parked at the curb. The couple stood with an assumed intimacy, their dark heads tilting toward each other.

"Keep away from the window when you change your clothes," Paul heard him say. "I can see through the curtain. Couldn't you get a room at the back?" Paul stepped off his bike at a slight distance from them, adjusted the straps of his backpack. He was uncomfortably aware that he was shabbily dressed—in shorts, and Birkenstocks, and an old Dartmouth T-shirt, his pale legs covered with matted blond hair. The boyfriend wore perfectly fitted faded jeans, a white shirt, a navy-blue blazer, and brown leather shoes. His sharp features commanded admiration without being imposing. His hair, in contrast, was on the long side, framing his face in a lavish, unexpected style. He looked several years older than Sang, Paul decided, but in certain ways he strongly resembled her, for they shared the same height, the same gilded complexion, the same sprinkle of moles above and below their lips. As Paul walked toward them, Sang's boyfriend was still inspecting the house, searching the yellow-and-ochre Victorian facade as if for defects, until he looked away suddenly, distracted by the bark of a dog.

"Your roommates have a dog?" the boyfriend asked. He took an odd, dancelike step to the left, moving partly behind Sang.

"No, silly," Sang said teasingly, running her hand down the back of his head. "No dogs, no smokers. Those were the only listings I called, because of you." The barking stopped, and the ensuing silence seemed to punctuate her words. There was a necklace around her neck, lapis beads she now fingered in a way that made Paul think they were a gift. "Paul, this is Farouk. Farouk's afraid of dogs." She kissed Farouk on the cheek.

"Freddy," Farouk said, nodding rather than extending a hand, his words directed more to Sang than to Paul. She shook her head.

"For the millionth time, I'm not calling you Freddy."

Farouk glanced at her without humor. "Why not? You expect people to call you Sang."

She was unbothered. "That's different. That's actually a part of my name."

"Well, I'm Paul, and that's pretty much all you can call me," Paul said. No one laughed.

Suddenly, she was never at home. When she was, she stayed in her room, often on the phone, the door shut. By dinner, she tended to be gone. The items on her shelf of the refrigerator, the big tubs of yogurt and the crackers and the tabouli, sat untouched. The yogurt eventually sported a mantle of green fuzz, setting off shrieks of disgust when Sang finally opened the lid. It was only natural, Paul told himself, for the two of them to want to be alone together. He was surprised to run into her one day in the small gourmet grocery in the neighborhood, her basket piled high with food she never brought back to the house, purple net bags of shallots, goat cheese in oil, meat wrapped in butcher paper. Because it was raining, Paul, who had his car with him, offered her a ride. She told him no thank you, and headed off to the T stop, a Harvard baseball cap on her head, hugging the grocery bag to her chest. He had no idea where Farouk lived; he pictured a beautiful house on Brattle Street, French doors and pretty molding.

It was always something of a shock to find Farouk in the house. He visited infrequently and seemed to appear and disappear without a trace. Unless Paul looked out the window and saw the BMW, always precisely parked under the shade of a birch tree, it was impossible to tell if he was there. He never said hello or good-bye; instead, he behaved as if Sang were the sole occupant of the house. They never sat in the living room, or in the kitchen. Only once, when Paul returned from a bike ride, did he see them overhead, eating lunch on the deck. They were sitting next to each other, cross-legged, and Sang was extending a fork toward Farouk's mouth, her other hand cupped beneath it. By the time Paul entered the house, they had retreated into her room.

When she wasn't with Farouk, she did things for him. She read through proofs of an article he'd written, checking it for typos. She scheduled his doctor's appointments. Once, she spent all morning with the Yellow Pages, pricing tiles; Farouk was thinking of redoing his kitchen.

By the end of September, Paul was aware of a routine: Mondays, which Sang had off from the bookstore, Farouk came for lunch. The two of them would eat in her room; sometimes he heard the sounds of their talking as they ate, or their spoons tapping against soup bowls, or the Nocturnes of Chopin. They were silent lovers—mercifully so, compared with other couples he'd overheard in the house through the years—but their presence soon prompted him to go to the library on Mondays, for he was affected nevertheless, embarrassed by the time her door had been partly open and he'd seen Farouk zipping his jeans.

Three years had passed since Theresa, the one girlfriend he'd ever had. He'd dated no one since. Because of Theresa, he'd chosen a graduate school in Boston. For a few months, he had lived with her in her apartment on St. Botolph Street. For Thanksgiving, he'd gone with her to her parents' house in Deerfield. It was there that it had ended. "I'm sorry, Paul, I can't help it, I just don't like the way you kiss me," she told him once they'd gone to bed. He remembered himself sitting naked on one side of the mattress, in a room he was suddenly aware he was never again to see. He had not argued; in the wake of his shame, he became strangely efficient and agreeable, with her, with everyone.

Late one night, Paul was in bed reading when he heard a car pull up to the house. The clock on his desk said twenty past two. He shut off his lamp and got up to look through the window. It was November. A full moon illuminated the wide, desolate street, lined with trash bags and recycling bins. There was a taxi in front of the house, the engine still running. Sang emerged from it alone. For close to a minute, she stood there on the sidewalk. He waited by the window until she climbed up to the porch, then listened as she climbed the staircase and shut the door to her room. Farouk had picked her up that afternoon; Paul had seen her stepping into his car. He thought perhaps they'd fought, though the next day he detected no signs of discord. He overheard her speaking to Farouk on the phone in good spirits, deciding on a video to rent. But that night, around the same time, the same thing happened. The third night, he stayed awake on purpose, making sure she got in.

The following morning, a Sunday, Paul, Heather, and Sang had pancakes together in the kitchen. Sang was playing Louis

Armstrong on the CD player in her room while Paul fried the pancakes in two cast-iron skillets.

"Kevin's sleeping over tonight," Heather said. She'd met him recently. He was a physicist at MIT. "I hope that's okay."

"Sure thing," Paul said. He liked Kevin. He had been coming over often for dinner and brought beers and helped with the dishes afterward, talking to Paul as much as he talked to Heather.

"I'm sorry I keep missing him. He seems really nice," Sang said.

"We'll see," Heather said. "Next week is our one-month anniversary."

Sang smiled, as if this modest commemoration were in fact something of much greater significance. "Congratulations."

Heather crossed her fingers. "I guess the next stage is when you assume you're going to spend weekends together."

Paul glanced at Sang, who said nothing. She got up, returning five minutes later from the cellar with a basket full of laundry.

"Nice Jockeys," Heather said, noticing several pairs folded on top of the pile.

"They're Farouk's," Sang said.

"He doesn't have a washing machine?" Heather wanted to know.

"He does," Sang said, oblivious of Heather's disapproving expression. "But it's coin-operated."

The arguments started around Thanksgiving. Paul would hear Sang crying into the phone in her room, the gray plastic cord stretched across the linoleum and then across the landing, disappearing under her door. One of the fights had something to do with a party Sang had been invited to, which Farouk didn't want to attend. Another was about Farouk's birthday. Sang had spent the day before making a cake. The house smelled of oranges and almonds and Paul heard the electric beater going late at night. But the next afternoon, he saw the cake in the trash can.

Once, returning from school, he discovered that Farouk was there, the BMW parked outside. It was a painfully cold December day; early that morning, the season's first flakes had fallen. Walking past Sang's room, Paul heard her raised voice. She was accusing: Why didn't he ever want to meet her friends? Why didn't he invite her to his cousin's house for Thanksgiving? Why didn't he like to spend the night together? Why, at the very least, didn't he drive her home?

"I pay for the cabs," Farouk said quietly. "What difference does it make?"

"I hate it, Farouk. It's abnormal."

"You know I don't sleep well when you're there."

"How are we ever going to get married?" she demanded. "Are we supposed to live in separate houses forever?"

"Sang, please," Farouk said. "Try to be calm. Your roommates will hear."

"Will you stop about my roommates," Sang shouted.

"You're hysterical," Farouk said.

She began to cry.

"I've warned you, Sang," Farouk said. He sounded desperate. "I will not spend my life with a woman who makes scenes."

"Fuck you."

Something, a plate or a glass, struck a wall and broke. Then the room went quiet. After much deliberation, Paul knocked softly. No one replied. A few hours later, Paul nearly bumped into Sang as she was emerging from her bathroom, wrapped in a large dark pink towel. Her wet hair was uncombed and tangled, a knot bulging like a small nest on one side of her head.

For weeks, he had longed to catch a glimpse of her this way, and still he felt wholly unprepared for the vision of her bare legs and arms, her damp face and shoulders.

"Hey," he said, sidling quickly past.

"Paul," she called out after a moment, as if his presence had registered only then. He turned to look at her; though it was barely past four, the sun was already setting in the living-room window, casting a golden patch of light to one side of her in the hallway.

"What's up?" he said.

She crossed her arms in front of her, a hand concealing each shoulder. A spot on her forehead was coated with what appeared to be toothpaste. "I'm sorry about earlier."

"That's okay."

"It's not. You have an exam to study for."

Her eyes were shining brightly, and she had a funny frozen smile on her face, her lips slightly parted. He began to smile back when he saw she was about to cry. He nodded. "It doesn't matter."

For a week, Farouk didn't call, though when the phone rang she flew to answer it. She was home every night for dinner. She had long conversations with her sister in London. "Tell me if you think this is normal," Paul overheard her say as he walked into the kitchen. "We were driving one time and he told me I smelled bad. Sweaty. He told me to wash under my arms. He kept saying it wasn't a criticism, that people in love should be able to say things like that to each other." One day, Charles took Sang out and in the evening she returned, with shopping bags from the outlets in Kittery. Another night, she accepted an invitation to see a movie at the Coolidge with Paul and Heather and Kevin, but once they'd reached the box office she told them she had a headache and walked back to the house. "I bet you they've split up," Heather said, once they'd settled into their seats.

But the following week Farouk called when Sang was at work. Though Farouk hadn't bothered to identify himself, Paul called the bookstore, leaving her the message.

The relationship resumed its course, but Paul noticed that Farouk no longer set foot in the house. He wouldn't even ring the bell. He would pause at the curb, the engine of his car still running, beeping three times to signal that he was waiting for her, and then she would disappear.

Over winter break, she went away, to London. Her sister had had a baby boy recently. Sang showed Paul the things she bought for the baby: playsuits full of snaps, a stuffed octopus, a miniature French sailor's shirt, a mobile of stars and planets that glowed in the dark. "I'm going to be called Sang Mashi," she told him excitedly, explaining that *Mashi* was the Bengali word for "Aunt." The word sounded strange on her lips. She spoke Bengali infrequently—never to her sister, never to her suitors, only a word here and there to her parents, in Michigan, to whom she spoke on weekends.

"How do you say 'bon voyage'?" Paul asked.

She told him she wasn't sure.

Without her there, it was easier for Paul to study, his mind spacious and clear. His exam was less than six months away. A date and time had been scheduled, the first Tuesday in May, at ten o'clock, marked with an "X" on the calendar over his desk. Since summer, he had worked his way, yet again, through the list of poems and critical essays and plays, typing summaries of them into his computer. He had printed out these summaries, three-hole-punched them, put them in a series of binders. He wrote further summaries of the summaries on index cards that he reviewed before bed, filed in shoe boxes. For Christmas, he was invited to an aunt's house in Buffalo, as usual. This year, with his exam as an excuse, he declined the invitation, mailing off gifts. Heather was away, too; she and Kevin had gone skiing in Vermont.

To mark the new year, Paul set up a new routine, spreading himself all over the house. In the mornings, he reviewed poetry at the kitchen table. After lunch, criticism in the living room. A Shakespeare play before bed. He began to leave his things, his binders and his shoe boxes and his books, on the kitchen table, on certain steps of the staircase, on the coffee table in the living room. He was slouched in the papasan chair one snowy afternoon, reading his notes on Aristotle's Poetics, when the doorbell rang.

It was a UPS man with a package for Sang, something from J. Crew. Paul signed for it and took it upstairs. He leaned it against the door of her room, which caused the door to open slightly. He closed it firmly, and for a moment he stood there, his hand still on the knob. Even though she was in London, he knocked before entering. The futon was neatly made, a red batik bedspread covering the top. The green walls were bare but for two framed Indian miniatures of palace scenes, men smoking hookahs and reclining on cushions, bare-bellied women dancing in a ring. There was none of the disarray he for some reason pictured every time he walked by her room; only outside, through the windows, was there the silent chaos of the storm. The snow fell in disorderly swirls, yet it covered the brown porch railing below, neatly, as if it were a painted trim. A single panel of a white seersucker curtain was loosely cinched with a peach silk scarf that Sang sometimes knotted at her throat, causing the fabric of the curtain to gather in the shape of a slim hourglass. Paul untied the scarf, letting the curtain cover the windowpane. Without touching his face to the scarf, he smelled the perfume that lingered in its weave. He went to the futon and sat down, his legs extending along the oatmeal carpet. He took off his shoes and socks. On a wine crate next to the futon was a glass of water that had gathered bubbles, a small pot of Vaseline. He undid his belt buckle, but suddenly the desire left him, absent from his body just as she was absent from the room. He buckled his belt again, and then slowly he lifted the bedspread. The sheets were flannel, blue and white, a pattern of fleur-de-lis.

He had drifted off to sleep when he heard the phone ring. He stumbled barefoot out of Sang's room, into the kitchen, the linoleum chilly.

"Hello?"

No one replied on the other end, and he was about to hang up when he heard a dog barking.

"Hello?" he repeated. It occurred to him it might be Sang, a poor connection from London. "Sang, is that you?"

The caller hung up.

That evening, after dinner, the phone rang again. When he picked it up, he heard the same dog he'd heard earlier.

"Balthazar, shush!" a woman said, as soon as Paul said hello. Her voice was hesitant. Was Sang in? she wanted to know.

"She's not here. May I take a message?"

She left her name, Deirdre Frain, and a telephone number. Paul wrote it down on the message pad, under Partha Mazoomdar, a suitor who'd called from Cleveland in the morning.

The next day, Deirdre called again. Again Paul told her Sang wasn't there, adding that she wouldn't be back until the weekend.

"Where is she?" Deirdre asked.

"She's out of the country."

"In Cairo?"

This took him by surprise. "No, London."

"In London," she repeated. She sounded relieved. "London. Okay. Thanks."

The fourth call was very late at night, when Paul was already in bed. He went downstairs, feeling for the phone in the dark.

"It's Deirdre." She sounded slightly out of breath, as if it were she, not he, who'd just rushed to the phone.

He flicked on the light switch, rubbing his eyes behind his glasses. "Um, as I said, Sang's not back yet."

"I don't want to talk to Sang." She was slurring her words, exaggerating the pronunciation of Sang's name in a slightly cruel way.

Paul heard music, a trumpet crooning softly. "You don't?"

"No," she said. "Actually, I have a question."

"A question?"

"Yes." There was a pause, the clink of an ice cube falling into a glass. Her tone had become flirtatious. "So, what's your name?"

He took off his glasses, allowing the room to go blurry. He couldn't recall the last time a woman had spoken to him that way. "Paul."

"Paul," she repeated. "Can I ask you another question, Paul?"

"What?"

"It's about Sang."

He stiffened. Again, she had said the name without kindness. "What about Sang?"

Deirdre paused. "She's your housemate, right?"

"That's right."

"Well, I was wondering, then, if you'd know if—are they cousins?"

"Who?"

"Sang and Freddy."

He put his glasses on again, drawing things into focus. He was unnerved by this woman's curiosity. It wasn't her business, he wanted to tell her. But before he could do that, Deirdre began quietly crying.

He looked at the clock on the stove; it was close to three in the morning. It was his own fault. He shouldn't have answered the phone so late. He wished he hadn't told the woman his name.

"Deirdre," he said after a while, tired of listening to her. "Are you still there?"

She stopped crying. Her breathing was uneven, penetrating his ear.

"I don't know who you are," Paul said. "I don't understand why you're calling me."

"I love him."

He hung up, his heart hammering. He had the urge to take a shower. He wanted to erase her name from the legal pad. He stared at the receiver, remnants of Sang's mole-colored fingerprints still visible here and there. For the first time since the winter break had begun, he felt lonely in the house. The call had to be a fluke. Some other Sang the woman was referring to. Maybe it was a scheme on behalf of one of her Indian suitors, to cast suspicion, to woo her away from Farouk. Before Sang left for London, the fights had subsided, and things between Sang and Farouk, as far as Paul could tell, were still the same. In the living room, she'd been wrapping a brown leather satchel, a pair of men's driving gloves. The night before she left, she made a dinner reservation for the two of them at Biba. Farouk had driven her to the airport.

The ringing of the phone woke Paul the next morning. He remained in bed, listening to it, looking at the ashen branches of the tree outside his window. He counted twelve rings before they stopped. The phone rang half an hour later, and he ignored it again. The third time, he was in the kitchen. When it stopped, he unplugged the cord from the jack.

Though he studied in silence for the remainder of the day,

he felt fitful. Sitting in the kitchen that evening with a bricklike volume of Spenser, he was unable to concentrate on the lines, irritated by the footnotes, by how much there was left to learn. He wondered how many times Deirdre had tried to call him since he'd unplugged the phone. Had she given up? The calling seemed obsessive to him. He wondered whether she was the type to do something. To take a bottle of pills.

After dinner, he plugged the phone back into the jack. There were no further calls. And yet his mind continued to wander. Something told him that she'd try again. He'd made the mistake of telling her when Sang would be back. Perhaps Deirdre was waiting to speak to her directly. Perhaps Deirdre would tell Sang the same thing she'd told him, about loving Farouk. Before going to bed, he poured himself a glass of Dewar's, a gift sent by his aunt in Buffalo. Then he dialed the number Deirdre had given him. She picked up right away, with a lilting hello.

"Deirdre, it's Paul."

"Paul," she said, slowly.

"You called me last night. I'm Sang's housemate."

"Of course. Paul. You hung up on me, Paul." She appeared to be drunk again, but in a sunnier mood.

"Listen, I'm sorry about that. I just wanted to make sure you were okay."

Deirdre sighed. "That's sweet of you, Paul."

"And to ask you to please stop calling me," he said after a considerable pause.

"Why?" There was panic in her voice.

"Because I don't know you," he said.

"Would you like to know me, Paul?" she said. "I'm a very likable person."

"I have to go," he said firmly, hoping not to provoke her. "But maybe there's someone else you could talk to? A friend?"

"Freddy's my friend."

The mention of Farouk, the use of the nickname, unsettled Paul as it had the night before. Yesterday, he'd surmised that Deirdre might be a student of Farouk's at Harvard, practically a teenager, infatuated with an older man. He imagined her sitting at the back of a lecture hall, visiting him in his office, getting the wrong idea. Now a simple, reasonable question, which was at the same time a poisoned question, formed in Paul's mind.

"So, how exactly do you know Farouk?" Paul asked lightly, as if they were chatting at a party.

He didn't think she'd tell him, thought she might even hang up on him as he had on her, but they slipped easily into a conversation. It was Deirdre who did most of the talking. She told Paul that she was from Vancouver originally, and that she'd moved to Boston in her twenties, to study interior design. She'd met Farouk one Sunday afternoon, a year and a half ago, when she was walking out of a café in the South End. He had followed her halfway down the block, tapped her on the shoulder, looked her up and down with unconcealed desire. "You can't imagine," Deirdre said, remembering it. "You can't imagine how something like that feels." Nevertheless, he'd been gentlemanly. For their first date, they had gone to Walden Pond. Afterward, they bought corn and tomatoes, and grilled salmon in her backyard. Farouk loved her home, an old farmhouse on five acres. He asked her to draw up the plans for redoing his kitchen. On Labor Day, they had hiked Mount Sunapee together. She said other things Paul listened to, unsure of how much he should believe. For either they were true, and Farouk and Deirdre were having a full-blown affair, or Deirdre was simply inventing it all, the way lonely, drunk people sometimes invent things. At one point, he wandered into the hallway and opened Sang's door, making sure the curtain was tied as he'd remembered it.

"What about you?" Deirdre asked suddenly.

"What about me?"

"Well, here I am going on and you haven't said a thing. What are you like, Paul? Are you happy?"

He had sacrificed an hour to this woman. The edge of his ear ached from pressing the phone to it for so long. "This isn't about me." He swallowed, shutting the door to Sang's room. "It's about Sang."

"They're cousins, right?" Deirdre said. He could barely hear her. "Aren't they?"

The desperation with which she asked him brought with it a crushing certainty. He knew that all she had told him was true, the knowledge of something having gone terribly wrong leveling him the way his exam had. The way Theresa's words had.

"Sang and Farouk are not cousins," he said. He felt a strange, inward power as he spoke, aware that the information could devastate her.

She was silent.

"They're boyfriend and girlfriend, Deirdre," he said. "A serious couple."

"Oh, yeah?" Her tone was challenging. "How serious?"

He thought for a moment. "They see each other four or five nights a week."

"They do?" To Paul's satisfaction, Deirdre sounded wounded by this information.

"Yes," he said, adding, "they've been together for over three years."

"Three?" The word trailed off weakly, in a way that made Paul wonder if she might cry again. But when she spoke next her voice was clear. "Well, we're a serious couple, too. I picked him up from the airport yesterday when he came back from Cairo. I saw him tonight. He was here for dinner, here in my house. He made love to me on my staircase, Paul. An hour ago, I could still feel him dripping down my thighs."

. . .

Sang returned from London with presents for the house, KitKats in red wrappers, tea from Harrods, marmalade, chocolate-coated biscuits. A snapshot of her nephew went up on the refrigerator, his small smiling face pressed against Sang's. Paul, from his room, saw that it was Farouk who dropped her off at the house. Eventually, Paul had gone downstairs, down the magnificent staircase, which he was now unable to descend without a fleeting image of Farouk naked on top of a woman who was not Sang. In the kitchen he opened his cupboard and pulled down the Dewar's.

"Wow. Things have really changed around here," Sang said, smiling, her eyebrows raised in amusement, watching him pour the drink.

"What do you mean?"

"You're drinking Scotch. If I'd known, I would have bought you some single malt in duty-free, instead of the KitKats."

The thought of her buying him a gift depressed him. They were friendly, but they were not friends. He offered her a glass of the Scotch, which she accepted. They sat together at the table. She clinked her glass against his.

She began sorting through the mail Paul had collected for her. Her hair was a few inches shorter; she smelled intensely of a spicy perfume.

"I don't know any Deirdres," she said, reading her messages on the legal pad. "Did she say why she was calling?"

He'd drained his glass and was already pacified by the drink. He shook his head.

"I wonder what I should do."

"About what?"

"Well, should I call her back?"

He stood up and opened the freezer to get ice cubes for a

second drink. When he returned to the table, she was crossing out the name with a pencil. "Forget it. She's probably a tele-marketer or something."

Avoiding Sang was easy. The university library, which Paul nor-mally found so charmless, with its cement floors and gray metal shelves and carrels full of anonymous ballpoint philosophy, was where he began to spend his days. At home, he discovered that it was just as easy to take a sandwich up to his room. Winter gave way to a wet, reluctant spring, full of wind and slanted rains that lashed the window by Paul's bed. Whenever the phone rang, he didn't answer. In the first few days after Sang's return, he was convinced, each time, that it would be Deirdre, demanding to talk to Sang. But Deirdre never called. He waited for her voice, the things she had told him, to fade from his memory. But the conversations had lodged themselves stubbornly in his mind, alongside all the plays and poems and essays. He saw two people swimming in Walden Pond, their heads above the surface of the water. But then there was Sang, day after day, disappearing to eat dinner at Farouk's. There she was, sitting at the kitchen table, booking Farouk's tickets to Cairo for the summer, his credit card number written on a sheet of paper. After two months, Deirdre still hadn't called, and Paul finally stopped fearing that she would.

Paul took the week of his spring break off from studying. "Stop cramming. That's probably what happened the first time. Go to the Caribbean," his adviser suggested. Instead, Paul stayed at home, but declared himself officially on vacation. He went to movies at the Brattle, spent two days making a cas-soulet. He drove to Wellfleet one day, forcing himself not to take a book. He decided to ride out to Concord on his bike, to see Emerson's house; on Saturday morning, he discovered that the chain needed to be fixed, and he brought the bike up to the deck. When he looked up, Sang was standing there, the phone in her hands, the cord stretched as far as it could go.

"Something weird just happened, "she said.

"What?"

"It was that Deirdre woman. The one you took the message from when I was away."

Paul bent down, pretending to root around for something in his toolbox. "She was asking for Farouk," Sang continued. "She says she's a friend of his, visiting from out of town."

"Oh. So that must have been why she was calling," he said, relieved to hear that this was all Deirdre had said.

"He's never mentioned a Deirdre."

"Oh."

Sang sat down in a beach chair, the phone in her lap, her body leaning into it. She straightened, staring at the phone, pressing numbers at random without picking up the receiver. "Farouk doesn't have any friends," she said. "Ever since I've known him, he's never introduced me to a single friend. I'm his only friend, really." She looked intently at Paul, and for a second he feared she was about to draw some sort of parallel, point out that Paul didn't have friends, either. Instead, she said, "How did she get my number, anyway?"

She'd looked it up in Farouk's address book; Deirdre had confessed this to Paul. Farouk had made it easy for her, writing it under "S" for Sang, the name of the cousin he had mentioned in a way that made her suspicious. Paul shook his head, standing up, squeezing the hand brakes on the bicycle. "Don't know. I guess I'd ask Farouk."

"Right. Ask Farouk." She stood up and went back into the house.

That evening, when Paul returned from Concord, he found Sang at the kitchen table. She said nothing as he went to the refrigerator to pull out the remains of the cassoulet.

"Farouk isn't in," she said, as if responding to a question on Paul's part. "He hasn't been in all day."

He lifted the lid of the baking dish and sprinkled a few drops of water on top of the cassoulet. "You want some of this?"

"No, thanks." She was frowning.

Paul put the cassoulet in the oven and poured a Scotch. The muscles in his arms and his thighs ached pleasantly. He wanted to take a shower before eating.

"So, when exactly did this Deirdre person call?" Sang said, stopping him as he walked out of the kitchen.

He turned to face her, pivoting on his heels. "I don't remember. It was when you were away."

"And did she say anything to you?"

"What do you mean?"

"What did she say to you, exactly?"

"Nothing. I didn't talk to her," he said, his pulse racing; he was thankful that he was already coated with sweat. "She just wanted you to call her back."

"Well, I can't call her back. She didn't even leave her number. It was weird. Did she sound like a weird sort of person to you?"

He remembered Deirdre's tears. "I love him," she'd told Paul, a perfect stranger. He looked at Sang, manipulating his face into an uncomprehending expression. "I'm not sure what you mean."

She sighed impatiently. "Can you hand me that?" she said, pointing to the message pad.

Paul watched as Sang began flipping through the pages that had been turned over, running her finger down each line.

"What are you looking for?" he said after a moment.

"Her number."

"Why?"

"I want to call her back."

"Why?"

She looked up at him, exasperated. "Because I want to, Paul. Is that a problem with you?"

He went upstairs to take his shower. It wasn't his business, he told himself as the hot water washed over him, and, later, as he dried himself, then combed back his hair, enveloped in steam. When he came downstairs again, he found her on her hands and knees, going through the recycling bin, newspapers and magazines piled around her.

"Damn it," she said.

"Now what are you looking for?"

"The number. I remember ripping out that page for some reason. I think I threw it away." She began to put the newspapers and magazines back into the bin. "Damn it," she said again. She stood up, kicking the bin lightly with her foot. "I don't even remember her last name. Do you?"

He inhaled, as if to seal the information inside himself, but then he shook his head, relieved at the opportunity, at last, to be honest with her. He, too, had forgotten Deirdre's last name. It was a name of one syllable, but apart from that detail it had vanished from his brain.

"Hey, Paul," Sang said after a moment. "I'm sorry if I sounded harsh back then."

He walked across the kitchen, opened the oven. "Don't worry about it."

Her stomach growled, loudly enough for Paul to hear. "God, I just realized I haven't eaten a thing today. I think I'll have some of that cassoulet, after all. Should I make a salad?" This would be their first dinner together, alone, without Heather. He used to yearn for such an occasion. He used to feel clumsy and tongue-tied when Sang was in the room. Now he felt dread.

"I guess she was a little weird," he said slowly, gazing at the back of Sang's head, bent forward over the sink where she was ripping lettuce. She turned around.

"How? How did she seem weird to you?"

He was so nervous that for a terrible instant he worried that he might laugh out loud. Sang was regarding him steadily. The faucet was still running. She reached back to turn it off, and now the room was silent.

"She was crying," he said.

"Crying?"

"Um—yeah."

"Crying how?"

"Just—crying. Like she was upset about something."

Sang opened her mouth, as if to speak, but for a while it simply hung open. "So let me get this straight. This woman Deirdre called and asked for me."

Paul nodded. "Right."

"And you said I wasn't there."

"Right."

"And then she asked you to have me call her back."

"Right."

"And then she started crying?"

"Yeah."

"And then what happened?"

"That was it. Then she hung up."

For a moment, Sang seemed satisfied with the information, nodding slowly. Then she shook her head abruptly, as if to flick it away. "Why didn't you tell me this?"

He regretted having offered her the cassoulet. He regretted ever having picked up the phone that day. He regretted that Sang and not another person had moved into the room, into his house, into his life. "I did," he said calmly, drawing a line between them in his mind. "I told you she called."

"But you didn't tell me this."

"No."

She opened her eyes wide, incredulous. "Didn't it occur to you I might want to know?"

He curled his lips together, looking away.

"Well?" she demanded, shouting at him now. "Didn't it?"

When he still did not reply, she marched up to him, her hands clenched in fists, and he braced himself for a blow, twisting his face to one side. But she didn't strike him. Instead she gripped the sides of her own head, as if to steady herself. "My God, Paul." Her voice was so shrill it was nearly inaudible. "What the hell is wrong with you?"

Now it was she who began to avoid him. For a few nights, she was not at home. Paul saw her getting into Charles's truck with a weekend bag. Because Heather had by then all but officially moved in with Kevin, once again Paul found himself alone in the house. A week passed before he saw Sang again. Thinking himself alone, he hadn't bothered to shut his door. She came up to his room, wearing a pretty dress he'd never seen, a white cotton short-sleeved dress, fitted at the waist. The neck was square, showing off her collarbones.

"Hey," she said.

"Hey." He had not missed her at all.

"Look. I just wanted to tell you that it's all a huge confusion. Deirdre really is an old friend of Farouk's, from way back. From college."

"You don't have to explain it to me," Paul said.

"She lives in Canada." Sang continued. "In Vancouver."

"I see."

"They talk, like, once a year. Farouk mentioned my name to her years ago, when we first got together, when he lived in another apartment, and she remembered it. She was trying to get in touch with him because she's getting married, and she wanted to send Farouk an invitation. She didn't have Farouk's new address or his number, and he's not listed. That's why she tried here."

She seemed strangely excited by her convoluted explanation. Some color had come to her cheeks.

"There's only one thing, Paul."

He looked up. "What's that?"

"Farouk called Deirdre to ask about what you said."

"What I said?"

"About the crying." Sang shrugged her shoulders, dropped them carelessly. "He told me she has no idea what you were talking about." Her voice sounded compressed, the words running together quickly.

"Are you saying I made it up?"

She was silent.

For her sake, he'd told her about the crying. That night in the kitchen, watching her make the salad, he'd felt the walls collapsing around her. He'd wanted to warn her somehow. Now he wanted to push her from the door frame where she stood.

"Why would I make up a story like that?" He could feel a nerve on one side of his head throbbing.

Instead of arguing with him, she gave a sympathetic glance, letting her head rest against the door frame. "I don't know, Paul." It occurred to him that this was the first time she'd visited him in his room. For a moment, she appeared to be searching for a free place to sit. She straightened her head.

"Did you really think it would make me leave him?"

"I didn't think it would make you do anything," Paul said. He was clenching his teeth now. His body felt heavy from her accusation, numb. "I didn't make it up."

"I mean, it's one thing for you to like me, Paul," she continued. "It's one thing for you to have a crush. But to make up a story like that—" She stopped, her mouth now straining into something that was not a smile. "It's pathetic, really. Pathetic!" And she walked out of the room.

. . .

When they crossed paths again, she didn't apologize for the outburst. She didn't appear angry, only indifferent. He noticed that a copy of the *Phoenix,* which she'd left on top of the microwave, was folded to the real estate section, and that a few of the listings were circled. She came and went from Farouk's. She looked up at Paul briefly when she happened to see him, with a mechanical little smile, and then she looked away, as if he were invisible.

The next time Sang worked at the bookstore, Paul stayed up in his room until he heard her leave the house. Once she was gone, he went to the kitchen, emptying out the recycling bin, which had not been taken out all winter. He flipped though each magazine, unfolded every newspaper, searching for the sheet of paper with Deirdre's number. It would be like Sang, he thought, to look for it and not find it. But Paul couldn't find it, either. He pulled out the White Pages and opened it at random, searching for a Deirdre, not caring how ridiculous he was being. Then he remembered it. Her last name. It swam effortlessly back to his memory, accompanied by the sound of Deirdre's voice as she introduced herself to him that night on the telephone months ago. He turned to the "F's," saw it there, a D. Frain, an address in Belmont. He dragged the nail of his index finger beneath the listing, leaving a faint dent in the paper.

He called the next day. He left a message on her machine, asking her to call him back. He felt giddy, having done it. In a way, it was his fear that Deirdre would not call him back, knowing that she, too, was now keeping her distance, that emboldened him to keep calling, to keep leaving messages. "Deirdre, this is Paul. Please call me," he said each time.

And then one day she picked up the phone.

"I need to talk to you," he said.

She recognized his voice. "I know. Listen, Paul—"

He cut her off. "It's not right," he said. He was sitting in a booth in the lobby of the library, watching as students flashed their ID cards to the security guard. He fished in his pocket for extra quarters.

"I listened to you. I was kind to you. I didn't have to talk to you."

"I know. I'm sorry. It was wrong of me." She no longer sounded drunk or flirtatious or desperate or upset in any way. She was perfectly ordinary, polite but removed.

"I didn't even tell her the other stuff you told me." He saw that a student was standing outside the booth, waiting for him to finish. Paul lowered his voice. He felt mildly hysterical. "Remember all that stuff?"

"Look, please, I said I'm sorry. Can you hold on a second?" Paul heard a doorbell ring. After a minute, she came back to the phone. "I have to go now. I'll call you back."

"When?" Paul demanded, afraid that she was lying to him, that it was a ploy to be rid of him. In January, when Paul had wanted to get off the phone with Deirdre, she had pleaded with him to stay on the line.

"Later. Tonight," she said.

"I want to know when."

She told him she'd call at ten.

The idea came to him immediately after getting off the phone, the receiver still in his hand. He left the library, went to the nearest RadioShack. "I need a phone," he told the salesman. "And an adapter with two jacks."

It was a night Sang worked at the bookstore; as usual, she was home by nine. She said nothing to Paul when she came into the kitchen to get her mail.

"I called Deirdre," Paul said.

"Why don't you stop involving yourself this way?" Sang said evenly, leafing through a catalogue.

"She's calling me at ten o'clock," Paul said. "If you want, you can listen in without her knowing. I got another phone and hooked it up to our line."

She dropped the catalogue, noticing the second phone. "Jesus, Paul," she hissed. "I can't fucking believe you."

She went into her room; at five to ten she came out and sat next to Paul. He'd set the phones together on the table. At exactly one minute past ten, both phones rang. Paul picked up one. "Hello?"

"It's me," Deirdre said.

He nodded, motioning to Sang, and slowly, carefully, Sang picked up the other phone and put it to her ear without allowing it to touch her. She held it unnaturally, the bottom of the receiver turned away from her mouth, pointed toward her shoulder.

"Like I said, Paul, I'm sorry for calling you. I shouldn't have," Deirdre said.

She seemed relaxed, willing to talk, in no apparent rush. Paul relaxed a little, too. "But you did."

"Yes."

"And you cried about Farouk."

"Yes."

"And then you made me into a liar."

She was silent.

"You denied the whole thing."

"It was Freddy's idea."

"And you went along with it," Paul said. He was looking at Sang. She was pressing her top teeth into her lower lip in a way that looked painful.

"What was I supposed to do, Paul?" Deirdre said. "He was furious when he found out I'd called you. He refused to see me. He unplugged his phone. He wouldn't answer the door."

Sang put a palm against the table's edge, as if to push it away, but she ended up pushing herself back in her chair, scraping the linoleum. Paul put a finger to his lips, but then he realized that, to Deirdre, it was he who'd made the sound. She kept talking.

"Listen, Paul, I'm sorry you're in the middle of all this. I really am sorry I called. It was just that Freddy kept telling me Sang was his cousin, and when I asked him to introduce me to her he refused. I didn't care at first. I figured I wasn't the only woman in his life. But then I fell in love with him." She wanted to believe him, she explained. She was a thirty-five-year-old woman, already married and divorced. She didn't have time for this.

"But I've ended it," she said, matter-of-factly. "You know, there was a point when I actually believed he couldn't live without me. That's what he does to women. He depends on them. He asks them to do a hundred things, makes them believe his life won't function without them. That was him this afternoon when you called, still wanting to see me, still wanting to keep me on the side. He doesn't have any friends, you see. Only lovers. I think he needs them, the way other people need a family or friends." She sounded reasonable and reflective now, as if she were describing an affair she'd had years before. Sang's eyes were closed and she was shaking her head slowly from side to side. The dog was barking.

"That's my dog," Deirdre said. "He's always hated Freddy. He's the size of a football, but every time Freddy comes over he makes me put a guardrail across the stairs."

Sang inhaled sharply. She put the receiver down quietly on the table, then she picked it up again.

"I should go," Paul said.

"Me, too," Deirdre agreed. "I think you need to tell her now."

He was startled, afraid Deirdre had discovered his trick, that she knew that Sang was listening in. "Tell her what?"

"Tell her about me and Farouk. She deserves to know. It sounds like you're a good friend of hers."

Deirdre hung up, and for a long time Paul and Sang sat there, listening to the silence. He had cleared himself with Sang, and yet he felt no relief, no vindication. Eventually, Sang hung up her phone and stood up, slowly, but made no further movements. She looked sealed off from things, holding herself as if she still needed to be perfectly stealthy, as if the slightest sound or gesture would betray her presence.

"I'm sorry," Paul said finally.

She nodded and went to her room, shutting the door. After a while he followed her, stood outside. "Sang? Do you need anything?"

He remained there, waiting for her to reply. He heard her moving around the room. When the door opened, he saw that she had changed, into a black top with long tight-fitting sleeves. Her pink raincoat was draped over her arm, her purse hanging over her shoulder. "I need a ride."

In the car, she directed him, saying what to do and where to turn only at the last possible minute. They drove through Allston and down Storrow Drive. "There," she said, pointing. It was an ugly high-rise, bereft of charm and yet clearly exclusive, on the Cambridge side of the river. She got out of the car and started walking.

Paul followed her. "What are you doing?"

She speeded up. "I need to talk to him." She spoke in a monotone.

"I don't know, Sang."

She walked even faster, her shoes clicking on the pavement.

The lobby was filled with beige sofas and potted trees. There was an African doorman sitting at the desk who smiled at them, recognizing Sang. He was listening to a radio tuned to the news in French.

"Evening, Miss."

"Hello, Raymond."

"Getting cold again, Miss. Maybe rain later."

"Maybe."

She kept her finger pressed on the elevator button until it came, while she fixed her hair in the mirror opposite. On the tenth floor, they stopped, then walked to the end of the hallway. The doors were dark brown, thickly varnished. She tapped the door knocker, which was like a small brass picture frame hinged to the surface. Inside, there was the sound of a television. Then there was silence.

"It's me," she said.

She tapped it again. Five consecutive taps. Ten. She pressed the top of her head against the door. "I heard her, Farouk. I heard Deirdre. She called Paul, and I heard her." Sang's voice was quavering.

"Please open the door." She tried the knob, a strong metal knob, which would not budge.

There were footsteps, a chain being undone. Farouk opened the door, a day's stubble on his face. He wore a flecked fisherman's sweater, corduroy pants, black espadrilles on bare feet. He looked nothing like a philanderer, just bookish and slight. "I did not invite you here," he said acidly when he saw Paul.

In spite of all he knew, Paul was stung by the words, unable to speak in his own defense.

"Please leave," Farouk said. "Please, for once, try to respect our privacy."

"She asked me," Paul said.

Farouk lurched forward, arms extended rigidly in front of him, pushing Paul away as if he were a large piece of furniture.

Paul took a step back, then resisted, grabbing Farouk's wrists. The two men fell to the floor of the hallway, Paul's glasses flying onto the carpet. It was easy for Paul to pin Farouk to the ground, to dig his fingers into his shoulders. Paul squeezed them tightly, through the thick wool of the sweater, feeling the give of the tendons, aware that Farouk was no longer resisting. For a moment, Paul lay on top of him fully, subduing him like a lover. He looked up, searching for Sang, but she was nowhere. He looked back at the man beneath him, a man he barely knew, a man he hated. "All she wants is for you to admit it," Paul said. "I think you owe her that."

Farouk spat at Paul's face, a cold spray that made Paul recoil. Farouk pushed him off, went into his apartment, and slammed the door. Other doors along the hallway began to open. Paul could hear Farouk fastening the chain. He found his glasses and stood up, pressed his ear to the varnished wood. He heard crying, then a series of objects falling. At one point he could hear Farouk saying, "Stop it, please, please, it's not as bad as you think." And then Sang saying, "How many times? How many times did you do it? Did you do it here on the bed?"

A minute later, the elevator opened and a man walked toward Farouk's apartment. He was a lean man with gray hair and a big bunch of keys in his hand. "I'm the super in this building. Who are you?" he asked Paul.

"I live with the woman inside," he said, pointing at Farouk's door.

"You her husband?"

"No."

The super knocked on the door, saying neighbors had complained. He continued to knock, rapping the wood with his knuckles until the door opened.

Inside was a hallway illuminated by track lights. Paul glimpsed a bright white kitchen without windows, a stack of cookbooks on the counter. To the right was a dining room, painted the same sage-green as Sang's room. Paul followed the super into the living room. There was an off-white sofa, a coffee table, a sliding glass door that led to a balcony. In the distance was a view of the Citgo sign, draining and filling with color. There was a bookcase along one wall which had fallen to the floor, its books in a heap. The receiver of a telephone on a side table hung from a cord, beeping faintly, repeatedly. In spite of these things, the room had a barren quality, as if someone were in the process of moving out of it.

Sang was kneeling on an Oriental carpet, picking up the pieces of what appeared to have been a clear glass vase. She was shivering. Her hair was undone, hanging toward the floor, partly shielding her face. There was water everywhere, and the ruins of a bouquet of flowers, irises and tiger lilies and daffodils. She worked carefully with the glass, creating a pile of shards on the coffee table. There were petals in her hair and stuck to her face and neck, and plastered to the skin exposed above her black scoop-necked top, as if she had smeared them on herself like a cream. There were welts emerging above her neckline, fresh and bright.

The men stood there, looking at her, none of them saying anything. A policeman arrived, his black boots and his gun and his radio filling up the room, static from his radio replacing the silence. Someone in the building had called the station to complain, he said. He asked Sang, who was still on the floor, if Farouk had struck her. Sang shook her head.

"Do you live here?" he asked.

"I painted the walls," Sang said, as if that would explain everything. Paul remembered her painting her own room, barefoot, listening to Billie Holiday.

The policeman leaned over, inspecting the broken glass and flower debris on the carpet, noticing the welts on her skin. "What happened?"

"I bought them," she said, tears streaming quickly down her cheeks. Her voice was thick, ashamed. "I did this to myself."

After that, everything proceeded in an orderly way, with people moving in separate directions, not reacting to anyone else. The policeman filled out a form, then lent an arm and took Sang to the bathroom. The super left, saying something to Farouk about a fine. Farouk went to the kitchen, returning with a roll of paper towels and a garbage bag, and knelt by the carpet, cleaning up the mess Sang had made. The policeman looked at Paul, as if assessing him for the first time. He asked if Paul was an involved party.

"I'm her housemate," Paul replied. "I just gave her a ride."

The next morning, Paul was awakened by the noise of a car door closing. He went to the window and saw the trunk of a taxi being pressed down by the driver's hand. Sang had left a note on the kitchen table: she was going to London to visit her sister. "Paul, thanks for yesterday," it said. Along with this was a signed check for her portion of the rent.

For a few days, nothing happened. He collected her mail. The bookstore called to ask where she was. Paul told them she had the flu. Two weeks later, the bookstore called again. This time it was to fire her. The third week, Farouk began to call, asking to speak to her. He didn't identify himself, didn't press Paul when he said, night after night, "Sang's not in." He was polite to Paul, in a way he had never been before, saying, thank you, that he'd try later. Paul relished these calls. He liked depriving Farouk of the knowledge of where Sang was. But then, one day when he called, Heather, holed up in the house that week to study for an exam, happened to answer and said, "She's left the country," putting an end to Farouk's calls.

At the end of the month, the rent was due. Paul and Heather didn't have enough to cover it. Instead of contacting Sang's parents, he looked up her sister's phone number in London on an old telephone bill. A woman answered, who sounded just like her.

"Sang?"

The phone switched hands, and a man came on the line. "Who is this?"

"This is her housemate in America, in Brookline. Paul. I'm trying to reach Sang."

There was a long pause. After some minutes had passed, he wondered if he ought to hang up and try again. But then the man picked up the phone. He didn't apologize for the delay. "She's indisposed at the moment. I'm sure she'll appreciate your call."

Charles came that weekend to pack up Sang's things. He tossed her clothes into garbage bags, stripped the futon of its sheets, and asked Paul to help him put it out on the sidewalk. Wrapping the framed Indian miniatures in newspaper at the kitchen table, he told Paul he'd talked to Sang on the phone, said that she'd be living in London with her sister through the summer. "You know, I kept telling her to leave him. Can you believe, I never even met the guy?"

Charles loaded up the back of his truck, until all that was left of Sang in the house was the sage and mole paint on the walls of her room, and the hanging plant over the dish drainer. "I guess that's everything," Charles said.

The truck disappeared, but Paul stood a while longer, looking at the houses lining the street. Though Charles was her friend, she had not told him. She had not told Charles that Paul had known for months about Deirdre. That night at Farouk's apartment, after washing up in the bathroom, Sang had got down on all fours and crawled into Farouk's coat closet, weeping uncontrollably, at one point hitting herself with a shoe.

She'd refused to emerge from the closet until the policeman lifted her by the armpits and dragged her forcefully from the apartment, telling Paul to see her home. Tiny pieces of flower petals and leaves were still stuck in her hair. She had taken Paul's hand in the elevator, and all the way back to the house. In the car, she had cried continuously with her head between her knees, not letting go of Paul's hand, gripping it even as he shifted gears. He had put the seatbelt on her; her body had been stiff, unyielding. She seemed to know, without looking up, when they turned in to their road. By then, she had stopped crying. Her nose was running. She wiped it with the back of her hand. A light rain had begun to fall, and within seconds the windows and the windshield seemed covered with scratches, similar to the ones she'd inflicted on herself, the drops beading up in small diagonal lines.

The day Paul passed his exams, two of his professors took him to the Four Seasons bar for a drink. He had many drinks that afternoon, ice-cold Martinis on an unseasonably warm spring day. He drank them quickly on an empty stomach and little sleep the night before, and suddenly he was drunk. He had answered every question, passed with honors the three-hour ordeal. "Let's pretend it never happened," his committee told him, alluding to his previous embarrassment. After they left him, shaking hands a final time, patting him on the back for good measure, he went to the men's room, splashed water on his face. He pressed a plush white towel to his temples, sprayed himself with some cologne from a leather-encased bottle by the sink. Returning to the lobby, the reception desk, the massive bouquets of flowers, the well-dressed guests, the brass carts piled with expensive luggage—all of them had spun round him like a carrousel, then floated one by one in an arc across his vision. For a while, he stood watching these images appearing and fading like fireworks, not wanting them to end. He wanted money all of a sudden, enough of it to march up to the desk and request a room, a big white bed, silence.

Outside, he turned a corner, crossed a street. He walked toward Commonwealth Avenue, so different at this end from the way it was by the university. Here it was an elegant, tree-lined boulevard, flanked by spectacular homes, and benches on which to sit and admire the architecture. The cross streets progressed alphabetically—Berkeley, Clarendon, Dartmouth. He walked slowly, still drunk, looking now and then for a taxi to take him home. At Exeter Street, he noticed a couple on a bench. It was Farouk and a woman, willowy but haggard. Her bony nose was a little too large for her face. Her slim legs were crossed. Her eyes, a limpid turquoise blue, were topped with mascara-coated lashes and she blinked rapidly, as if irritated by a grain of sand.

There was an empty bench across from them. Paul walked to it and sat down. Loosening his tie, he looked directly at Farouk. For this man, Deirdre had called a perfect stranger, made a fool of herself. For this man, Sang would rush from the house, had refused all her suitors. Because the suitors didn't know her, they hadn't had a chance. "It's not love," she used to say. They still called for her now and again, their voices eager, their intentions plain. "Do you know her number in London?" some asked, but Paul had thrown it away. His head tilting this way and that way, he studied Farouk carefully. Paul had lain on top of this man. He had felt those legs, that chest, beneath his own, had smelled his skin and hair and breath. It was a knowledge he shared with Sang and Deirdre, a knowledge each had believed to be her own. Farouk and the woman exchanged glances. Let them, Paul thought, smiling, a quiet snicker escaping him. There was nothing Farouk could do to stop him; not with this new woman at his side. He slouched down, his head against the wood of the bench now, allowing the afternoon sun to warm his body, his face. He was tempted to stretch out. He closed his eyes.

He felt a poke in the side of his arm. It was Farouk, standing in front of him.

"You should be grateful I didn't sue," Farouk said. He spoke precisely yet without rancor, as if he were making casual conversation.

Paul rubbed his eyes behind his glasses, displacing them. "What?"

"You've damaged my shoulder. I had to get an MRI. I may need surgery."

The woman, now standing a few feet behind Farouk, said something Paul was unable to hear.

"He should know," Farouk said to the woman, his voice rising unpleasantly. Then he shrugged, and they walked off together. There was something curious about the way they were walking, together and yet with a space between them. It was only then that Paul noticed a small yellow dog at the end of a very long leash, stretched taut in the woman's hand, pulling her along the path.

PART TWO

HEMA AND
KAUSHIK

Once in a Lifetime

I had seen you before, too many times to count, but a farewell that my family threw for yours, at our house in Inman Square, is when I begin to recall your presence in my life. Your parents had decided to leave Cambridge, not for Atlanta or Arizona, as some other Bengalis had, but to move all the way back to India, abandoning the struggle that my parents and their friends had embarked upon. It was 1974. I was six years old. You were nine. What I remember most clearly are the hours before the party, which my mother spent preparing for everyone to arrive: the furniture was polished, the paper plates and napkins set out on the table, the rooms filled with the smell of lamb curry and pullao and the L'Air du Temps my mother used for special occasions, spraying it first on herself, then on me, a firm squirt that temporarily darkened whatever I was wearing. I was dressed that evening in an outfit that my grandmother had sent from Calcutta: white pajamas with tapered legs and a waist wide enough to gird two of me side by side, a turquoise kurta, and a black velvet vest embroidered with plastic pearls. The three pieces had been arrayed on my parents' bed while I was in the bath, and I stood shivering, my fingertips puckered and white, as my mother threaded a length of thick drawstring through the giant waist of the pajamas with a safety pin, gathering up the stiff material bit by bit and then knotting the drawstring tightly at my stomach. The inseam of the pajamas was stamped with purple letters within a circle, the seal of the textile company. I remember fretting about this fact, wanting to wear something else, but my mother assured me that the seal would come out in the wash, adding that, because of the length of the kurta, no one would notice it anyway.

My mother had more pressing concerns. In addition to the quality and quantity of the food, she was worried about the weather: snow was predicted for later that evening, and this was a time when my parents and their friends didn't own cars. Most of the guests, including you, lived less than a fifteen-minute walk away, either in the neighborhoods behind Harvard and MIT or just across the Mass Avenue Bridge. But some were farther, coming by bus or the T from Malden or Medford or Waltham. "I suppose Dr. Choudhuri can drive people home," she said of your father as she untangled my hair. Your parents were slightly older—seasoned immigrants, as mine were not. They had left India in 1962, before the laws welcoming foreign students changed. While my father and the other men were still taking exams, your father already had a PhD, and he drove a car, a silver Saab with bucket seats, to his job at an engineering firm in Andover. I had been driven home in that car many nights, after parties had gone late and I had fallen asleep in some strange bed or other.

Our mothers met when mine was pregnant. She didn't know it yet; she was feeling dizzy and sat down on a bench in a small park. Your mother was perched on a swing, gently swaying back and forth as you soared above her, when she noticed a young Bengali woman in a sari, wearing vermilion in her hair. "Are you feeling all right?" your mother asked in the polite form. She told you to get off the swing, and then she and you escorted my mother home. It was during that walk that your mother suggested that perhaps mine was expecting. They became instant friends, spending their days together while our fathers were at work. They talked about the lives they had left behind in Calcutta: your mother's beautiful home in Jodhpur Park, with hibiscus and rosebushes blooming on the rooftop, and my mother's modest flat in Maniktala, above a grimy Punjabi restaurant, where seven people existed in three small rooms. In Calcutta they would probably have had little occasion to meet. Your mother went to a convent school and was the daughter of one of Calcutta's most prominent lawyers, a pipe-smoking Anglophile and a member of the Saturday Club. My mother's father was a clerk in the General Post Office, and she had neither eaten at a table nor sat on a commode before coming to America. Those differences were irrelevant in Cambridge, where they were both equally alone. Here they shopped together for groceries and complained about their husbands and cooked at either our stove or yours, dividing up the dishes for our respective families when they were done. They knitted together, switching projects when one of them got bored. When I was born, your parents were the only friends to visit the hospital. I was fed in your old high chair, pushed along the streets in your old pram.

During the party it started snowing, as predicted, stragglers arriving with wet, white-caked coats that we had to hang from the shower curtain rod. For years, my mother talked about how, when the party ended, your father made countless trips to drive people home, taking one couple as far as Braintree, claiming that it was no trouble, that this was his last opportunity to drive the car. In the days before you left, your parents came by again, to bring over pots and pans, small appliances, blankets and sheets, half-used bags of flour and sugar, bottles of shampoo. We continued to refer to these things as your mother's. "Get me Parul's frying pan," my mother would say. Or, "I think we need to turn the setting down on Parul's toaster."

Your mother also brought over shopping bags filled with clothes she thought I might be able to use, that once belonged to you. My mother put the bags away and took them with us when we moved, a few years later, from Inman Square to a house in Sharon, incorporating the clothes into my wardrobe as I grew into them. Mainly they were winter items, things you would no longer need in India. There were thick T-shirts and turtlenecks in navy and brown. I found these clothes ugly and tried to avoid them, but my mother refused to replace them. And so I was forced to wear your sweaters, your rubber boots on rainy days. One winter I had to wear your coat, which I hated so much that it caused me to hate you as a result. It was blue-black with an orange lining and a scratchy grayish-brown trim around the hood. I never got used to having to hook the zipper on the right side, to looking so different from the other girls in my class with their puffy pink and purple jackets. When I asked my parents if I could have a new coat they said no. A coat was a coat, they said. I wanted desperately to get rid of it. I wanted it to be lost. I wished that one of the boys in my class, many of whom owned identical coats, would accidentally pick it up in the narrow alcove where we rushed to put on our things at the end of the day. But my mother had gone so far as to iron a label inside the coat with my name on it, an idea she'd got from her subscription to *Good Housekeeping*.

Once I left it on the school bus. It was a mild late winter day, the windows on the bus open, everybody's outerwear shed on the seats. I was taking a different bus than usual, one that dropped me off in the neighborhood of my piano teacher, Mrs. Hennessey. When the bus neared my stop I stood up, and when I reached the front the driver reminded me to be careful crossing the street. She pulled back the lever that opened the door, letting fragrant air onto the bus. I was about to step off, coatless, but then someone cried out, "Hey, Hema, you forgot this!" I was startled that anyone on that bus knew my name; I had forgotten about the name tag.

By the following year I had outgrown the coat, and to my great relief it was donated to charity. The other items your parents bequeathed to us, the toaster and the crockery and the Teflon pots and pans, were gradually replaced as well, until there was no longer any physical trace of you in the house. For years our families had no contact. The friendship did not merit the same energy my parents devoted to their relatives, buying stacks of aerograms at the post office and sending them off faithfully every week, asking me to write the same three sentences to each set of grandparents at the bottom. My parents spoke of you rarely, and I imagine they assumed that our paths were unlikely to cross again. You'd moved to Bombay, a city far from Calcutta, which my parents and I never visited. And so we did not see you, or hear from you, until the first day of 1981, when your father called us very early in the morning to wish us a happy New Year and say that your family was returning to Massachusetts, where he had a new job. He asked if, until he found a house, you could all stay with us.

For days afterward, my parents talked of nothing else. They wondered what had gone wrong: Had your father's position at Larsen & Toubro, too good to turn down at the time, fallen through? Was your mother no longer able to abide the mess and heat of India? Had they decided that the schools weren't good enough for you there? Back then international calls were kept short. Of course, your family was welcome, my parents said, and marked the date of your arrival on the calendar in our kitchen. Whatever the reason you were coming, I gathered from my parents' talk that it was regarded as a wavering, a weakness. "They should have known it's impossible to go back," they said to their friends, condemning your parents for having failed at both ends. We had stuck it out as immigrants while you had fled; had we been the ones to go back to India, my parents seemed to suggest, we would have stuck it out there as well.

Until your return I'd thought of you as a boy of eight or nine, frozen in time, the size of the clothes I'd inherited. But you were twice that now, sixteen, and my parents thought it best that you occupy my room and that I sleep on a folding cot set up in their bedroom. Your parents would stay in the guest-room, down the hall. My parents often hosted friends who came from New Jersey or New Hampshire for the weekend, to eat elaborate dinners and talk late into the evening about Indian politics. But by Sunday afternoon those guests were always gone. I was accustomed to having children sleep on the floor by my bed, in sleeping bags. Being an only child, I enjoyed this occasional company. But I had never been asked to relinquish my room entirely. I asked my mother why they weren't giving you the folding cot instead of me.

"Where would we put it?" she asked. "We only have three bedrooms."

"Downstairs," I suggested. "In the living room."

"That wouldn't look right," my mother said. "Kaushik must practically be a man by now. He needs his privacy."

"What about the basement?" I said, thinking of the small study my father had built there, lined with metal bookcases.

"That's no way to treat guests, Hema. Especially not these. Dr. Choudhuri and Parul Di were such a blessing when we first had you. They drove us home from the hospital, they brought over food for weeks. Now it's our turn to be helpful."

"What sort of doctor is he?" I asked. Though I had always been in good health, I had an irrational fear of doctors then, and the thought of one living in the house made me nervous, as if his mere presence might make one of us sick.

"He's not a medical doctor. It refers to his PhD."

"Baba has his PhD and no one calls him a doctor," I pointed out.

"When we met, Dr. Choudhuri was the only one. It was our way of paying respect."

I asked how long you would be staying with us—a week? Two? My mother couldn't say; it all depended on how long it took your family to get settled and find a place. The prospect of having to give up my room infuriated me. My feelings were complicated by the fact that, until rather recently, to my great shame, I'd regularly slept with my parents on the cot in their room, and not in the room where I kept my clothes and things. My mother considered the idea of a child sleeping alone a cruel American practice and therefore did not encourage it, even when we had the space. She told me that she had slept in the same bed as her parents until the day she was married and that this was perfectly normal. But I knew that it was not normal, not what my friends at school did, and that they would ridicule me if they knew. The summer before I started middle school, I insisted on sleeping alone. In the beginning my mother kept checking on me during the night, as if I were still an infant who might suddenly stop breathing, asking if I was scared and reminding me that she was just on the other side of the wall. In fact, I was scared that first night; the perfect silence in my room terrified me. But I refused to admit this, for what I feared more was failing at something I should have learned to do at the age of three or four. In the end it was easy; I fell asleep out of sheer anxiety that I would not, and in the morning I woke up alone, squinting in the eastern light my parents' room did not receive.

The house was prepared for your arrival. New throw pillows were purchased for the living-room sofa, bright orange against the brown tweed upholstery. The plants and the curios were rearranged, my school portrait framed and hung above the fire-place. The Christmas cards were taken down from around the front door, where my mother and I had taped them one by one as they came in the mail. My parents, remembering your father's habit of dressing well, bought robes to wear in the mornings, my mother's made of velour, my father's styled like a smoking jacket. One day I came home from school and found that the pink-and-white coverlet on my bed had been replaced by a tan blanket. There were new towels in the bathroom for you and your parents, plusher than the ones we used and a prettier shade of blue. My closet had been weeded, bare hangers left on the rod. I was told to clear out a couple of draw-ers, and I removed enough things so that I would not have to enter the room while you were in it. I took my pajamas, some outfits to wear to school, and the sneakers I needed for gym. I took the library book I was reading, along with the others stacked on my bedside table. I wanted you to see as few of my things as possible, so I cleared away my jewelry box full of cheap tangled chains and my bottles of Avon perfume. I removed the locked diary from my desk drawer, though I'd written only two entries since receiving it for Christmas. I removed the seventh-grade yearbook in which my photograph appeared, the endpapers filled with silly messages from my classmates. It was like deciding which of my possessions I wanted to take on a long trip to India, only this time I was going nowhere. Still, I put my things into a suitcase covered with peeling tags and stickers that had traveled various times back and forth across the world and dragged it into my parents' room.

I studied pictures of your parents; we had a few pasted into an album, taken the night of the farewell party. There was my father, his stiff jet-black hair already a surprise to me by then. He was dressed in a sweater vest, his shirt cuffs rolled back, pointing urgently at something beyond the frame. Your father

was in the suit and tie he always wore, his handsome, bespecta-
cled face leaning toward someone in conversation, his greenish
eyes unlike anyone else's. The middle part in your mother's
hair accentuated the narrow length of her face; the end of her
raw-silk sari was wrapped around her shoulders like a shawl. My
mother stood beside her, a head shorter and more disheveled,
stray hairs hanging by her ears. They both appeared flushed,
the color high in their cheeks, as if from drinking wine, even
though all they ever drank in those days was tap water or tea,
the bond between them clear. There was no evidence of you,
the person I was most curious about. Who knows where you
had lurked in that crowd? I imagine you sat at the desk in the
corner of my parents' bedroom, reading a book you'd brought
with you, waiting for the party to end.

My father went one evening to the airport to greet you. It
was a school night for me. The dining table had been set since
the afternoon. This was my mother's way when she gave parties, though she had never prepared such an elaborate meal in
the middle of the week. An hour before you were expected, she
turned on the oven. She had heated up a panful of oil and
begun to fry thick slices of eggplant to serve with the dal, filling
the room with a haze of smoke, when my father called to say
that though your plane had landed, one of your suitcases had
not arrived. I was hungry by then, but it felt wrong to ask my
mother to open the oven door and pull out all the dishes for my
sake. My mother turned off the oil and I sat with her on the
sofa watching a movie on television, something about the Second World War, in which a group of tired men were walking
across a dark field. Cinema of a certain period was the one thing
my mother loved wholeheartedly about the West. She herself
never wore a skirt—she considered it indecent—but she could
recall, scene by scene, Audrey Hepburn's outfits in any given
movie.

I fell asleep at her side, and the next thing I knew I was

sprawled on the sofa alone, the television turned off, voices filling another part of the house. I stood up, my face hot, my limbs cramped and heavy. You were all in the dining room, eating. Pans of food lined the table, and in addition to the water pitcher there was a bottle of Johnnie Walker that only your parents were drinking, planted between their plates. There was your mother, her slippery dark hair cut to her shoulders, wearing slacks and a tunic, a silk scarf knotted at her neck, looking only vaguely like the woman I'd seen in the pictures. With her bright lipstick and frosted eyelids, she looked less exhausted than my mother did. She had remained thin, her collarbones glamorously protruding, unburdened by the weight of middle age that now padded my mother's features. Your father looked more or less the same, still handsome, still wearing a jacket and tie, a different style of glasses his concession to the new decade. You were pale like your father, long bangs combed over to one side of your face, your eyes distracted yet missing nothing. I had not expected you to be handsome. I had not expected to find you appealing in the least.

"My goodness, Hema, already a lady. You don't remember us, do you?" your mother said. She spoke to me in English, in a pleasant, unhurried way, with a voice that sounded amused. "Come, poor thing, we've kept you waiting. Your mother told us you went hungry because of us."

I sat down, embarrassed that you had seen me asleep on the sofa. Though you had all just flown halfway across the world, it was I who felt weary, despite my nap. My mother served me a plate of food, but her attention was on you and the fact that you were refusing seconds.

"We had dinner before we landed," you replied, a faint accent present in your English, but not the strong accent our parents shared. Your voice had deepened, no longer a child's.

"It's remarkable, the amount of food you get in first class," your mother said. "Champagne, chocolates, even caviar. But I saved room. I remembered your cooking, Shibani," she added.

"First class!" my mother exclaimed, with an intake of breath. "How did you end up there?"

"It was my fortieth birthday gift," your mother explained. She looked over at your father, smiling. "Once in a lifetime, right?"

"Who knows?" he said, clearly proud of the extravagance. "It could become a terrible habit."

Our parents spoke of the old Cambridge crowd, mine telling yours about people's moves and accomplishments, the bachelors who had married, the children who had been born. They spoke about Reagan winning the election, all the ways that Carter had failed. Your parents spoke of Rome, where you'd had a two-day layover to tour the city. Your mother described the fountains, and the ceiling of the Sistine Chapel you had stood three hours in line to see. "So many lovely churches," she said. "Each is like a museum. It made me want to be a Catholic, only to be able to pray in them."

"Do not die before seeing the Pantheon," your father said, and my parents nodded, not knowing what the Pantheon was. I knew—I was, in fact, in the middle of learning about ancient Rome in my Latin class, writing a long report about its art and architecture, all of it based on encyclopedia entries and other books in the school library. Your parents spoke of Bombay and the home you had left behind, a flat on the tenth floor, with a balcony overlooking palm trees and the Arabian Sea. "A pity you didn't visit us there," your mother said. Later, in the privacy of their bedroom, my mother pointed out to my father that we had never been invited.

After dinner I was told to show you the house and where you would sleep. Normally I loved to do this for guests, taking a proprietary pleasure in explaining that this was the broom closet, that the downstairs half-bath. But now I lingered over nothing, for I sensed your boredom. I was also nervous at being sent off with you, disturbed by the immediate schoolgirl attraction I felt. I was used to admiring boys by then, boys in my class who were and would remain unaware of my existence. But never someone as old as you, never someone belonging to the world of my parents. It was you who led me, climbing quickly up the stairs, opening doors, poking your head into rooms, unimpressed by it all.

"This is my room. Your room," I said, correcting myself.

After dreading it all this time, now I was secretly thrilled that you would be sleeping here. You would absorb my presence, I thought. Without my having to do a thing, you would come to know me and like me. You walked across the room to the window, opened it, and leaned out into the darkness, letting cold air into the room.

"Ever go out on the roof?" you asked. You did not wait for me to answer, and the next thing I knew you'd lifted the screen and were gone. I rushed over to the window, and when I leaned outside I couldn't see you. I imagined you slipping on the shingles, falling into the shrubbery, my being blamed for the accident, for standing by stupidly as you did such a brazen thing. "Are you okay?" I called out. The logical thing would have been to say your name, but I felt inhibited and did not. Eventually you came back around, seating yourself on the incline over the garage, gazing down at the lawn.

"What's behind the house?"

"Woods. But you can't go there."

"Who said?"

"Everyone. My parents and all the teachers in school."

"Why not?"

"A boy got lost in them last year. He's still missing." His name was Kevin McGrath, and he'd been two grades behind

me. For a week we'd heard nothing but helicopters, dogs barking, searching for some sign of him.

You did not react to this information. Instead, you asked,
"Why do people have yellow ribbons tied to their mailboxes?"

"They're for the hostages in Iran."

"I bet most Americans had never even heard of Iran before
this," you said, causing me to feel responsible both for my
neighbors' patriotism and for their ignorance.

"What's that thing to the right?"

"A swing set."

The word must have amused you. You faced me and smiled,
though not kindly, as if I'd invented the term.

"I missed the cold," you said. "This cold." The remark
reminded me that none of this was new to you. "And the snow.
When will it snow again?"

"I don't know. There wasn't much snow for Christmas this
year."

You climbed back into the room, disappointed, I feared, by
my lack of information. You glanced at yourself in my white-
framed mirror, your head nearly cut off at the top. "Where's
the bathroom?" you asked, already halfway out the door.

That night, lying on the cot in my parents' room, wide
awake though it was well past midnight, I heard my mother
and father talking in the dark. I worried that perhaps you
would hear them, too. The bed where you slept was just on the
other side of the wall, and if I had been able to stick my hand
through it, I could have touched you. My parents were at once
critical of and intimidated by yours, perplexed by the ways
in which they had changed. Bombay had made them more
American than Cambridge had, my mother said, something she
hadn't anticipated and didn't understand. There were remarks
concerning your mother's short hair, her slacks, the Johnnie
Walker she and your father continued to drink after the meal
was finished, taking it with them from the dining room to the

living room. It was mainly my mother who talked, my father listening and murmuring now and then in tired consent. My parents, who had never set foot in a liquor store, wondered whether they should buy another bottle—at the rate your parents were going, that bottle would be drained by tomorrow, my mother said. She remarked that your mother had become "stylish," a pejorative term in her vocabulary, implying a self-indulgence that she shunned. "Twelve people could have flown for the price of one first-class ticket," she said. My mother's birthdays came and went without acknowledgment by my father. I was the one who made a card and had him sign it with me on the first of every June. Suddenly my mother sat up, sniffing the air. "I smell smoke," she said. My father asked if she had remembered to turn off the oven. My mother said she was certain she had, but she asked him to get up and check.

"It's a cigarette you smell," he said when he came back to bed. "Someone has been smoking in the bathroom."

"I didn't know Dr. Choudhuri smoked," my mother said. "Should we have put out an ashtray?"

In the morning you all slept in, victims of jet lag, reminding us that despite your presence, your bags crowding the hallways, your toothbrushes cluttering the side of the sink, you belonged elsewhere. When I returned from school in the afternoon you were still sleeping, and at dinner—breakfast for you—you all declined the curry we were eating, craving toast and tea. It was like that for the first few days: you were awake when we slept, sleeping when we were awake; we were leading antipodal lives under the same roof. As a result, apart from the fact that I wasn't sleeping in my own room, there was little change. I drank my orange juice and ate my bowl of cereal and went off to the bus stop as usual. I spoke to no one of your arrival; I almost never revealed details of my home life to my American friends. As a child, I had always dreaded my birthdays, when a dozen girls would appear in the house, glimpsing the way we lived. I don't know how I would have referred to you. "A family friend," I suppose.

Then one day I came home from school and found your parents awake, their ankles crossed on top of the coffee table, filling up the sofa where I normally sat to watch *The Brady Bunch* and *Gilligan's Island*. They were chatting with my mother, who was in the recliner with a bowl in her lap, peeling potatoes. Your mother was dressed in a nylon sari of my mother's, purple with red dots in various sizes. Distressing news of your mother's missing suitcase had come: it had been located in Rome but had been placed on a flight to Johannesburg. I remember thinking that the sari looked better on your mother than on mine; the intense purple shade was more flattering against her skin. I was told that you were outside in the yard. I did not go out to look for you. Instead I practiced the piano. It was nearly dark by the time you came in, accepting the tea that I was still too young to drink. Your parents drank tea as well, but by six o'clock the bottle of Johnnie Walker was on the coffee table, as it would be every night that you stayed with us. You had gone out in only a pullover, your father's costly camera slung around your neck. Your face showed the effects of the cold, your eyes blazing, the borders of your ears crimson, your skin glowing from within.

"There's a stream back there," you said, "in those woods."

My mother became nervous then, warning you not to go there, as she had so often warned me, as I had warned you the night you came, but your parents did not share her concern. What had you photographed? they asked instead.

"Nothing," you replied, and I took it personally that nothing had inspired you. The suburbs were new to you and to your parents. Whatever memories you possessed of America were of Cambridge, a place that I could only dimly recall.

You took your tea and disappeared to my room as if it were yours, emerging only when summoned for dinner. You ate quickly, not speaking, then returned upstairs. It was your parents who paid me court, who asked me questions and complimented me on my manners, on my piano playing, on all the things I did to help my mother around the house. "Look, Kaushik, how Hema makes her lunch," your mother would say as I prepared a ham or turkey sandwich after dinner and put it in a paper bag to take to school the next day. I was still very much a child, while you, just three years older, had already eluded your parents' grasp. You did not argue with them and yet you did not seem to talk to them very much, either. While you were outside I'd heard them tell my mother how unhappy you were to be back. "He was furious that we left, and now he's furious that we're here again," your father said. "Even in Bombay we managed to raise a typical American teenager."

I did my homework at the dining table, unable to use the desk in my room. I worked on my ancient Rome report, something that had interested me until your arrival. Now it seemed silly, given that you'd been there. I longed to work on it in privacy, but your father talked to me at length about the structural aspects of the Colosseum. His civil engineer's explanations went over my head, were irrelevant to my needs, but to be polite I listened. I worried that he would want to see whether I had incorporated the things he said, but he never bothered me about that. He hunted through his bags and showed me postcards he'd purchased, and though it had nothing to do with my report, he gave me a ten-lire coin.

When the worst of your jet lag had subsided we went to the mall in my parents' station wagon. Your mother needed bras, one item that she could not borrow from my voluptuous mother. At the mall our fathers sat together in a sunken area of benches and potted plants, waiting, and you were given some money and allowed to wander off while I accompanied our mothers to the lingerie department in Jordan Marsh. Your mother led us there, with the credit card your father had handed to her before they parted. Normally we went to Sears. On her way to the bras she bought black leather gloves and a pair of boots that zipped to the knee, never looking at the price before taking something off the shelf. In the lingerie department it was me the saleswoman approached. "We have lovely training models, just in," she said to your mother, believing that I was her daughter.

"Oh, no, she's far too young," my mother said.

"But look, how sweet," your mother said, fingering the style the saleswoman presented on a hanger, lacy white with a rosebud at its center. I had yet to get my period and, unlike many of the girls at school, still wore flower-printed undershirts. I was ushered into the fitting room, your mother watching approvingly as I took off my coat and sweater and tried on the bra. She adjusted the straps and attached the hook at the back. She tried things on as well, topless beside me without shame, though it embarrassed me to see her large, plum-colored nipples, the surprising droop of her breasts, the dark patches of underarm hair that gave off a faintly acrid but not altogether unpleasant smell. "Perfect," your mother said, running her finger below the elastic, along my skin, adding, "I hope you know that you're going to be very beautiful one day." Despite my mother's protests, your mother bought me my first three bras, insisting that they were a gift. On the way out, at the makeup counter, she bought a lipstick, a bottle of perfume, and an assortment of expensive creams that promised to firm her throat and brighten her eyes; she was uninterested in the Avon products my mother used. The reward for her purchases at the makeup counter was a large red tote bag. This she gave to me, thinking that it would be useful for my books, and the next day I took it to school.

. . .

After a week your father began his new job, at an engineering firm forty miles away. At first my father got up early and dropped him off before returning to Northeastern to teach his economics classes. Then your father bought an Audi with a stick shift. You stayed home with our mothers—your parents wanted to wait until they'd bought their home to see which school you would go to. I was stunned, and envious—half a year without school! To my added chagrin, you were not expected to do anything around the house, never to return your plate or glass to the sink, never to make my bed, which I would see from time to time through the partly open door to my room in a state of total disarray, the blanket on the floor, your clothes heaped on my white desk. You ate enormous amounts of fruit, whole bunches of grapes, apples to their cores, a practice that fascinated me. I did not eat fresh fruit then; the textures and intensity of flavors made me gag. You complained about the taste, or lack of taste, but nevertheless decimated whatever my parents brought home from Star Market. I would find you, when I came home in the afternoons, always at the same end of the sofa, the toes of your thin bare feet hooked around the edge of the coffee table, reading books by Isaac Asimov that you'd picked off my father's shelves in the basement. I hated *Doctor Who,* the one show you liked on television.

I did not know what to make of you. Because you'd lived in India, I associated you more with my parents than with me. And yet you were unlike my cousins in Calcutta, who seemed so innocent and obedient when I visited them, asking questions about my life in America as if it were the moon, astonished by every detail. You were not curious about me in the least. One day a friend at school invited me to see *The Empire Strikes Back* on a Saturday afternoon. My mother said that I could go, but only if you were invited as well. I protested, telling her that my friend did not know you. Despite my crush, I didn't want to have to explain to my friend who you were and why you were living in our house.

"You know him," my mother said.

"But he doesn't even like me," I complained.

"Of course he likes you," my mother said, blind to the full implication of what I'd said. "He's adjusting, Hema. It's something you've never had to go through."

The conversation ended there. As it turned out, you were uninterested in the movie, not having seen *Star Wars* in the first place.

One day I found you sitting at my piano, randomly striking the keys with your index finger. You stood up when you saw me and retreated to the couch.

"Do you hate it here?" I asked.

"I liked living in India," you said. I did not betray my opinion, that I found trips to India dull, that I didn't like the geckos that clung to the walls in the evenings, poking in and out of the fluorescent light fixtures, or the giant cockroaches that sometimes watched me as I bathed. I didn't like the comments my relatives made freely in my presence—that I had not inherited my mother's graceful hands, that my skin had darkened since I was a child.

"Bombay is nothing like Calcutta," you added, as if reading my mind.

"Is it close to the Taj Mahal?"

"No." You looked at me carefully, as if fully registering my presence for the first time. "Haven't you ever looked at a map?"

On our trip to the mall you'd bought a record, something by the Rolling Stones. The jacket was white, with what seemed to be a cake on it. You had no interest in the few records I owned—Abba, Shaun Cassidy, a disco compilation I'd ordered from a TV commercial with my allowance money. Nor were you willing to play your album on the plastic record player in my room. You opened up the cabinet where my father kept his turntable and receiver. My father was extremely particular about his stereo components. They were off-limits to me, and even to my mother. The stereo had been the single extravagant purchase of his life. He cleaned everything himself, wiping the parts with a special cloth on Saturday mornings, before listening to his collection of Indian vocalists.

"You can't touch that," I said.

You turned around. The lid of the player was already lifted, the record revolving. You held the arm of the needle, resting its weight on your finger. "I know how to play a record," you said, no longer making an effort to conceal your irritation. And then you let the needle drop.

How bored you must have been in my room full of a girl's things. It must have driven you crazy, being stuck with our mothers all day long as they cooked and watched soap operas. Really, it was my mother who did the cooking now. Though your mother kept her company, occasionally peeling or slicing something, she was no longer interested in cooking, as she had been in the Cambridge days. She'd been spoiled by Zareen, the fabulous Parsi cook you had in Bombay, she said. From time to time she would promise to make us an English trifle, the one thing she said she always insisted on making herself, but this didn't materialize. She continued to borrow saris from my mother and went to the mall to buy herself more sweaters and trousers. Her missing suitcase never arrived, and she accepted this fact calmly, saying that it gave her an excuse to buy new things, but your father battled on her behalf, making a series of irate phone calls to the airline before finally letting the matter go.

You were in the house as little as possible, walking in the cold weather through the woods and along streets where you were the only pedestrian. I spotted you once, while I was on the school bus coming home, shocked at how far you'd gone. "You're going to get sick, Kaushik, always wandering outside like that," my mother said. She continued to speak to you in Bengali, despite your consistently English replies. It was your mother who came down with a cold, using this as an excuse to stay in bed for days. She refused the food my mother made for the rest of us, requesting only canned chicken broth. You walked to the minimart a mile from our house, bringing back the broth and issues of *Vogue* and *Harper's Bazaar*. "Go ask Parul Mashi if she wants tea," my mother said one afternoon, and I headed upstairs to the guestroom. On my way I needed to use the bathroom. There was your mother, wrapped up in a robe, perched morosely on the edge of the bathtub, legs crossed, smoking a cigarette.

"Oh, Hema!" she cried out, nearly falling into the tub, so startled that she crushed the cigarette against the porcelain and not into the tiny stainless-steel ashtray she held cupped in her palm, and which she must have brought with her from Bombay.

"I'm sorry," I said, turning to leave.

"No, no, please, I was just going," she said. I watched as she flushed away the cigarette, rinsed her mouth at the sink, and applied fresh lipstick, blotting it with a Kleenex, which then fluttered into the garbage pail. Apart from her bindi, my mother did not wear makeup, and I observed your mother's ritual with care, all the more impressed that she would go to such lengths when she was unwell and spending most of her day in bed. She looked into the mirror intently, without evasion. The brief application of lipstick seemed to restore the composure that my sudden appearance had caused her to lose. She caught me looking at her reflection and smiled. "One cigarette a day can't kill me, can it?" she said brightly. She opened the window, pulled some perfume out of her cosmetics bag, and sprayed the air. "Our little secret, Hema?" she said, less a question than a command, and left, shutting the door behind her.

In the evenings we sometimes went house-hunting with you. We took the station wagon; the beautiful car your father had bought could not comfortably accommodate us all. My father drove, hesitantly, to unknown neighborhoods where the lawns were all a little bigger than ours, the houses spaced a little farther apart. Your parents searched first in Lexington and Concord, where the schools were best. Some of the homes we saw were empty, others full of the current occupants and their possessions. None, according to the conversations I overheard at night as I tried to fall asleep, were the sort my parents could afford. They stepped to the side as your parents discussed asking prices with the real estate agents. But it wasn't money that stood in the way. The houses themselves were the problem, the light scant, the ceilings low, the rooms awkward, your parents always concluded, as we drove back to our house. Unlike my parents, yours had opinions about design, preferring something contemporary, excited when we happened to pass a white boxlike structure obscured by a thicket of tall trees. They sought an in-ground pool, or space to build one; your mother missed swimming at her club in Bombay. "Water views, that's what we should look for," your mother said, while reading the classified section of the Globe one afternoon, and this limited the search even further. We drove out to Swampscott and Duxbury to see properties overlooking the ocean, and to houses in the woods with views of private lakes. Your parents made an offer on a house in Beverly, but after a second visit they withdrew the bid, your mother saying that the layout was ungenerous.

My parents felt slighted by your parents' extravagant visions, ashamed of the modest home we owned. "How uncomfortable you must be here," they said, but your parents never complained, as mine did, nightly, before falling asleep. "I didn't expect it to take this long," my mother said, noting that almost a month had gone by. While you were with us there was no room for anyone else. "The Dasguptas wanted to visit next weekend and I had to say no," my mother said. Again and again I heard how much your parents had changed, how we'd unwittingly opened our home to strangers. There were complaints about how your mother did not help clean up after dinner, how she went to bed whenever it suited her and slept close to lunchtime. My mother said that your father was too indulgent, too solicitous of your mother, always asking if she needed a fresh drink, bringing down a cardigan if she was cold.

"She's the reason they're still here," my mother said. "She won't settle for anything less than a palace."

"It's no easy task," my father said diplomatically, "starting a new job, a new way of life all over again. My guess is she didn't want to leave, and he's trying to make up for that."

"You would never put up with that sort of behavior in me."

"Let it go," my father said, turning away from her and tucking the covers under his chin. "It's not forever. They'll leave soon enough and then all our lives will go back to normal."

Somewhere, in that cramped house, a line was drawn between our two families. On one side was the life we'd always led, my parents taking me to Star Market every Thursday night, treating me to McDonald's afterward. Every Sunday I studied for my weekly spelling test, my father quizzing me after *60 Minutes* was over. Your family began to do things independently as well. Sometimes your father would come home from work early and take your mother out, either to look at properties or to shop at the mall, where slowly and methodically she began to buy all the things she would need to set up her own household: sheets, blankets, plates and glasses, small appliances. They would come home with bags and bags, amassing them in our basement, sometimes showing my mother the things they'd bought, sometimes not bothering. On Fridays your parents often took us out to dinner, to one of the overpriced mediocre restaurants in town. They enjoyed the change of pace, having mysteriously acquired a taste for things like steak and baked potatoes, while my parents had not. The outings were intended to give my mother a break from cooking, but she complained about these, too.

I was the only one who didn't mind your staying with us. In my quiet, complicated way I continued to like you, was happy simply to observe you day after day. And I liked your parents, your mother especially; the attention I got from her almost made up for what I didn't get from you. One day your father developed the photographs from your stay in Rome. I enjoyed seeing the prints, holding them carefully by the edges. The pictures were almost all of you and your mother, posing in piazzas or sitting on the edge of fountains. There were two shots of Trajan's Column, nearly identical. "Take one for your report," your father said, handing me one. "That should impress your teacher."

"But I wasn't there."

"No matter. Say your uncle went to Rome and took a snap for you."

You were in the picture, standing to one side. You were looking down, your face obscured by a visor. You could have been anyone, one of the many passing tourists in the frame, but it bothered me that you were there, your presence threatening to expose the secret attraction I felt and still hoped would be acknowledged somehow. You had successfully wiped away all the other crushes I harbored at school, so that I thought only of being at home, and of where in the course of the afternoon and evening our paths might intersect, whether or not you would bother to glance at me at the dinner table. Long hours were devoted, lying on the cot in my parents' room, to imagining you kissing me. I was too young, too inexperienced, to contemplate anything beyond that. I accepted the picture and pasted it into my report, but not before cutting the part with you away. That bit I kept, hidden among the blank pages of my diary, locked up for years.

Your wish for snow had not been granted since you'd arrived. There were brief flurries now and again, but nothing stuck to the ground. Then one day snow began to fall, barely visible at first, gathering force as the afternoon passed, an inch or so coating the streets by the time I rode the bus home from school. It was not a dangerous storm, but significant enough to break up the monotony of winter. My mother, in a cheerful mood that evening, decided to cook a big pot of khichuri, which she typically made when it rained, and for a change your mother insisted on helping, standing in the kitchen deep-frying pieces of potato and cauliflower, melting sticks of butter in a saucepan for ghee. She also decided that she wanted, finally, to make the long-promised trifle, and when my mother told her that there weren't enough eggs your father went to get them, along with the other ingredients she needed. "It won't be ready until midnight," she said as she beat together hot milk and eggs over the stove, allowing me to take over for her when she tired of the task. "It needs at least four hours to set."

"Then we can have it for breakfast," you said, breaking off a piece of the pound cake she'd sliced, stuffing it into your mouth. You seldom set foot in the kitchen, but that evening you hovered there, excited by the promise of trifle, which I gathered you loved and which I had never tasted.

After dinner we crowded into the living room, watching the news as the snow continued to fall, excited to learn that my school would be closed and my father's classes canceled the next day. "You take the day off, too," your mother said to your father, and to everyone's surprise he agreed.

"It reminds me of the winter we left Cambridge," your father said. He and your mother were sipping their Johnnie Walker, and that night, though my mother still refused, my father agreed to join them for a small taste. "That party you had for us," your father continued, turning to my parents. "Remember?"

"Seven years ago," my mother said. "It was another life, back then." They spoke of how young you and I had been, how much younger they had all been.

"Such a lovely evening," your mother recalled, her voice betraying a sadness that all of them seemed to share. "How different things were."

In the morning icicles hung from our windows and a foot of snow blanketed the ground. The trifle, which we had been too tired to wait for the night before, emerged for breakfast along with toast and tea. It was not what I'd expected, the hot mixture I'd helped beat on the stove now cold and slippery, but you devoured bowl after bowl; your mother finally put it away, fearing that you would get a stomachache. After breakfast our fathers took turns with the shovel, clearing the driveway. When the wind had settled I was allowed to go outside. Usually, I made snowmen alone, scrawny and lopsided, my parents complaining, when I asked for a carrot, that it was a waste of food. But this time you joined me, touching the snow with your bare hands, studying it, looking happy for the first time since you arrived. You packed a bit of it into a ball and tossed it in my direction. I ducked out of the way, and then threw one at you, hitting you in the leg, aware of the camera hanging around your neck.

"I surrender," you said, raising your arms. "This is beautiful," you added, looking around at our lawn, which the snow had transformed. I felt flattered, though I had nothing to do with the weather. You began walking toward the woods and I hesitated. There was something you wanted to show me there, you said. Covered in snow on that bright blue-skied day, the bare branches of the trees concealing so little, it seemed safe. I did not think of the boy, lost there and never found. From time to time you stopped, focusing your camera on something, never asking me to pose. We walked a long way, until I no longer heard the sounds of snow being shoveled, no longer saw our house. I didn't realize at first what you were doing, getting on your knees and pushing away the snow. Underneath was a rock of some sort. And then I saw that it was a tombstone. You uncovered a row of them, flat on the ground. I began to help you, unburying the buried, using my mittened hands at first, then my whole arm. They belonged to people named Simonds, a family of six. "They're all here together," you said. "Mother, father, four children."

"I never knew this was here."

"I doubt anyone does. It was buried under leaves when I first found it. The last one, Emma, died in 1923."

I nodded, disturbed by the similarity of the name to mine, wondering if this had occurred to you.

"It makes me wish we weren't Hindu, so that my mother could be buried somewhere. But she's made us promise we'll scatter her ashes into the Atlantic."

I looked at you, confused, and so you continued, explaining that there was cancer in her breast, spreading through the rest of her body. That was why you had left India. It was not so much for treatment as it was to be left alone. In India people knew she was dying, and had you remained there, inevitably, friends and family would have gathered at her side in your beautiful seaside apartment, trying to shield her from something she could not escape. Your mother, not wanting to be suffocated by the attention, not wanting her parents to witness her decline, had asked your father to bring you all back to America. "She's been seeing a new doctor at Mass General. That's where my father often takes her when they say they're going to see houses. She's going to have surgery in the spring, but it's only to buy her a little more time. She doesn't want anyone here to know. Not until the end."

The information fell between us, as shocking as if you'd struck me in the face, and I began to cry. At first the tears fell silently, sliding over my nearly frozen face, but then I started sobbing, becoming ugly in front of you, my nose running in the cold, my eyes turning red. I stood there, my hands wedged up under my cheekbones to catch the tears, mortified that you were witnessing such a pathetic display. Though you had never taken a picture of me in your life, I was afraid that you would lift the camera and capture me that way. Of course, you did nothing, you said nothing; you had said enough. You remained where you were, looking down at the tombstone of Emma Simonds, and eventually, when I calmed down, you began to walk back to our yard. I followed you along the path you had discovered, and then we parted, neither of us a comfort to the other, you shoveling the driveway, I going inside for a hot shower, my red puffy face assumed by our mothers to be a consequence of the cold. Perhaps you believed that I was crying for you, or for your mother, but I was not. I was too young, that day, to feel sorrow or sympathy. I felt only the enormous fear of having a dying woman in our home. I remembered standing beside your mother, both of us topless in the fitting room where I tried on my first bra, disturbed that I had been in such close proximity to her disease. I was furious that you had told me, and that you had not told me, feeling at once burdened and betrayed, hating you all over again.

Two weeks later, you were gone. Your parents bought a house on the North Shore, which had been designed by a well-known Massachusetts architect. It had a perfectly flat roof and whole walls of glass. The upstairs rooms were arranged off an interior balcony, the ceiling in the living room soaring to twenty feet. There were no water views but there was a pool for your mother to swim in, just as she had wanted. Your first night there, my mother brought food over so that your mother would not have to cook, not realizing what a favor this was. We admired the house and the property, the echoing, empty rooms that would soon be filled with sickness and grief. There was a bedroom with a skylight; underneath it, your mother told us, she planned to position her bed. It was all to give her two years of pleasure. When my parents finally learned the news and went to the hospital where your mother was dying, I revealed nothing about what you'd told me. In that sense I remained loyal. Our parents were only acquaintances by then, having gone their separate ways after the weeks of forced intimacy. Your mother had promised to have us over in the summer to swim in the pool, but as her health declined, more quickly than the doctors had predicted, your parents shut down, still silent about her illness, seldom entertaining. For a time my mother and father continued to complain, feeling snubbed. "After all we did for them," they said before drifting off to sleep. But I was back in my own room by then, on the other side of the wall, in the bed where you had slept, no longer hearing them.

Year's End

I did not attend my father's wedding. I did not even know there had been a wedding until my father called early one Sunday during my final year at Swarthmore. I was roused from sleep by a fist pounding on my door, followed by the voice of one of my hallmates saying my last name. I knew before answering that it was my father; there was no one else who would have called me before nine. My father had always been an early riser, believing that the hours between five and seven were the most profitable part of the day. He would use that time to read the newspaper and then go for a walk, along Marine Drive when we lived in Bombay and on the quiet roads of our town on the North Shore, and as much as he used to encourage my mother and me to join him I knew he preferred being alone. Things were different now, of course; those solitary hours he'd once savored had become a prison for him, a commonplace. I knew that he no longer bothered to go for walks and that since my mother's death he hardly slept at all. I had not spoken to my father in several weeks. He had been in Calcutta, visiting my grandparents, all four of whom were still alive, and when I picked up the phone, left for me hanging upside down by its cord, I expected him to say only that he had returned safely to Massachusetts, not that I now had a stepmother and two stepsisters.

"I must tell you something that will upset you," he began, and I wondered if perhaps one of my grandparents had fallen ill, if my mother's parents, in particular, could no longer endure the loss of their only daughter at the age of forty-two. It had been the hardest thing, in those first months after she was gone: having to go to Calcutta with my father and enter the home where my mother had been a girl, having to see the man and woman who had raised her, who had known her and loved her long before my father and I did. My grandparents had already lived in a state of mild mourning since 1962, when my parents were married. Occasionally my mother would return to them, first from Boston and then Bombay, like Persephone in the myth, temporarily filling up and brightening the rooms, scattering her creams and powders on the dressing table, sipping tea from cups she'd known since she was a girl, sleeping in the room where she'd been small. After we called my grandparents from Massachusetts to tell them my mother was dead, they had held on to the hope that it was only a matter of time, and that she would board a plane and walk through the door once again. Even after my father and I entered the house, my grandmother asked if my mother was still in the taxi that had already driven away, this in spite of the fact that a photograph of my mother, larger than life and draped with a tuberose garland, hung on their living-room wall. "She's not with us, Didun," I said, and it was only then both my grandparents broke down, grieving freshly for my mother as neither my father nor I had done. Being with her through her illness day after day had denied us that privilege.

But my grandparents were fine, my father reported now. They missed me and sent their love, he said, and then he told me about Chitra. She had lost her spouse two years ago, not to cancer but encephalitis. Chitra was a schoolteacher and, at thirty-five, nearly twenty years younger than my father. Her daughters were seven and ten. He offered these details as if responding diligently to questions I was not asking. "I don't ask you to care for her, even to like her," my father said. "You are a grown man, you have no need for her in your life as I do. I only ask, eventually, that you understand my decision." It was clear to me that he had prepared himself for my outrage—harsh words, accusations, the slamming down of the phone. But no turbulent emotion passed through me as he spoke, only a diluted version of the nauseating sensation that had taken hold the day in Bombay that I learned my mother was dying, a sensation that had dropped anchor in me and never fully left.

"Is she there with you?" I asked. "Would you like me to say something?" I said this more as a challenge than out of politeness, not entirely believing him. Since my mother's death, I frequently doubted things my father said in the course of our telephone conversations: that he had eaten dinner on any given night, for example, at the Italian restaurant he usually took me to when I went home, and not simply polished off another can of almonds and a few Johnnie Walkers in front of the television.

"They arrive in two weeks. You will see them when you come home for Christmas," my father said, adding, "Her English is not so good."

"Worse than my Bengali?"

"Possibly. She will pick it up, of course."

I didn't say what came to my lips, that my mother had learned English as a girl, that she'd had no need to pick it up in America.

"The girls are better at it," my father continued. "They've gone to English-medium schools. I've enrolled them in their grades to start in January."

He had known Chitra just a few weeks, had met her only twice before their marriage. It was a registry wedding followed by a small dinner at a hotel. "The whole thing was arranged by relatives," he explained, in a way that suggested that he was not to blame. This remark upset me more than anything my father had said so far. My father was not a malleable man, and I knew that no one would have dared to find him a new wife unless he had requested it.

"I was tired, Kaushik," he said. "Tired of coming home to an empty house every night."

I didn't know which was worse—the idea of my father's remarrying for love, or of his actively seeking out a stranger for companionship. My parents had had an arranged marriage, but there was a touch of romance about it, too, my father seeing my mother for the first time at a wedding and being so attracted that he had asked, the following week, for her hand. They had always been affectionate with one another, but it wasn't until her illness that he seemed fully, recklessly, to fall in love with her, so that I was witness to a courtship that ought to have faded before I was born. He doted on her then, arriving home at our Bombay flat with flowers, lingering in bed with her in the mornings, going in late to work, wanting to be alone with her to the point where I, a teenager, felt in the way.

"I thought," he continued, "since your bedroom is a good size, of putting the girls together there. Would you mind terribly staying in the guestroom when you visit, Kaushik? Most of your things are with you now anyway. It is just a matter of where to sleep. But please tell me if you mind." He seemed more concerned about my reaction to a new room than the fact that I had just acquired a new family.

"It's fine."

"You are being honest?"

"I said I don't mind."

I returned to my dorm room. There was a girl in my bed that morning; she had remained asleep as I pulled on my clothes and stumbled barefoot into the hallway to answer the phone. Now she was lying on her stomach, a pen in her hand, finishing a crossword I'd abandoned. Her name was Jessica, and I'd met her in my Spanish class.

"Who was that?" she asked, turning to look at me. Strong sunlight angled in from the window behind her, darkening her to the point that her features were obscured.

"My father," I said, squeezing back into the bed beside her. For a while she continued pondering the puzzle as I lay curled at her side, the unfamiliar smell of her still thrilling. She knew nothing about my family, about my father's recent visit to Calcutta or about my mother's death the summer before I started college. In the course of our few weekends together I had told Jessica none of those things. That morning, after crying briefly against her body, I did.

After my exams I drove to Massachusetts, dropping off Jessica on the way at her parents' farmhouse in Connecticut. When I decided to attend Swarthmore my father gave me the Audi he'd bought after we moved back from Bombay. He said that it would make it easier for me to come home from Pennsylvania during weekends and holidays, but I knew it was really an excuse to get rid of yet another thing my mother had touched, known, or otherwise occupied. The day we came back from the hospital for the last time, he took every single photograph of her, in frames and in albums, and put them in a shoebox. "Choose a few, I know pictures are important to you," he told me, and then he sealed the box with tape and put it in a closet somewhere. He had wasted no time giving away her clothes, her handbags, her boxes of cosmetics and colognes. That is probably the last time I remember you from that period, you and your mother coming to the house one day and spending an afternoon going through my mother's drawers as many others already had, fingering her things, lifting her sweaters and shawls to their chests to see if they would flatter them, testing to see if Chanel No. Five would react as favorably with their skin. The items you and your mother and the other Bengali women had no need for were sent to charities in India, as there was nowhere in New England to donate all those saris with their matching blouses and petticoats. This was according to my mother's instructions. "I don't want all that beautiful material turned into curtains," she'd told us from her hospital bed. Her ashes were tossed from a boat off the Gloucester coast that a coworker of my father's, Jim Skillings, had arranged for, but her gold went back to Calcutta, distributed to poor women who had worked for my extended family as ayahs or cooks or maids.

It didn't matter to me that her things were gone. After Bombay she had little occasion to wear jewels and saris, saying no to most of the parties she and my father were invited to. Coming home from school toward the end, I would find her sitting wrapped in a blanket, looking out at the pool she no longer had strength to swim in. Sometimes I would take her outside for fresh air, walking carefully through the birches and pines behind the house and sitting with her on a low stone wall. Occasionally, feeling ambitious, she would ask me to drive her to the sea. "Be sure to keep my ruby choker and the pearl and emerald set for the person you will marry," she said during one of these walks. "I'm not planning on getting married any time soon," I told her, and she said that she wished she could say the same for dying. Ultimately, I disobeyed her. After she was gone I was unable to open up and examine the contents of all those flat red boxes she'd kept hidden in a suitcase on her closet shelf, never mind set something aside for the sake of my future happiness.

Late in the afternoon I climbed the road that led to our driveway. Our house was the only source of light for miles, amid isolated patches of hardened snow. It was not an easy, typically inviting place. Stone steps had been built into the uneven ground, flanked by overgrown rhododendrons leading to the entrance. I saw from the other car in the driveway that my father was home, and he stood behind the storm door, waiting for me to come in with my things.

"We were expecting you earlier," he said. "You said you would be here by lunchtime."

I knew then that it was true, that there was another person inside the house, a person who made it possible for my father, without hesitating, to say "We" instead of "I." I said nothing about my detour to Jessica's home and the two hours I'd spent there. Instead I said the traffic had been bad. I wondered if my father had left work early for my sake, or if perhaps he had not gone into the office that day. I could not tell from his appearance. He had given up wearing suits and was dressed as he might be for the weekend, in dark blue pants and a cream-colored sweater. There was more gray in his hair than I remembered, and though he was still vigorously handsome, old age was creeping into his face, the skin sagging at the sides of his nose, his pale greenish eyes—a trait that made my mother insist that there was Irish blood on his side of the family—less curious than they had once been. I tried to imagine him, just weeks before, in a silk kurta, a groom's topor on his head. I wondered who had taken photographs of the wedding, whether my father would show them to me.

I was unused, stepping into the house, to the heavy smell of cooking that was in the air. Otherwise things appeared unchanged, the black-and-white photographs I'd taken of the surrounding woods, which my mother had insisted on framing, still lining one wall of the entryway. The house had always maintained an impersonal quality, full of built-in cupboards concealing the traces of our everyday lives. Now that I no longer lived there I was astonished by how enormous it was, the soaring double-height ceiling of the living room and the great wall of glass looking out onto the trees, more befitting of an institution than a private home. There was a window-seat running along the length of the glass wall, enough space for twenty people to sit side by side, as they had during my mother's funeral.

As soon as I removed my coat, my father hung it in a cupboard, then led me to the dining table. My mother had insisted on furnishing the house with pieces true to its Modernist architecture: a black leather sectional configured in a U, a chrome floor lamp arcing overhead, a glass-topped kidney-shaped cocktail table, and a dining table made of white fiber-glass surrounded by matching chairs. She had never allowed a cloth to cover the table, but one was there now, some-thing with an Indian print that could just as easily have been a bedspread and didn't fully reach either end. In the center, instead of the generous cluster of fresh fruit or flowers my mother would have arranged, there was a stainless-steel plate holding an ordinary salt shaker and two jars of pickles, hot mango and sweet lime, their lids missing, their labels stained, spoons stuck into their oils. A single place had been set for me at one end, with translucent luchis piled on a plate, and sev-eral smaller bowls containing dal and vegetables arrayed in a semicircle.

"Sit down," my father said. "You must be hungry." He was nervous, as I was. There was no drink in his hand, no bottle of Johnnie Walker set out, as it usually was by this time, on the cocktail table.

I remained standing, uninterested in the food, staring down at the table. I was no longer accustomed to Indian food. At school I ate in the cafeteria, and during my time at home after my mother's death my father and I either went out or picked up pizzas, so that the impressive gas stove that my mother was so excited about when we moved in, with the inset grill where she said she would make kebabs, was used only to boil water for tea. I looked above the table at one corner of the ceiling and saw that it was discolored by a leak.

"When did that happen?" I asked.

"A while back."

"Aren't you going to fix it?" My father, sensitive to how buildings were put together, had always been particular about that sort of thing.

"It's a big project," he said. "There's a reason roofs should be sloped in this part of the world."

I heard no voices or footsteps, no sound of cooking or water running in the kitchen. It was as if Chitra and her daughters were discreetly hidden in one of the many cupboards of the house, swallowed up as so many other things were. "Where are they?" I asked finally.

She appeared then, walking through the swinging doors that led to the kitchen. She was closer to my age than my father's. I had known this beforehand, but seeing her was a shock. Her hair was long and dark and she had a broad nose on an otherwise pleasant face, though it was too round for me to find beautiful. She was taller than I expected her to be, a little taller than my mother. She wore vermilion in her hair, a traditional practice my mother had shunned, the powdery red stain the strongest element of her appearance.

"I would like for you to call me Mamoni," she said in Bengali. Her voice was of a lower pitch than my mother's, with a faint huskiness that was oddly calming. "Do you have any objection to that?" She asked this kindly, smiling, wary of my reaction, and I shook my head, not smiling back.

"Please," she said, this time in English, motioning to the chair.

I turned to my father and asked, "Aren't we all eating?"

"We already have." Chitra said, switching back to Bengali. "You have driven from so far. More is coming."

She returned abruptly to the kitchen and I sat down. My mouth watered, in spite of my reluctance to eat, and I was suddenly grateful for the vast amount of food in front of me. The last thing I'd eaten was a slice of fruitcake baked by Jessica's mother, whom I'd met in the course of dropping Jessica off. It was a delicious cake and Jessica's mother cut off some extra pieces for me, wrapping them in foil for the road, but I had forgotten them on the coffee table in their living room, distracted after Jessica kissed me on the four-poster bed of her childhood room.

"Start, Kaushik," my father said, sitting down in a chair beside me. "It's getting cold."

The arrangement of the bowls, small glass bowls in which we normally had ice cream, felt too formal to me. This was the old-fashioned, ceremonious way I remembered my grandfathers eating in Calcutta, being treated each day like kings after their morning baths. I wondered what was the best way to go about it, whether to take a spoonful of each dish as I went or to dump everything onto the plate at once. In the meantime I ate the luchis, still warm and impressively puffed, on their own. I was reminded of Sunday mornings in Bombay, eating luchis prepared by our Parsi cook, Zareen. I could hear my mother complaining cheerfully in the kitchen, telling Zareen to try another batch, that she was frying them before the oil was hot enough.

When Chitra returned she was followed by her daughters, two girls who at first glance, apart from a few inches in height, were indistinguishable. They were overdressed in our comfortably heated house, in thick sweaters and socks, incongruous Indian things that would soon be rejected, I knew, in favor of clothes from the mall. The sweaters were made of the same sickeningly bright shade of pink wool. The girls did not resemble Chitra very strongly. They were darker and sweeter-looking, with heart-shaped faces and two black ponytails on either side of their heads, adorned with red ribbons.

"Would you like some of this?" I asked, pointing to the luchis still on my plate, and to my surprise they stepped forward and both put out a hand, cupping their giggling mouths with the other. I saw that one of the girls, the shorter one, was missing a front tooth.

"Let Dada eat in peace," Chitra said. She had treaded cautiously in terms of what I was to call her, but now referred to me without hesitation as the girls' older brother.

"You can call me Kaushik," I said to the girls, and this made them put their hands back over their mouths and giggle more forcefully.

"What about KD?" my father suggested.

We all turned to him, puzzled, this man for whom we were now gathered together.

"Short for Kaushik Dada," he explained. I wondered if this was something that had just popped into his head or if he'd considered it carefully beforehand. He had always possessed an inventive streak when it came to words, writing Bengali poems on weekends and reading them aloud to my mother. From her comments I gathered that the poems were witty. It had been one of our family secrets, the fact that my civil engineer father was also a poet. Though I never asked about it, I'd assumed he'd stopped writing after my mother's death, as he'd stopped doing so many things.

"That's clever," Chitra said, speaking directly to my father for the first time since my arrival. She spoke approvingly, with the tone of someone who is used to acknowledging small achievements, and it was then that I remembered that she had been a schoolteacher in her former life. "Yes, KD is better."

I found the nickname inane, but my father seemed proud of

it, and it was preferable to Chitra's alternative. "And what do I call you?" I asked my stepsisters.

"I am Rupa," said the taller one, her voice husky, like her mother's.

"And I am Piu," said the one missing the tooth.

"We are very glad to be in your room," Rupa added. She spoke stiffly, a bit distantly, as if reciting something she'd been forced to memorize. "We are very much appreciating."

They spoke to me in English, their accents and their intonation sounding as severe as mine must have sounded to your fully American ear when we arrived as refugees in your family's home. I knew the accents would soon diminish and then disappear, as would their unstylish sweaters, their silly hairstyles.

"Rupa and Piu are eager to see the Aquarium and the Science Museum," my father said. "Perhaps you can take them one day, Kaushik."

I didn't reply to this. "Very tasty," I said instead in Bengali, referring to the food, something my mother had taught me to say after eating in the homes of other people. I got up to bring my plate to the kitchen.

"You have not eaten," Chitra said, intercepting me. She attempted to take the plate from my hand, but I held on to it and went to the kitchen to pour myself some of the Johnnie Walker my father stored in the cupboard over the dishwasher.

"What do you need? I'll get it for you," Chitra said, following me. I was suddenly sickened by her, by the sight of her standing in our kitchen. I had no memories of my mother cooking there, but the space still retained her presence more than any other part of the house. The jade and spider plants she had watered were still thriving on the windowsill, the orange-and-white sunburst clock she'd so loved the design of, with its quivering second hand, still marking the time on the wall.

Though she had rarely done the dishes, though it was in fact I who had mostly done the dishes in those days, I imagined her hands on the taps of the sink, her slim form pressed against the counter. Ignoring Chitra, I opened one cupboard for a glass and another for the Scotch, but all I found there now were boxes of cereal and packets of chanachur brought back from Calcutta.

My father came into the kitchen as well. "Where's the Scotch?" I asked him.

He glanced at Chitra, and after some small silent communication between them she walked out. "I put it away," he said once we were alone.

"Why?"

"I've stopped taking it. I sleep better at night, I find."

"Since when?"

"For some time now. Also, I didn't want to alarm Chitra."

"Alarm her?"

"She's a bit old-fashioned." He pulled out the stepstool that lived in a space beside the refrigerator and unfolded it. He climbed to the top and opened up a cupboard above our refrigerator that was difficult, even with the stepstool, to reach, and took out a half-empty bottle.

I wanted to ask my father what on earth had possessed him to marry an old-fashioned girl half his age. Instead I said, taking the bottle from his hand, "I hope it's all right if I alarm her."

"Just be quiet about it, especially around the girls."

My parents had never been quiet about their fondness for Johnnie Walker, around me, around anyone. After my mother's death, just after I turned eighteen, it was I who filled her shoes, nursing one watered-down glass and then another in the evenings in order to keep my father company before we could both justify going to bed. I almost never drank the stuff at college, preferring beer, but whenever I came home I craved the taste, unable to avoid the thought of my mother when I happened to see an ad for it on a billboard or in a magazine.

"I thought tomorrow, while I'm at work, you could go pick up a tree," my father said. "There's a place not too far down 128. Perhaps the girls would want to join you. They're terribly excited about it."

I looked at him, confused. Until now it had not fully registered that my father would be at work during the days, that I would be alone with Chitra and her daughters.

"You mean a Christmas tree?" For the past three years, since my mother's death, we had not celebrated the holiday at our house. Instead we had fallen into a pattern of accepting invitations at the homes of friends, appearing in the mornings fully dressed while the other family would still be in their pajamas. I would receive a single box containing a sweater or a buttondown shirt and watch the family's children open dozens of gifts. In Bombay my mother had always thrown a party on Christmas Day, stringing lights throughout our flat and putting presents under a potted hibiscus. It was a time of year she spoke fondly about Cambridge, about your family and the others we had left behind, saying the holiday wasn't the same without the cold weather, the decorated shops, the cards that came in the mail.

"I suppose we'll have to get some presents," my father added. "We still have a few days. It needn't be extravagant."

I knew Chitra and her girls were probably huddled together in the dining area listening to every word my father and I exchanged, but that didn't stop me from saying, "Those girls are barely half my age. Do you expect me to play with them?"

"I don't expect you to do anything," my father replied evenly. He was unshaken by my remark, perhaps even relieved that we were now officially in opposition, that there was no longer a need to pretend. It was as if he had already played out this scene several times in his mind and was weary of it. "I am only asking if you mind picking up a tree."

I had yet to pour my drink. I'd been standing with my back to the kitchen counter, one hand holding a glass, the other the bottle my father had retrieved for me from its hiding place. I poured it now, taking it as my mother did, with one ice cube, not adding water. I drank what I poured, then poured another.

"Easy," my father said.

I glanced in his direction. After my mother's death he had acquired an expression that permanently set his features in a different way. It was less an expression of sadness than of irritated resignation, the way he used to look if a glass slipped and broke from my hands when I was little, or if the day happened to be cloudy when we had planned a picnic. That was the expression that had come to his face the morning we stepped into my mother's hospital room for the last time, that subsequently greeted me whenever I came home from college, that still seemed directed at my mother for letting him down. But the expression was missing now. "Not easy," I said, shaking my head at my own reflection suspended against the black backdrop of evening. "It's not easy for me."

My father had already left for work by the time I woke up the next morning. For a while I remained in bed, not knowing what time it was, confused, initially, as to why I was in the guestroom and why I could hear the sound of muffled girlish laughter drifting down through the ceiling. The guestroom was located on the first floor of the house, in its own wing off a corridor behind the kitchen. I occupied a double bed, the mattress positioned on a platform low to the ground. On the opposite wall was a sliding glass door facing the backyard and the pool, covered by a black tarp. When we first moved into the house my mother had devoted a disproportionate amount of attention to setting up the guestroom, shopping for the grasshopper-green quilt on the bed, curtains for the sliding glass door, an alarm clock for the bedside table, a soap dish for the adjoining bathroom, asking me to hang a pink and purple Madhubani painting over the chest of drawers. I didn't know who she was expecting to come and stay with us, but by then we indulged her in whatever pastime lifted her spirits. I was grateful for it now, glad not to be upstairs in my old bedroom which shared a wall with my parents' room. It had been awful enough hearing my mother's raspy breathing at night, her moans. Now it would be Chitra and my father I would have heard conversing before bed, their bodies I would have to imagine under a blanket side by side.

To my knowledge the only person who'd ever occupied our guestroom was a nurse named Mrs. Gharibian, who had come to tend to my mother after her needs became too much for my father and me and before my mother decided that she wanted to die in the hospital and not at home. Mrs. Gharibian was a middle-aged woman with short brown hair and a soft Southern accent. She had married an Armenian and learned to make all sorts of snacks from her mother-in-law. She would bring Tupperware containers full of lamb turnovers and stuffed grape leaves, food that now reminds me of my mother dying, putting them in the refrigerator for my father and me to eat, also stocking the house with milk and bread without being asked. Normally she left in the evenings, but for two weeks she spent the nights with us, administering morphine injections and emptying the bedpans, making notes in a little cloth book that looked as if it ought to contain recipes. Something about her quietly optimistic manner made me believe that Mrs. Gharibian had the power to sustain my mother, not to cure her but to keep her alive indefinitely. "This is the worst part," she told me once. "You're holding your breath, thinking it's still ahead, but this really is the worst of it, for you and for her." At the time her words had not soothed me; I could imagine nothing worse than the moment my mother no longer drew air in and out of her lungs, no longer took us in through her weary eyes. I could imagine nothing worse than not being able to look at her face every day, its beauty grossly distorted but never abandoning her. But in the days after her death I realized Mrs. Gharibian had been right, there had been nothing worse than waiting for it to come, that the void that followed was easier to bear than the solid weight of those days.

I pulled on a sweater, cracked open the sliding door, lit a cigarette. The season's leaves had not been raked, were scattered everywhere and drifting in the breeze. The swimming pool had made my summer vacations from college tolerable, but last summer, which I'd spent house-sitting in Brooklyn with a friend whose parents had gone to Europe, my father had not bothered to fill it with water, and last night at dinner he mentioned that the filter needed to be replaced. Our first summer in the house my mother had used the pool religiously, forty lengths back and forth before breakfast. By the following summer, when she was weak from chemotherapy, she would only wade or dangle her legs on hot days, and at the end of that summer she died.

Inside, I could hear the television—as soon as I emerged from the guestroom I would have to see them. I put on my jeans, annoyed that I could not simply walk through the house in boxers. In the bathroom I brushed my teeth and took the time to shave. I craved coffee but not food. Dinner had been another embarrassment of riches. Chitra hovered over my father and me and the girls, eating privately after we were done, the way our maids would in Bombay. I imagined another crowded plate waiting for me on the dining table, but there was no breakfast prepared, nothing offered when I approached Chitra and her daughters in the living room. They were sitting with their feet up on the sectional, watching an episode of

Family Feud. They were dwarfed by the soaring ceiling, washed out by the morning sun the room received. The girls were dressed, but Chitra was wearing a zippered housecoat in a frumpy red-and-yellow calico print. Without makeup or jewelry she looked even younger. She was drinking a cup of tea, my mother's biscuit tin open beside her.

"Good morning," I said.

"Good morning," Piu and Rupa chimed back, their eyes quickly returning to the television.

"I'll get your tea," Chitra said, putting her cup on the cocktail table and preparing to get up. "I didn't make any for you. Your father told me you like to sleep late when you visit home."

"It's okay," I told her. "Don't get up. I don't need any."

She spoke to me in Bengali, I to her in English, as had been the case the night before. I thought that my slack Americanized pronunciation would be lost on her, but she seemed to follow what I said.

Chitra frowned, confused. "No tea in the morning?" The girls also looked away from the television, waiting for my answer.

"I need coffee. It's what I have at school. I'm used to it now."

"But there is no coffee in the kitchen. Not that I have seen."

"Don't worry about it. I'll grab some at Dunkin' Donuts." Before she had the chance to ask, I continued, "It's a place that sells donuts. Donuts are a kind of cake, with a hole in the center."

"The store is far?"

"Just a few minutes."

"But you must take the car?"

I nodded, and she looked disappointed. "Without a car there is nowhere to go?"

"Not really. Can you drive?"

She shook her head.

"It's not hard. I'm sure you could get a license."

"Oh, no," she said, not as if she were incapable, but as if driving were beneath her. "I would not like to learn."

"I'll be back in a while," I said. I noticed that the girls were looking up at me and I hesitated. "Would you like to come along?"

"Yes, please," Rupa and Piu said at the same time. They looked at Chitra, and she nodded in assent.

I went back to the guestroom to get my wallet and keys, and when I returned the girls were already in their coats, matching red parkas that my father must have bought for them after they arrived. The thick zippers and bright nylon shells of the coats transformed their appearance, suddenly lending them a legitimately American air. They sat together in the back of my car among the newspapers, empty soda bottles, course books, cassette tapes. "Sorry for the mess," I said, tossing everything off the seat and onto the floor. They fastened their seat belts carefully, prying one of the buckles out of its gap, Rupa helping Piu. Chitra stood in her housecoat looking through the storm door. She was trusting me to take her children to a place she'd never heard of and would not be able to find. Still, she waved and forced a small smile. I stepped on the clutch, about to reverse the car, when Chitra opened the storm door, poking her head out. "And I will be all right?"

"What do you mean?"

"I will be safe alone, in this house?"

"Of course," I said, stunned that it would be the first time, nearly laughing at her. "Enjoy it."

"She does not allow us to go outside," Piu said. "Not without her."

"She is afraid because she cannot see neighbors," Rupa added.

"And that we will fall into the swimming pool."

I did not know how to respond to any of this, so I said nothing as I backed out of the long driveway and drove toward town. The closest Dunkin' Donuts was less than fifteen minutes away, and when I approached it felt too soon. I wanted to continue driving, and so I kept going, heading toward the next town, where there was a beach my mother used to like for an occasional change of scenery. This required getting on the highway, and I found it satisfying, accelerating for a short while along the empty, impersonal road. The girls asked no questions about where we were going, each looking steadily out the back windows, the journey still brief enough that the lack of conver- sation did not feel strange. I entered the next town and took a road from which the gray line of the ocean was visible. I pointed this out to Rupa and Piu, but they said nothing. "We can either go into the drive-through or inside," I said once we reached the donut shop. "You guys have a preference?"

"Which way is best?" Rupa asked.

"With the drive-through I get my coffee and drink it as we go back to the house. The other way, we sit inside."

Rupa voted for the drive-through, Piu to go inside. "Tell you what," I said. "We'll go in, and on our way home I'll get a refill in the drive-through."

They seemed pleased that neither option would be denied to them and got out of the car, holding hands as they walked across the parking lot. The Dunkin' Donuts was part of a shopping plaza with a liquor store, a Bed and Bath, and a place that sold party supplies. The lot was crammed with the cars of last-minute Christmas shoppers, but Dunkin' Donuts was empty. Christmas carols played on the sound system, their trite melodies foreign to Rupa and Piu. I ordered my coffee and asked the girls what they wanted. They stared at the selections, Piu straining on tiptoe, Rupa with her mouth slightly open and her tongue planted in one corner of it. The decent thing to do was to lift Piu up so that she could get a better view, and when I offered, she raised her hands and came into my arms. She was heavier than I expected, and I placed her on the counter, where she continued to stare.

"Which is your favorite, KD?"

"Boston Cream."

"I want that one, then."

"Me, too," Rupa said.

"Make it three," I told the cashier.

We sat in a booth, me on one side of the Formica table, my stepsisters on the other. They began eating enthusiastically, not pausing until they were finished, exchanging glances and a sisterly commentary I was not privy to. I ate my donut as well, surprised by how much smaller their mouths were, how much longer it took them to finish compared to me. I felt separate from them in every way but at the same time could not deny the things that bound us together. There was my father, of course, but he seemed to be the least relevant in a way. Like them I'd made that journey from India to Massachusetts, too old not to experience the shock of it, too young to have a say in the matter. They would recall all of this, perhaps not as clearly as I remember those first months at your parents' home, but nevertheless they would remember. Like them I had lost a parent and was now being asked to accept a replacement. I wondered how well they remembered their father; Piu would only have been five at the time. Even my memories of my mother had begun to break apart in the three and a half years since her death, the thousands of days I had spent with her reduced to a handful of stock scenes. I was lucky, compared to Rupa and Piu, having had my mother for as long as I did. The knowledge of death seemed present in both sisters—it was something about the way they carried themselves, something that had broken too soon and had not mended, marking them in spite of their lightheartedness.

"Liked that?" I asked.

Both girls nodded, and Piu said, "Another tooth is loose."

She opened her mouth and pressed a tiny chocolate-stained lower tooth forward with her tongue.

The coffee was too hot to drink, so I removed the lid and set it on the counter. Piu was looking out the window, at the cars pulling in and out of the lot. Rupa was eyeing the donuts on display, the dispensers of coffee, the tanks of bubbling red punch.

"Would you like another?"

She shook her head, avoiding my gaze. She was more reserved than Piu and seemed, at times, unimpressed by her new surroundings. "I would like to bring one home for Ma."

"The one with the colors on top," Piu said, kneeling up in the booth and pointing. "That is prettiest."

Rupa disagreed. "I like the one that is covered in snow."

"Here's a dollar," I said, lifting my hips and reaching for my wallet. "Would you guys like to buy a couple more?"

"We are not allowed to touch money," Rupa said.

"It's only a dollar. Even if you were to lose it between here and there," I said, glancing back at the cash register, "it wouldn't be a big deal."

"Big deal?" Piu asked, knitting her dark brows together.

"Not important."

They slid out of the booth and walked toward the counter, each of them holding a corner of the dollar bill as if it were a miniature banner in a parade. I had my back to the counter so I turned partway around to watch. I saw Rupa pointing, once and once more, then both of them sliding the dollar to the cashier. He folded over the top of the bag and moved it back and forth, unsure which of the girls to hand it to, eventually leaving it on the counter for Rupa.

"Why didn't you say anything?" I asked when they returned.

Rupa handed me the change, looking defensive. "We have done something wrong?"

"No. But you could have said the kind of donuts you wanted

instead of pointing, you could have thanked the cashier when he gave them to you. And you should always start off by saying hello."

Rupa looked down at the table. "Sorry."

"Don't apologize. I'm just saying, you guys don't have to be shy. The more you use your English in these situations, the better it will be. It's already good."

"Not like yours," Rupa said. "They will laugh at us in school."

"I am afraid to go to school," Piu said, shaking her head and covering her eyes with her hands.

It was not my intention to reassure them, but it seemed cruel not to. "Look, I know how you feel. A few kids might laugh in the beginning, but it doesn't matter. They laughed at me, too. I came here from Bombay when I was sixteen and had to figure things out all over again. I was born here but it was still hard, leaving and then coming back again."

"It was before your mother died?" Piu asked. She asked this reverently, a bit sadly, as if she'd actually known my mother, or perhaps because it reminded her of her father, I could not tell.

I nodded.

"What was she like?"

"She was—she was my mother," I said, caught offguard by the question. I felt suddenly vulnerable in front of two little girls I'd known less than a day and yet who understood me better, in many ways, than friends who had known me for years. Four years ago my mother would have been the one sitting across from me, sipping her tea, complaining how tasteless it was, after one of our windy walks along the beach.

"Do you have a picture of her?" Rupa asked. For a moment her gaze held mine.

"No," I lied, not wanting to show them the one I carried stuffed behind the ID cards in my wallet. It had been taken during a party in our flat in Bombay, long before her illness, from such a distance that it gave little impression of her face. I had put the photograph, cut down to size, into my wallet after she died, but since then I had never taken it out to look at it.

"Why is there no picture of her in the house?" Rupa asked.

"My father didn't want any."

"Ma has been looking," Piu said. "She has looked in every room. But she cannot find one."

Chitra was sitting on the window seat when we got back, watching for my car. The anxiety in her face was obvious, but she didn't ask what had taken us so long. Piu and Rupa didn't give her a chance, rushing up as if they hadn't seen her for days, handing her the donuts and telling her what a fun trip it was, how generous I'd been, Piu reporting that they'd paid for the donuts themselves. It was obvious that the girls liked me and that, because of her daughters' approval, Chitra was willing to like me, too. But I needed to be alone. The open plan of the house meant it was impossible to watch television or listen to music without engaging with them. Instead I sat on the bed in the guestroom, looking at the yard and leafing through the *Globe*. Then I went for a run, five cold miles on the winding roads. When I returned, they were eating a heavy Bengali lunch, hunched over plates of rice and dal and the previous night's leftovers. I turned down Chitra's invitation to join them and instead, after my shower, dragged the phone into the guestroom and called Jessica.

"Why don't you just come here?" she suggested. I wished I could, wished I could simply get into my car and drive to her parents' home. But I wasn't capable of walking out, not yet. When I went to return the phone to its place in the hallway, I realized that they were all upstairs, napping, the way my rela-

tives did in India. For the first time since my arrival I stretched
out on the sectional, to watch television, and without meaning
to I fell asleep myself. They were downstairs when I woke up,
within arm's reach but behaving as if I were not there. It was
already getting dark outside, the arcing lamp spreading its light
over the cocktail table. The channel had been changed to a talk
show. Chitra was combing and retying the girls' hair and then
proceeded to comb her own. She worked through it with her
fingers, a stunning mass that had been contained, until now, in
a braid, the smooth strands cascading nearly to her waist. The
sight of it repulsed me; I could not help thinking of the hair
that had fallen out in clumps from my mother's head, the awful
wig she'd worn even in the hospital, up until the day she died,
that artificial part of her more healthy-looking than anything
else.

Rupa sat behind Chitra, massaging her mother's scalp and
plucking out a few gray hairs while Chitra leaned back and
closed her eyes. I gathered that this was a regular routine,
something that took place without the need for instructions or
comment. I sat up and watched, imagining the rest of Chitra's
hair turning gray one day, imagining her growing into an old
woman alongside my father the way my mother was meant to.
That thought made me conscious, formally, of my hatred of
her. As if aware of what I was thinking, Chitra opened her eyes
and looked at me, embarrassed, quickly gathering her hair
around her hand. She got up and went to the kitchen, returning a few minutes later with a pot of tea and cups of Ovaltine on
a tray. There were two types of chanachur in cereal bowls, and
on a small plate, a donut cut into four pieces.

"Now will you take tea?" she asked me.

I accepted, lifting from the tray the cup she'd already prepared, with separately heated milk and too much sugar.

"This is from Haldiram," she said, passing me one of the cereal bowls. "Best in all Calcutta."

"No, thank you."

"This room is cold," she continued. "The wind comes straight through the glass. Why aren't there curtains?"

"It would spoil the view," I said.

"The steps are also slippery." She pointed to the floating staircase leading to the second floor. "And there is no railing. I am afraid Rupa and Piu will fall."

I turned to look at the thick pieces of wood arranged like empty shelves ascending the white walls. Even at her weakest, my mother had gone up and down them without protest.

"Why is there no railing?" Chitra repeated.

"Because we liked it that way," I said, aware that I sounded pedantic. "Because that's what makes it beautiful."

We had nothing else to say to one another. We sat and watched one program and then the next as Chitra worked on something with a crochet hook, and I wondered how I was going to survive the next four weeks in her company. We were all waiting for my father, waiting for him to return and explain, if only by his presence, why we were sitting together drinking tea. When he did, he asked me to give him a hand outside; there was a Christmas tree tied to the roof of his car. "I would have gone tomorrow," I said, helping him to untie the rope that held it in place. I was without gloves, a fact that made the task, in the frigid evening air, both easy and painful. We dragged the tree inside and propped it in one corner of the living room, next to the high stone fireplace. Chitra and the girls gathered around.

"But it's just like all the other trees outside," Chitra said, pointing through the glass wall.

"It's different, actually." I said. "On the property we have pine trees. This is a spruce."

Somewhere in the basement there was a box, my father said, containing the stand, the lights, ornaments to hang from the branches. They were from our first winter in the house, the last

Christmas my mother celebrated, and I was surprised my father hadn't tossed them out. He asked me to go down and look for the box. Our basement lacked the sedimented clutter of most, given that we'd lived in the house only a handful of years and that for most of that time my mother had been dead and I had been away at college. There had been no period of haphazard accumulation, only events that had caused things to be taken away. Still, there were a number of boxes stacked up against the walls, empty ones that once contained the television and the stereo speakers, others still taped up, full of inessential items my parents had had shipped from Bombay and never bothered to unpack.

I slit the tape with my car key and lifted the flaps of a few of the boxes. One contained old engineering books of my father's. Another had a dinner set wrapped in pages of *The Times of India,* plates I had eaten off for years but forgotten until now, with a pattern of small orange diamonds around the rim. I found my enlarger, tongs, a set of trays, and old bottles of fixer for the darkroom I'd set up during my last year of high school. There were times my mother came down and kept me company, sitting quietly in the blackness as I struggled to load film onto the developing reel. Together we would breathe in the chemical smells, their corrosiveness, from which my hands were protected by rubber gloves, nothing compared to what was taking place inside her body. She would keep time for me with her watch, familiarizing herself with the process enough to be able to tell me when to pour the series of fluids in and out of the processing tank, both of us knowing that I'd have to buy a timer, eventually. "It must be something like this," she said once in that perfectly dark, silent, sealed-up space, and I understood without her saying so that she was imagining what it might be like to be dead. "This is how I want to think of it."

The box I was looking for was labeled "X-MAS" in my

mother's hand, not on the side so that it was easily identifiable, but in a corner on top. I had no sentimental attachment to the items inside, and yet I didn't want to see them. The thought of Chitra going through the box, watching her sift through every-thing, upset me just as it had upset me, throughout the day, to watch her handle the cutlery, the teakettle, at one point to hold the telephone and speak with my father to learn that he was on his way home. When my father had tried to remove the signs of my mother from the house I blamed him for being excessive, but now I blamed him for not having done enough.

"I can't find it," I said, after returning upstairs. My father did not press the issue, did not insist on going down and look-ing for it himself. He behaved differently around Chitra, was more accepting of the minor defeats of life. I offered to go to a drugstore and buy what we needed, glad to have another reason to leave the house. When I came back my father and I trimmed the tree together, Chitra and the girls watching us from the sec-tional. We placed the tree in the stand and tightened the screws and draped lights over the branches. There was nothing per-sonal or idiosyncratic to put on it, just a box of sapphire blue balls, so that it looked less like a tree in someone's home and more like one in the corner of a bank or an office lobby. But Rupa and Piu were delighted, exclaiming that they'd never seen anything more beautiful. My father went upstairs and returned with a shopping bag full of gifts. They'd all been wrapped at whatever store he bought them in, the same green-and-gold paper professionally taped and tied. He distributed them under the tree, eight boxes altogether. "Two for each of you," he said to no one in particular. Rupa and Piu got up and went to look at them then, excited to find their names written on the tags.

"Can we open them?" Piu asked Chitra, Chitra who did not know the answer.

"Not until Christmas morning," I said. "Until then you can just look. And maybe shake them a little."

"So lovely," Chitra said, impressed now that the tree had been trimmed.

"Kaushik, what about a picture?" my father suggested.

I shook my head. I had left my camera, my father's old Yashica, at school.

"But you always have it with you." That look of irritated disappointment, the one that had appeared the day my mother died and was missing now that he'd married Chitra, passed briefly across my father's face.

"I forgot it," I said. It was true, I did always have the camera with me. Even on quiet weekends when I came home and my father and I saw no one I would bring it, taking it with me on walks. This time I had left it behind, knowing that I would not want to document anything.

"I don't understand," my father said.

"Neither do I," I replied. "You haven't wanted a picture of anything in years."

"That's not true."

"It is."

We were stating facts and at the same time arguing, an argument whose depths only he and I could fully comprehend. I went to the kitchen to pour myself a drink, bringing it with me to the dining table when Chitra announced, a few minutes later, that dinner was ready. No one said anything during the meal. When we were done eating, Chitra cleared all the plates and took them into the kitchen, just as she had the night before, allowing my father and me to relax after dinner in a way that we'd never been able to during the last years of my mother's life. We no longer had to assume the responsibility of scraping the plates and loading the dishwasher so that my mother could rest. I sat finishing my drink, and Rupa and Piu slithered out of their seats and returned to the sectional to watch more television. My father got up and followed them, settling into his recliner with the newspaper. He opened it to a large ad for Lechmere that featured cameras for sale, circling things with a ballpoint pen.

Two days later was Christmas Eve, and my father stayed home from work, suggesting that we all go, the five of us, into Boston to show Chitra and the girls the city. I had no excuse and so I joined them, sitting in the backseat of my father's car, between Rupa and Piu. Though we were only going for a short ride, the trip felt strangely momentous. For the last two years of my mother's life, when she was always in and out of the hospital, we had gone nowhere, taken no trips for pleasure apart from those occasional walks along the beach. The last thing in my life that was anything close to a vacation was the layover in Rome with my parents, on our way back from Bombay. All I had learned about New England was the immediate region that surrounded our house, and the way to Mass General, making the trip back and forth until it was no longer necessary.

My father drove us first into Cambridge to look at Harvard and MIT, Chitra asking me why I had chosen a college so far away when I could have attended those schools instead. I ignored her question, as I ignored so many of the things she said to me. "He wanted to get out of Massachusetts," my father explained.

I had thought we would get out of the car at various points and walk around, but Chitra said it was too cold and my father agreed. After circling around Kendall Square he drove over the Mass Avenue Bridge and turned onto Commonwealth Avenue, which was decorated with lights and wreaths, and then drove around the Public Garden and the Common. He pointed out the golden dome of the State House, and the beautiful homes that lined the steep streets of Beacon Hill. Behind those homes was Mass General, where my father and I had gone together so many times. A phone call had woken us in the early hours one morning, and we had driven down to Boston just as the first light was intruding with harsh orange streaks in the sky. She looked the same as the night before, lying in the bed with her eyes closed, only all the machines were shut off, making the room in which we had spent so many quiet hours all the more silent. Her skin felt chilled when I touched it, as if she had just returned from a brisk walk in winter. I looked up now at the windows of the hospital, but my father turned toward Chitra. "This is where America's Brahmins live," he said, laughing at his own joke, and in the front seat Chitra smiled in a way that revealed to me that she was falling in love.

For Christmas my father bought me a sweater and a shirt, but later he gave me an envelope containing ten hundred-dollar bills. "You will need it for this and that," he said when I told him it was too much. My father had also arranged to go to Disney World for five days; this, along with the toys under the tree, was his present to the girls. "You are welcome to join us," my father said when he announced this news on Christmas morning, but I said no, making up something about there being a winter session at Swarthmore. My father did not convince me to join them. But Rupa and Piu were devastated. "Why don't you want to come?" they kept asking, all the more bewildered when they discovered that I had never been to Disney World. I sensed that they needed me to guard them, as I needed them, from the growing, incontrovertible fact that Chitra and my father now formed a couple. My presence was proof that my mother had once existed, just as they represented the physical legacy of their dead father. "Won't you be lonely staying all by yourself?" Chitra asked me more than once. At the same time I gathered that she, like my father, was relieved to hear my plans. I had no plans, of course, other than to be in the house alone.

Once I knew that they were leaving I felt more charitable toward the girls, and in an effort to make up for not going to Disney World I took them to the Science Museum one day, and another day to the Aquarium. They behaved impeccably on these outings, never complaining or demanding, overjoyed when I bought each of them a cheap rubber lobster. They were with me, having ice cream at Herrell's in Harvard Square, where I'd gone to buy a record, when Piu's loose tooth fell out as she crunched on her cone, and I sopped up the blood in her mouth with napkins and put the sticky tooth in my pocket, telling them about the tooth fairy as we drove home. Though I was only twenty-one I remember wondering, just then, what it might be like to have a child. I did not hold it against them that they had begun calling my father Daddy. They never spoke of their own father, but one night I woke up to the sound of Piu screaming, locked inside a nightmare, asking for her Baba again and again.

A few days before New Year's Eve, my father and Chitra were invited to a holiday party at the home of some of my parents' friends. How strange it was, seeing Chitra carefully descending the floating staircase, dressed up in a dark green sari and a garnet necklace, and then my father behind her, then beside her, always beside her now, his hair neatly combed, wearing a tweed sports jacket I had not seen since my mother died. I was not expected to attend the party, but Rupa and Piu were going, had put on matching dresses with red-and-black-checkered skirts and black velvet headbands in their hair. At the last minute, just as my father was taking the coats out of a cupboard, Rupa turned to Chitra and asked, "Can we stay home?"

"Of course not," Chitra said. "It would be rude."

"But KD isn't going."

"Actually, it may be rather dull for them," my father said. "I don't believe there will be any children close to their ages."

"I haven't made dinner for them," Chitra said. "They haven't eaten."

"I can get a pizza," I offered, looking up from the sectional. I winked at Rupa and Piu. "We can have our own party."

The girls clapped their hands, Piu smiling to reveal the new gap in her teeth. Chitra told me to have them in bed by nine, and then she and my father buttoned their coats and went off to the party. It was the first time they had gone out alone, and it occurred to me, once they were gone, that I had done a favor to them as well as to Rupa and Piu. The girls took off their shoes but kept their tights and party dresses on, and sat with me to watch television. We passed a bag of potato chips back and forth, and when it was empty I called in for pizzas. I put on my coat to go to the restaurant. Rupa and Piu stared at me.

"Where are you going?" Piu asked.

"To get our dinner."

"You are leaving us alone?"

"It's ten minutes away. I'll be back before you know it."

They said nothing, but they looked genuinely scared. It annoyed me that Chitra had instilled in them such fear. "Well, come if you want."

We drove to the restaurant and ended up eating the pizza there. I drank a beer and smoked a few cigarettes during the meal, and Rupa and Piu sipped Cokes from tall paper cups. They asked me again if I would go with them to Disney World. I told them I would think about it, and the lie was enough to fill them with new hope. The phone was ringing when we returned to the house. It was Jessica, so I poured myself a drink and took the phone into the guestroom. When I told her about my father taking Chitra and the girls to Disney World, Jessica suggested coming up to visit me while they were away. I missed her, I thought about her and desired her at night in bed, and yet I did not want to see her in my parents' house. I didn't say this, but she sensed my reluctance and we began to quarrel for the first time. It was an awkward conversation, full of long pauses, draining, even though it never escalated into a real argument. I felt guilty about avoiding her, just as I felt guilty saying no to Disney World, but I knew that were I to agree to either proposition I would feel worse. I told Jessica the same lie that I told the girls, that I would think about it, and got off the phone.

When I opened the door to refresh my drink I saw that Rupa and Piu were no longer watching television, which was what I'd assumed they'd been doing all this time. I called for them, checking the kitchen, the bathroom, then went upstairs, to the door of my old room. I didn't hear them talking and, seeing from my watch that it was already ten o'clock, thought maybe they were asleep. I opened the door, looking into the room for the first time since I'd come home. The lights were on, and I saw my old bed, and a folding cot placed beside it without any gap. The things I'd had on the walls, the poster of Jimi Hendrix and a copy of Paul Strand's "Blind Woman" I'd ripped out of a magazine, had not been removed. The closet door was open, and there was a chair in front of it, as if positioned to pull something down from the shelf. I had thought the room would be transformed with Rupa and Piu's things, but there was no sign of them apart from the extra bed and the small pile of toys they'd gotten for Christmas neatly stacked in one corner. Close to this pile sat Rupa and Piu in their party dresses. They had their backs to me, were hunched over something on the carpet that I couldn't see. "She looks sad in this one," I heard Piu whisper in Bengali, and then Rupa, saying, "She and KD smile the same way."

"What are you doing?" I said.

They leapt apart, startled, realizing I was there. Spread out on the gray carpet, arranged like a game of Solitaire, were about a dozen photographs of my mother taken from the box my father had sealed up and hidden after her death. Even from a distance the banished images assaulted me: my mother wearing a swimsuit by the edge of the pool at our old club in Bombay. My mother sitting with me on her lap on the brown wooden steps of our house in Cambridge. My mother and my father standing before I was born in front of a snow-caked hedge.

"What the hell do you think you're doing?" I said now.

Rupa looked at me, her dark eyes flashing, and Piu began to cry. I walked into the room and picked up the pictures, putting them face down on my old dresser. Then I grabbed Rupa by the shoulders from where she sat crouched on the floor, shaking her forcefully. Her body had gone limp, her thin legs wobbling in their cabled black tights. I wanted to throw her against the wall, but instead I managed to direct her to the folding cot and forced her to sit, knowing that I was squeezing too hard. "Tell me, where did you find these?" I demanded, just inches from her face.

Now Rupa began to cry as well, but she pointed to the closet. I walked toward it, but Piu, still sobbing on the carpet and shaking her head, said "It is not there anymore." She crawled toward the cot where her sister was sitting and pulled out a black shoebox, white at the edges, the masking tape that had once bound it shut lifted away. This time it was Piu that I grabbed, dragging her away from the shoebox as if her proximity would contaminate it, and thrusting her aside.

"You have no right to be looking at those," I told them. "They don't belong to you, do you understand?"

They nodded, Rupa trembling as if with cold, Piu's lips pressed tightly together. Tears fell down their faces but words continued to pour out of me, words that should not have been uttered, should not have been heard. "Well, you've seen it for yourselves, how beautiful my mother was. How much prettier and more sophisticated than yours. Your mother is nothing in comparison. Just a servant to wash my father's clothes and cook his meals. That's the only reason she's here, the only reason both of you are here."

Now the girls were no longer crying, their shiny black heads staring down at the carpet, not moving, saying nothing in reply. I took the shoebox and the rest of my mother's photographs and left the room. I wanted to remove the pictures from the house, as far as I could. I returned to the guestroom, hastily packed my things, and then got into my car, telling myself that my father and Chitra would be back from their party soon enough. My actions felt spontaneous, almost involuntary, propelled by the adrenaline of a state of emergency, but I realize now that on some level I had been thinking of running away for days. Rupa and Piu never came out of their room, never opened the door to see or question what I was doing, and when I started the car they did not rush out of the house to beg me to stay.

I had no idea where to go, but I got on the highway and started driving north. I quickly left Massachusetts, driving through a small piece of New Hampshire and over the bridge into Maine. As I approached Portland, I turned onto a smaller, two-lane road that occasionally hugged the sea. I drove down dark, empty stretches punctuated now and then by a cluster of churches and restaurants and homes. I could not see the ocean but detected its salty smell and the jerking sound of the wind, a sound like that of a fire burning, penetrating the closed doors and windows of my car. I thought at first that I would drive through the night, but eventually I began to feel tired and looked for a place to sleep. Most of the hotels and motels were shut for the season, and the ones that looked open were closed because it was so late. I was considering pulling onto the shoulder to nap when I spotted a motel with a twenty-four-hour sign glowing in the parking lot.

The next day I was woken by the calls of sea birds. I sat up in a sagging brass bed and saw the water for the first time, outside my window. I remember that the window was disproportionately small for the room, as if the motel itself were a ship. The water was choppy, a gray a shade or two darker than the sky, its nearness and activity unknown to me as I'd slept. The room was dank and clammy, wallpapered with small blue anchors against a white ground, and the empty medicine cabinet in the bathroom was edged with rust. The desk clerk told me that there was a restaurant a few miles down the road, and that I was somewhere on Penobscot Bay.

After breakfast I walked around the town and along the harbor, past boarded-up businesses and homes of people who would occupy them in summer. But I spent most of the day in the motel, either looking at the ocean from the armchair in my room or downstairs at the bar, drinking, feeling sick to my stomach about what had happened the night before, afraid of myself and ashamed. I kept seeing Rupa and Piu with their heads bent, their bodies prepared to be shaken again, absorbing all the things I was too afraid to tell my father and Chitra. And I thought of them in the house after I'd left them there, knowing how frightened they were to be alone. I wondered what had happened when my father and Chitra returned from the party, what Rupa and Piu had told them. I assumed they'd told everything, that they had done the dirty work of expressing what I could not. I was aware that by disappearing I was causing my father concern, though I felt worse about my treatment of the girls. It was to Rupa and Piu that I owed the greater apology, but at the same time I knew that what was done was done, that no matter what I said now I would never be able to make it right.

In the afternoon I went to a pay phone and called my father at work. "I know that you aren't happy, that this is hard for you," he told me, as if my disappearance were something he'd been prepared for. "But you could have done the decent thing and waited until morning. You could have said good-bye."

I didn't offer an explanation. I had none. Instead, I asked how the girls had been when my father and Chitra returned.

"They were asleep," my father said. "Still, you shouldn't have abandoned them in the house, Kaushik, not so late at night. Anything might have happened. Chitra was quite disturbed. She's worried that it's her fault you've run off, that she's said or done something to upset you. She's trying her best, you know."

I realized then: the girls had said nothing. Chitra had no idea that I had ranted at her daughters, that I had harmed and terrified them.

"We leave for Florida day after tomorrow," my father said. "Do you plan to return by then?"

"I don't think so."

"You will get back to college on time?"

"Yes."

"We will speak in a few weeks, then."

He hung up the phone. He had not bothered to ask me where I'd gone.

The next morning I got back in my car, and for days I did the same thing: driving up the coast, eating in restaurants when I was hungry, finding motels when I was tired, paying for it with the money my father had given me for Christmas. I didn't bother getting a map. A gas station attendant told me that eventually I would hit Canada. Now and again I saw the water, little islands and striped lighthouses and tiny spits of land. It was too brutally cold to get out of the car, but occasionally I did, to look at the ocean or explore a bit of trail. It was like no other place I'd seen, nothing like the North Shore of Massachusetts. The sky was different, without color, taut and unforgiving. But the water was the most unforgiving thing, nearly black at times, cold enough, I knew, to kill me, violent enough to break me apart. The waves were immense, battering rocky beaches without sand. The farther I went, the more desolate it became, more than any place I'd been, but for this very reason the landscape drew me, claimed me as nothing had in a long time.

Most of the fishing villages were shut down, the lobster boats out of the water for winter, the wooden traps stacked and empty. At times I wished that I'd had my camera with me, but there is no documentation of those days. The food was generally terrible, but when I think of it I still savor the taste of diner coffee that was at once bitter and insipid, the waffles drowned in syrup, the gummy chowder and greasy eggs, as if no other food had nourished me before then. The bars were the only consistent sign of life, strange small places that felt more like people's living rooms, with clamshells for ashtrays and nets draped on the walls. I had nothing to say to the fishermen and the other people who drank there and had lived in those villages all their lives, their tobacco-stained beards concealing their faces, their hands raw and chapped, their accents unfathomable. They were neither friendly nor unfriendly, and I kept to myself, aware that I stood out, watching whatever was on the television, observing whatever pool game was in progress. I did not crave anyone's company. I had never traveled alone before and I discovered that I liked it. No one in the world knew where I was, no one had the ability to reach me. It was like being dead, my escape allowing me to taste that tremendous power my mother possessed forever.

I spent five days getting to the border of Canada, another four heading back, using my father's money almost to the penny. Somewhere during that time the year ended; I was aware of it thanks only to a free shot of whiskey I received one night in a bar. I was certain that if my mother had lived to visit that part of the world, she would have persuaded my father to buy her one of the hundreds of homes I passed, overlooking the open sea, many occupying islands all to themselves. The bars and diners always had stacks of pamphlets listing waterfront properties, everything from simple timeshares to turreted mansions, and sometimes, lacking anything else to read, I looked through them. It reminded me of my parents' search for our house after leaving Bombay. And it was then, wandering alone that winter up the coast of Maine, that I thought of you, and our weeks in your house during another winter five years before.

You would have been in college by then, on Christmas vacation as I was. But I remembered you not much older than Rupa, and I remembered a day after a snowstorm, when something I'd said caused you, like Rupa and Piu, to cry. I had hated every day I spent under your parents' roof, but now I thought back to that time with nostalgia. Though we didn't belong there, it was the last place that had felt like a home. In pretending that my mother wasn't sick and being around people who didn't know, a small part of me had been able to believe that it was true, that she would go on living just as your mother had. The second house was different. There phone calls were made freely to the doctors, medicine bottles were strewn about, the paraphernalia of her illness taking over every corner of every room. In spite of all the effort and money my mother put into that house, we had never been able to inhabit it properly, and because of what was happening to her we never felt happy. It was there that my mother prepared to depart for another place altogether, one where we would be unable to join her, and from which she would not return.

One day close to the Canadian border, walking along cliffs overlooking the Bay of Fundy, I found a spot that was particularly striking. A sign told me I was in the easternmost state park in the country. The trail was not easy, falling through rich-smelling pine forests. The tops of the trees were spindly, their lower boughs dusted with snow. The wind ripped and chewed through everything, and the water was a sheer drop down. I crossed paths with no one. For a long time I watched the approach and retreat of the waves, their thick caps crashing apart against the rocks, that eternally restless motion having an inversely calming effect on me. The following day I returned to the same spot, this time bringing with me the shoebox of my mother's photographs. I sat on the ground, opened the box, and began going through the pictures one by one, as if they were pieces of mail that I was quickly scanning and would read later on. But there were too many pictures, and after a few I, like my father, could no longer bear their sight. A slight lessening in the pressure of my fingertips and the ones I was holding would have blown away into that wild sea, scattering down to where my mother's ashes already resided. But I could not bear that either, and so I put them back in the box and began to break the hardened ground. I only had a stick and a sharp-edged rock to work with and the hole was not impressive, but it was deep enough to conceal the box. I covered it with dirt and stones. The moon's first light was shining down when I was done, and I walked back, aided by that same beam of light, to my car.

A few weeks before my college graduation my father called to say that he was selling our house, that he and Chitra and the girls were moving to a more traditional one in a less isolated suburb of Boston. There were other Bengalis nearby and an Indian grocery in the town, things that were more important to Chitra than the proximity of the ocean and Modernist architecture had been for my mother. I would not be following my father to that new house; I had made plans to travel in South America after graduating. The events over Christmas had never been discussed, never acknowledged. Along with my father, Chitra and Rupa and Piu watched my commencement sitting on folding chairs on the grass, clapping when it was my turn to walk to the dais, posing beside me for photographs in my cap and gown. The girls were polite to me, respectful of the fact that it was my day, but at the same time it was as if we'd never met. I knew that they had never revealed anything to Chitra or to my father about the things I had said and done that night, that it would remain between the three of us, that in their silence they continued both to protect and to punish me. The memory of that night was now the only tie between us, eclipsing everything else. In their utterly polite way they made that clear. They spoke only to each other, and though their accents had turned American, my stepsisters, the closest thing I would ever have to siblings, seemed more impenetrable to me now than just after they'd arrived. "Everyone closer," my father directed from behind his new camera, and Rupa and Piu held their shoulders tensely as I draped an arm around each. "We are both moving forward, Kaushik," my father told me after the ceremony. "New roads to explore." And without our having to say it, I knew we were both thankful to Chitra for chafing under whatever lingered of my mother's spirit in the place she had last called home and for forcing us to shut its doors.

Going Ashore

Again she'd lied about what had brought her to Rome. A grant had relieved her, this autumn, of teaching at Wellesley. But Hema was not in Italy in any official capacity, only to take advantage of a colleague's empty apartment in the Ghetto. She had invented something that sounded impressive, a visiting lectureship at an institute of classical studies, and neither Navin nor her parents had questioned her. Her scholarly life was a mystery to them, something at once impressive and irrelevant. It had earned her a PhD and a tenure-track job, that was the important thing. The colleague, Giovanna, had arranged for Hema to have library privileges at the American Academy and given her the numbers of a few people to call in Rome, and in October, Hema had packed her laptop and clothes and flown across the ocean for an improvised leave of absence. Just before Christmas she would go to Calcutta, where her parents had returned after a lifetime in Massachusetts and where, in January, she would marry Navin.

Now it was November, the week before Thanksgiving. When Hema thought of the existence she had evaded this semester, she saw the trees on Wellesley's campus stripped of their leaves, patches of Lake Waban already freezing over, darkness descending through classroom windows as her students struggled through sentences from Wheelock's Latin: *id factum esse tum non negavit.* In Rome the leaves were also falling, untended copper piles heaped on either side of the Tiber. But the days felt languorous, warm enough to wander the streets in a cardigan, and the tables outside the restaurant where Hema went each day for lunch were still full.

The restaurant, five minutes from Giovanna's apartment, was next to the Portico di Ottavia. There were of course hundreds of other restaurants she might have tried, hundreds of versions of cacio e pepe and carbonara and deep-fried artichokes she might have eaten. But the few times she wandered into different places, she was either disappointed by the food or flustered by her broken Italian, and so she remained faithful to the one she knew, the one where she was no longer questioned. At this restaurant the waiters knew by now to bring her a bottle of acqua gassata, a half-litre of vino bianco, swiftly to clear the second place setting away. They left her alone with the book she would bring, though mostly she sat and looked at the remains of the Portico, at its chewed-up columns girded with scaffolding, its massive pediment with significant chunks missing. Well-dressed chattering Romans would pass by without a glance, while tourists would pause, gazing down at the excavations before proceeding on to the Theater of Marcellus. In front of the Portico was a little piazza where, according to the plaque Hema had managed to translate, over a thousand Jews had been deported in October 1943.

She could not take credit for discovering the restaurant on her own. She had eaten a meal there many years ago, with Julian, the other time she'd come to Rome under false pretenses. And though she had not intended to eat there again, she had found it during her first jet-lagged walk around Giovanna's neighborhood in search of food. She had accompanied Julian secretly, still confident in those days that his divorce was a matter of time. It was May, the city clogged with people, already too hot for the clothes she'd brought. She and Julian stayed together at a hotel behind the Colosseum, and he presented a paper at a conference, a recycled chapter from his study of Petronius. Under normal circumstances Hema might have presented her own paper. This was what she had told her parents she'd be doing, and they had not questioned her. But she had just defended her dissertation and was determined to take a few months off.

Before that, Hema had been to Rome only once, traveling with a girlfriend after graduating from Bryn Mawr. That first visit, when she and her friend, both classics majors, earnestly walked from landmark to landmark, translating inscriptions and subsisting on panini and gelato, had left a lasting impression on Hema. But the trip with Julian was a heap of rubble that added up to nothing. She remembered breakfasts with him on the roof of the hotel, sitting among small brown birds that hopped at her feet, eating fresh ricotta and mortadella and salami under a glaring blue sky. She had been disconcerted by those salty, fleshy meats so early in the day, yet never able to resist them. She remembered the hotel room, the pink damask wallpaper, the broad bed. Every few days Julian spoke to his wife and daughters, asking them how things were in Vermont, on Lake Dunmore, where Julian and his family spent the summers. So much of their affair had taken place in hotel and motel rooms, little places Julian would seek out along the North Atlantic coast; he preferred them to the apartments Hema shared with other students throughout graduate school at CUNY. It was never possible to see each other at Julian's home in Amherst. Even their first date had taken place at a hotel, Julian inviting her back to The Mark for a drink after her department had treated him, following his lecture, to dinner.

There was no question of Navin coming to Rome. Before getting engaged they had spent just three weekends together, spaced out over as many months, Navin coming each time from Michigan to see Hema. They wandered chastely around Boston, going to museums and movies and concerts and dinners, and then, beginning on the second weekend, he kissed Hema goodnight at the door of her home and slept at a friend's. He admitted to her that he'd had lovers in the past, but he was old-fashioned when it came to a future wife. And it touched her to be treated, at thirty-seven, like a teenaged girl. She had not had a boyfriend until she was in graduate school, and by then she was too old for such measured advances from men.

In Rome, she communicated with Navin by e-mail and spoke to him a few times on the phone, conversations heavy with the weight of things to come but lacking the foundation of any lived history between them. They talked about their honeymoon in Goa, something Navin was planning, deciding together which of the resorts they preferred. She did not miss him but looked forward to Calcutta, to marrying him and returning with him on the plane in time to resume teaching at Wellesley. Navin was what her parents termed a "non-Bengali," that is, someone from any province in India other than West Bengal. His parents were Hindu-Punjabis living in Calcutta, and Navin had come to America for his PhD. Navin was also a professor, of physics, at Michigan State. But MIT had promised him a job in the fall, and so he was moving to Massachusetts to be with Hema.

She refused to think of it as an arranged marriage, but knew in her heart that that was what it was. Though she'd met Navin before her parents, they had found him for her. They had asked Hema if he might phone her, and finally, after years of refusing similar requests, after years of believing that Julian would leave his wife, she'd agreed. Her parents assumed that she was single because she was shy, too devoted to her studies to bother with men. Her mother even asked, on Hema's thirty-fifth birthday, if she preferred women. They'd had no idea, for all those years, that she was involved with anyone, never mind a married man. Even as she looked for the home her parents had helped her to buy in Newton, even as she sat signing the closing papers in the lawyer's office, putting her solitary signature where there was always space for another, she believed that eventually she would have to add Julian's name. It was her inability, ultimately, to approach middle age without a husband, without children, with her parents living now on the other side of the world, and yet to own a home and shovel the driveway when it snowed and pay her mortgage bill when it came—though she had proven to herself, to her parents, to everyone, that she was capable of all of those things—it was her unwillingness to abide that life indefinitely that led her to Navin.

From the beginning it was assumed that as long as she and Navin were attracted to each other, as long as they got along, they would marry. And after years of uncertainty with Julian, Hema found this very certainty, an attitude to love she had scorned in the past, liberating, with the power to seduce her just as Julian once had. It allowed her to find Navin physically appealing, to like his tranquil brown eyes, his long tan face, the black line of mustache that grounded it. After Navin there were no more surprise visits by Julian, no more bells ringing in the middle of the afternoon demolishing the rest of her day. No more waiting for the situation to change. After nearly a decade, a single phone conversation had ended it. "I'm engaged to be married," she told Julian the last time he wanted to arrange a weekend away, and he accused her of deceiving him, called her heartless, and then he did not call again.

Now she was free of both of them, free of her past and free of her future in a place where so many different times stood cheek by jowl like guests at a crowded party. She was alone with her work, alone abroad for the first time in her life, aware that her solitary existence was about to end. In Rome she savored her isolation, immersed without effort in the silent routine of her days. At night, after a bath, she slept soundly in Giovanna's bed, in a room with meager square footage but breathtaking height, enormous shuttered windows that shielded her from the sun but let in every sound: the scooters and cars on Via Arenula, the grates of the shops being raised for business, the perpetual singsong of ambulance sirens that she found strangely soothing. Certain elements of Rome reminded her of Calcutta: the grand weathered buildings, the palm trees, the impossibility of crossing the main streets. Like Calcutta, which she'd visited throughout childhood, Rome was a city she knew on the one hand intimately and on the other hand not at all—a place that fully absorbed her and also kept her at bay. She knew the ancient language of Rome, its rulers and writers, its history from founding to collapse. But she was a tourist in everyday Italy, and apart from Giovanna, who was in Berlin on sabbatical, she did not have a single Roman friend.

In the mornings she made espresso and heated up milk and spread jam on squares of packaged toast, and by eight she was at Giovanna's desk, colonized now with the ferment of Hema's books, her notebooks, her laptop, her Latin grammar and dictionary. In spite of the hundreds of things she might be doing or seeing in the city, until one o'clock each day she maintained this routine. This was her anchor, this had been her anchor for years. She was a professor now, her dissertation on Lucretius a bound, published, quietly praised thing. And yet it was the aspect of her job that required her to sit for hours alone at a desk that still fulfilled her more than anything. Since eighth grade, reading Latin had been an addiction, every line a puzzle to coax into meaning. The knowledge she'd slowly accumulated, the ancient words and declensions and syntax that dwelled in her brain, felt sacred, enabling her to bring a dead world to life.

The Etruscans were her focus now. A few months ago she had attended a lecture in Boston about Etruscan references in

Virgil, and this had ushered her headlong into that mysterious civilization prior to Rome, people who had possibly wandered from Asia Minor to central Italy and flourished for four centuries, who had ruled Rome for one hundred years before turning obsolete. Their literature was nonexistent, their language obscure. Their primary legacy was tombs and the things that were put in them: jewels, pottery, weapons to accompany the dead. She was learning about the *haruspices,* augurs who interpreted the will of the gods through the entrails of animals, lightning bolts, dreams of pregnant women, flights of birds. She wanted to put a seminar together when she returned to Wellesley, about Etruscan influence in Roman antiquity, and possibly, based on her research, a proposal for a second book. She had gone to the Vatican to see the Etruscan collection at the Gregorian Museum, and also to the Villa Giulia. She was combing through Cicero and Seneca, Livy and Pliny, reading fragments of the occultist senator Nigidius Figulus, typing notes into her laptop, marking up the many books she read.

And so Hema had not yet called anyone, not contacted any of Giovanna's friends so that they could meet her for a coffee or drive her out to Tivoli or to Ostia, as Giovanna assured her they would. She was content to spend the days alone, working, reading, and then having lunch by the Portico. In the afternoons she wandered in and out of churches, along dark cramped streets that opened into enormous light-filled squares. She walked everywhere, almost never resorting to a bus or the metro. In the evenings she retreated, preparing dinner at home, simple meals she ate while watching Italian television. It felt wrong to be out alone at night, more awkward to sit by herself at dinner than lunch. During her years with Julian, even when she was by herself, men had sensed that her heart was taken, that she would not pause to consider them, as if she were a passing taxi with its off-duty light on. But now, though she was engaged, she was aware of the Roman men who looked at her, sometimes called out. And though she was flattered by their attention, it reminded her that her heart did not belong to Navin in the same way.

Saturday mornings, instead of working, she would go to the Campo de' Fiori, watching the stylish mothers in their high heels and jewels and quilted jackets pushing strollers and buying vegetables by the kilo. These women, with their rich, loose tangles of hair, their sunglasses concealing no wrinkles, were younger than Hema, but she felt inexperienced in their company, innocent of the responsibilities of rearing children and running a household and haggling flirtatiously with vegetable vendors. She had grown used to this feeling over the years with Julian—her position as the other woman, which had felt so sophisticated when their affair began, was actually a holding pen that kept her from growing up. She had denied herself the pleasure of openly sharing life with the person she loved, denied herself even the possibility of thinking about children. But Navin had changed that, too. They were both aware of her age, and as soon as they were married, Navin told her, he was eager to begin a family.

One day after lunch, feeling energetic, she walked all the way to Piazza del Popolo, and then over to the Villa Giulia for another visit. In the museum she was moved once again by the ancient cups and spoons, still intact, that had once touched people's lips; the fibulae that had fastened their clothes, the thin wands with which they had applied perfume to their skin. But this time, looking at the giant sarcophagus of the bride and groom enclosed in a box of glass, she found herself in tears. She couldn't help but think of Navin. Like the young smiling couple sitting affectionately on top of a shared casket, there was something dead about the marriage she was about to enter into. And though she knew it had every chance, over the years, of coming to life, on her way home, in the yellow light of evening, she was conscious only of its deadness. She shopped for her dinner in an *alimentari* on Via dei Giubbonari, and now she carried a bag containing lettuce, a box of spaghetti, and mushrooms and cream to turn into a sauce. She walked through the studded doorway of Giovanna's building, past a window like a ticket booth where one of two porters greeted her each day as she left and returned. In the courtyard a stone lion continually poured water from his mouth. And then up the stone steps, unlit, unyielding beneath her tired feet, three generous flights that felt like ten.

In the long hallway of Giovanna's apartment she saw the answering machine blinking. She played back the tape. It was not Navin's voice but a friend of Giovanna's. Normally these friends left messages in Italian that Giovanna retrieved from Berlin. But this message, in English, was for Hema. It was a person named Edo, a name she recognized from Giovanna's list of people to call. For weeks, Edo said in his message, he had been expecting Hema to get in touch. Was everything all right? He sounded kind, and genuinely distressed enough for Hema to return the call. She assured Edo that all was well, and because she had no other excuse, she accepted his invitation to have lunch with him and his wife the following Sunday.

Edo's wife, Paola, was a photo editor at *L'Espresso*, but Kaushik had met her in Netanya, a resort town on the Israeli coast, where they'd both gone to cover the bombing of a hotel banquet hall, the victims about to begin their Passover meal. It was only rarely that he worked in Italy, the odd photo essay about Senegalese immigrants in Brescia, or shots of the nineteen caskets containing the soldiers in Iraq being carried past the Colosseum. For most of the past five years, Rome had simply been a place from which to get to where he needed to go, and if he looked back at his pocket calendars, each with their three hundred and sixty-five sky-blue pages, and counted the days, he could have confirmed that most of them had been spent taking pictures in Gaza and the West Bank.

His life as a photojournalist had begun nearly twenty years ago. He was wandering through Latin America in 1987, living off the money his father gave him after he graduated from college. He'd gone with his friend Douglas, and they began in Tijuana, hoping to end up in Patagonia. They spent a few months in Mexico, working their way south, through Guatemala and then into El Salvador. And it was there that Douglas decided he'd had enough of Central America, enough of being harassed for looking so obviously American, and bought a ticket to Madrid. Like the Mexicans and Guatemalans, the Salvadorans were never sure what to make of Kaushik, not the soldiers who patrolled the streets with guns nearly as big as their bodies, not the children who posed eagerly for pictures when they saw him with his camera. He began to explore the country alone, a country that was smaller, he'd read in his guidebook, than Massachusetts. He took pictures of the volcano that loomed west of the capital, buildings pocked by bullets and cracked in half by the earthquake earlier that year.

He'd never been in a place so obviously at war with itself. He'd understood, in Guatemala, that the guerrillas were active, gathered from other backpackers that there were parts of the country to avoid. An overnight bus he and Douglas took to Tikal was stopped, and they and the rest of the passengers were ordered to step out and show their passports, flashlights aimed at their faces by a group of drunken checkpoint guards. One of the guards asked to see Douglas's wallet, took the cash, and tossed the wallet back in Douglas's face. In Guatemala, that had been the worst of it. But in El Salvador things were more violent, more gruesome, the tourists more scarce. In Santa Ana, Kaushik befriended a Dutch journalist named Espen and began to travel around, absorbing the history of the conflict, the stories Espen told him of the death squads, decapitated bodies strewn on highways, teenagers hanging from trees with fingernails missing and thumbs tied behind their backs. With Espen he watched air force planes dropping bombs at night on FMLN territory, went to visit a refugee camp across the Honduran border. He absorbed the fear of the place and of its people, grew used to the sound of machine-gun fire, accepted as everyone did the fact that he could at any moment, anywhere, crossing a road or asleep at night, be killed. But he'd never felt afraid, back then, for himself.

While sitting with Espen one afternoon, eating lunch in a village outside Morazán, the table began to shake, dark stew spilling from bowls. By then he'd grown used to occasional tremors, the earth's violence yielding a moment's pause. They picked up their spoons, continued eating, but then people began exclaiming, running past them through the small square. He and Espen leapt up, following the crowd, thinking perhaps a building had fallen, but the commotion had nothing to do with the tremors. They turned a corner to see a young man lying on the street. He'd been shot in the head, blood pouring like a slowly widening river away from his skull, but not a speck of blood, or even dirt, Kaushik still remembered, staining his tan shirt and trousers. He was curled on the pavement, eyes closed as if napping, the faintest sound escaping from his throat, a cheap gold watch telling the time on his wrist.

A group of people gathered around the body, calling for a doctor, while a young woman, a wife or a girlfriend in a pink sleeveless blouse, sat on the ground weeping with her fist in her mouth. Kaushik's camera was around his neck as usual, and Espen told him to take a picture. He did not have a long lens with him, had to get in close, expecting at each step for someone in the group to obstruct him, curse at him, shoo him away. But no one paid attention, and so he crept forward and lifted the camera to his face. When he thought back to that afternoon, he remembered that his hands were shaking but that otherwise he felt untouched by the situation, unmoved once he was behind the camera, shooting to the end of the roll. When he was finished, the calls for a doctor had stopped; the man was dead.

Kaushik was the only person to document what had happened. And though he had not saved the man's life he'd felt useful, aware that he had done something to mitigate the crime. Still, he never believed that the pictures would be published until Espen sent them to the right people. A week later, one ran in a Catholic newspaper published out of Amsterdam. He received a small check, and then, when the photo was picked up by a European newsmagazine, a larger one. And so he began taking pictures for a living. At first he simply woke up and followed the news, sticking close to Espen, staying in El Salvador through the elections, the transportation strike, the killing of the six Jesuit priests and their housekeepers. He photographed bodies with faces smashed and throats slit and penises hacked from between their legs, handing the images over to a human rights agency so that relatives could attempt to identify the disappeared. Thanks to a connection of Espen's he was hired as a stringer for AP, and so he remained in Latin America, first in Mexico, then Buenos Aires, working for wire services and English-language papers. When he was thirty he was hired by *The New York Times,* and they sent him to Africa and then to the Middle East. He could no longer remember all the corpses he'd photographed, their faces bloated, their mouths stuffed with dirt, their vacant eyes reflecting passing clouds over their heads.

The demands of the job allowed him permanently to avoid the United States. Occasional trips to New York to meet with an editor, to pick up equipment—this was the extent of his time in America, and there were trips when he'd not bothered to tell his father he was in the country, when he'd avoided the miserable day trip to Massachusetts to see his father's new life, though by now that life had surpassed, in years, the old. His father was in his seventies now, living off a generous pension and devoting most of his time to golf. From sporadic e-mails Kaushik learned that Rupa, the older of the girls, had married an American named Peter and taught art to elementary school students in Colorado. He had received an invitation to the wedding, but thanks to his work, his excuse for so many things, he had not gone. The little one, Piu, was in medical school at Tufts. And yet, also thanks to his work, Kaushik continued to wash up on his father's doorstep, in the form of his photo credit in one of the newsmagazines his father read, announcing that he was alive, indicating where he'd been and what he'd seen.

He kept a place in Trastevere, a tiny apartment off Piazza di San Cosimato with a generous terrace where, between assignments, he recovered. A woman had brought Kaushik to Italy. Until Franca he had preferred Latin America to Europe, and even now the Spanish he had learned all those years ago got in the way of his serviceable Italian. Franca had convinced him to follow her back to Milan. She came from a family of minor nobility, her heart-shaped face and deep-set gray eyes speaking for a refinement she had not been able to hide when he first met her working for a relief agency in Cameroon. For years he had drifted across the globe without making meaningful ties, and suddenly he was sharing an apartment with Franca, driving out to Bergamo on Sundays to eat polenta and roasted rabbit at her nonna's home, aware that her grandmother, who had spent years hand-stitching and embroidering a trousseau of night-gowns and bedjackets for Franca, approved of him. It had ended bitterly; though at the time he could never come up with a reason not to, he could not bring himself to propose. She had not taken hold of him; he could see now that that was the prob-lem. And so he left the tears and fury in Milan and took the train down to Rome. At first he thought he'd stay a week, to see a little bit of the city, then move back to Buenos Aires. But the Second Intifada drew him back to the Middle East, and he stayed on in Europe, never telling Franca that he was living in her country, never once running into her.

He remembered Rome, of course, from the only other time he'd gone there, on the way back from Bombay to Massachusetts with his parents. His mother was dying, but at the time, apart from her thinness, there had been no signs. She had just turned forty, Kaushik's age on his next birthday. He remembered the look of the hotel where they stayed, the marble steps they would ascend to go to the breakfast room. The strong shaft of light that poured through the dome of the Pantheon, and the glances of admiration the waiters could not conceal as his mother perused a menu. He remembered walking along the Janiculum and seeing clusters of swallows like giant thumbprints swiping the sky. And he had returned like a pilgrim to those places, recalled that the hotel was close to the Spanish Steps and managed to find it somehow.

Last year his father and Chitra had visited him in Rome, spending four days on their way to Calcutta. He had obliged, reserving a room for them at the Hotel d'Inghilterra and taking them everywhere. He stood in line with them to see the Colosseum and walked with them through the Forum. He took pictures of their stay, handing his father the rolls of film before they left as if it had been any other job. He ordered Chitra tea with milk in every restaurant, every café, because she did not like the taste of Italian coffee. But they had left no dent on the place, and he never thought of their presence on the streets of Rome as he continued to think, now and again, of his mother's.

It was in the course of those days with his father and Chitra that a faint gray speck, smaller than the head of a pin, began floating across his left eye. He first noticed it the afternoon they went to Testaccio, his father wanting to visit Keats's grave. In the lush grounds of the Protestant Cemetery, Kaushik had thought that a gnat was circling his head, and he kept swatting at it, putting out his fingers trying to flick it away. But the speck continued to accompany him wherever he went, quietly tormenting him, and he realized it was within him, that it was not possible to remove it or make it stop. An optometrist explained that it was caused by vitreous gel clumping and pulling away from the wall of his eye, that it was a harmless symptom of getting older. He was told he would grow used to it, and he had, more or less, not bothered these days unless he were in a bright room with white walls, or outside without his sunglasses. It did not affect his driving, or his picture-taking. And yet it felt like an invasion of the part of his body, the physical sense that was most precious: something that betrayed him and also refused to abandon him.

On Sunday he set out in his Fiat for Edo and Paola's, in a suburb south of the city. The thought of leaving the city, the streets he now navigated with ease, made him melancholy. For he was leaving; in the new year he would be gone. A position as a photo editor for an international newsmagazine had opened up in Hong Kong, and he had accepted. Apart from a few visits to Tokyo, he knew little of East Asia. It would be the first time in his life that a job would mean waking up and going to the same place each day, the first time he would have an office, a desk, an assistant to schedule his appointments and take his calls. The first time he would not wake up unprepared, until he was chasing after it, for what the day would bring. In that sense he would taste a version of the professional life his father had maintained for decades. He imagined he would hate it. Paola told him he was making a mistake, warning him that it was death to the photographer, that since becoming an editor she hadn't taken a decent picture. The money would be better, but that wasn't what had attracted Kaushik. It was his need for a different life that was taking him to Asia. The promise, for the next few years at least, that he would be still.

The magazine was paying for his move, but apart from the Fiat, which he'd already arranged to sell to a friend, he owned little. It was nothing like the times he moved with his parents, those two colossal upheavals he had experienced as a boy, first leaving America, then returning seven years later, the furniture and paintings and tea sets his mother thought she could not live without following them slowly, both times, on cargo ships. His mother had set up households again and again in her life. It didn't matter where she was in the world, or whether or not she was dying; she had always given everything to make her homes beautiful, always drawn strength from her things, her walls. But Kaushik never fully trusted the places he'd lived, never turned to them for refuge. From childhood, he realized now, he was always happiest to be outside, away from the private detritus of life. That was the first thing he'd loved about taking pictures— it had gotten him out of the house. His earliest memories, of Cambridge, Massachusetts, where he'd been born, were all outdoors. A chain-link fence matted with forsythia. The herringbone pattern of bricks on a sidewalk. His mother's voice calling his name as he ran across the Common.

He was reminded of his family's moves every time he visited another refugee camp, every time he watched a family combing through rubble for their possessions. In the end, that was life: a few plates, a favorite comb, a pair of slippers, a child's string of beads. He wanted to believe that he was different, that in ten minutes he could be on his way to anywhere in the world. But he knew that it was impossible, wherever he landed, not to form attachments. He would miss the short, tinted wine glasses in his Trastevere cupboards, the shrinking trapezoid of sunlight cast on his bed in the afternoons. And he knew that in his own way, with his camera, he was dependent on the material world, stealing from it, hoarding it, unwilling to let it go. The move to Asia was official now. His landlord, the owner of the *gelateria* on the corner, had found a new tenant. And just yesterday he had booked his ticket, arranging for a layover in Thailand, where he planned to spend the last week of December before continuing on to Hong Kong.

Edo liked to cook, specializing in the cuisine of his native Cremona. Kaushik imagined a gathering like all the others Edo and Paola liked to organize, an international crowd of journalists and photographers and academics, always three or four languages spoken at the table. Today, Paola had mentioned, an American novelist was coming, someone homesick for Thanksgiving and bringing an apple pie. There would also be an Indian woman, Paola said—a scholar, a friend of a friend of Edo's. He pictured someone middle-aged in spectacles and a sari, an archeologist like Edo. He had so little to do with India. He had not gone back since the year his mother died, had never gone there for work. As a photographer, his origins were irrelevant. And yet, in Rome, in all of Europe, he was always regarded as an Indian first.

A few blocks from Edo and Paola's he parked the car and got out. The neighborhood was spectacular in its own way: broad avenues lined with cypress, concrete postwar buildings with glass entrances and protruding balconies stacked one on top of the next. He realized he would probably not return here before leaving Italy, wanted to take a picture, but he had left his camera at home. Paola and Edo lived on a high floor, in an airy apartment overlooking a park. Turning onto their street, Kaushik noticed a woman standing on the sidewalk, long hair concealing her face, staring down at a map. *"Signorina, dove deve andare?"* he asked.

The woman looked up, confused, and he realized, in spite of her dark hair and fitted leather coat, that she was not Italian. That in fact she was Indian. That he needn't have used the polite form in addressing her, that her face was one he'd known.

.　.　.

From the moment they arrived together at Paola and Edo's, it was assumed, by the other guests, that they were old friends. One of the guests had even assumed they were lovers, asking how long they had been together, how they had met. "Our parents," Kaushik had said lightly, but Hema thought back, saddened by those two simple words. She was aware that he had not corrected the guest's assumption. Aware, too, of the way he looked at her across the table during lunch, surprised by the allure that had come to her late. He looked the same to her, that was the astonishing thing. The sharp-faced boy who had stepped reluctantly into her parents' home. Only the eyes appeared tired, the skin surrounding them now darker, faintly bruised. He was dressed like an Italian, wearing jeans and a thin black pullover, brown-and-white sneakers with Velcro straps. She still remembered her first impression of him, a quiet teenager in a jacket and tie, refusing her mother's food. She remembered the ridiculous attraction she had felt that night, when she was thirteen years old, and that she had secretly nurtured during the weeks they lived together. It was as if no time had passed.

After lunch he drove her back, inviting her to his place, in a quiet neighborhood where laundry hung between apricot-colored houses and old men sat in folding chairs on the streets. The men watched, silently, as Kaushik unlocked the bolts and Hema waited at his side. It was unquestioned that they would not part yet, unquestioned that though they had not seen or thought of each other in decades, not sought each other out, something precious had been stumbled upon, a newborn connection that could not be left unattended, that demanded every particle of their care. The building was nothing like Giovanna's, the door easily overlooked, an enclosed staircase leading directly into his small world. The apartment was a room and a bathroom and a two-burner stove. He led her to the terrace to see the neighboring rooftops, the Romanesque belltower of the church on the piazza. "You're that way," he said, putting his hands lightly on her shoulders, orienting her. He told her that he'd returned to Rome recently, that a week before he'd been in Ramallah, covering Arafat's funeral. Twenty thousand people had turned up, he said, scaling walls and tearing down barbed wire for a glimpse of the coffin.

They remained on the terrace, talking into the evening. She told him about college and graduate school, learning that during her first year at Bryn Mawr he'd been close by, at Swarthmore. She told him about her years in New York, getting her PhD, her job at Wellesley. And while she mentioned nothing about Julian—that long involvement, enough to make her feel, at times, like a divorced woman, was rendered meaningless in the official chronicle of her past—eventually she told him that she was going to marry Navin.

Kaushik leaned toward her across the small metal table where they were sitting. They had long ago digested Edo's pumpkin tortelli and bollito misto with mostarda, their heads clear again after many glasses of wine, but there was no food in Kaushik's refrigerator, only a box of salted biscotti he'd put between them along with two glasses and a bottle of mineral water. He smoked a few cigarettes. She had her hands flat on the table, as if to derive heat from its surface, and he hooked one of his fingers, lightly but possessively, around the gold bangle on her wrist, causing her hand to shift slightly in his direction.

"You wore this when you were a kid."

It was a gift from her grandmother, something she'd had since she was ten. It was the only piece of jewelry she never bothered to remove. She had always loved the design, small four-petaled flowers threaded along a vine, and when her wrist grew thick she'd had the bangle cut off and enlarged. "You remember."

"But you don't wear an engagement ring."

"I don't have one."

He studied the bangle, turning it slowly around. "What kind of man proposes without a ring?"

She explained, then, that there had not been a proposal, that she hardly knew Navin. She was looking away, at a dried-out plant on the terrace, but she felt his eyes on her, intrigued, unafraid.

"Then why are you marrying him?"

She told him the truth, a truth she had not told anybody. "I thought it might fix things."

He did not question her further. Unlike her friends back in America, who either thought she was doing something outrageously stupid or thrillingly bold, Kaushik neither judged nor commended her, and the formal presentation of the facts, the declaration that she was taken, opened the door. Only his kisses, rough, aggressive kisses that were nothing like Navin's schoolboy behavior at her door, made Hema feel guilty. But the rest of what they did that night felt fresh, new, because she and Navin had never done them before, and there was nothing with which to compare. Navin had never looked at her body unclothed, never explored her with his hands, never told her she was beautiful. Hema remembered that it was Kaushik's mother who had first paid her that compliment, in a fitting room shopping for bras, and she told this to Kaushik. It was the first mention, between them, of his mother, and yet it did not cause them to grow awkward. If anything it bound them closer together, and Hema knew, without having to be told, that she was the first person he'd ever slept with who'd known his mother, who was able to remember her as he did. His bare feet were warm, surprisingly smooth against her soles as they lay afterward side by side. He slept on his back and at one point was startled awake by a nightmare, lunging forward and springing off the edge of the bed before falling asleep again. It was Hema who stayed awake, listening to him breathing, craving his touch again as light came into the sky. In the morning, looking into the small mirror over the sink in Kaushik's bathroom, she saw that the area around her lips, at the sides of her mouth, was covered with small red bumps. And she was pleased by that unbecoming proof, pleased that already he had marked her.

At first Hema tried to stick to her morning routine at Giovanna's desk. But by eleven the phone would ring, and twenty minutes later she would be crossing the Ponte Garibaldi to meet him, or he would pull up to Giovanna's building in his Fiat to take her out for the day. And so she put away her books, lowered the screen of her laptop, knowing she would not touch them again until she returned to Wellesley. At night he took her to out-of-the-way restaurants and bars, to fountains in abandoned squares where they sat like a teenaged couple, kissing. They went outside the city walls, to places she'd never been and that he wanted to see for the last time. It was Kaushik who drove her to Ostia and Tivoli, and to Cerveteri to visit the hilly tombs of the Etruscan necropolis.

Hema told him about the history of those places, who had built them and why. She told him what she was learning about the Etruscans, that it was they who taught the Romans how to build their roads and irrigate their fields. She told him about the Etruscans' love of the natural world, their belief in signs and portents, their obsession with the journey out of life. They did not speak of their own future, of where their days together would lead. Nor did they discuss the past, the months during which he had lived in her home, the friendship between their parents that was already dying, along with his mother, during that time. Their parents had liked one another only for the sake of their origins, for the sake of a time and place to which they'd lost access. Hema had never been drawn to a person for that reason, until now.

Almost always, an international news channel played without sound on the small television in Kaushik's apartment. His work depended wholly on the present, and on things yet to come. It was not the repeated resurrection of texts that had already been composed, of a time and people that had passed, and it made Hema aware of the sheltered quality not only of her life but her mind. One day, after she asked him to, he showed her his Web site. He left her alone to look at it, going out to buy food for their dinner. She sat on his bed, wrapped in a sheet, his laptop humming against her legs.

There were countless images, terrible things she'd read about in the newspaper and never had to think about again. Buses blasted apart by bombs, bodies on stretchers, young boys throwing stones. He had witnessed these things, unseen and uninvolved, yet with an immediacy she had never felt. Because he had become her lover, these images upset her. Kaushik had told her about fellow photographers who were killed on the job, about the time an Israeli police officer bashed his camera in his face. And she was secretly glad, as his mother would have been, that his work would soon be different, that he would be behind a desk in Hong Kong presiding over meetings. That he would not be constantly in harm's way.

There were also shots of dusty streets and villages, markets and homes and shop windows, arid, barren landscapes, pictures of people. An old man sat peeling an orange under a tree, a flea-bitten dog dozing at his feet. A group of women in head scarves threw back their heads, laughing. A young girl poked her head out from behind a studded metal gate, baring a gap-toothed smile. As she looked at the pictures, she began to appreciate his ability, perhaps his need, to connect to strangers in this way, and the willingness of strangers to connect to him. She began to understand his willingness—and she thought perhaps this was also a need—to disappear at any moment. He lived in a rented room with rented furniture, rented sheets and towels. In the corner his camera bags and tripods were always packed, his passport always in his pocket. Apart from a detailed map of the West Bank there was nothing on his walls. She suspected that even if it were possible to turn back the clock, to never have met Navin and wait to bump into Kaushik in Rome, it would not have made a difference. She guessed that he had casually been with many women, that she should consider herself no different. And she refused to go to that miserable place Julian had dragged her to so many times, to hope for a thing that was unchangeable.

The key turned in the lock, and then Kaushik was with her again. He set down the bags of food on a small square table set with two chairs, the only furniture, apart from the bed, in his apartment. For the first time he seemed hesitant in her presence, not kissing her first thing. He hung his coat on a hook, loosened the thin red wool scarf at his throat.

"They're amazing," she said.

"They don't all pay the bills."

"Does it affect you, seeing these things?"

He shrugged, opened the cupboard, took out two glasses for wine. "It doesn't help anyone if I'm affected."

They stayed in that night, eating the bread and cheese he'd bought, the sliced meats and wine. Kaushik spent a while uploading images from his camera onto his Web site, writing captions. She helped him to pack stacks of contact sheets into boxes for the movers, gather up old photo magazines for the trash. He showed her a portfolio of pictures he hoped someday might form a book. For the first time they fell asleep without sex, not for lack of desire but because a familiarity was growing.

But then she felt him pressing up against her, felt his breath and his lips on the back of her neck, and she turned to face him, gave him her mouth. He could be aloof in bed as he could be in general, focusing on some part of her body to the point of seeming to forget her. But that distance no longer threatened her. It was only in bed that he uttered her name, the hot word filling her ear. It was a Saturday night, lingering voices in the piazza giving way to silence and at times the distant barking of dogs.

"It does affect me," he said afterward as they lay in the dark, awake.

"What?"

"Taking pictures. Not always, but sometimes. Sometimes in ways I don't like." He lit a cigarette, and then he told her about a day last summer, when he was driving back from Fregene and passed an accident: two cars had collided at an intersection. A crowd gathered, but the police had not yet arrived. Inside one of the cars, a child was crying. It turned out that the passengers were not badly hurt. Kaushik had pulled over, rushed out, but the first thing he'd done was take a picture. "The first thing," he told Hema. "Before even asking if they were okay."

Three weeks had passed. One evening in December as they were returning to Giovanna's, Navin called. The phone rang and then Navin left a message on the answering machine, calling to say hello as Kaushik pressed Hema against the door and began unbuttoning her jacket, the top of her blouse, uncovering her breasts and causing the keys to drop from her hands onto the terra-cotta floor. From the very beginning she had felt clear-eyed, aware that in a matter of weeks it would end. In another two weeks everything would be wiped clean—they would be in different countries, the keys to both Kaushik's and

Giovanna's apartments in the hands of other people. And this knowledge allowed her once more to step out of her jeans as Navin's voice spoke into the room. Even the fact that Kaushik had to wear a condom helped to keep him in his place, reminding her, whenever he paused to rip open the little packet, that in spite of what they were about to do, they would remain separate. Such thinking was a consequence of Julian, she knew. She supposed that all those years of loving a person who was dishonest had taught her a few things.

She told Navin that she was going to travel during her last week in Italy, another lie to prevent him from contacting her again, and this gave Hema and Kaushik the idea to take a trip together. They decided to go north, to Volterra, a town founded by Etruscans, and it was in that austere, forbidding, solitary place that they spent their remaining days together. They went in Kaushik's car, up the coast into Tuscany, then cutting through the misted blue Maremma and the white chalk hills of the Cecina Valley, climbing and descending a thin slip of road. Volterra appeared in the distance, perched on a cliff high above the open countryside like an island surrounded by land. The rough, restrained architecture, the coats of arms and the hard dark walls, were something new for Hema. The medieval buildings were more recent than the Forum, yet Volterra felt more remote, impervious to tourists and time. Rome had hidden them, enabled them, their affair one of thousands, but here she felt singled out, exposed. She also sensed an indifference; they were among a handful of people who seemed not to belong to Volterra, and she felt that the people who lived there were waiting for them, politely but firmly, to pass on.

It was a nearly silent place, apart from the sharp sound of their footsteps, the insistent coupled notes of the bells, the shriek of the wind. At that great height the wind was constant, striking their faces and agitating their hair. It was the week before Christmas, the town discreetly decorated, holly draped over the antipasti tables in restaurants. They went into the workshops where alabaster was cut and polished, the translucent material quarried in Volterra for thousands of years.

It was colder than Rome, a cold that emanated from stone, and instead of her leather jacket Hema now wore a peacoat of Kaushik's, grateful for the weight over her shoulders, remembering that other coat of Kaushik's she'd so hated wearing when she was a girl, back when they were nothing but already something to each other.

They stayed in a hotel that had once been a convent, slept in the former quarters of nuns. The food was plainer, bowls of ribollita, bread without salt, bittersweet hot chocolate in the afternoons. As they ate their meals and rested their feet from walking, they, too, felt fortified, tranquil, much like the town. Kaushik took a few photographs, not many, never of Hema, less of the town itself than the spectacular views it provided, the Carrara Mountains to the north and the Ligurian Sea distantly gleaming, one cloudless afternoon, thirty miles to the west. They looked down at the ruins of a Roman amphitheatre, and over the walls at the Balze, a precipice beneath which the earth had fallen away, once claiming a church, always threatening to take more of the town. Beneath the Porta all'Arco, the Etruscan gateway, three featureless blackened heads gazed down like sentinels upon them, and upon the world they had left behind.

Mainly, because it was so cold, they took refuge in the churches and museums. They saved the Guarnacci Etruscan Museum for last, and there they saw, lined on shelves, hundreds of urns in which the ancient people of Volterra had stored the ashes of their dead. They were called urns but were more like little caskets, made of alabaster or terra-cotta, the lids topped with figures with large heads and disproportionately small bodies, grotesquely but indisputably alive. The women were veiled, held fans or pomegranates in their hands. The sides were covered with carvings showing so many migrations across land and departures in covered wagons to the underworld, so many fantastic beasts and fish-tailed gods of the sea. Hema and Kaushik were the only visitors to the museum that day, alone apart from the heat that hissed from the radiators, the guards sitting patiently in their folding chairs. In the museum there was another sarcophagus of a husband and wife. But they were nothing like the languid, loving pair Hema had seen in Rome. Here they were older, cruder, still bristling after years of marriage, ill at ease.

After the museum they went to lunch, in a restaurant on Piazza dei Priori they had already tried and liked. After eating they would drive back to Rome, and the following day Hema would fly to India. They had checked out of the hotel that morning, their bags already in the car. The padrone seated them at the table in the corner where they had sat before. They ordered bruschetta with black cabbage, soft pappardelle flecked with wild boar. Hema looked at the postcards she'd bought at the museum, lining them up on the table as they drank the first glass of wine. One thing they'd seen there had been unlike anything else: a bronze sculpture of a severely elongated boy's body, a skeleton more than flesh, standing with his arms at his sides. At the center of the restaurant, at a long messy table, a slightly raucous group was gathered, mostly men in their thirties wearing suits.

"An office holiday party," Kaushik explained, after listening for a while to the conversation. "They work in the bank." He continued listening, then said, "They have lived here, in each other's company, all their lives. They will die here."

"I envy them that," Hema said.

"Do you?"

"I've never belonged to any place that way."

Kaushik laughed. "You're complaining to the wrong person."

"What if you hate Hong Kong? Where will you go?"

"I don't know."

"Will you come back to Italy?"

"No."

"Why not?"

He poured more wine into her glass, then his. He leaned forward slightly, looking at her, then seeming to change his mind about what he wanted to say. "I've reached an end here, that's all."

The meal ended without conversation, with vin santo and a slice of chestnut cake. They stepped outside, into the first twilight, for a last look at the town. It was the hour of the *passeggiata,* the older people promenading arm-in-arm through the streets. The men were with men, women with women, segregated as Hema's and Kaushik's parents once tended to be at parties. There was a uniformity to their appearances, their faces and their clothing, the flat woolen caps on the men's heads, the straight skirts and low-heeled black and navy-blue shoes of the women. With them, alongside them, were children and grandchildren, the generations knit casually and fondly together.

"Come with me," Kaushik said.

"Where?"

"To Hong Kong." And then he said, "Don't marry him, Hema."

She stopped walking. They were on a street of steps, lined with cypress trees, working their way down. Those behind her in the collective procession murmured *permesso* and pressed past. She felt the lurch of a head rush. The boy who had not paid attention to her; the man who'd embarked on an affair knowing she could never be his; at the last moment he was asking for more. A piece of her was elated. But she was also struck by his selfishness, by the fact that he was telling her what to do. Unlike Navin, he was not offering to come to her.

"Don't answer now," he said, pulling her toward him, guiding her down a few more steps, his arm around her waist. "Go to India first, straighten things out. I can wait."

She moved away, upset for the first time by his touch. "It's too late, Kaushik."

He extended a finger toward her jaw, turned her gently to look at him, into the tired eyes she had begun to love. His face glowed with affection for her, with hope, and she knew then that it was not just the wine talking, that he meant what he'd said. "In a few weeks it will be. Not yet."

He sought her hand again, and they continued walking. They entered a small piazza where she was aware everywhere of children, boys and girls of five and seven, eight and ten, swarming around them as if a school had just been dismissed. She had known Kaushik at that age, she had worn his coat, given him her bed, dreamed of him kissing her, these facts of the past haunting her and steadying her at the same time. The Italian children, eager for Christmas's approach, calling out *Buon Natale* as they greeted one another, were embracing in the cold air, their youthful excitement infectious and pure, so much so that Hema's heart leapt with theirs. In ten years, she imagined, these boys and girls would begin to fall in love with one another; in another five, their own children would be at their feet.

On the drive down from Volterra, as the landscape disappeared and they traveled through the night, she told him. She explained her reasons, reasons that had nothing to do with Navin. She told Kaushik she was not able to give up her life, not able to follow him that way. And that she didn't expect it of him. She said she didn't want to try to change him, didn't want to be accused, one day, of pinning him down.

"It doesn't mean we can't continue to see each other," she said, afraid to suggest it, more afraid not to.

"I'm not interested in any sort of arrangement," he said, in the cold tone she had not heard since they were teenagers. It was the only thing he said during the drive, until he pulled up in front of Giovanna's apartment in the middle of the night. Then he said, "You're a coward." She began to cry, unable to control herself, aware that he would never forgive her for refusing him, that even if she were to change her mind he had already retracted his invitation. He had told her not to marry Navin, but he had not asked her to marry him, and Hema knew that it was not a fair trade. As she cried he sat there, unmoved, as he must have been when he took his pictures, as he'd been that morning when she was thirteen and he had uncovered graves in the snow. She realized he had nothing more to say, that he was only waiting for her to get out of the car. They spent the night apart, and she did not expect to see him again. But the next morning he called to make sure she was packed, told her that he'd be there in an hour.

He drove her to Fiumicino and accompanied her to check in, speaking Italian on her behalf. He walked her over to Security, kissed her lightly on the mouth. And then he was gone, leaving her to wipe her tears, to take off her shoes and empty her pockets of the pretty coins that would soon buy her nothing. She navigated her way to the gate, riding an air train. She sat by a window, with a view of Alitalia jets crisscrossing slowly on the tarmac, watching other passengers, mostly Indians, fill up the seats. She sat alone, flipping though Italian fashion magazines until the flight was called.

It wasn't until she was on the ramp leading to the plane that she realized what she'd left behind. Her bangle, the one she never removed, the one Kaushik had hooked his finger through that first night, drawing her to him. She saw it now in her mind, sitting in the gray plastic tray she'd placed it in before passing through the security gate. She turned around, began walking in the opposite direction, back to the woman who had taken her boarding pass.

"Everyone is being seated now," the woman said in English. "The plane is about to take off."

"I've left something behind," Hema said. "Jewelry."

The woman looked at her, vaguely interested. "What type of jewels?"

"A bangle," she said. A hand went to her naked wrist.

"You would like us to check where you have been sitting?"

"No." She remembered the ride on the air train, all the shops along the way. "It's at Security. I went through this morning."

The woman shook her head. The whole time she was doing her job, taking boarding passes from the other people. "There is no way to reach Security now. If you like, we send a message."

She went back down the ramp, onto the plane, and found her seat. She fastened her seat belt, her right arm feeling foreign, missing the sound the bangle would have made coming into contact with the metal buckle. It would be replaced tenfold in the course of her wedding. And yet she felt she had left a piece of her body behind. She had grown up hearing from her mother that losing gold was inauspicious, and as the plane began to climb, in those moments she was still aware of it moving, a dark thought passed through her, that it would crash or be blasted apart in the sky. Then the fear turned numb. Already on the screen at the center of the plane there was a map with a white line emerging away from Rome, creeping toward India. And this simple graphic composed her, making clear the only road available now.

. . .

He was in a place where he knew no one. He was staying at a small resort a little north of Khao Lak, in a one-room thatched bungalow on stilts. This was his third day on the beach, and already he felt drugged by the routine: getting out of bed, eating fruit and sticky rolls for breakfast, lying in his swimming trunks on the hot sand. He glanced at back issues of the magazine where he was about to work. But mainly he dozed. He had stopped shaving, an uneven beard beginning to form on his face. The food reminded him a little of his childhood: steaming rice, dense brown and yellow curries, whole red and green chilies floating in sauce. Normally he harbored no nostalgia for the particular elements of his upbringing, adapting to so many cuisines throughout his adult life. But this food caused him to feel strangely sentimental. His eye distracted him, the shifting speck visible whenever he happened to remove his sunglasses and confront the untempered brightness of the day.

The beach faced west, and each evening he ordered a beer and watched the sun set over the water. The water was calm and shallow, but he preferred swimming in the pool. There had been an occasion off the coast of Venezuela, many years ago, when the undertow caused him a genuine struggle, his throat choking on salt water to the point where he feared he would not make it back. A neighboring bather lent a hand, but since then he had not swum in the ocean, no longer trusting it, knowing that his mother, who loved water so much that she would have swum in a pool of algae, would have scoffed. Behind the beach, rubber trees rose thickly on the hills. Somewhere across the water, beyond the Andaman Sea, was the Bay of Bengal, and Calcutta, where Hema was.

On the plane from Italy his anger had dissolved, and now, in Thailand, he was left only with longing for her. He wondered if he should have brought things up earlier, wondered if he had sounded halfhearted. He regretted his surliness when she had refused. She was the only person he'd met in his adult life who had any understanding of his past, the only woman he wanted to remain connected to. He didn't want to leave it up to chance to find her again, didn't want to share her with another man. That last day in Volterra he had searched for a way to tell her these things. She had not accused him, as Franca had, of his own cowardice, of his inability to form attachments. But Hema's refusal to accuse him made him feel worse, and without her he was lost.

There was a Swedish family in the neighboring bungalow, with a boy and a girl who both sunbathed and swam in their underpants, as if they had forgotten to pack their swimsuits. The children were tall for their ages; he was startled to learn, overhearing the mother tell one of the women who served drinks at the resort, that they were only five and seven. The mother was attractive, with a lean, freckled face and closely cropped hair, and seemed to wear a new bathing suit every few hours. In the mornings she would sit at their little round table in front of the bungalow, peeling fruit, offering pieces of coconut and papaya to the children, wearing a thin robe that was the color of a watermelon's flesh. While the children played and chased each other on the sand she sat in a chair and read, swatting them affectionately with a magazine when they attempted to involve her in their games. The woman and her husband made an incongruous couple. The husband was a large man, his skin burnt, straw-blond hair to his shoulders, hair longer than his wife's, a face like a ham. He spent most of the days sleeping in a hammock strung up between two trees, straining the knots that held him. As far as Kaushik could tell, it was just himself and the Swedish family; the third bungalow at this end of the resort, down a path from the main hotel building, was empty.

He'd thought about moving around a bit, going down to Phuket after Christmas, but for now he wasn't inspired to go anywhere else. He'd taken a few pictures, of the view from his bungalow, longtail boats on the water, the Swedish children playing on the sand. He felt no inclination to go walking through the hillside to photograph the shrines or to take a boat to the Similan Islands. In three days he left the resort only once, walking to a strip of souvenir and dive shops that bored him. He found an Internet center, considered going inside to see if Hema had written. Then he remembered that he had not given her his e-mail address. Instead, he uploaded new pictures onto his Web site: of Volterra, where Hema had been standing pressed up next to him, her hair flapping in the wind, strands of it sometimes intruding in front of the lens, and a few pictures of the Andaman Sea.

He spent Christmas on the beach as he had every other day. The restaurant at the resort had put up a small fake tree. He had dinner on the patio as a full moon poured its shimmering light across the water. The Swedish family occupied the neighboring table, conversing, laughing, eating their meal. The children's long limbs were dark from the sun. The family had ordered an array of dishes, were messily picking at a whole curried fish. Kaushik thought of Hema and anger coursed through him, thinking of her about to enter the world of marriage, of children, of taking trips and sleeping for the rest of her life with someone she did not love.

The wife stood up when they were finished, kissed the husband on the forehead, and took the children away. "Join me for a drink?" the man called out to Kaushik after they'd gone.

They walked indoors into the air-conditioned bar and ordered whiskey. A band was setting up to play. The Swedish man, Henrik, worked as a film editor for a television station in Stockholm. They spoke about the press in Sweden and Italy, about the war in Iraq. "Our jobs, they are similar," Henrik said. "Our names, too."

Kaushik nodded.

It was the fourth Christmas the family had spent at this resort, Henrik said. "The first year, Lars was just a baby."

"Your families don't mind?"

"What?"

"Your going to Thailand for Christmas?"

"My wife's parents complain. But we come anyway. They are in Stockholm, living across the street. My parents are divorced, both remarried." Henrik shook his big head. "Too many people to see. And you, where is your family?"

"My mother's dead. My father lives in the United States."

"But you are Indian, no?"

"Yes."

"You live in India?"

"I don't live anywhere at the moment. I'm about to move to Hong Kong."

"Married?" Henrik asked.

He shook his head.

"But you are thinking of someone. My wife says so. Missing her."

He had not thought that he had been obvious, that the family had been paying attention to him. He thought about denying it. "Now and again."

"You will see her soon?"

"No."

Henrik shrugged. "Alone is good, too." He drained his whiskey.

Kaushik's mood darkened. As much as he'd wanted Hema to be with him now, he knew it would be easier to begin life in Hong Kong alone. He knew there was nothing for her to do there, that the move would have stripped her of her work, her world. The band started to play, the stale cover music grating. He wanted to be alone, to lie down and think. "I'm going to bed," he said.

"Goodnight," Henrik told him. He ordered another whiskey. "One last for me."

Once more the day was flawless. Kaushik got up, walked over to the restaurant for breakfast. Henrik was sitting at the bar where Kaushik had left him the night before, but he was freshly showered, dressed in swimming trunks and a Hawaiian shirt, drinking coffee, breaking apart his rolls. "You felt your bed shake this morning?"

Kaushik shook his head.

"They said in the hotel, a small earthquake," Henrik said. "Over now."

Whatever had happened, Kaushik had slept through it. He thought back to the day in El Salvador when he'd taken his first real picture, and the tremor that had come just before: the stew spilling from its bowls, the young man in impeccably clean tan trousers lying in a pool of blood on the street.

"There is a shallow coral reef not far from here. Like to come? My wife and the kids want to buy things in town."

Kaushik looked out at the water. "I'm not a very good swimmer."

Henrik laughed. "Someone else will be doing the swimming for us." He pointed to a fishing boat resting on the shoreline. "I've arranged for a good price. When we get there, you can relax while I poke around."

After breakfast they walked over to the boat. The owner, a bare-chested teenage Thai boy wearing long red shorts, was clearing it of leaves and withered frangipani petals. Two small lime-colored frogs hopped out, leaping onto the sand. Henrik scooped up one in each of his large hands and brought them over to his children, who began chasing the frogs around in circles, their heads bent toward the ground. The Thai boy began to pull the boat into the water, Kaushik following, white foam like soap suds hissing around his ankles. He had brought one of his cameras, wearing it around his neck. Henrik had an extra set of snorkeling gear, in case Kaushik changed his mind.

They got into the boat, the boy taking his place at the front. On the beach Henrik's wife raised a thin arm from where she was sitting, gave a lazy wave. The children looked up briefly as Henrik and Kaushik settled themselves inside. There was plenty of room on board, and when Henrik called out to his wife and said something in Swedish, pointing to the empty seats, Kaushik guessed that it was to ask her and the children to join them. But she replied in the negative, shaking her head and retreating behind one of her magazines.

He experienced a moment's nervousness because Henrik was so large, but the boat absorbed their shared weight. The Thai boy lifted his oar and they began to move. Kaushik felt the swell of the sea beneath the hull, close to his body, not touching him but penetrating him at the same time. The resort retreated from view, the bungalows beneath the palms and the darting forms of Henrik's children turning to specks, the familiar coastline curving away like a flat smiling beast. The boy spoke a little English, told Henrik about a school of parrotfish he'd seen the day before. The morning sun was already strong, and after a while Henrik took off his shirt. Kaushik looked at Henrik's broad pink back, glistening with sweat. They were skirting an abandoned cove. "It's getting hot," Henrik said. He tapped the boy on the shoulder. "I take a dip here to cool off."

The boy nodded, rested his oar. Henrik dived over the edge of the boat and started to swim, his ungainly body turning graceful as it cut through the water with swift, skillful strokes. And alongside Henrik, for a moment, Kaushik saw his mother also swimming, saw her body still vital, a brief blur that passed as effortlessly as the iridescent fish darting from time to time beneath the boat. His torso cast a shadow into the sea. He thought of the thin bronze sculpture of the boy he'd seen with Hema in Volterra, in the Etruscan Museum. It was called *L' Ombra della Sera:* the Shadow of Evening. But in Khao Lak it was morning, the sun burning down on Kaushik, his shadow still in proportion to his body.

When he looked up, he saw that the boy had guided them close to shore. Henrik emerged from the water, waded clumsily toward the deserted cove. The white sand was spotless, limestone cliffs looming behind. Kaushik lifted the camera to his face, took a picture, and set the camera down at his feet. He dipped his hands into the water, cooling off his neck and face, not expecting its salty taste. Then he unbuttoned his shirt, felt the sun strike his skin. He wanted to swim to the cove as Henrik had, to show his mother he was not afraid. He took off his sunglasses, leaving them in the boat next to his camera. The speck in his vision rose and fell, erasing its random trail. He held on to the edge of the boat, swinging his legs over the side, lowering himself. The sea was as warm and welcoming as a bath. His feet touched the bottom, and so he let go.

All day I was oblivious. I was out with my mother and two aunts, being fitted for blouses, selecting jewels. We had spent hours on a thin futon, drinking Cokes and eating mutton rolls, as men in a sari shop unfolded the greater part of their inventory. I went along with all of it, chose a red Benarasi to wear. But the whole time I was thinking of you, fearful of the mistake I was making. I was still slightly jet-lagged, hungry for meals we were used to eating together, for the taste of good coffee and wine. On the crowded street, walking back to my parents' flat off Triangular Park, I searched foolishly for your face. "A terrible thing has happened," the gatekeeper told us when we arrived.

On television, in a pink sitting room with stark fluorescent light, I saw images of the Indian and Sri Lankan coastline, glimpses from vacationers' video cameras never intended to capture such a thing. I saw a massive surge of water moving so quickly that the tape seemed to be playing at an unnatural speed. At first it was only the damage in South India and Sri Lanka I was aware of, the fishing villages that had been obliterated, tourists stranded on Vivekananda's Rock. And then I learned that Thailand had also been hit very badly.

I did not know where you were in Thailand, only that you planned to be on a beach. I had not asked you the details, thinking, as I prepared to leave you, that such information would make it worse. The next morning I went to the newsstand and bought the papers, studying every picture, looking for your name in one of the credits, hoping you had been lucky and that you had continued to do your work. I went to an Internet center, drew up your Web site. I saw the last images you had posted. A faint sliver of the shoreline we had seen from Volterra. Three blackened faces, supposed to be Etruscan divinities, that loomed over our heads. And then, scenes of another coast. Two children playing, a gentle turquoise sea.

At the end of that week, Navin arrived to marry me. I was repulsed by the sight of him, not because I had betrayed him but because he still breathed, because he was there for me and had countless more days to live. And yet without his even realizing it, firmly but without force, Navin pulled me away from you, as the final gust of autumn wind pulls the last leaves from the trees. We were married, we were blessed, my hand was placed on top of his, and the ends of our clothing were knotted together. I felt the weight of each ritual, felt the ground once more underfoot. Our honeymoon in Goa was canceled. Navin said it didn't feel right to swim in the polluted waters that surrounded India at that time.

I returned to my existence, the existence I had chosen instead of you. It was another winter in Massachusetts, thirty years after you and your parents had first gone away. In February, Giovanna got in touch to say she had heard the news from Paola. A small obituary ran in *The New York Times*. By then I needed no proof of your absence from the world; I felt it as plainly and implacably as the cells that were gathering and shaping themselves in my body. Those cold, dark days I spent in bed, unable to speak, burning with new life but mourning your death, went unquestioned by Navin, who had already begun to take a quiet pride in my condition. My mother, who called often from India to check on me, had heard, too. "Remember the Chaudhuris, the family that once stayed with us?" she began. It might have been your child but this was not the case. We had been careful, and you had left nothing behind.

A Note About the Author

Jhumpa Lahiri's debut collection, *Interpreter of Maladies*, won the 2000
Pulitzer Prize for fiction, as well as the PEN/Hemingway Award, the *New
Yorker* Debut of the Year, and an Addison M. Metcalf Award from the
American Academy of Arts and Letters. It was an international best seller,
translated into more than thirty languages. *The Namesake*, her first novel, was
a *New York Times* Notable Book, a finalist for the *Los Angeles Times* Book
Prize, and was selected as one of the best books of the year by *USA Today*
and *Entertainment Weekly*, among others. Ms. Lahiri was the recipient of a
Guggenheim Fellowship in 2002, and a fellowship from the National
Endowment for the Arts in 2006. She lives in Brooklyn, New York,
with her husband and two children.

A Note on the Type

This book was set in Galliard, a typeface drawn by Matthew Carter
for the Mergenthaler Linotype Company in 1978.

Carter, one of the foremost type designers of the twentieth century, studied
and worked with historic hand-cut punches before designing typefaces for
Linotype, film, and digital composition. He based his Galliard design on
sixteenth-century types by Robert Granjon. Galliard has the classic feel of
the old Granjon types as well as a vibrant, dashing quality that marks it
as a contemporary typeface and makes its name so apt.

Composed by Creative Graphics,
Allentown, Pennsylvania

Printed and bound by R. R. Donnelley,
Harrisonburg, Virginia

Designed by Iris Weinstein